Readers everywhere are "Coming Home to Brewster," North Dakota...

Here's what they're saying about *After Anne*:

From California: "A dear dear friend gave me *After Anne* several weeks ago...Your book was awesome and should be sold with a box of Kleenex!"

From North Carolina: "I felt as though the characters were my best friends. The last time I cried this much was when I read James Patterson's *Suzanne's Diary for Nicholas.*"

From Canada: "I laughed and cried. It made me reflect on my life. We all assume we have lots of time and put off telling people what we feel...It was a wonderful book."

From Oregon: "I could hardly put the book down. Oprah should know about this!"

From Christianbook.com: "*After Anne* is probably my favorite [book of the year]. This moving story of an unlikely friendship between two women will have you laughing and crying and longing for a relationship like theirs."

From Brandywine Books: "*After Anne* depicts the kind of friendship every woman craves. Henke reveals her characters' deep emotions without caricature...It rings true..."

From an Amazon.com reader: "I don't know how I got this copy of *After Anne*, but however I got it, I am so glad I read it!...It's just beautifully written—and so true...It is one of the must-reads for the coming year, if not tomorrow."

And book number two, *Finding Ruth*:

From Virginia: "I read *Finding Ruth* after I finished *After Anne*, and I thought this book couldn't be as good...but, sure enough, you did it again! You are my favorite author."

From Ohio: "After reading *Finding Ruth* and enjoying it so much...I felt compelled to thank you for such a wonderful story...I am an 80-year-old...and I love Christian fiction."

From California: "I just finished reading the last page of *Finding Ruth*...the tears went down my cheeks as I read it...But what kept me so on the edge...was your showing me Brewster town. I could see everyone, even their laugh lines."

From Kentucky: "Your book couldn't have come to me at a better time. I struggle with contentment or lack of. Thank you for a touching story that fit quite nicely into my life. I was moved by it...If I had my way, your book would be topping all the bestseller lists."

From Indiana: "I chose your book from the new fiction section at our public library without realizing it was a Christian book...I could hardly bear to put it down."

Via e-mail: "I love your characters, all of them, even the broken ones. Even the selfish ones. Even the unlovable ones. I can't remember the last time a book has made me feel such empathy for a fictitious person, first with Anne and Libby, and now with Ruth's friends and family. I feel like I know them personally."

"Ruthie's emotions and outlook seemed so similar to mine. Unlike Ruthie, I am not yet 'home,' but your book has touched my life in a way I can't quite explain...Thank you for writing such a heartfelt story."

And book number three, *Becoming Olivia:*

From Indiana: "I've been burning up the e-mail lines telling anyone who will listen that your books are required reading. Please hurry with number four!!!!"

From North Carolina: "Just finished *Becoming Olivia*—loved it!...Your Christian insight and faith shine through as realistic and practical without coming off 'preachy.' "

From South Dakota: "I could not put it down! I could relate to so many of the things Olivia went through, especially the struggle with depression and anxiety...*Becoming Olivia* was the first of your books that I have read, and I look forward to reading the others. Thank you!"

From Ohio: "I've just read *Becoming Olivia* and am so moved. There are many words to describe the book, but none seem adequate enough."

Via e-mail: "It was a brave thing you did in writing this, and it has touched me. There were times when I had to stop reading because I couldn't continue. Yet I was compelled to return to the story...I am a voracious reader, and many authors have touched me, moved me, and changed me, but you are the first one I've written to. I needed you to know how important your writing is to people like me. Thank you."

"I just finished *Becoming Olivia* and *had* to write and tell you how much I loved it. I have read all three of your books...but *Becoming Olivia* especially spoke to me...I know that this had to have been a difficult book for you to write, but you did a superb job, as always."

"I quickly began to discover why God brought your book to me. I felt as if I were living right there in Olivia's life. Not only could I relate to this story, but I knew God had a strong message for me among these pages."

"*[Becoming Olivia]* is amazing for its healing powers...I'm going to use the book in my clinical practice to give to patients who know they don't feel right but don't think it's bad enough to be classified as depression. Thanks for telling the story so beautifully."

"I cried and laughed through the whole book, finishing it in under two days!! This was the very first Christian fiction book I have read, and I want more! I cannot wait to find your other two books so I can read them."

Always Jan

ROXANNE HENKE

HARVEST HOUSE PUBLISHERS

EUGENE, OREGON

Cover by Koechel Peterson & Associates, Inc., Minneapolis, Minnesota

Cover photo © Getty Images/Photodisc Green/Doug Menuez

Published in association with the literary agency of Janet Kobobel Grant, Books & Such, 4788 Carissa Avenue, Santa Rosa, California 95405

ALWAYS JAN
Copyright © 2005 by Roxanne Henke
Published by Harvest House Publishers
Eugene, Oregon 97402
www.harvesthousepublishers.com

Henke, Roxannne, 1953–
    Always Jan / by Roxanne Henke.
        p. cm. — (Coming home to Brewster ; bk. 4)
    ISBN 0-7369-1150-2 (pbk.)
    1. North Dakota—Fiction. I. Title II. Series: Henke, Roxanne, 1953- Coming home to Brewster ; bk. 4
PS3608.E55A79 2005
813'.6—dc22

                                                                    2004015418

Printed in the United States of America

06 07 08 09 10 11 12 / BC-KB / 10 9 8 7 6 5 4 3

Charm is deceptive, and beauty is fleeting;
but a woman who fears the LORD is to be praised.
—PROVERBS 31:30

Get wisdom, get understanding...
Wisdom is supreme; therefore get wisdom.
Though it cost all you have, get understanding.
—PROVERBS 4:5-7

To my mother,
Jean Jensen Sayler Klein.
Thank you
for your loving and laughing heart!

Acknowledgements

As I began to write *Always Jan,* I learned that writing a book on the topic of "aging" could very easily *make* me "old." Thank goodness I had some *great* role models: three graceful and godly women, who taught me that getting older only means getting better.

The first of these women was my aunt, Lillian Sayler, who passed away recently at the age of ninety. Until the week she died, she lived alone, even though she was legally blind. She volunteered at a soup kitchen and often told me, "I pray for you every day when I'm walking on my treadmill." Aunt Lillian's enthusiasm for life is my goal!

I also had my "Grandma Herr." She wasn't my grandma by blood, but she was the grandma of my heart. She taught me to love God…every day, and that following Jesus could be filled with laughter. And that's what I remember when I think of Grandma Herr…her faith and laughing!

Another aunt inspires me: Christine Mueller. Ninety-one and so interested in life, we never run out of things to talk about. While our relationship is woven through a complicated family arrangement, our friendship is simple: We love each other.

There are many others who helped me with this book. A big thank you to Curt and Linda Michaelson, owners of Curt's Service Station. They allowed me to snoop around the "garage" and answered questions about their work, which lent an air of reality to this story. And to Shelli Sayler, COTA/L, at the Wishek Nursing Home, who let me pick her brain and her exercise files. Thanks…it was just what I needed!

As always, a big thank you to Nick Harrison, editor extraordinaire! Janet Grant, agent and advisor. And Kim Moore, who makes line edits practically painless.

I also want to thank my mom. Her many years of volunteer work at our local nursing home taught me there is blessing in the wisdom of those older than me.

A journey wouldn't be complete without someone waiting to greet you at the end of it. My husband, Lorren, has become an expert at putting up with me when my mind is more involved in imagination than reality. And my daughters, Rachael and Tegan, are more than daughters; they are also my friends. And I can't forget Gunner, our English cocker spaniel, who lays at my feet each day while I write and never forgets to remind me, mid-afternoon, that it's time to GET UP!!

Through all of these people, my friends, and readers, God has blessed me indeed.

Brewster, North Dakota. Middle America, USA. The kind of town where everybody knows your name. Where everybody knows what everyone else is doing...or thinking of doing. A place where neighbors run cookies over with the latest gossip. Where the waitress at the café is your next-door neighbor. Nine-man football. A twenty-bed hospital. A grocery store that offers home delivery on Thursdays. All these things can be found in Brewster.

What else can be found there? People with hopes and dreams. People in love and people with broken hearts. Friends and foes. Families and faith. When you get to know the people of Brewster, you'll find it isn't all that different from where you live.

Welcome to Brewster...it's a good place to call home.

Prologue

Ian

I Lost My Youth at Pizza Hut!

Trying to ignore the screaming headline, I pushed my grocery cart toward the checkout, past the tabloids lining the way like wallpaper.

"Hi." The clerk behind the cash register at the CashSavers grocery store in Carlton tapped her fingers across the keys, apparently itching to begin ringing up my order. Or she was extremely bored. One look at her face and I voted for bored. I began unloading my cart, putting her out of her misery.

I Lost My Youth at Pizza Hut! The annoying headline flashed through my brain again. It wasn't the first time the words had appeared out of nowhere. And probably not the last. I pulled a package of frozen corn from my cart, closed my eyes, opened them, and dared myself to look back and see if the headline was still there.

I glanced quickly. *Famous Soap Star Dumps Young Lover!* Of course it wasn't there. By now I should know that stupid headline was a product of my imagination. I yanked groceries from my cart. Yogurt. Cottage cheese. Three veggie pizzas.

Pizza. How appropriate. *I Lost My Youth at Pizza Hut!*

I pushed both sides of my desperately needing-highlights hair behind my ears and continued putting items on the revolving belt on the counter. I might as well let the tabloid-like story play out in my head. It always did when I shopped. The memory had spun through my mind at least once a week this past year. A headline from the *National Enquirer.* Or the title of a movie. A bad movie. One that starred me. The scene would unfold in my mind as though it were a slow-motion segment of a cheesy film clip.

There I was, Jan Edwards at the time, newly divorced, not quite the culmination of carefree innocence walking down the sidewalk toward the Carlton Pizza Hut. My blonde hair, mostly natural, was blowing behind me in the light summer breeze. I had no doubt the sun was picking up the highlights in my hair. Highlights I'd paid good money to have put there.

I remembered exactly what I'd been wearing. A pair of tight-fitting denim cutoffs. Short. A white tank top, tucked in. Low neckline. Gold hoop earrings. Big. A pair of strappy, black sandals with heels. High. Black sunglasses. That's all. I looked hot. Or cool. Either way, my appearance had nothing to do with the temperature.

I'd almost forgotten about my thirteen-year-old niece, Julie, who was walking one step behind me. It was her choice to eat lunch at Pizza Hut, part of my belated birthday present to her. She was my sister's oldest child and someone I only got to see once a year. Julie lived in Texas with my only sister, my *older* sister, my *smart* sister, Maureen, and her husband. They also had two young sons, but it was Julie who came to visit her Auntie Jan in Carlton, North Dakota, each summer.

I'd taken a week of vacation from my job as a bookkeeper at a jewelry store in the mall that July, making sure the four days I had with Julie were packed with fun. My sister had gotten married and pregnant when she was only twenty...not that *that* was so smart. But still, she'd managed to finish college. Two more kids and a series of great jobs followed. Her savvy brain had served her well.

Maureen's our smart child. You're our pretty one. My mother's mantra still echoed. For the past five years, brainy Maureen had been sending Julie north to spend a little time alone with me each summer. Maybe she hoped Julie would get her mom's brains and my beauty. Now that would be a lethal combination.

So far that week we'd painted each other's nails twice. Well, actually, I painted Julie's; I wouldn't let her touch mine. I paid someone to make mine look good. We'd gone to a movie one evening and shared a large tub of buttered popcorn. I'd skipped supper that night and made sure Julie ate most of our snack. I didn't need the calories or the greasy fingers. The morning of the last day of her visit, I French-braided Julie's hair and then showed her how to dab on eye shadow and blush before pressing a bit of pink lipstick between her lips just so. She might as well learn from an expert. Goodness knows, my sister had never tried a makeup tip in her life; she'd been too busy studying, or chasing babies. Lunch at Pizza Hut was Julie's grand finale. I'd be driving her to the airport after that for her flight back to Texas.

So there we were at Pizza Hut that hot July day. I'd turned twenty-nine a week before, and I was strutting the stuff I knew I had.

The sidewalk leading to the front door was long—long enough to pretend it was the runway of a fashion show for summer clothes. I placed one high-heeled, sandaled foot in front of the other, hoping Julie would pick up just a bit of my moxie. We were halfway down the sidewalk when the door of the Pizza Hut swung open. I slowed my steps, raised my chin, and looked slightly downward through the dark lens of my black sunglasses. I knew enough to look just above the shoulders of the two young men who were exiting the Pizza Hut door. I didn't need to make eye contact to get their approval. I'd wait until they were close enough down the sidewalk so they'd smell my perfume instead of pepperoni, and then I'd toss them a look over the top of my sunglasses that would put a blush on their late-teen cheeks.

Thrills were easy back then.

From behind my sunglasses I watched as the boys drew near. Saw as one elbowed the other, tilting his head with a subtle dip, making sure they were both looking at the same thing. Me.

They were four steps in front of me. Three. Two. Okay, now. I lowered my chin and grazed my shadowed brown eyes just over the rim of my sunglasses, ready to meet their young, lustful gazes.

Only they weren't looking at me. Their eyes weren't on me at all. They were looking over my shoulder, past me. I turned my head as they walked by to see just what was more enticing than I was.

Julie. My niece. My thirteen-year-old niece.

The boys had stopped walking, had stepped off the sidewalk to let Julie glide by. She'd picked up my moxie, all right. A shy smile tugged at the corners of her Pink Passioned lips.

Funny, how I suddenly noticed the brown tufts of grass at the edge of the sidewalk. The unevenness of the cement under my feet. The peeling paint on the side of the building. One of my high-heeled sandals snagged on a crack in the walk. I stumbled and then caught myself. Took in a quick breath. Watched as my youth took a tumble and died, right there on the sidewalk in front of Pizza Hut.

Charm is deceptive...

Jan

I woke up crabby and knew the day wasn't going to get any better. Maybe not the perfect day to paint my clothesline poles Lapis Blue. I swung my feet over the side of the bed. Best get on with it. Lazing around wasn't going to change one minute of my birthday.

My friends had been teasing me for weeks. They knew how much I hated this day, and they had made no effort to hide the fact that they loved my irritation over the party Connie and Brenda had planned for tonight. I'd threatened not to show up. Turning forty-three would be that much closer to moving into my room at the Brewster Nursing Home. That much closer to my downhill slide to senility. I might as well prove my friends right by painting my clothesline poles Lapis Blue.

Painting clothesline poles as rebellion. Quite the rebel, aren't you? Oh, my, you are getting old.

I pulled on a pair of faded jeans and a gray T-shirt. Slipped my feet into a pair of plastic thongs. I could already hear what my neighbors would say. Or the coffee crowd at Vicky's café. *She painted them BLUE! Have you ever heard of clothesline poles being painted blue? She always was a little bit flashy...but BLUE poles?*

I hadn't actually bought the paint yet. Maybe I'd change my mind before the morning was over. But, considering how owl-y I was feeling, I doubted it. Off to scrape rust.

The early August sun was already hot as I sat on the damp grass and pushed the stiff wire brush across the boring white paint,

13

concentrating my efforts on the orange rusty patches. I stopped for a moment to roll up the short sleeves of my tee. It would look dumb if I got weird tan lines the day of my birthday. Face it, it would look dumb anytime. I scooted around the pole, trying to get a tan on my face. I looked much better with a little color. Not like my friend, Olivia Marsden, who avoided the sun as if she were part vampire. A little color would do her good. But, I had to admit, her skin was gorgeous. Oh, I knew what all the beauty magazines said about staying out of the sun to keep your skin supple and all. I hadn't read those magazines for the past thirty-some years and not had that advice drilled into me. What they didn't say was how insipid women look without a tan. Bland. Boring. I compensated by lathering on moisturizer every night.

"Happy birthday, Jan." My neighbor, Arlene Harris, was dragging a bag of trash down her back steps.

What? Was there a sign on Main Street? How did Arlene know it was my birthday? Sure, she might have been my son Joey's English teacher last year, but that didn't mean she would know about my birthday.

I pasted a smile on my face. "Thanks." *Change the subject.* "I suppose you'll be getting ready to start back to school pretty soon."

Arlene pulled the heavy trash bag off the foot of the steps and across the lawn, toward the alley. "Don't mention school. This summer has simply disappeared. I don't know where time goes."

I did. I knew exactly how time disappeared. Forty-three today. I didn't want to talk about it. Or think about it. I stood, turning my back toward the Harris' yard, pretending I needed all my brain power to scrape a clothesline pole. I could hear the clank as Arlene pulled the cover from the garbage can in the alley, the thud as she hoisted the heavy bag over the side, and then the clank again as she closed the lid. I hoped she'd go quietly back into her house. Arlene was nice enough, but I didn't feel like talking to her much. Especially not today.

She was a teacher, with four important years of education I'd never had. Not that she'd ever said anything about it. And it wasn't as though I'd ever needed a college degree to get a job. My eyes traced the front of my body in a quick swipe. My slim figure, long blonde hair, and big brown eyes had won me more than one decent job.

"See you at your party tonight," Arlene called before she went back into her house.

Had Connie and Brenda invited the whole town? I jabbed at the last of the rust spots on the crossbar over my head. The scraping job I'd started yesterday was done and I still hadn't changed my mind. Lapis Blue. I tossed the wire brush onto the grass, dusted off my hands, and then placed them on the small of my back, stretching into the pressure. Ouch. My back was stiff from the work I'd done yesterday. Maybe I'd be too stiff and tired to go to the party tonight.

As if you'd ever admit that!

I straightened slowly. My back really didn't hurt all that much.

I walked into the house and changed clothes for my trip to Cal's Hardware. I wouldn't be caught alive, downtown, in my old painting clothes. I ratted at my hair, poufing it with tangles and hairspray. As a final touch I swiped some Pink Passion across my lips. There, all set.

⌒

"Hey there, Jan. Happy Birthday!" Cal, the owner of the hardware store, greeted me as the creaky wooden door to his shop announced my arrival.

"Thanks," I mumbled, making my way to the aisle with the paint samples, pretending it was nothing but a passing comment. There *had* to be a sign on Main Street or something. How did everyone in town seem to know it was my birthday?

"Saw the sign on Main Street," Cal added, as if in answer to my thought.

"What!?" I stopped.

"Right there." Cal pointed to the streetlight pole outside the window of his store. "Right in front of Vicky's café." He chuckled. "Wonder who did that?"

I hurried back out the door and over to the pole. Sure enough, nailed to it was a metal sign that read: "Old Person's Parking Only.

Reserved for—" Underneath, someone had written in black marker: Jan Jordan.

Funny. Very funny. That sign was coming down. Now. If only I could reach it. I jumped. The metal edge of the sign barely grazed my fingers. I jumped again, not nearly as high as I'd imagined I could. I jumped again, my stiff back reminding me I wasn't as agile as I'd thought I was. I took a step back to survey the situation as Paul Bennett, one of Brewster's bankers, and his brother-in-law, Dave Johnson, left Vicky's café. They stopped beside me, chuckling loud enough for me to cringe.

"Good one," Paul said, looking up at the sign.

"Wonder who did it?" Dave chimed in.

"I don't care who did it," I said. "I just want it down." I wasn't about to take another leap at the sign with both of them standing there. Borrowing a ladder from Cal was my next plan. Unless... I batted my big brown eyes, first at Paul and then at Dave. They got the hint.

Paul was taller; he reached up first. He had no trouble grabbing the edge of the sign with his right hand. He pulled. His hand fell, the sign didn't.

"Here, let me try." Dave managed to get a pretty good grip, but he had about as much luck as Paul. "Man, whoever put that up there used a spike instead of a nail. I think I'd better grab a chair."

"I'll see if I can borrow a hammer from Cal," Paul said as Dave turned to go back into his wife's café for something to stand on.

I waited, my hands on my hips, staring at the sign. This was turning into a major production. Next, I'd be on the front page of the *Brewster Banner*. Good thing the weekly paper had come out yesterday. I'd already read it. I wasn't in it. At least not this week.

Dave came out of the café with a chair and three curious customers. Oh, great. I'd forgotten all about the morning coffee klatch at Vicky's. Everyone had seen the sign. Dave stood on the chair. Paul handed off the hammer. Cal came out to watch, too.

A bubble of laughter tickled the back of my throat. I highly doubted whoever had done this had meant to be mean. Tricks like this weren't played on someone people didn't like. It was supposed to be funny. Make me laugh.

And it just might have…if I didn't feel so much like crying.

⁓

I leaned into the bathroom mirror turning my head from side to side. No, it wasn't my imagination. I touched the corner of my right eye. Crow's-feet. Definitely crow's-feet. I was surprised my mom hadn't pointed them out when I visited her in Carlton last week. She noticed that sort of thing. I closed my eyes, lifting my eyebrows as if that could smooth away the lines. I peeked again, squinting my eyes and trying to imagine what dim lighting might do. Blurry crow's feet. Well, that wasn't my only worry. I straightened, tilting my chin up…down…trying to find just the right angle. There would be photos tonight. Probably lots of them. Of me.

You're the pretty one.

I wasn't looking forward to tonight. This celebration of aging. What a joke. Well, if the magazines said forty was the new thirty, I'd just have to become the poster woman for the cause.

I tugged at the V-neck of my new pink shirt. Maybe a little cleavage would divert attention. No, I didn't need that much attention. Not there, anyway. I pulled it back up.

Leaning over the bathroom counter, I put a hand on either side of my face and gently pushed the skin back toward my ears. No, too much. I wasn't going for the deer-in-the-headlights look. Just trying to erase ten years. Fifteen. There. Like *that*. Where was a plastic surgeon when I needed one?

"Happy birthday, Jan." Dan came up behind me, kissing the back of my neck and ruining my impromptu face-lift. He pulled his electric razor from a drawer and ran it over his chin. "Ready for the party soon? I'd like to take a swing by the softball diamond on the way over. See how the guys are doing. They're playing the team from Flanders tonight. They're supposed to be tough."

At least there was something in this world more important to someone in town than my birthday. Dan understood. I knew if we didn't have this party to go to, he would be on the bleachers watching the game. He'd played on the team for years, quitting two years before we got married. He'd been Brewster's most eligible bachelor when I'd met him. Nine years older than me and still quite the catch. He made me feel so much younger. He'd quit playing only because he'd broken his ankle sliding into third on a close play. "But I was safe," he liked to add when he told the story. I used to love to sit and watch the games with him. It was a good way to get a tan. But, leave for the party early just so we could watch a couple innings? No.

Dan tapped his razor against the sink; a peppering of whiskers sprinkled the porcelain. I gave him "the look," the one that meant "don't do that." Then I remembered I was trying to quit using that expression. It was causing wrinkles between my eyebrows. "Da-an."

"Sorry." He looked sheepish. "Habit." He reached for the garbage can instead. He put his razor back into the drawer and picked up his aftershave. "So, you ready?"

Ready? If dread counted, I'd been getting ready for this party for the last ten years. No, I quickly did the math. Make that thirty-one years.

I'd been twelve when my grandmother died. The grandmother I adored. Grandma Gloria had been the person who'd cajoled me through piano practice, rewarding me with a pile of M&M's when I played a piece right and subtracting them one-by-one with a sly wink each time I hit a wrong note. To this day I credited Grandma Gloria with my ability to play the piano. And spell. She'd pick me up after school on cold winter days with a small thermos of hot chocolate waiting on the car seat, and then she would take me back to her house until my parents got off work. There she'd help me with my homework, teaching me silly ways to remember hard spelling words.

I remember the day my mother came to school. I was in sixth grade. It was right after lunch and we were getting ready for math. I was glad. I was good at math. I'd just pulled my book out of my flip-top desk when there was a knock on the classroom door. Every head in the room turned. Any interruption in our routine was exciting. I could see my mom standing next to the glass partition that sided the doorframe. Without even looking at my teacher, I got out of my desk and walked to the door. I don't remember why I thought my mother might be there. She was supposed to be at work. I didn't have a dentist appointment or anything. I opened the door. She put her arm around my shoulder and I knew. I just knew. Grandma Gloria had died.

"A heart attack," relatives said as they sat around the living room later that night. I was curled up by my mom on the couch, listening to stories about my grandma, knowing my memories were the best. "She had eighty-six glorious years," they said. "We should be happy she was healthy for so long."

All I knew was that eighty-six meant you died. For some unknown reason, as I sat curled on the couch, I'd divided the number eighty-six by two. Maybe it was one for my grandma and one for me. The two of us. And now it was just me. Two into eighty-six equaled forty-three. For most people, turning *forty* was the big one. For me, every birthday loomed large, but forty-three would be the biggest of all. The day my grandma died, I did the math. When I turned forty-three, my life would be half over.

"Are you looking forward to the party?" Dan's words broke through my memory, bringing me suddenly back to my bathroom, back to my crow's-feet, back to my life being half over.

An unattractive snort puckered my lips. "Hardly." I grabbed my blush compact and stabbed the brush into the powder.

"Come on, Jan." Dan met my eyes in the mirror. "Your friends want you to have a good time. They're celebrating your life." His words hung in the air as he rubbed my favorite aftershave across his neck, put the cover back on, and walked to the door of the bathroom. He paused, then he stepped back, reached out, and rubbed my back. "Think of the alternative."

I rolled my eyes as he walked out of the bathroom. I knew that cliché by heart. *Think of the alternative.* Ha.

Death. Growing old. Death. Growing old. Such a lovely choice.

I pushed the blush brush across my cheeks, twice on each side. One light, sun-kissed bounce of the brush on the end of my nose. I dabbed white highlighter under the arch of each of my eyebrows. Applied another coat of mascara to my lashes. I appraised myself in the mirror, then tugged the "V" of my shirt a little lower. Gold hoop earrings. Two gold chains around my neck. A bracelet on each arm. I smoothed my hands over my clingy black knit skirt and then hiked it above my knees an extra inch. Two. There. That would do it. I stood back and looked into the full-length mirror on the back of the bathroom door.

I could almost hear the words of my high school career counselor. *You should think about being a model. You've got the looks for it. I hear they make a lot of money, too.* I remembered the wide-eyed way I'd stared back at him. I'd been waiting for him to tell me I should be an accountant because of my good grades in math.

"Are you coming?" Dan's voice shattered my memory.

"Ready," I called. Ready as I'd ever be to mark this milestone. This *mill*stone. My life was half over, and what did I have to show for it?

You're the pretty one.

Well, at least I had that. I sprayed my wrists with expensive perfume and rubbed them together. I wasn't sure which was the worst of the two evils…death or growing older. But I did know one thing. I might have to *get* old, but I didn't have to *look* old.

What are you afraid of?

I fumbled with the perfume cap. *I'm not afraid.* The lie came quickly.

You're afraid of dying, aren't you?

Wasn't everyone?

Of not doing anything with your life?

I stared at myself in the mirror, not seeing me, seeing, instead, what lay ahead. I hoped far ahead. Getting older only meant one thing. Death.

What I feared was what came next. After that…

Or, more importantly, what didn't.

Kenny

Whack! The sting of the swing zipped down the bat into my hand a fraction of a second before the sharp crack registered in my ears. The softball went sailing high, heading for the right field fence. The runners on second and third took off, and I shook the satisfying tingle from my hand as I headed for first base. I tagged the bag, then tugged at the waistband of my uniform as I rounded the base. I really needed to do something about this gut I was getting. I watched as a young kid dashed behind the outfield fence in search of the ball. It was the bottom of the eighth, and we'd been down by one. With two men on base, it was a good time to hit a homer. They hadn't made me cleanup batter for nothing.

"Way to go, Kenny!" My teammates on the bench.

"Woo-hoo, Dad!" My six-year-old son, Billy. I glanced over at the bleachers as I headed toward second. He was jumping, pumping one fist in the air. My thirteen-year-old daughter, Renae, was leaning back on the bleachers, her nose in a book. She was supposed to be keeping an eye on Billy, or at least look up when her dad hit a home run.

We hadn't meant to have those two kids so far apart, but Diane had had two miscarriages in between, one too early to know what the baby was, the second a tiny boy, stillborn at six months. We'd quit trying for a while after that. Then Billy came along. We'd planned on naming that first little boy Kenny Jr., but when Billy showed up, it'd been too much of a reminder of all our hoping before to put the name on him. We'd decided on Billy, William, actually, after Diane's grandpa. But no one called my towheaded son anything but Billy.

I did a slow jog around the bases, wishing Diane were here to watch me hit my home run. It wasn't often she came to games anymore. She'd said it was too hot tonight, and she hadn't felt great all day. She'd about given me a heart attack when she said she felt the weird kind of way she did when she was first pregnant with each of the kids. But I quickly realized that would be next to impossible considering the few times we'd actually had...well...*sex*...since Paige had been born. Having another baby a couple of years ago had put a crimp in that sort of thing. Not to mention our finances. I probably shouldn't have closed the station early for the softball game, but heck, Kenny's SuperPumper Station was the team sponsor.

I ran across home plate, high-fiving Paul Bennett, who was up next to bat. He'd probably hit a home run, too, but I had cleaned off the bases. I slapped the hands of a couple more teammates and then made a swing by the bleachers. "Hey, Renae!" She looked up from her book, a distracted expression on her face. "Did you see your old dad out there?"

She smiled. Shook her head.

Billy rolled his chin through the air, disbelief in the whites of his eyes. "He hit a home ru-un." Wisely, he left off the "dummy" he'd been tacking on to sentences lately. He was a smart kid. Like his mom. "Can I have some money for an ice cream cone?" He didn't miss a beat...or a good mood.

Automatically, I reached for my wallet and then caught myself. Diane had reminded me just yesterday that we had to watch our expenses, even the little things. "The kids are going to need their eyes checked before school starts, not to mention new clothes and shoes. We're going to need every dollar."

I reached out and ruffled Billy's blond hair. "Nice try, kiddo, but I didn't bring my wallet, and, besides, they don't even sell concessions at the amateur softball games."

"I was going to ride my bike to the Dairy Freeze."

"What about the rest of the game?"

Billy shrugged one shoulder. "It's over."

It wasn't officially, but I knew what he meant. I liked the kid's attitude. He knew his dad had won the game for the team. "Go look in my duffel bag." I tilted my head toward my bag under the team bench. "There's a couple dollars in the side pocket." He took off like a shot. "Make sure your sister goes with you," I called to his back. I poked the spine of Renae's book with my finger. She looked up. "Take Billy to the Dairy Freeze, and then you guys head straight home. Tell your mom I'll be in after the game."

Renae moved her bookmark to where her nose had been and then stood while waiting for her brother. I reached out and tickled her hard.

"Dad! Stop it!" Rolling her eyes, she angled away from me.

I tickled her again. She was a good kid, but sometimes I worried about all that reading she did. She needed to lighten up. Life wasn't that serious. If she didn't even notice when her dad hit a ball over the fence, what else was she missing?

I walked back to the team bench and grabbed my glove. The inning was over, and it was time to get into left field and put the other team out of their misery. The sooner we did that, the sooner we could get to the best part of the game…talking about the highlights. Like my homer. Or the double I'd hit in the third.

I took my place in the outfield and smacked my hand into the glove. "Batter-batter-batter," I chattered, hoping for a quick strikeout, wanting this game to be over for real. There was nothing better than analyzing a good game over a couple beers. It might get late tonight.

Diane wouldn't wait up. She knew the drill. I took the two oldest with me to the local games so she'd have some time to get the house picked up without everyone underfoot. Usually our toddler, Paige, cooperated by going to bed early. But it wasn't easy to predict what a two-year-old would, or wouldn't, do. I hoped Diane at least had time to tackle that stack of bills I'd brought home from the station.

The batter hit a single down the middle. I watched as he tossed the bat, tucked in his head, and barreled toward first. He didn't have a prayer. Well, he wouldn't have, if our second baseman, Greg Dosch, hadn't bobbled the ball. He was doing that more and more. Where was his head? He must be getting old. I'd have to tell him.

Man on base.

I smacked my hand into the glove, crouching as if I meant business. "Let's get this game over," I called as our pitcher fired one across the plate. Swing and a miss. "Strike!" That was better. I relaxed and stood up. This guy would be an easy out. My mind wandered.

Before Paige had come along, Diane had come to the station for a few hours every day, taking care of the books while I waited on customers and did service work out in the garage. Lots of times she'd even fill gas if I had my head far enough under a vehicle on the hoist.

I missed her at the station, but at least she was still helping as much as she could. I was going to have to remember to thank her tonight. Maybe a back rub that could lead to something else...

The crack of a bat pulled my head back into the game.

I looked up. The evening sun was in my eyes. Where was the ball? "I got it," I called, still searching the hazy August sky for the ball. I held my glove aloft, trying to block the sun, trying to find the ball.

"Back! Back!" Ben yelled from fifteen feet to my left.

I backpedaled big time. Without seeing the ball, all I could do was rely on Ben's coaching. "It's in there," I called a fraction of a second before I heard the ball drop beside me.

"Home! Home! Home!" I could hear the third base coach urging his front runner around third.

I bent, sensing where the ball had landed before seeing it. My fingers brushed at it, missed. Oh, man, was I going to hear about this after the game. Finally, I got my hand around the ball and wound up for the throw. The batter was ready to tag third. He touched the base. Hesitated. So did I. Our eyes met. He was daring me to throw home. He ran. I threw. Hard.

Not hard enough. The ball bounced short. The catcher ran to meet it as the runner slid past onto the plate. Tie game. My error. I kicked at the brown grass. Swore under my breath. Rubbed my shoulder. I'd heard something pop. Must have pulled something with that throw. At least the guys would know I'd tried to make up for my error. So much for getting this game over early.

Between the possible extra innings and the razzing I'd have to listen to after the game, I doubted Diane would be awake for a back rub, much less up for anything else. Oh, well. She'd understand. She always did. She knew how important softball was to me.

The next three batters hit easy, infield pop flies that the pitcher caught as if he did that sort of thing in his sleep. It was our turn to bat. We needed just one run to get this game over. I hustled in, hanging my head to let everyone know the tie game was my fault.

"Shake it off." Ben slapped me on the back as he ran by. He'd been born exactly one minute before me and took his role as older brother seriously. Sometimes too seriously.

He'd tried to talk me out of dropping out of college. What he didn't understand was that just because we were twins didn't mean we had the exact same interests. He liked numbers. I liked cars. He earned his business degree and after ten years working in hospitals around the state, he'd ended up back in Brewster, the big-time administrator of our small-town hospital. The clinic, too.

I took a seat on the bench and watched as Ben stepped up to the plate. Maybe I should have listened to him, but going to tech school and then slowly buying the gas station hadn't been a bad decision. Just a different one. So what if Kenny's SuperPumper didn't bring in near as much money as Ben and his wife, Cindy, made? She was the director of nurses for the Brewster Retirement and Nursing Home and pulled in a chunk of change all by herself. I sure wouldn't mind if Diane made that kind of money, but then who'd help me at work? Money was always tight for us, but I wasn't going to begrudge Ben and Cindy their good jobs.

Ben took a couple practice cuts with the bat before positioning himself for the pitch. My brother would give me the shirt off his back if I needed it. Too bad his shirts wouldn't fit me anymore. I couldn't figure out how he managed to stay so trim with a desk job, while I spent my days pumping gas and rolling tires around and had nothing but a big gut to show for it. And now a sore shoulder, too.

I was glad my turn in the lineup wouldn't roll around for a while. I needed some time to nurse my injury and my pride. The only reason we were batting again was my stupid error.

I noticed Dan Jordan's Crown Vic parked in the grassy area that bordered first base. Nice car. I'd changed the oil in it last week. He was a good customer and a huge sports fan. We always had lots to talk about when he pulled in for a fill. I hoped he hadn't been sitting there too long watching. Maybe he'd missed my slipup. If not, I'd hear about it tomorrow. I wondered why he wasn't in his usual spot, high on the bleachers. I squinted. Maybe he'd been in the bleachers and I hadn't seen him. Maybe I needed my eyes checked. It was getting harder and harder to read the auction sale posters hanging at the station. Maybe that's why I hadn't seen the ball. Nope. Dan's spot on the bleachers was empty. I narrowed my eyes, trying to see into his car.

Hoo-hee, my vision was operating just fine. I could see Dan's wife, Jan, sitting in the front seat with him. It didn't take squinting to notice the hot pink top she was wearing. If memory served, it was probably low cut. More than likely, tight. Whoo-hoo, I wouldn't mind a wife who looked like that! I wouldn't mind a lot of things about Jan Jordan. Like—

"Dad!" Billy's voice.

I whipped my head around. He didn't need to see me ogling Jan or not paying attention to the game. How many times had I told him when he went to T-ball, "Keep your head in the game, kiddo." I'd do well to take my own advice. After all, it had been my wandering mind that had us still up to bat.

Billy was weaving his bike around the bleachers, heading toward the players' bench where I was sitting. I stood, hiked up my pants, and then walked his way. I'd told that kid to go to the Dairy Freeze and then straight home. Where was Renae? She was supposed to be watching him. No wonder I couldn't keep my head in the game. I tried to keep the irritation out of my voice as Billy stopped his bike at the foot of the bleachers and straddled the crossbar. "Where's your sister?"

Billy heaved two deeps breaths. He'd obviously been riding fast...with no helmet. Something his mom wouldn't be happy about.

I chucked him under the chin. "Helmet," I said, trying to sound stern. Diane had told me she needed me to back her up on this. I was trying, but wearing a helmet to ride a bike seemed as though it took all the fun out of it.

Billy nodded and rolled his eyes. "Mom said to tell you to come home."

A crack of the bat and a loud cheer caused me to turn my head. It looked as though Ben might have hit a double, maybe a triple. With any luck this game would be over with the next swing of a bat.

I turned back to Billy, who was watching his uncle round the bases. "Tell Mom I'll be home in an hour." I'd better cover my own bases. "Or so," I added, starting my walk back to the bench. "Now you get home."

The next three batters struck out. Game tied. Extra innings. I picked up my glove and ran to left field. I could see Billy straddling his bike, still watching the game. Diane might worry if he didn't come right home, but she'd figure out what happened. She knew how these games went. She'd sat through enough of them herself.

By the bottom of the tenth, the sun was setting. If my Kenny's SuperPumper team didn't get a run this time at bat, the game would be called for darkness. There were no fancy lights on this dry, grass field. I was on deck, slicing my favorite bat through the air while the other team fired the ball around. Here was my chance to redeem my error. All I needed was a good solid hit.

Before heading to the plate I glanced over my shoulder to see if Billy was still watching. He was, but bad news was walking up behind him. There was Diane striding toward the field. It didn't take a genius to tell, even from here, that she was upset. Poor Billy, he should have gone straight home. Diane could be an alley cat when she had a mad on. I ducked my head and swung the bat. I didn't want to see the look on Billy's face when his mom caught up to him.

I couldn't help it. I swung again and then peeked. Shoot, Diane had walked right past Billy and was angling in on me. She paused when she saw I was on deck to bat.

"Batter up!" The ump was Austin Vetter, a young man with one year of college under his belt and home for the summer. He wouldn't have a clue that having a wife show up in the bottom of the tenth could not mean good news.

"Gimme a sec." I held my palm out to the pitcher, indicating he should hold his pitch. Good thing this was amateur ball. The pitcher had a wife; he'd understand. I jogged over to Diane, feeling my teammates' eyes on my back. This had better be important.

"What?" I could feel my eyebrows practically touching. Out of the corner of my eye I could see Billy hoist himself onto his bike seat and start pedaling our way. He was as curious as my teammates, apparently. "Hurry up." My voice, though whispered, was harsh. "I'm supposed to be batting. What is it?"

"I came to find Billy. It was getting dark and I was worried. And—" Diane's eyes filled with tears. She pressed her lips together. They still trembled slightly. She shook her head. "It can wait." She turned to go.

The sun was setting and the guys in the outfield were hollering to get the game going. Talk about a rock and a hard place.

I had to live with Diane. I touched her shoulder. She looked back at me, her eyes brimming. Tired. Old for thirty-seven.

"What?"

"I'm pregnant again." The tears spilled down her cheeks about as fast as my heart dropped to my stomach.

"Woo-hoo!" Billy punched a fist in the air. "I'm gonna have a brother!" he yelled. "Or a sister," he added, not quite as enthusiastically. His outburst clearly alerted everyone within earshot to our family news. Chuckles and cheers came from behind me. Ben came over and threw an arm around my shoulder. "Congratulations, Kenny!"

I pasted a smile on my face and then turned to my teammates as they crowded around.

"Game over," Austin Vetter called as the last bit of light dropped from the sky.

I'd let the rest of the team decide what they wanted to do about the tie. Someone else could pick up the bats and balls tonight. Billy tore out ahead of us, a miniature Paul Revere, anxious to tell his two sisters the news.

I wrapped an arm around Diane's shoulders and pulled her close as we walked the six blocks to our house. In the darkness I tried to tell her that everything would be okay.

I ran out of words.

Instead, I kicked at a rock as I silently tried to convince myself.

Jan

"Congratulations!" Brenda rushed out the door to give me a hug. "Come in, come in. Everyone's here."

I hesitated in the doorway. Usually I loved being the center of attention, but not tonight. Not when it meant everyone would be focused on how old I was. Or, how young I *wasn't*. Discreetly, I tugged at the hem of my pink sweater, sucked in my stomach, and pulled my shoulders back. No slouching. Slouching added a good five years, according to my mom. Five years I wasn't about to claim with poor posture. I forced a smile onto my face and stepped into Brenda's living room.

"Happy birthday!" The chant went up. Connie and her husband, Gary. Olivia and Bob Marsden. Arlene and John Harris. Four, five other couples.

I started my mental clock. I had two, possibly three hours to endure. Might as well make the best of it. I flung my hands up in the air and struck a pose. "It's the birthday girl," I announced. "Over forty and proud of it," I lied. There. Maybe now they'd drop it.

"Over forty is right." Connie stepped forward and hugged me. One of those stiff, insincere hugs that made me wonder why she even bothered. "Forty-*three*, if my math is right." Was it my imagination, or did Connie raise her voice as she announced my age?

Her husband, Gary, leaned forward to kiss my cheek. "Well, if this is what forty-three looks like, I can't wait until Connie gets there." He winked.

A real smile spread across my face as I caught the look on Connie's face. The look her husband missed. *Thank you, Gary.* Connie wasn't one to let a comment like that drop. I knew he'd hear about his remark later, but for now she simply turned her back.

"You look fabulous." My good friend, Olivia, wrapped me in a warm hug. Held me tight for a few seconds. Long enough to allow some of the tension I'd carried about this night to disappear. Then she held me at arm's length. "If Connie hadn't announced it, I'd swear you were *thirty*-three." Olivia seemed to understand I needed reassurance.

"Thanks." I pulled her back into a hug, half hoping I could stay in the warm envelope of her arms and bypass the rest of the night. Maybe her assurance would rub off on me.

No such luck. She pulled away, cupping her warm hands around my jaw line. "Enjoy the new year ahead of you," she said softly, just to me. "It's a gift." She smiled, as if she knew something about this year I didn't. I smiled back, pretending I knew what she meant. If I could have half the confidence Olivia seemed to carry in the tip of her unpolished little finger, I'd be a happy camper.

"Come on everybody and sit down." Brenda herded us into the living room. "Time for our first game!" Brenda was holding a bowl with several folded slips of paper in it.

A groan went up in unison from the men as we all found seats. "I'll pay you not to play." The comment from Brenda's husband, Eric, began a round of bidding as if Brenda were auctioning off the bowl she was holding.

"Five!"

"Ten!"

"You guys, stop it." Brenda couldn't help but laugh. The guys did something like this every time.

"Ten-fifty!"

They all knew better. And I knew best of all. We were going to play this game no matter what, and I only had myself to blame. I was the one who'd started the silly game playing among this group.

I'd lived in Brewster for almost three years when I met Dan. By then I'd made my own circle of friends and he had his, some dating back to high school. When we were married five years ago, we'd tried to merge our circles as if they were Olympic rings. It turned out they were more like magician's rings in the hands of an amateur, clunking together in an awkward attempt to mingle that wasn't working.

You'd think in a town the size of Brewster that everyone would know everyone else. Well, they did. Sort of. They *knew* who everyone else was; they just didn't hang around with them. Until Dan and I had our first, joint, pre-wedding party.

I quickly learned that Dan's idea of a party was to call a few guys, set some cans of Coke and beer on a coffee table, open a large bag of Doritos, and turn on the television. Monday night football, preferably. His years of bachelorhood had left him relying on other people to actually entertain.

So there we were, on a Friday night, his usual buddies and their wives, my girlfriends and their husbands and no TV allowed. Idle chatter was the polite description. Utterly boring was the truth.

"Okay, everybody." I'd clapped my hands as if I were a kindergarten teacher, desperate gaiety in my voice. "We're going to play charades!" The first and only time the men didn't groan out loud. I think they were relieved to quit racking their brains for conversation. "Guys against girls." Connie shot me a stern look. "Men against women, then." Connie was a stickler for what she called "empowering women." To me, her attitude felt more like un-empowering men, but I wasn't about to argue with her. Not that night, anyway.

I grabbed one of the Jordan Real Estate notepads Dan had lying by his phone and started dealing paper like cards. Passing out rules with the pencils.

And that was how it started. The game playing. All because of desperate me. Now it was my birthday. We had come full circle, the original group plus a couple more. I was still desperate, but this time I didn't want to play any games.

"Listen up." Brenda wasn't taking groans for an answer. "Before Jan got here I had everyone write down a prediction of something good that will happen to her this year. I'm going to read them out loud, and then we'll try and guess who wrote it. We'll keep track of who guesses the most."

Maybe this wouldn't be so bad. All I had to do was sit here and smile. I crossed my arms and my legs, making myself comfortable.

Brenda dug her hand into the bowl and pulled out a piece of paper that had been wadded into a tiny, golfball-like ball.

"That's Jerry's." Jerry's wife, Tami, shook her head. "It's pretty pathetic when you're almost forty-five and everything you do still comes in the form of a ball."

"Hey," Jerry said, "can I help it that I love my job?" It was no secret his position as Brewster High's basketball and golf coach, in addition to social studies teacher, came as natural to him as breathing.

"People," Brenda said, tossing the minuscule ball at Jerry, "we're supposed to guess who wrote these *after* I read them."

"Yeah." Jerry lobbed the balled-up paper at Tami. "*After* she reads them."

"Okay, here's the *first* one." Brenda unfolded a piece of paper and read, "Jan will get her nails done every three weeks." She held up the paper. "Okay, who wrote this?"

Someone who knew my routine, apparently. I didn't even have to guess. "Connie." You'd think a freelance interior designer would be more creative.

"I didn't mean to be that obvious."

"One point for Jan." Brenda pulled out another paper. "Jan will have a baby."

"Oh-ho!" Gary rubbed his hands together. "That's a good one. Dan, did you write that?"

"Duh," Connie poked Gary with an elbow. "Think about it. They weren't even here when we wrote this stuff. Besides, she's forty-*three*. Who'd want a baby at forty-three? Whoever wrote that is delusional. Must have been a man."

Brenda's eye caught mine. She flushed. I knew it had been either her or Olivia who'd written that. They were the only two people I'd told about my desire. But Olivia knew better than to treat my longing as fodder for a party game. I felt myself turn red. Not a good contrast with the hot pink top I was wearing. I hadn't expected Brenda to broadcast my wish to the world. But then, she didn't know the rest of the story. Olivia did. About how my third husband, Dan, and I had been trying to have a baby ever since we got married. My son, Joey, the only good thing to come from my short, second marriage, was already an eighth-grader. I had a notion having a baby with Dan would keep both of us young.

Or give you something meaningful to do?

There was that, too. But I wasn't about to admit it.

Forty-three wasn't out of the question to have a baby these days. Was it? Connie seemed to think so. I stared at my hands, wishing the floor would open up and swallow me. Or her.

A very pregnant silence hung in the air. It wasn't often this group lacked for conversation. Brenda cleared her throat as if trying to speak, trying to clear the air, but no words would do it.

"Speaking of sports, Jerry." Dan, my lovable husband, grabbed an old ball that had been lying on the conversational field and ran with it. "Jan and I stopped by the softball diamond on our way over here tonight. Man, what a game. Kenny's team was ahead going into the top of the ninth and then…"

As if a tidal wave of relief had swooshed through the room, the men somehow shifted toward the couch, the guessing game forgotten.

"Well, now." Brenda stuck the paper-filled bowl on a shelf behind her, tucking it neatly behind a framed picture of their dog as if it belonged there in the first place. My guess was we'd never be playing that game again. Thank goodness.

Brenda turned to face us. We women were looking at her as if she were the activities director on a cruise ship. We'd paid good money for this trip, and it had suddenly run aground. What was she going to do about it? We were waiting for our life jackets. Quick.

Brenda opened her mouth. Closed it. Shot me a desperate look. What was I supposed to do? Bail her out? *I've been drowning all day.* If anyone should be jumping in to help, it should be Connie. It was her big mouth that had sunk this party.

"Why don't we have Jan open her gifts?" Leave it to Olivia to throw a life preserver into the water.

"Libby, thank you!" Brenda jumped on the idea. "Can someone help me get the presents?"

She mouthed a cringed "*sorry*" as she scooted past me. Tami and Connie got up to help, leaving Olivia and me together on the loveseat. The two other women in the room had picked up a photo album from under Brenda's coffee table and were paging through it. Distracting themselves from this fiasco.

Libby's hand reached out and covered mine. "You okay?"

Automatically, I nodded. What was I going to do? Throw a hissy fit at my birthday party? I wanted to appear young, but not like a three-year-old. "I'm fine." I pressed my lips together in the semblance of a smile.

"You sure?" She lowered her chin and looked at me with something that felt like compassion in her eyes.

Where had the lump in my throat come from? I moved my eyes from Libby's. Swallowed. Shook my head. The truth was I wasn't okay. Not at all. I felt my lips tremble. I blinked fast. It had been a while since I'd let anyone but Dan see me cry. But Libby had a way of cutting through my smiling mask with two simple words that made tears the easiest answer of all.

I'd met Libby at Brewster's one and only hair salon…well, the only one worth going to, in my opinion. There were a couple of other ladies in town who cut hair out of their kitchens, but to look at their own hair, the last time they'd paged through a hair styling magazine and paid attention was the eighties.

Our friendship started one day when my hair appointment followed Libby's. Jacob, the only male hair stylist within a hundred miles, was running late, so I sat myself in the next chair so he wouldn't get carried away with Libby's highlights and forget about mine. Libby made a smart remark I could have thought was snotty, but it struck me as funny instead. By the time Jacob was finished blow-drying her hair, we simply switched chairs and continued our conversation. It spilled over into coffee at Vicky's cafe and that was that. We were friends. I mostly talked, Libby mostly listened, and it worked out fine.

Until Anne Abbot moved to town. Something in Olivia started changing. She wasn't quite as anxious to hear the latest gossip anymore. And after Anne was diagnosed with breast cancer, Olivia started driving Anne to her doctor appointments. Then she changed her standing hair appointment. I hardly saw Olivia the year Anne was sick. That's when Brenda and I became good friends. I had to talk to someone, and Olivia wasn't available. But I still considered Libby my friend. My good friend. And in the last couple years we'd grown close again, in a different sort of way. She was the kind of person I knew I could count on, even if we hadn't talked in ages. She was there for me. I just knew it.

She squeezed my hand now. "Come on." She stood and pulled me from the couch, leading me down the hall, through the master bedroom, and into the bathroom. She shut the door, put down the lid of the toilet seat, and said, "Sit." I did. She perched on the edge of the tub. "It's okay to cry. I know where Brenda keeps her makeup."

Tears came with my sudden laugh. "It's so stupid," I said, covering my face with my hands for a second. "But I want a baby so bad. Dan does too. And then I got my period yesterday, which isn't helping matters any." I sighed, trying to push away the heaviness on my chest. "I've had Joey for thirteen years, and now he's getting older and I'm not ready *not* to be a mom anymore. Do you know what I mean?"

Libby nodded. "I do," she said softly, her own tears rimming her eyes.

It was then I remembered that her youngest, Emily, had graduated from Brewster High School this past May. She'd be leaving for college in just a couple weeks. Libby had to know how I was feeling, maybe even better than I did.

Another wave of tears filled my throat. I talked through them. "I'm sorry, Libby. I should have remembered Emily's leaving. You don't need to hear me moaning about not being ready to give up mothering." I tapped myself on the side of my head with the heel of my hand. "I'm such a clod sometimes. Open mouth, insert foot. You'd think by my age I'd know better." For the first time this day I was finally admitting I was getting older.

Tell her the rest. About what you really want.

What did I really want?

Meaning. You want meaning to your life. Something to show you made a difference.

I opened my mouth. Closed it. I didn't know if I dared—

Libby reached out and put a hand on my knee. "It's okay. We all have struggles at different times in our lives. Sometimes at the same time." With a nod she acknowledged our mutual ache. "It's okay to want a baby. Just don't let it keep you from growing in other ways."

I dabbed under my eyes with a square of toilet paper. I must look a mess. "Going in other ways? I'm not sure I know what you mean."

"Not going. *Growing.*" She shifted herself on the side of the tub as if trying to find a more comfortable spot. Or maybe getting into a better position to talk seriously to me. "Sometimes we get so caught up in our own ideas that we forget to keep an eye out for God's plans. While we're holding on for dear life to the fraying rope of our old dream, afraid of letting go for fear of getting hurt, we might be missing the stunning silk cord God is holding out to us instead of that ratty old rope."

"You should be a writer," I said, seeing in my mind the vivid image she'd painted.

"I am," she said.

"Oh, duh." Again, I hit myself gently on the side of my head. I'd forgotten all about the semimonthly column Olivia wrote for the *Brewster Banner* and the book she'd been working on for ages. "But I still don't see how not wanting a baby would make me feel better about Joey growing up."

Or getting older? Or having an empty life.

Olivia didn't need to know about that.

"Just think about it, okay?" Libby straightened her back, putting her hands on her knees. "I'm not saying you shouldn't have a baby. Maybe that *is* God's plan for you. All I'm saying is, if that path ends up in a dead end, don't forget to look around once you get to the end of the trail. There might be a beautiful footpath hidden in the grass that God has put there just for you. It might lead to somewhere wonderful. Somewhere you never imagined."

I nodded, pretending I understood. "I'll think about what you've said." That much I could promise to do. Libby's way of talking often had my mind fingering her words long after we'd parted. For now we needed to get back to the party. I smoothed the black knit of my skirt and checked the clasps on my hoop earrings. "Now…" I said, standing. "Where does Brenda keep her makeup? I think I need some major repair work." I glanced in the mirror. Oh, my. "I *know* I need work." I certainly wasn't the *pretty one* now.

There was a light knock on the door. Brenda poked her head around the doorframe, a sheepish look on her face. "There you two are." She stepped inside, closed the door behind her, and then leaned her back against it. She wasn't going to let us out until she'd said whatever was on her mind. "I thought maybe you both got mad at me and left." She took a deep breath as if relieved we were still here. "If you're in here planning how to tell me what a dork I am, you can forget it. I already know." She pressed the palms of her hands together in front of her chest, a little kid pleading for understanding. "Jan, please forgive me for writing that stupid prediction. I don't know what I was thinking. You told me you wanted to have a baby, and I don't know what possessed me to think it was my news to broadcast to the world. I wouldn't blame you if—"

"Stop." I held up one palm. "Enough. Apology accepted." I brushed my fingers through my long hair, pushing it behind my ears and flipping it over my shoulders. "Good grief, you two should know by now that I am the Queen of the Big Mouths. I've blabbered more news I shouldn't have than you two ever will. And I haven't exactly kept it a secret that Dan and I have been trying to have a baby. I guess it was just the way Connie blurted that thing about me being too old to want one—" There was that lump in my throat again. "Do you think I'm too old?"

"To want a baby?" Brenda asked. "No. I think there's something in most women that always has us wanting to mother something. A baby is just the easiest answer to that urge." She laughed. "Maybe you should get a puppy. You can wipe up accidents to your heart's content. It took care of any baby urges *I* had, I can tell you that."

"Don't either of you even breathe the word 'dog' to Bob," Libby cautioned. "He's been talking about getting a hunting dog for years. That's all I need. Now that I'll finally have the house empty and time to write, I certainly don't want a dog under my feet. That is not an option no matter what kind of urge I might have after Emily leaves." She looked back and forth between us. "Remind me of that if I ever even start to consider a dog. Or a baby."

"Brenda?" Eric's voice came from the hall. "Do you know where Jan and Olivia are?"

"Uh—" she stuck her head around the bathroom door. "They're in here with me?" It came out as a question, not an answer to one.

"All three of you are in the bathroom? What are you doing?"

Brenda's eyes flashed between Olivia and me.

"Don't you dare say 'talking about *dogs*,'" Libby whispered.

"Or *babies*," I added, not sure anymore *what* I wanted.

"Um, Jan's having trouble with—"

The don't-you-dare look in my eyes must have looked like two "Stop" signs. Her voice came to an abrupt halt.

"Her bra strap!" Libby called out. "Almost fixed. We'll be out in a second." A bubble of laughter popped from between her lips.

Mine too. Pretty soon all three of us were holding our stomachs and bending over as we tried to keep our giggles inside the bathroom walls. If this was what getting older was like, maybe it wasn't so bad after all.

Brenda was the first to stand up straight. She looked into the mirror, catching our eyes as she grabbed a powder puff and dabbed at her nose. "Some hostess I am. Having the best of the party in the bathroom. We'd better get back out there. At least I'd better."

As she left Libby stepped into her spot in front of the mirror and did a once-over with her eyes. "I guess it's true. Laughter does do good like medicine…or like makeup. I thought I'd look worse." She turned to me and pointed. "You, however, have raccoon eyes." She waved her hand as she bowed her way out of the bathroom. "It's all yours. Left-hand drawer. Have at it."

I grabbed a tissue and wrapped it around my index finger, moistening the tip with a drop of the scented hand lotion Brenda had on the counter. I scrubbed at the black smudges beneath my eyes. I'd learned the beauty tip from my mother when I'd been crying at Aunt Beth's funeral. *Can't look like that.* My mom was seventy now, but dressed each day as if the Queen of England might drop by. She'd given up on changing Maureen's tomboy tendencies years ago. Instead, I became her Barbie doll.

I rummaged in the drawer Libby had directed me to. I daubed on some blush and powder, but I was hesitant to use Brenda's eye makeup. I'd read too many beauty tips about eye infections to dare dig in. I leaned into the mirror. My face needed far more work than this makeshift makeup counter offered. My hand hovered over the fat-bristled hairbrush on the counter. I doubted Brenda had head lice. I'd take my chances.

I tugged the brush through my hair. Any style I'd had at the start of the night had long since disappeared. There was a ponytail band wrapped around the end of the brush. That might do the trick. I flipped my head upside down, gathered my hair together just in back of the crown of my head, and wrapped the stretchy black band around and around, pulling it tight. I whipped my head back up, tugging at my make-do ponytail, making it tighter. Ouch. That was as tight as it would go. I turned to the mirror.

Oh. One look told me my hair looked awful. A second look told me my face didn't. Where the skin around my eyes and mouth had drooped a bit minutes before, it was now taut and smooth. *You're the pretty one.* My makeshift hairdo had turned into an improvised facelift. Mom would approve.

I leaned into the mirror, inspecting my quick handiwork. If I could do this with a hairbrush and an elastic band, just think what a skilled plastic surgeon with a scalpel could do.

"Sometimes we get so caught up in our own ideas that we forget to keep an eye out for God's plans. While we're holding on for dear life to the fraying rope of our old dream, afraid of letting go for fear of getting

hurt, we might be missing the stunning silk cord God is holding out to us instead of that ratty old rope."

Maybe a *baby* wasn't what God wanted me to have to keep me young. Maybe He meant for me to have a *face-lift.* Maybe *that* was the stunning silk cord Libby had talked about.

I pulled the black elastic band from my hair. No way would I let anyone see the new me just yet. I pulled the brush through my hair, coaxing it back onto my shoulders, suddenly very glad I had come to this party. By this time next year I'd make forty-four look like thirty-four.

We'd see what Connie would say then.

Kenny

A baby? *Four* kids? How in the world was I ever going to be able to support a wife and four kids on the measly income I got from this place? I unlocked the door to the gas station and walked through the cluttered room that doubled as office and sales space. The faint scents of oil and gas mingled with the smell of overcooked coffee and cigarettes. You think people would know enough not to smoke in a gas station, but try telling that to the coffee crew that stopped here every day around ten.

I let myself through the side door into the coolness of the large, two-stall garage. The familiar smell of oil was thick in here. I was used to it, but it would air out as soon as I opened the two big garage doors. First I needed to turn on the pumps. Never could tell when one of the semis that hauled grain through town might need an early morning fill. I walked to the fuse box in the rear of the garage and flipped two switches. A slight hum told me the pumps were ready for the day.

Better get the coffee going and then fill the pop machine outside. It was going to be a warm one today. I grabbed the coffeepot and a key before heading outside, around the corner of the station to the bathrooms to get some water. I went into the women's bathroom; it was always cleaner. One of these days I was going to have to think about moving the bathrooms inside. There was hardly a station around that didn't have inside bathrooms anymore. But that would cost money. Money I was going to need to feed another mouth around our table.

Pot filled, coffee brewing, I walked back to the small storeroom behind the office, hiked at the belt around my jeans, and then hoisted three cases of pop into my arms. Yikes! My shoulder! It had been tender this morning when I woke up, but not like this. Ouch! What in the world was going on? I lifted my knee, trying to balance the cases of pop that were falling from my right arm.

I managed to slide the cases back onto the stack in a jumbled pile. Oh, man, was my arm throbbing. The arm I'd made that dumb error with at last night's softball game. I was going to have to ice it or something. I sat on the cases of soda and rubbed at the tender muscles. Maybe I could wrap it with something. Tape it up. But then I wouldn't be able to reach above my head and do the underbody work I had coming in today. No, I was just going to have to tough it out.

I stood, testing my shoulder by circling it forward and then back. Man, that hurt. Okay, so maybe I shouldn't carry three cases of pop all at once. I'd have to carry them one at a time.

I lifted one case, twenty-four cans. Man! Even that caused my shoulder to spasm. I set the case back down. *Wimp!*

Better wimp than outright bawling. Not a pretty picture. Not at Kenny's SuperPumper, anyway.

I heard a diesel truck pull up outside. I would just have to grit my teeth and get out there. Pumping gas was money.

Roy Wahl was climbing out of his vehicle. "Fill 'er up." He spit onto the concrete and then stood, looking at the sky. "Good day for combining. Soon as it dries off."

If gas was money for me, the weather was money for the farmers around here. Trouble was, when one wanted sun, another wanted rain. I'd learned just to agree with whoever was doing the talking.

"Sure is," I said, reaching for the gas pump. "What're you working on now? Wheat?"

I lifted the pump handle and my shoulder cramped. Ooooh! I held my arm close to my body, using my left hand to prop up my elbow, searching for whatever support I could find, managing, somehow, to fit the nozzle into the truck's gas tank. If Roy had answered me, I didn't hear. My shoulder was screaming. "Windows need cleaning?"

Please say, no.

"Yup."

I gripped the squeegee, stepped on the running board, and reached for the over-sized windshield. There was no way my right arm would reach across that bug-infested glass, much less have the pressure I was going to need to eliminate bug guts. I transferred the squeegee handle to my left hand, wondering why I hadn't converted this station to self-serve years ago. Now there was an idea whose time had come.

The Sentex station down the street had put in credit card-operated pumps a year ago. The station operator didn't even have to set eyes on whoever was at the pump if they didn't want to. I could hardly imagine what my day might be like if I didn't have my customers to gab with. That's what made work seem not so much like work. Until today, anyway.

I stepped off the running board. Roy's windows were streaked, but it was the best I could do with my left arm. Maybe he'd just be grateful I still washed windshields at all. If he went to the Sentex station, he would have to pump his own gas, wash his own windows, and pay a penny more for gas.

"Missed a spot there." Roy pointed to a bug blotch in the middle of the window.

A quick flash of anger burned in my chest. What did he expect for free? I swallowed what I wanted to say. "Sorry about that. My arm's giving me a little bit of trouble today." I lifted my shoulder so he'd get my drift.

"Arthritis?"

Oh, brother, just because he was getting old and his body was giving out didn't mean mine was. "Nah." I'd better set him straight. "Last night at the softball game I was trying to throw out a guy running home. From left field," I added, just so he'd know how hard I'd had to throw.

"Get him?" He had to ask.

"No," I mumbled, taking Roy's credit card and heading to the office. I'd spent long enough on his nine-gallon purchase. I had oil to change and tires to rotate. Jobs where I didn't have to explain my error of last night over and over again.

I wasn't about to bring up my second big error. The one where I'd confessed to Diane that I wasn't one bit excited about having another kid.

No, that was one blunder I didn't plan to repeat to anyone. Not even myself.

⌐

"Diane?" I tried hard to make sure she'd hear the note of apology in my voice over the phone. Other than necessary conversation, we hadn't spoken for two days. Two *long* days, in which I'd tiptoed around the house trying not to make waves...or eye contact, knowing that would be an invitation for either anger or tears. Two days, in which I'd spent as much time at the station as possible. Just like now. I knew she was expecting an apology for my comment about not wanting this baby, but I was trying to come to grips with what I'd say and still be honest. Besides that, my shoulder was hurting something awful, and it didn't help that I didn't dare complain to her. I could use some sympathy, too.

"What?" Her voice was flat. She still hadn't forgiven me. I could hear Paige and Billy yelling in the background.

"Is Renae there?" I was hoping I could bypass Diane on this one.

"No."

Great. "Where is she?"

"Babysitting at the Jangulas'." Diane wasn't about to give me an inch more than necessary.

"When will she be done?"

"I don't know." Her voice was tight, wound up like a kinked air hose.

Oh, man. I blew into the phone. I should have called Mike Anderson, the high school kid who pumped gas for me three evenings a week so I could go home and have supper with Diane and the kids. Mike would be leaving for college soon. I'd been thinking about looking for someone else, but now, with another kid on the way, that extra few bucks might be better in my pocket. It had hardly seemed worth calling him to cover for me for an hour. All of a sudden

I felt like doubling his pay. I was simply going to have to bite the bullet and ask Diane. "Do you think you could come to the station for about an hour this afternoon?"

"No. I have two small children to care for." She paused, too long for me not to squirm at what I guessed must be coming. "Someone in this house has to care for them. Plus, I have one on the way. *Remember?*"

I caught every layer of her meaning. The two kids who were screaming in the background. The one kid we hadn't talked about yet.

"Diane, I'm sorry. I really am. I love our kids, all *four* of them." The words fell out of my mouth. They hadn't been near as hard to say as I'd imagined. I only wished I'd had the nerve to say them face-to-face to her. And soon. A hug right now would feel plenty good and do wonders to soothe things between us. I hated it when we fought…with words or with silence. I really was sorry about what I'd said two nights ago. My thoughtless comment had hurt me, too. I didn't want to resent having a baby. I knew every one of my kids was a gift from God. It's just that I was still trying to be happy about the present I hadn't expected.

"I wish you would have said that two days ago." A huge sigh came through the phone line just as a Brewster Badgers school bus pulled up to the pump outside.

Lousy timing on my part and the bus driver's. I was going to have to make quick work of this off-the-cuff apology. "I know. I'm really sorry." I could see the bus driver, Marvin Bender, climbing out from behind the wheel. School was starting in two weeks, and it was time to get the buses ready for the country routes. I relied on my business with the school for a major part of my income. I needed to hustle out there. Honesty would be the quickest route. "Diane, someone just pulled up, but I promise you we'll talk about this tonight. What I wanted was for Renae to come watch the pumps around two. But if she can't come, could you do it? Please? Bring the kids if you have to. I have an appointment I have to keep." The door of the station opened, and Marvin walked in. I could hear Diane talking to me, questioning, as I moved my mouth from the receiver. "Hey, Marv, be right with you." I spoke back into the phone, interrupting Diane's questions. "Gotta go. See you a little before two. Thanks, hon." I hung up the phone.

There. Oh, man, did I feel better. Bases covered. An apology and someone to watch the station this afternoon all in one phone call. Not bad. What I'd thought was lousy timing on Marv's part actually turned into a lucky thing. If I'd have had to explain to Diane that I was going to the doctor for my bum shoulder in the same sentence I'd apologized, it might have started another argument. Diane had cautioned me often enough about being careful on the job. Our insurance deductible was about as high as five months of our insurance premiums. No way would she be happy to hear my softball injury was sending me to the doctor. Or about the bills that would follow.

I looked at the large clock hanging on the wall. I had four hours to cover this next base. Four hours to come up with an explanation that would satisfy my bookkeeper. The bookkeeper also known as my wife.

~

"Well, it's too late now." I could hear the exasperation in Diane's voice. She stood in the doorway of the office as I finished up an oil change out in the garage. She was standing there, trying to serve as a human shield, keeping Paige away from the greasy floor of the garage. Good thing I had the hoist and John Harris's Buick as my shield. Good thing one of Billy's friends had a birthday party this afternoon, too. One less kid for Diane to supervise while she managed the station for an hour.

Diane scooped Paige into her arms and walked as near to me as she dared. I knew she didn't like getting under the hoist. She was always certain it would fall on her or me. I'd told her a thousand times there were safety features built in, but she chose to keep her distance. Fine with me on a day like today, when things were still touch and go between us. "Have you ever thought about quitting softball?" she asked.

"Not really," I answered, not liking how unsure I sounded. The day I couldn't play sports was the day I'd know I was officially old. I didn't plan to get there for quite some time. If ever. I tightened the lug nut with the air gun, using my left hand. Technology had made working on vehicles a lot easier, but trying to do my usual work with the wrong hand was an exercise in frustration.

"What if the doctor says you need an operation?" Diane shifted Paige to her other hip. "Then what?"

I stepped out from under the Buick on the opposite side from where Diane and Paige stood and pressed the lever that began lowering the hoist. "That's what we pay insurance for." She should know that; she wrote the checks for the premiums.

"Oh, yeah." She laughed, not a funny, ha-ha laugh. "You've obviously forgotten that even with our high deductible we still have a co-pay."

Co-pay? She was wrong, I hadn't forgotten. I just wasn't sure I knew what it was. I didn't think it would help to mention that right now. "We'll manage," I muttered, reassuring myself as much as her.

"Um-hmm," she nodded, clearly not reassured. "And when you're in the hospital, recovering from this operation, who do you think is going to run the station? Renae? Billy? Maybe Paige?"

As if on cue, Paige chimed in, "Me-me."

"See," I said, grabbing the Armor All and ducking my head into the Harris' car, "she'll do it."

"Very funny." Diane wasn't in the mood for jokes. She opened the door on the other side of the car and stood Paige on the seat, bending down so she could see me. Criminy, a guy couldn't have a moment's peace around here. "Even if we could afford a sitter, and I did have time to sit here all day and pump gas, you know I can't do any of the shop work. Did you ever think of *that* when you threw that crummy softball?"

I knew better than to even try and answer her question. I shined the dashboard of the car and kept my mouth shut.

"Well, did you?" All I could see of Diane now was her torso and her hands planted stubbornly on her hips.

If she was going to demand an answer, I'd give her one. I threw the rag into the car and stood on my side, glaring at her over the top of the car. "No, I didn't think about it. I was too busy trying to enjoy the few hours I had away from work for a change. All I ask is one night a week to play softball, and even then I have to take the kids along and try to keep an eye on them at the same time. I can't get one minute for myself, and now we've got another kid on the way." I stepped aside and slammed the car door just as the driveway bell sounded. I glared toward the pumps. Old Mr. Ost was there, tooting his horn, thinking he was doing me a favor by letting me know he was giving me his three-dollar, top-off-the-tank business. I took off my cap, dragged my fingers through my hair, and set my cap back on. Tight. Stared defiantly at Diane. "One minute. That's all I ask."

Diane slowly closed her eyes, stood stock still, and then opened them. She gestured with her chin. "Go to your appointment. I'll take care of Mr. Ost." She reached into the car and took Paige in her arms. I could see tired tears welling in Diane's eyes. She turned away from me. It didn't take a genius to understand she probably wanted a minute to herself, too.

I held out my arms even though she couldn't see them. "Here, I'll take Paige."

Diane stopped walking and spoke to the air in front of her. "What about your precious minute?"

Funny, how that minute didn't seem so great when it was a mad minute. Dropping the whole thing might be a good idea. I stepped closer to her and stuck my index finger into Paige's curled fist. "They have that play corner at the clinic. Paige can come with me." I pulled my chunky little girl from Diane's arms, gritting my teeth against the pain. "Can't you?" I nuzzled Paige's stomach, making her squirm. Giggle.

Mr. Ost tapped at his horn again. Diane shook her head. I wasn't sure if she was exasperated at me or Mr. Ost. Probably both of us. I leaned over and kissed her on the cheek. "Thanks, hon." I knew when the getting was good.

I got.

⤳

"You did something all right." Dr. West dug her fingers into the skin surrounding my shoulder. "Move your shoulder forward...now back. Can you lift your arm?"

At this point I wasn't too proud to wince. "Ouch." I hadn't been all that thrilled to be seeing Dr. West in the first place, but when I'd called for an appointment, I'd been told Brewster's only other doctor, the only *male* doctor, was "on vacation all this week." Great. Just great. That left Dr. West. Dr. *Ellen* West. Well, at least this appointment didn't involve any private parts. Having her poke around my shoulder I could handle.

"You can put your shirt back on." She walked to the small desk that hung from the wall, sat on the stool, and picked up a pen. Tapped it on my chart.

I didn't like the expression on her face. "What seems to be wrong?" With a grimace I slid my arm back into the sleeve of my shirt. "Am I going to need an operation?"

Her face cleared. She shook her head. "No. That's the good news. For now, anyway. We have several options we can try before we resort to that. You might have torn a ligament. Damaged your rotator cuff. I'm going to order an X-ray on that shoulder so we can see what's going on—"

"Is that expensive?" I had to ask. Diane would.

Dr. West flipped through my chart. "You have insurance, don't you?"

"Yeah, but our deductible is high and there's that co-pay business." Good thing Diane had mentioned that.

"Okay then." She rolled her tongue between her lips, over her teeth, thinking. "Let's try this first. It might just be a bad sprain. I'm going to order a cortisone shot to try to bring the swelling down."

"A shot?" I could feel the blood draining from my face. Needles and me...uh-uh.

"An injection will be the fastest route to try at this point. I'm also going to put you on an anti-inflammatory for a few days, and want you to rest that arm."

Oh, man. Now my blood started racing. "I have two oil changes to do yet this afternoon and a set of brake pads to replace. How am I supposed to rest my arm when I've got a business to run?"

Dr. West looked at her watch. "Don't you have someone to help you?"

"Well, there's Diane, but no way is she going to change oil. She'll pump gas and that's about it." Did Dr. West really think my wife was going to do engine work?

"You don't have another mechanic? Someone who can cover strenuous tasks for the next few days?"

"No-oo." She knew this was Brewster. She should know most of the businesses around here ran on a shoestring. Mom and Pop. And at Kenny's SuperPumper it was mostly "Pop." I was hoping when Billy got older he'd take an interest, but Diane would hardly let him set foot out in the garage at his age now. I snuck him under the hoist with me now and then, but whenever Diane found out she threw a fit. And I could forget about Renae. About all she'd be interested in doing was reading the owner's manuals in car cubbyholes.

Dr. West cleared her throat. "Let's try the injection and medication. You do the best you can trying to rest that arm. Don't overdo it. We want to prevent further injury. And, I suppose it goes without saying that you shouldn't be playing ball until the swelling and pain subside."

Not exactly what I wanted to hear with Class C play-offs next week. We'd have to see about those instructions. Maybe the shot would do the trick. I'd worry about the play-offs later. "You're the doctor," is what I said.

She scrawled a prescription and stood. "I'll send a nurse in with the injection." She walked to the door, put her hand on the knob, and then turned. Cleared her throat again. "I don't know if you know my son, Pete? He's between jobs right now, but he's got a knack for work-ings on motors. If you decide you need help…" Her words hung in the air.

I knew her son, Pete, all right. Pete West. Loser with a capital "L," as the kids would say. Everyone in Brewster knew about Pete West. I knew he was over eighteen because he stopped at the station all the time to buy cigarettes. I'd checked his ID for a couple years, just to make a point. Smoking wasn't good for anyone, especially a punk who had enough strikes against him already. He'd been involved in some drug sniffing thing at the school a bunch of years ago, coulda killed him from what I heard, and that had been simply the start of his downhill slide. You'd think a doctor's son would be smart enough to know better. Drugs. Drinking. The grapevine had him doing all of that and more. I myself had seen him driving his dressed up '97 Grand Prix down Main Street at a good twenty miles over the speed limit more than once. Car was flaming red, hard for a guy to miss. Or a cop. The kid was bad news. If you could call him a kid anymore. He had to be… "How old is Pete now?"

Dr. West pressed her lips together before answering, "Old enough to know better." She dropped her head for just a second. "Guess his reputation has preceded him. Sorry." She sighed. "His dad, my ex-husband, died three weeks ago. A heart attack. Pete's been…" She wavered a hand through the air. "He's having a tough time. I just thought maybe…" She lifted one shoulder. "It's the 'mom' in me. I still have hope for that kid." She stopped. "Young man," she corrected. "I had to try." She looked at her watch again. "Well, I have another appointment. I'll see you next week."

All of a sudden I felt sorry for her. I knew how much I wanted the best for my kids. She couldn't be a whole lot different. She'd been a single mom for a lot of years. Raising a kid alone couldn't be easy. Diane and I had enough trouble raising ours, and we were doing it together. And we had just started the teen years. Who knew what the future held for our family?

I'd never really thought about it before today, but just because Ellen West was a doctor and made a slug of money, I'd somehow figured she'd have it made. Life would always be easy for her, or something.

I looked at her then and could see something in her eyes. Tiredness? Resignation? I wasn't the sharpest guy in the world, but it looked to me as if Dr. Ellen West might like some hope for her kid. I wasn't planning to hire him, but what I said was, "I'll keep him in mind."

"Thanks," she said. "I'd appreciate that." She held out her right hand.

I stuck out mine. "Yeow!" I pulled my arm back in. "You should know better." I grinned at the same time I rubbed my shoulder.

She smiled back at me. "You're right, I should." She nodded. "Take care."

$\sim$

I sat back down, looked the other way, and gritted my teeth through the cortisone shot.

"You can go now." The nurse patted a Band-Aid onto my arm. "Stop by the front desk and make an appointment for sometime next week."

I rolled down my sleeve as I walked into the waiting area of the clinic, suddenly remembering I'd forgotten all about Paige. I'd left her in the waiting room watching a cartoon when I'd been called for my appointment. The two gals at the reception desk had promised to keep an eye on her and come get me if she got fussy. "We do this all the time," they told me.

I glanced at the play corner now. No Paige! My heart did a flop into my stomach a second before I noticed Jan Jordan on the far end of the room, holding Paige in her lap and reading her a storybook.

Once I saw Paige, I wasn't sure if my heart was pounding over the fear of losing her or because of the low-cut top Jan had on. If my arm weren't hurting so much I would have shook my hand in the air. She was *hot!* There was no other word for that top she had on than Electric Green. I didn't even know if that was a color, but if it wasn't, that's what they should call it. Electric.

I tugged at the belt of my jeans. Jan didn't need to be watching Paige. I should go get her right now, but I was feeling suddenly tongue-tied. Man, if Diane looked like *that* we'd never have a fight; I simply wouldn't be able to speak around her.

Quit staring, man.

Oh, yeah. I gave my head a quick shake. It was hard not to be a red-blooded American male around someone like Jan Jordan.

A red-blooded, middle-aged American male.

I looked down at my stomach, hanging over my belt like a kangaroo pouch.

With a kid in it.

I sucked in my stomach as I walked toward Jan.

And Paige, remember?

Oh, yeah. And Paige. I racked my brain, trying to think of something to say. Something clever. "Babysitters didn't look like that when I was a kid."

Oh, man, what a downright stupid thing to say. You might as well have said, "I think you're hot," and be done with it.

Jan looked up from the book, a slow smile spreading across her face. I could swear she batted her eyes at me. They were brown. And big.

"Kenny! Hi!" She snuggled Paige against that electric top of hers. I tried not to look where Paige's chubby cheek was just then. "What a little sweetheart you have here. I hope you don't mind that I read her a story?"

"As long as insurance covers your fee." I laughed at my lame attempt to be clever, embarrassed for a reason I couldn't understand.

Brilliant, Kenny. Go ahead and drool, and then put yourself out of your misery.

Jan's laughter wrapped around mine. Like we were friends or something. Maybe she didn't think I was overweight and a blubbering idiot. She smoothed Paige's hair with her shiny fingernails. "I know, aren't these insurance companies nuts, these days? I swear, eventually they are going to simply do away with doctors and have us report directly to them."

"Yeah." I laughed. I wasn't sure I knew what she just said, but it didn't really matter when someone was that pretty. I wondered if Jan was this nice to everyone, or if it was something about me.

It's your turn. Say something, stupid.

"You have Blue Cross?"

No! Not something stupid. You're the one who's stupid!

She smiled. Polite-like. Maybe she was used to guys saying dumb things. "Yes, we do have Blue Cross. It's expensive, but good. What about you?"

Insurance. Insurance. Who was our company? I opened my mouth. Closed it. A fish. I must look like a fish. Out of water. Diane took care of all that insurance stuff. I shoved my hands in the pockets of my pants. "I—uh—"

"Jan Jordan?" Saved by the nurse. "The doctor will see you now."

Jan slid Paige off her lap, kissing her on the cheek. "Bye, sweetie." She straightened, running her hands over the lower part of her bright green top. As if it needed instructions to cling to her waist like that. She picked up her purse and tossed it over her shoulder. She tilted her chin down a little, angled her eyes up. "Nice chatting with you." Big smile. At me.

Oh, boy.

"Daddy." Paige pushed at my leg. "Want up." She held out her arms.

I hadn't even realized I'd been standing there watching Jan Jordan's swaying walk, her hair that bounced around like a shampoo commercial. If only Diane—

"Up!"

Back to reality. I bent and scooped Paige into my arms, grimacing at the painful reminder of my sore shoulder. Or maybe it was the reminder that Jan Jordan was a fantasy and this was my life.

Jan

"Jan, how are you? It's been too long." Dr. West entered the room smiling and gave me a quick hug. "I haven't seen you or Olivia in...well, much too long." She set down my file as she settled herself on a small stool near my chair.

A couple times Libby had arranged a coffee date for the three of us on one of Ellen's rare days off. I wasn't sure why she included me. Maybe Libby thought my fashion sense would rub off on Ellen.

Or Dr. West's smarts would rub off on you? I flipped my hair over my shoulder. I wasn't dumb. I'd just never had to rely on anything but my looks. And if I didn't have that to depend on anymore...well, that's why I was here. I was making sure I *would* have my looks for some time to come. *You're the pretty one.* What other choice did I have?

Other than waving at Ellen as our cars passed on the streets of Brewster, I hadn't seen her in ages. Goodness, the woman could certainly use some help. Of course, she had to wear a lab coat, but I doubted there were rules against adding some nice color under that too-bright white. A fresh haircut, a little eye shadow and blush, and a shiny necklace and bracelet or two would do wonders to show off her good bone structure. Maybe I could work it into the conversation.

You're sounding just like your mother. I twisted my wedding ring around my finger. How many times had I inwardly groaned as my mom recited self-improvement tips in my ear as we people-watched at the mall? If Dr. West was happy with who she was, who was I to judge?

Maybe you should stop using your mother's standards to judge yourself. A quick wash of relief was quickly replaced by a stab of fear.

56

What other way was there? I sat back, thankful this was simply a consultation. I still had time to think things over.

I fingered the pendant on my necklace. I hated those flimsy, ugly, paper half-gowns they made a person wear for an annual PAP exam. I'd convinced the nurse there was no need for me to undress for this appointment, but she'd insisted on taking my temperature and blood pressure, anyway. Probably some insurance requirement. As it was, I was at the Brewster clinic because of our insurance policy. It had changed recently, and the only way our policy would cover anything was if I were referred to a specialist by my doctor-of-choice, or whatever fancy wording they used to try and disguise the fact they had me over their barrel.

I crossed my legs, hoping Ellen would notice the brown, suede heels I had on. Old habits were hard to break. Certainly, the powers that be wouldn't object to her wearing something fashionable on her feet. Ellen looked over my chart as she sat on the small stool near me. At least she had great posture, which reminded me that I should sit up straighter, too. I lifted my spine and pushed my shoulders back. There.

Janine, don't slouch. There. See how much better you look? Maureen, look at your sister. Doesn't she look much prettier when she stands up straight?

"So, what brings you to see me today?" Ellen turned from my chart, which contained some vague scratching. I'd purposely been evasive when the nurse had questioned why I was here. My face-lift was none of her business. If, a couple months from now, the folks in Brewster were whispering about how much younger I looked, I didn't need a blabbermouth nurse spilling my secret.

"Well," I lifted my chin and then quickly lowered it. I wanted Dr. West to be sure and see the double chin I was developing. "The reason I'm here today is for a referral. To a…" I hesitated, suddenly feeling self-conscious to be asking Ellen about a face-lift. Considering how unconcerned she seemed to be about her appearance, I didn't know how sympathetic she'd be to my concern about how I looked…or *wanted* to look. "I'm…uh…" The words stumbled on my tongue.

She held up one finger. "You don't have to be embarrassed about anything in this office, Jan. Everything we talk about is private, and, believe me, I've heard it all. Let me try and help you out. Is this of a sexual nature, by any chance?"

Oh, my. I laughed a little too loud. "Thank goodness, no."

Ellen tilted her head from one side to the other. "That's usually the topic most people have trouble with. I do remember the coffee conversation we had together with Olivia about a year ago. You made reference to the fact that you were hoping to have a baby, and, well…" Her eyes flitted to my stomach. "Obviously, that hasn't happened. I guess I assumed…"

For a fleeting second, I recalled how warm and precious little Paige had felt in my arms moments ago. How nice it would be to have a baby again. But, no, that apparently wasn't going to happen. I waved a hand in front of my face as if that were old news. "Oh, *that*. I gave that idea up…" It sounded shallow to say *a week ago*. I fudged. "A while ago. I decided I kind of like having a flat stomach." I laid a hand on my abdomen, forcing a chuckle, trying to make my comment sound like a joke. Through the fabric of my chocolate-brown knit skirt I could feel the firm elastic of the control-top pantyhose I was wearing. Even the one hundred sit-ups I did every morning couldn't keep up with gravity. My secret was Victoria's Secret. Without that support, my stomach resembled slightly firm pudding. Come to think of it, maybe a tummy tuck was in order, too.

I pushed one side of my hair behind my ear. Maybe Ellen would notice the crow's feet by my eyes. I certainly wasn't going to get anywhere unless I just said it. "I was hoping for a referral. To a…" The words "plastic surgeon" suddenly seemed so, well…*plastic*. Artificial. Fake. Surely, there must be another way of saying this. Think. Ah! "*Cosmetic* surgeon." There, that was exactly what I wanted. I nodded, proud of myself.

Dr. West blinked a couple of times and ran her tongue under her lips as she assessed my face with her eyes. "I see," she said, slowly.

There, I knew she'd see exactly what I meant once she took a good look. I nodded again, eager for her to explain the next step. I was hoping that by the end of the week I could be sitting in a doctor's office in Carlton for my presurgery consultation. "Can you recommend someone?" I tilted my head, smiled at her a little, and spoke quickly. "Someone *good*, of course. I don't want just anyone cutting on me." I stopped, giving her time to think.

She was quiet. Too quiet. Maybe there wasn't anyone she knew of in North Dakota. Come to think of it, there probably wasn't a high demand for plastic…*cosmetic* surgery in a rural state like this. A state where people wore their wrinkles as if they were linen…something that was *supposed* to be wrinkled.

"I wouldn't mind going to Minneapolis, if I had to." I wasn't quite sure how I was going to tell Dan I'd be off to the Twin Cities for surgery. He'd have to drive me there, probably stay a few days, and return with me for follow-up appointments. I swallowed hard. I hadn't told him about my face lift plan. I'd been hoping I could have the procedure done in Carlton. That way I could drive myself to most of my appointments, except the actual surgery, of course. I didn't think he'd mind one bit if I looked younger. What he might mind is having to take so much time off work for my little project. "Is there someone in Carlton?" Why did I sound so nervous? "Can you think of anyone?"

Slowly she nodded her head, pressed her lips together into a tight, thinking-hard line, and then spoke. "Oh, I can think of several qualified surgeons." She rested one elbow on the desk, fingering an imitation-pearl button on her lab coat. She continued to stare at me, eyeing every pore of my face. "What were you thinking of having done?" she finally asked.

This was the part I'd been waiting for. I sat up even straighter, leaned forward, and pointed to the sides of my eyes. "See these lines? I've been putting moisturizer around my eyes for fifteen years and has it done any good?" I answered my own question. "No. And look at this." I dipped my chin, poking at the folds that gathered beneath it. "Now, watch this." I sat back in the chair, put a hand on either side of my face just in front of my ears and pushed back, just a little. "Can you see? See how a tuck right there could take ten, fifteen years off my face?"

Dr. West picked up a pen and flipped to the front of my chart. Her eyes scanned the first page. "How old are you, Jan?"

"Forty-three." The first time ever I didn't mind saying the number. She had to understand this was middle age we were talking about.

She put down her pen. Looked at me. "Would you really want to look twenty-eight?"

"Ye-es." Why did she think I was here asking about plastic...*cosmetic* surgery?

Ellen folded her hands on her lap. She closed her eyes. It almost looked as if she were praying for an answer as to who would be the very best person to do my surgery. I crossed my arms over my chest, waiting.

After a few seconds, Ellen opened her eyes. "I'm wondering if you've explored other options?"

"Other options?" My heart did a quick little dance. I'd never thought there could be other options. Maybe there were nonsurgical techniques only doctors were privy to. You'd think my beauty magazines would have the latest scoop. I creased my brows before remembering I was trying to break that bad habit. I raised them instead. "You mean I might not need surgery?"

She leaned forward and put her hands on my knees. "Look at my face," she said.

Ellen was at least ten years older than I and looked it. Circles under her eyes, graying hair, those same, saggy lines I was getting around my nose and mouth. A good concealer would do a lot for her, but surgery could eliminate the need.

You're getting as good as your mother.

I winced at the reminder. I put one hand on top of Ellen's. The least I could do was empathize.

"Those lines beside *your* eyes?" Ellen said. "My eyes? You know what I call them?"

I knew what she was going to say. So I said it for her. "Too-much-sun-tanning-when-we-were-teenagers lines?"

Her eyes crinkled. More than they already were. She gave a soft laugh. "Funny, but true," she said. She touched the side of her eye with an unpolished fingernail. Tapped at her face. "I call these *character* lines." She sat back, taking her warm hand away from under mine. She looked down at her ringless hands, then up at me. "I got a couple of these lines when my husband walked out on me. Some of them might have come from squinting when I forgot to wear my sunglasses the week I took my son, Pete, to Disney World. I'm guessing a couple more were added when he started getting into trouble. Then my mom died. A couple friends. But there are good lines, too. A whole bunch of them came from laughing. Most of them, actually." She smiled, as if remembering some of those times, and then she looked at me. "I wouldn't trade any of these character lines. I earned them, especially the tough-times ones. I might appreciate them more than the others because I grew from them. Do you see what I'm getting at?"

I happened to be blonde, but I wasn't stupid. She might not mind remembering her broken marriage every time she looked in the mirror, but I wasn't quite so fond of the memories my eyes carried. I could still see the bad haircut of the secretary I'd caught my first husband fooling around with, and I could clearly remember the look on the face of my second husband when I'd told him I was pregnant. He bluntly announced, "I'm not ready to have a kid." He'd eyed me, a long look up, then down. "Besides," he said, a sly smile turning on his lips, "a kid'll make you fat and dumpy. I don't want a wife who looks like that." He'd given me two choices, and they both started with the letter "A." Abortion or alone. I'd shown him. I didn't end up alone or fat and dumpy. I ended up with Joey…and crow's feet. I could do without those memories and the two characters who had caused most of them. I could also do without the lines.

"Of course I understand," I said, flipping my hair back over my shoulder with a toss of my head. Dr. West might think her lines gave her character. To me they simply made her look as though she'd given up caring about how she looked. Maybe in ten years I'd feel the same, but in the meantime I planned to do all I could to maintain the image I wanted.

Image? Isn't that another word for "mask"? What are you trying to hide?

Nothing. I shifted in my seat. I wasn't trying to hide anything. My life was an open book. I'd never made any secret of my two failed marriages. Or the fact that I'd dyed my hair since high school. All I wanted was to look the best I could. The way God intended. What was so bad about that?

Trying to look good for Me? Are you sure? You're already perfect in My eyes.

I was so far from perfect it wasn't funny. I flipped the thought away with my chin.

Ellen sat back on the stool and closed my chart. She laid her pen on top of my file. "Surgery is a rather drastic step, Jan. And it can be very expensive. Most insurance companies won't cover an elective surgery like the one you're seeking, you know."

Oooo-hhh, now I got it, she was trying to talk me out of surgery because of the insurance angle. Did she get some kind of kickback from the insurance company if I didn't have an operation?

That doesn't even make any sense. She just said insurance doesn't cover plastic…cosmetic surgery. Maybe she's trying to save you from doing something you'll regret.

Fat chance. How could I ever regret looking better?

"I'd rather you tried some other options first." Dr. West's eyes flitted to her watch.

"I told you already, I've tried all kinds of creams, moisturizers, you name it. They don't work. If you know of something that does, I'm all ears."

She sighed. "Jan, there's no magic medicine to keep you from getting older. I was thinking more along the lines of filling your time with things that make you happy. Maybe a job, some volunteer work. Things that add meaning to your days. An operation can't give you any of those things, and you might end up spending a lot of money and not be pleased with the results."

"I've given this a lot of thought." *Yeah, one week.* "And I think I'd be very pleased to look ten years younger."

"Maybe." Dr. West tilted her head from side to side. "Maybe not. Once it's done you can't undo it. I've heard of women who say they don't feel as though they know themselves when they look in the mirror after a face-lift. It doesn't feel like *them* anymore. They kind of miss the person they were."

"That's dumb," I replied. "I'd still be the same person. I'd just look younger."

She waved a hand in the air. "You can seek youth from a jar or from a scalpel. I guess it depends on your definition of young. Some of the oldest, most discouraged people I know are in their twenties and thirties, and some of the youngest, most joyful people I know are in their eighties. It doesn't make much difference what the numbers say; what matters is what's in here." She tapped at her graying temples. She really needed a hair appointment. "And in here." She tapped again, at her chest. Which sagged.

There was a light knock at the door. It opened a couple inches and a nurse said softly, "Dr. West, an ambulance is coming in. You're needed over at the hospital."

"I'll be right there." Dr. West picked up my chart, nestled it into the crook of her arm, and stood. From that angle, the way the overhead light hit her face, she actually looked quite pretty. And that was saying something under fluorescent bulbs. "Sometimes, when we reach a certain age, a person can look back over their life and feel as if it's slipping away. We can feel the need to do something drastic to hang on to the past, rather than looking ahead and embracing the future. I'd really like you to think about this before you do anything you might regret." She bent over, quickly wrote on a prescription pad, and then handed a piece of paper to me. "If you decide to follow up on this, these are two of the best doctors in Carlton. But promise me you'll think about it. Okay?"

I nodded noncommittally as she left the room. I already had thought about it. Surely she knew that by age forty-three, half the women in the United States had already thought about plastic...*cosmetic* surgery.

What is it about the word "plastic" that bothers you so much?

Plastic doesn't bother me. It's just a word. "Cosmetic" sounds better, is all.

If plastic is just a word, why are you so uncomfortable saying it?

I wasn't uncomfortable saying it. I tossed my purse onto my shoulder and stood up. Plastic. Plastic. Plastic.

As in Tupperware lid? As in trying to preserve something that will decompose anyway?

I stomped down the hall of the clinic. I liked my Tupperware very much, thank you. I flashed a fake smile at the nurse who greeted me.

See? Fake. Plastic.

I stopped. Turned back. "Oh, hi." I wiggled my fingers at her as she disappeared into an exam room.

There. Now what would you call that?

Friendly.

Plastic.

I ducked my head, trying to avoid eye contact with anyone else who might expect a greeting. If I was indeed *plastic,* why couldn't I preserve myself the way I'd been twenty years ago?

I slipped on my sunglasses and pushed my way out the clinic door. I was going to have that surgery.

Kenny

"Dad!" Billy came barreling at me and then skidded short. Surprising how quickly, in the past week, he'd caught on that my sore shoulder couldn't handle his usual, after work jump-and-hoist hug. He tackled my knees instead.

"Hey, kiddo." I rubbed at his short spiked hair with my left hand. My right arm was feeling amazingly better considering the pain I'd been in just five days ago, but I wasn't taking any chances. The play-offs for the state tournament were tomorrow afternoon, and there was no way I was going to be sitting on the bench.

"Where are your sisters?" I asked.

"Daa-ad." Paige came running toward me, each chubby-legged step looking like it would be her last. She stopped when she ran into my legs. I knelt and gave her a hug. "No heavy lifting" was my self-imposed rule until after the play-offs. Billy had run off as fast as he'd appeared. More than likely he had a ten-car Matchbox race going in his bedroom…and his mind. The kid was a chip off his old dad.

I grabbed Paige by her sticky hand. "Let's go find your sister and your mom." I followed my nose into the kitchen. Something smelled good. Renae was standing at the stove, barely stirring something in a pan while she turned a page of the book she was reading on the counter. "Look who's home," I said, flexing my left arm like Popeye. I lowered my voice. "The king of the Pearson house!" Renae rolled her eyes at my old joke. I reached out and tugged at her ponytail. I thought it was funny.

Winding my arms around Diane from the back, I let my hands rest on the little pouch of stomach we'd hardly talked about. "How's Junior?" I whispered in her ear.

"Your Aunt Ida called," Diane said in greeting as she cut fresh broccoli into smaller pieces. "She wants you to come over and fix something."

I closed my eyes and rolled them underneath my eyelids. I'd told Mike he could close up the station tonight. I'd been planning on eating supper, putting my feet on the coffee table, holding the remote in one hand and maybe Diane's hand in my other…once she got the kids to bed. My shoulder held just a tiny bit of tenderness in the joint, and I wanted to give it a good rest before the game tomorrow.

I popped a piece of raw broccoli into my mouth and crunched. It felt good to chomp on the irritation I was feeling. "Can't it wait?" I reached for another piece.

Diane swatted at my hand with the flat side of the knife. "You try telling her that. Why don't you bring her back here for supper?"

There went the hand-holding idea. I pressed my teeth together. Expanded my chest with a deep, deep breath. "Okay. I'll take a 'decoy' with me." Diane knew I often used one of the kids to sidetrack Aunt Ida when I went to her house in answer to her frequent calls. While she fussed over her grandniece or nephew, I quickly fixed whatever little job she'd dreamed up for me. Without one of the kids along, I was often forced to wait while she brewed coffee, got cookies out of the freezer, sliced a few slices of who-knew-how-old banana bread, and made us what she called, in her heavily accented English, "A little snek."

"Billy!" I yelled down the hall. "Come with me to Aunt Ida's." I knew I wouldn't have to ask twice. I snuck another piece of broccoli before I walked out to the garage to get my toolbox. With any luck Aunt Ida's chore would be something simple. Like changing the batteries in her living room wall clock. A no brainer. If she had batteries.

I climbed into the pickup. Good grief, I could swear the seat was still warm from my short drive home from the station. Billy hopped into the shotgun seat, pulling a bulging backpack in with him. No doubt his fleet of cars. He'd keep Aunt Ida interested while I worked, telling her the makes and models and special features of each vehicle. He loved going to visit my mother's oldest sister. My Aunt Ida Bauer, who thought I was her personal handyman. Just about the time I'd start wondering why she never called my brother, Ben, to help her out, she'd say something like, "Ben's smart, but he's not handy." Well, actually, the way Aunt Ida said it, the words came out sounding more like, "Bence shmart, but heece not hendy."

Somehow, thinking about her thick German brogue smoothed the irritation I felt tonight about all the nitpicking chores she had me do around her house.

"She's lonely," was the way Diane rationalized the constant calls.

She probably was. But that didn't change the fact that I had a business to run, a family to raise, and a need for some free time now and then. Right now I was tired and hungry. And I really wanted to rest my arm.

What about talking with Diane about the baby?

Oh, yeah, that too. I backed out of the driveway. That subject could wait until after the play-offs. I mean, we had a good six months to discuss the extra mouth I was going to have to feed. The sooner I got to Aunt Ida's, the sooner I could get back home.

Almost twenty years older than my mother, Aunt Ida was the oldest of what I liked to think of as the Reichert baseball team…only trouble was, all nine of the Reicherts were girls…well, old women, now. But they were a lot of fun, the ones who were still alive. Aunt Ida's husband, my Uncle Fred, had died, gosh, I could hardly remember how long ago that had been. I had a vague memory of him giving me a whisker rub one Christmas and another of him and my dad trying to do cartwheels at a picnic in the park. Ben and I about died laughing when Uncle Fred landed on his rear in a mud puddle. I smiled now, remembering. No wonder Aunt Ida was lonely. He'd been a fun guy and had been gone a long time.

I pulled into her driveway determined to put my irritation away. Living alone for that long couldn't be easy.

"Dare's my boyce." Aunt Ida stood in the open doorway. No doubt she'd been watching for me from the chair by her living room window. The one where the springs sagged from too much sitting. "Come in." She waved a hand towards her chest. "Hurry your foots. I don't vant dose flies in the house."

Billy ducked under her arm. By the time I'd walked through the door, he had his cars dumped into a pile in the middle of the floor and was busy sorting them by color.

Aunt Ida shook her head. "He'ss chust like hiss dat. Carse, carse, carse. Vy, I remember vhen you vass liddle you—"

"What did you need done, Aunt Ida?" I cut her off at the crossroad. I'd heard the story of how I'd slept with my yellow steel Tonka truck a million times. All I wanted was to fix what needed fixing and then get home to eat. I held up my toolbox so she'd get the hint.

"Acht, you could haff left dat at home. It's only the lightbulp in the battroom. I shouldt do it myself, but I made dat promise to Diane dat I vouldn't stant on the chair. I can't see to take my medicines tonight vhen it's so dark in dere."

I made a beeline for the bathroom. This was the no brainer I'd hoped for. I'd be done in no time at all. Swiss steak, here I come. I could hear Aunt Ida telling Billy to come into the kitchen for cookies.

"Aunt Ida," I yelled, "don't give Billy anything to eat. Diane said you're supposed to come home and have supper with us."

"Vell, den," I heard her say as she and Billy walked through her small house, "we'll chust wrap dem up in a nepkin so you can haff them later."

"Good deal." Billy knew how to wrap an old aunt around a little finger.

I set my toolbox on the floor. Ida had laid a new bulb on top of a washcloth in the basin of the sink. I reached up and undid the three screws that held the light fixture in place, setting it carefully on the back of the toilet. Out with the old. In with the new. It was hard to believe how something so simple for me could be so hard for her. Even reaching up to turn in the new lightbulb with my left hand was easy. I gave one last twist.

The faint, tinkling sound did nothing to hide the swear word that slipped through my lips as the bulb shattered in my hand.

"Vhat heppenedt?" Ida hurried to the doorway, followed by Billy.

"Don't come in," I said. "There's glass on the floor. I'm going to need a broom." A small drop of blood pooled on the tip of my middle finger. "And a Band-Aid." Already I was wondering how I was going to get the broken end of the bulb out of the socket. I'd have to turn off the electricity and see if my needle nosed pliers could grip the sides of the broken bulb. I could imagine that Swiss steak drying in the oven.

"Billy, you get da broom from behindt the kitchen door," Ida directed. "I'll get a Bandt-Aid. Dere in the kitchen, too. And I'll get a potato." Off she went.

A potato? She must be as hungry as I was. Or senile. Let her go look for her spud; at least her mission kept her out of the bathroom.

I stood back and surveyed the damage. I could see a sliver of glass barely sticking out from the end of my finger. If I tried to brush it away, I might break off the bit that was inside. Better try tweezers first. I opened the medicine cupboard.

A virtual pharmacy of brown bottles and white bottles, all with prescription labels, met my eyes. Man-oh-man. Either Aunt Ida was a drug dealer or she looked a lot healthier than she really was. I picked up one bottle and read the label. Celebrex. I remembered enough TV commercials to know that was arthritis medication. Cumadin. Hydrochlorothiazide. I read the label. "Take one half tablet daily." Zocor. Prilosec. Man, no wonder she wanted me to come and change the lightbulb before it got dark. Even in broad daylight it would be hard to swallow this much medication.

"Here vee go." Aunt Ida stood in the doorway of the bathroom, holding a Band-Aid into the room as far as she could reach.

Quickly, I put the plastic bottle back into the medicine cabinet and rummaged through several containers of aspirin and vitamins before I found a tweezers. "Just a sec," I said as I plucked at the small sliver of glass.

How much does all that medicine cost?

I stuck my finger under the tap and rinsed off the drop of blood that had followed the sliver. My eyes flitted to the open medicine cabinet and the lineup of bottles. I had a vague idea what medicine cost when one of the kids had an ear infection...none of it was cheap. How did Aunt Ida possibly make ends meet on Uncle Fred's Social

Security check and the rent money she got from the little bit of farm land she owned and rented out?

That's probably why she helps out at Vicky's during Pumpkin Fest.

Probably. But, man, I didn't want to be working when I was eighty. Or whatever age Aunt Ida was. I wanted to be living the good life by then…providing I was still living, of course. I dried my hand with the washcloth Ida had used to cradle the new lightbulb.

Then you'd better manage your business and your health wisely now.

I tugged at the belt of my jeans. Maybe it'd be okay if I missed dinner tonight. "I'm ready for that Band-Aid now."

Aunt Ida handed me the bandage, took the broom from Billy, and swept her way into the room. "Here'ce the potato." She motioned to Billy to hand me a good-sized spud, cut in half.

Okay. I stood there with a half of potato in my hand. What was I supposed to do with this? Was it supper? So much for giving up Swiss steak. I was on the raw potato diet.

Or not.

I held the spud in midair. "I give up, Aunt Ida. What am I doing holding a potato in your bathroom?"

"Vhy, it's to help you chanch dat broken bulp. Don't you know dat oldt trick?"

"No. I guess I don't."

"You chust take the potato and push it on the broken part." She urged me to follow her directions as she spoke.

"Hardt. Use dose muscles of yours."

I pushed until the potato half was wedged good and tight.

"Dare. Now turn it like you vas taking out a bulp."

Sure enough. It worked. I was left standing with half a potato, speared by half a lightbulb. Billy hooted and I started laughing softly along with him. How could someone who talked as though she came straight from the old country be so ingenious?

What else do you think she could teach you if you gave her half a chance? Maybe instead of rushing in here, gulping down a glass of milk

*and a couple cookies, fixing whatever, and then running out...maybe
you should take some time to listen to her.*

My stomach rumbled. Maybe I'd have to think about that, but
not now. I was hungry. I tossed the broken bulb in the garbage. "Do
you have another bulb?"

"Acht, no." Ida carefully wiped out the basin of the sink with a
damp rag. "I chust keep vun extra." She pointed to the garbage can.
"And dat vas it." She shook the rag into the can, picked up the broom,
and walked toward the kitchen.

With my fingers tucked into the back pockets of my jeans I surveyed the situation. There was no store open in Brewster after six.
Maybe Diane would have an extra bulb at home and I could bring it
back when I drove Ida home. This no-brainer chore was beginning
to take all night.

Ida reappeared in the doorway. "Here." She held out a lightbulb.

I took it from her, looking at the bulb as if she'd produced it out
of thin air. "I thought you said you only had the one extra bulb."

"I took the bulp from the liffing room floor light. Dat shouldt
vork until I can get to Cal's hardtvare store in the morning."

You could have thought of that.

Yeah, but I didn't.

You could learn a lot from her if you gave her half a chance.

After I had the light fixture back in place, I brushed my hands
together. Maybe I'd give her a chance. Sometime when I had more
time. Right now I had a ball game to think about.

⌣

"Batter up!" The ump's voice called me to the plate.

I took a cut at the air and then stepped beside the base, digging
my feet into the dirt, making sure my spikes were positioned just
right. Top of the fourth and from the looks of the ragtag team we
were playing, Kenny's SuperPumper Station was on its way to its first
trip to the state tourney. I watched as the pitcher went through his
gyrations just to throw a wild ball that sent the catcher lunging onto
his side to catch it. This guy was clueless.

Let me show him where to throw it. I swung at the air. Right *here.* Straight across the plate. I held my bat ready for his next pitch. I wasn't quite sure how I was going to afford to send the team to state. I knew the guys would all chip in by paying for their own motel rooms and meals. But it would be nice if the team sponsor could buy a round of pizzas and beer one night. I kind of had an idea what my bookkeeper might have to say about that. *No.*

I swung at the next pitch, sending the ball high behind the home plate fence.

"Foul ball," the ump called.

I stepped away from the plate and swung a couple times to keep my shoulder loose. I'd taken three aspirin before the game. Insurance that my muscles would stay supple. Or at least not ache until the celebrations had begun. Diane had quizzed me long and hard before I'd left this morning for the Saturday afternoon, out-of-town play-off game.

"Are you sure you should be playing?" she'd asked, rolling a big blue ball to Paige on the sidewalk.

"No problem," I'd answered, rotating my arm through the air to prove my point. Oooo. I hoped she hadn't noticed the small grimace I'd made when I'd swung my arm overhead. This was my first chance at playing in the state tourney, and I didn't plan to miss it. My team had come close to qualifying two other times, but we'd choked when it counted. It wasn't going to happen this year. The game this afternoon would decide who represented our region at state. I could already see the free advertising Kenny's SuperPumper Station would get by simply being at the tournament.

I stepped back to the plate. Nodded at the pitcher. I was ready for his next pitch. Another one, wide and outside. If I was lucky I'd be walking to first.

Lazy. You could use the exercise a little jog would do you.

I circled the bat over my shoulder. I was ready. Put that ball over the plate, and I'd give the whole other team a little exercise to keep them in shape. The pitcher held up his hand.

"Time!" the ump called.

The pitcher ran in to talk to the catcher. I stepped back from the plate. What? Were they afraid of me? I put the bat behind my neck, looping my hands over each end. My right shoulder twinged a bit, then let go. I twisted, right, left, stretching to keep myself loose. It wasn't as easy to stay limber at thirty-seven, but I liked to think what I'd lost in speed I made up for in game smarts. I looked down at my belly. And brawn. Okay, so it wasn't all muscle, but a lot of it was. I could still give the ball a good poke when I had a decent pitch to work with. "Let's play ball," I called into the air. Let the other team know I was here to play and not jabber around the way they were doing.

I jogged in place. If I was going to be running the bases this week and next, I'd better be ready. My mind worked at how I was going to keep the station open the three days we'd be at the state tourney. Mike Anderson would be at a family reunion in South Dakota two days next week, and then he'd be off to college.

"Batter." The ump nodded me to the plate.

Oh, well. I'd worry about the station later. If I had to, I'd simply close it for a couple days. At my age a guy only got one chance at the big show, and I didn't plan to miss it.

The pitcher's spaghetti-thin arm released the ball. It floated toward me, a meatball served on a platter. This was going to be so easy. I picked my spot. Right there. Between center and left field. I moved my left foot forward, ready for the swing.

Crack! The ball cut a smooth, fast arc through the air, heading exactly where I'd planned. I took off running, tucking my head and barreling toward first. The first base coach, Donny Klein, a former Brewster track star, twirled his arm in the air. "Go! Go! Go!" I had to trust him. Unlike him, my speed wasn't good after a fast sprint. He knew that. "Go!" he shouted. They must be having trouble in the out-field.

I rounded the bag, one step, two, then took my first glance to the outfield. The left fielder had scooped up the ball and was winding up to throw. There was no way I was going to beat that ball to second. My feet scrambled under me as I quickly tried to change direction.

"Back! Back!" Donny shouted. Now was a fine time for that call. The ball flew past my head toward the tall first baseman. He had one foot on the bag, one stretched as far as his grasshopper legs would extend. The ball nicked his glove and bounced wide.

"Second!" Donny screamed. "Run to second! *Second!*"

Once again my feet scrabbled at the dirt. What did Donny think I was? Some sort of machine with a voice-activated reverse switch? My cleats caught the dirt. I pumped my arms and ran toward the base. The second baseman was crouched low, one step ahead of the base, looking over my shoulder, waiting for the ball I had no doubt wasn't far behind me.

"Slide!" Donny was going to bust a lung if he wasn't careful. "Slide!"

Every ball game I'd ever watched, played in, or read about combined to help me now. I even thought about my bum shoulder as I tucked my right foot behind my left and threw my arms together above my head. Classic feet-first slide position. Well, classic according to the way I'd done it since I was six. What I hadn't taken into consideration was the way my sore shoulder would cramp at the sudden upward movement. Yeow! I swung my right arm down, under my rear trying to protect it from something I didn't have time to think about. A cloud of dirt filled the air as my feet scraped the dirt into the bag. I felt the tag of a glove near my knee.

"Safe!" the base ump yelled.

"No…" The cheers of the crowd drowned out what I shouldn't have said anyway. I jumped to my feet, automatically brushing the dust from my uniform. My left hand cooperated. My right didn't. What the heck? I looked down. My limp right wrist hung there like a pansy…without water. Then the pain hit. Yeow! I cradled my drooping right hand with my left. Held it like a baby. I wanted to shake the pain away but knew, from the looks of my limp wrist, that wouldn't be possible. I gritted my teeth against the pain, danced in place on the bag while I waited for the ump to call for help.

Diane was going to have a conniption.

But, hey, I was safe!

"Were you safe?" The X-ray technician positioned my arm just so before stepping behind a barrier to take the picture.

"Oh, yeah," I answered, grinning, pretending the pain wasn't near as bad as it was. "I was safe." All of a sudden my big softball game didn't seem quite so important.

"Great." His voice was distracted. He was being polite. Already ready for the next case after me. "We'll get these films upstairs pronto."

I sat on a bed in the emergency exam cubicle at the Carlton hospital, my arm cradled limply in front of me, waiting for the doctor. A case of the chills had taken over my body, and a light film of sweat coated my upper lip. I wondered if the station was busy this afternoon. If Mike could handle it alone. Diane had said she'd try to stop by a couple of times to see if he needed help, but Paige was getting some kind of monster tooth and it all depended on how she cooperated. Maybe I should have sent the team to the tournament without me. Maybe I should have stayed at home and run my business. Maybe I should—

"Hey, Slugger!" The doctor eyed my softball uniform as he pushed aside the curtain of the exam area. "Were you safe?"

I pasted a smile on my mouth and nodded. The question wasn't one bit funny anymore. Not after I'd had time to imagine what Diane was going to say. Not after I'd started trying to add up how much all this might cost. Not to mention the repair work at the station I wasn't going to be able to do. Oh, man. What I'd done was stupid with a capital "S." I hung my head.

The doctor stuck two X-rays in front of a lighted panel. Stepped back and rubbed his chin.

Say something, already!

He swiveled his eyes to glance at my limp wrist and then looked back at the board.

I beat him to the punch line. "I suppose I'm going to need a cast on this." Without thinking I tried to lift my arm, as if he didn't know what I was talking about. Man, that hurt.

A slow nod of his head. "See this here?" He took a pen from his front pocket and pointed to the dim image in front of him. "There are eight bones in the wrist," he explained. "It looks like you have a scaphoid fracture." He waved his pen around on the cloudy picture as though I was supposed to know what he was talking about. "It appears you've crushed a couple of the carpel bones and…"

From that point on all I heard was, "Blah, blah-blah. Surgery." I felt a little faint. Sweat ran down my temples. I took a really deep breath. It didn't help. The room went into a slow blur. In. Out. Bad focus on a cheap camera. I wished Diane were here with me.

"Mr. Pearson! Mr. Pearson." A soft hand was patting my face. "Lift your head. I'm going to put this pillow under it."

My eyelids fluttered open. Fluorescent lights stabbed at the back of my eyes like knives. The pain was sharp, but fleeting. I was reminded of where I was by the dull throbbing in my right wrist.

Surgery. I remembered that word. The overhead lights floated like bright, fast-moving clouds. "Oh, man," I muttered, closing my eyes, "Diane is going to kill me."

"You're going to be fine." The nurse dabbed at my face with a cool, damp washcloth. Her name tag was near my face. Colette. "You scared us, falling over like that." She chuckled, entertaining only herself. "You men put on a good act." She pushed her chin into her neck and lowered her voice. "I'm a *tough* guy." She laughed again, took her hand, and flopped it backward into the air. "And then, ka-boom. Good thing Doctor Brevik saw you leaning. He caught you."

I'd had enough of her monologue. "Where is he?"

"He's arranging your surgical consult. Are you feeling better now?"

I had been until she mentioned surgery. I shook my head. She already knew my tough-guy image was a fake. Why spoil her conclusion? "Can someone call my wife?"

She nodded. "I think the teammate of yours who brought you here already did that."

"Oh, brother." I closed my eyes, gathering my wits. "You'd better get your security system ready. She is not going to be a happy camper."

Colette laughed. Obviously she'd never seen Diane on the warpath.

"Really," I told her. "She's going to be ticked. Big time."

Colette folded the washcloth and laid it on the rolling stand by my bed. "Don't worry, we're used to dealing with all sorts of trauma around here. If we have to, we'll anesthetize her." She grinned to let me know she was joking.

"You might have to," I replied, not so sure I was kidding.

⁓

"I'm sorry, Diane." Tears dropped out of the corners of my eyes and ran into my ears. I'd never cried much, and never on my back before. I turned my head from side to side, wiping my face against the scratchy cotton of the hospital pillow. My broken wrist lay by my side, operated on, pinned, and in a cast. Badger Blue. Always-practical Diane had chosen the color. "*Less likely to show dirt from the station,*" she'd said as I was being wheeled into surgery.

"I screwed up again." My voice was thick with emotion. "I'm sorry." I might have said those two words about a dozen times since Diane had appeared by my bedside. I blinked, sending another run of tears down my cheeks. A foggy part of my brain knew the painkiller I was on might be contributing to the emotion I was feeling, but that didn't stop the waterworks coming from my eyes.

Diane sat on the bed, pulled a tissue from the box on my bedside tray, and dabbed the corners of my eyes. "It was an accident," she said for the twelfth time.

"What'd you do with the kids?" I vaguely remembered asking her the same question before, but I didn't remember the answer.

"I dropped them off at your Aunt Ida's. Renae's old enough to help keep Billy and Paige in line."

"If she remembers to look up from her book," I added, smiling for the first time since I'd seen the X-ray of my wrist.

"I reminded her about that." She squeezed my left hand. Her try at comforting me only sent a wave of panic through my hazy mind.

"What're we gonna do? Oh, man, I am so sorry. I gotta get out of here and get to the station." I struggled to sit up. "I—"

Diane cut my words with a finger on my lips. "Shhh," she whispered. "You need to rest. Mike said he'd watch the station for the next few days."

I fell back against the pillow, suddenly exhausted. "Yeah, and then what?"

Diane was quiet as she looked at her folded hands. She looked up at me and said softly, "Then we pray. That you'll heal quickly. That we'll be able to keep the station going while you mend. That this baby that's on the way will have a dad who's ready to hold him...or her," she quickly added, smiling.

"Him," I said. I'd almost forgotten about the baby. Diane had been to the obstetrician in Carlton last week, and he'd confirmed what the at-home pregnancy test had shown—that she was indeed expecting. "It's a him." That much I knew for sure—even if Diane didn't.

"Well, then." She stroked the side of my face. Man, that felt good. "I guess we've got Kenny Jr. on the way."

Speaking of healing. If Diane was ready to name this new baby Kenny Jr., that meant we could move on from those two miscarriages. Oh, man. I swallowed back another round of tears. I needed to change the subject before I started blubbering.

"How'd the te-am do-o?" So much for croaking out a question.

Diane fingered the blanket covering my legs. "I'm not sure you want to know."

Uh-oh. They were going to state and I wouldn't be going with them. Shoot! My one shot at it and I'd blown it. I looked down at my cast. Just as well. I was going to need all the gas business I could get to pay the deductible on our insurance policy. Well, at least they'd rallied and won the game. Made my sacrifice worth it.

"They lost."

"What?!" I practically sat up.

"I told you you wouldn't want to know. They lost."

I laid back down. "You mean they—" I coughed. Loudly. "Choked."

A nurse poked her head into the doorway. "Everything okay in here?"

"Fine." Diane waved as though they were old friends. "We're fine." As the nurse left, Diane giggled. "You might not want to do that again. We'll have the paramedics in here. Just like *ER*."

I put my left hand on my neck and, soundlessly, pretended I was choking. Diane laughed, a light, loose, forgiving sound that sent a wave of relaxation coursing through my body. It was as powerful as if I'd been given an extra dose of pain medication. She leaned over, lifted my left hand away from my neck and threaded it around her shoulders. Then she bent close and put her head into the crook of my shoulder. I felt her kiss my chin and then close her eyes, a butterfly brushing against my face. Oh, man.

I closed my eyes, too. Suddenly so sleepy. I had no doubt what I was feeling was the result of some sort of drug. It could have been a timed-released painkiller.

More likely it was a drug called love.

Ida

Acht, I was too old for this. Babysitting. At my age. Well, you could hardly call Renae and Billy babies. And even that little sweetheart, Paige, would be called a toddler. But still, I wasn't used to that kind of commotion. Not for so many hours in a row. I shook my head, slipping my tired arms into my cotton nightgown. Ay! I'd better get some sleep. I had another busy day ahead tomorrow.

I lay back on the pillow. *Thank You, Lord, for pillows.*

Maybe I should get up and check on Paige one more time. Renae was sleeping in the extra room. Billy had fallen asleep on the sofa. Poor little Paige, who I was afraid might tumble out of a bed, got the floor. Folded covers were her make-do manger. I would say a prayer and check on her when I got up for my twice-a-night trip to the toilet.

What a day. When I'd opened my eyes this morning, all I'd had planned was to buy a lightbulb...

With both my hands, I gripped the metal edge of the countertop. *Godt, help my knees holdt me.* Slowly, I lowered myself to the linoleum floor. I knew it was clean. It had taken me two whole days to scrub it on my wrinkled hands and my poor knees.

"Acht, himmel," I said out loud as my knees gave way and dropped me the last inch to the floor. I kneeled there and surveyed for damage. All was well. *Thank You, Lord.*

Good thing I didn't have much planned for today. My arthritis was aching something fierce. My eyes had opened long before a rooster would crow this morning, but it had taken me a good hour to push my creaking legs over the side of the bed and into my slippers.

Even my slow shuffling to the bathroom and the kitchen hadn't done much to loosen my old joints. *Not complaining, Lord, just telling You I'm grateful they still get me around.*

I'd put my tin coffeepot in the sink and filled it only halfway to the top. On days like today I didn't trust my hands to pour boiling coffee from a plum full pot. And besides, two and a half cups of coffee were enough. No sense wasting good grounds. Fred had liked his coffee hot and strong. "Four scoops and don't you skimp, Ida," he'd tell me almost every morning. I didn't. Not when he was watching, anyway. But now that he was gone, one heaping tablespoon of grounds and a good, rolling boil flavored my "morning water," as Fred used to tease when he caught me holding back on the grounds. How I missed him.

From my kneeling spot on the floor I could see my old coffeepot on the stove. The coffee was cold now, but I'd saved half a cup in case I wanted to dunk a cookie in it later. If nothing else, I'd use it to water my African violet on the television in the living room. I didn't believe in wasting things the way the kids nowadays did.

I sighed. I had one errand to run today. I'd best get on with it. I opened the two cabinet doors in front of my hands and pulled out the soup kettle. It was too hot to make soup today, but what I wanted was the heavy quart jar I kept hidden behind the kettle. I bent down, not so easy when my knees were hollering at me, and grabbed the rim of the old blue jar with my fingertips, pulling it toward me. I carefully set the jar on the floor and then pulled myself toward the countertop. How some people climbed those high mountains…. My white-speckled countertop was mountain enough for me.

I stood for a moment, making sure my knees were under me good. Now for the tricky part. I bent at the waist, gripping the counter with one hand as I picked up the coin-filled jar with the other. It slipped out of my hand, too heavy for my ailing fingers. I was going to have to think of another way.

Ah. I pulled the cotton dish towel I'd ironed yesterday off the handle of the stove. It hardly seemed possible that I'd embroidered that bluebird on there before I'd even set eyes on Fred. I hated to set a good clean towel on the floor, but I'd learned an old dog had to resort to new tricks now and then.

I unfurled the towel onto the floor as if I were going to have an unexpected picnic. When was the last time I'd been on a picnic? Oh, my. The fun times we used to have when I was a kid. Three-legged races in the park. Mama's fried chicken. Watermelon. I caught my mouth smiling and waved my hand in front of my face. I had work to do.

I scrunched the dish towel around one edge of the jar bottom. With my thick-soled shoe I bumped the jar onto its side. Coins tipped out, but now it didn't matter. I bent, gathering the four corners of the towel into my hands. Better tie a knot to get a surer grip. I grasped the thick knot with both hands and lifted. Coins clinked against each other as I shuffled to the wooden kitchen table and with the help of my sore hip, nudged my bundle onto the tabletop. There.

I slipped into a chair and untied the knot, uncovering the pile of coins in the cloth. Last I remembered lightbulbs came two to a package. No buying just one of hardly anything these days. Oh, well. I'd have an extra lightbulb in the drawer as a backup. If I lived long enough to need it. I was becoming more and more aware of the little time I had left to walk on this earth. *Shuffle on it, Ida.* The corners of my mouth turned up. What would this world be like if we couldn't laugh a little at ourselves? *Laughter doeth good like medicine.* I was glad God had given me some funny bones. Goodness, some days the only thing that brought me through was remembering the laughing times. I often thought about that old gander we had growing up on the farm. That sneaky bird would come running out from behind the barn, lickety-split, trying to peck at us kids. We'd scream as though a coyote had got in the hen house and jump on the nearest hay bales or tractor or— Oh, goodness, where was my mind? I was never going to get my lightbulb bought at this rate.

I began sorting through the coins, pushing them into small piles. Pennies, nickels, a few dimes and, now and then, a lucky quarter. I usually kept the quarters in my billfold. They were what I used to pay for my afternoon coffee at Vicky's. An expensive treat I felt guilty about. But the days I didn't get to the café I found myself sitting in my chair by the window, staring out at nothing. Worrying about the squirrels that ran across the street without looking for cars. Wondering how I would ever rake all the leaves that were going to start falling in just a few weeks. Sometimes my heart would ache when I thought about all the years my Fred had been gone. I coughed at the sudden lump in my throat. It wasn't good to live in the past. That kind of thinking didn't bring me any closer to the Lord, but going to the café and being ready to listen to other folks tell me their troubles did. It gave me things to pray about at night when I couldn't sleep because of my crabby joints.

Ida, you are never going to get to the hardware store if you don't stop wandering in your mind like a jackrabbit.

This was true. Let's see…lightbulbs. One dollar apiece, do you think? I pushed two quarters and ten nickels into a pile. Better make it more. Everything was higher-priced these days. Not like when I was a young bride. If Fred could see how little that Social Security check bought these days… Good thing he never sold off that farmland when we moved to town. The rent I collected from those acres was the only reason I had enough money for my pills.

I counted out another dollar in coins and then added one more just to be on the safe side. At the last I pushed a handful of pennies into the pile. All I'd need was to get to Cal's and be a couple pennies short. Knowing him, he'd throw in his own pennies and let me have the bulbs. He'd lived through the Depression just like me; he knew pennies were worth more in a jar than lying on the street like rocks. With my own two eyes, I'd seen the neighbor kids walk right by two pennies on the sidewalk. In my day there would have been a squabble right on the cement if we'd seen two coins just lying there, waiting to be found. We could have filled our jaws with candy with two whole pennies. And now kids thought they weren't even worth bending over to pick up. Acht.

Ida! No wonder you get nothing done. You daydream like a cat in sunshine.

I would get a go on right now. I pulled my white purse over from the corner of the kitchen table where I kept it. I'd put the coins in my billfold and then off I'd be. I glanced at the clock hanging high on the wall above the sink. *What?* Had my clock batteries been filled with speed-up juice? It was noontime. Where had the morning gone away to? Cal closed up for lunch. Well, I'd fix myself some cottage cheese. Slice a couple of those tomatoes growing out in the backyard. If I had some that the pesky birds hadn't pecked up.

I opened the kitchen door. Windy today. I grabbed the chiffon scarf I kept by the door and tied it under my chin. Who could see to pick tomatoes with hair flying like prairie grass?

I hurried out to my small rectangle of dirt. My garden wasn't near what I'd put out when Fred was around to help. Every year I planted less, but growing tomatoes was one thing I'd do until I fell on the spade. Those pale red, cardboard balls they tried to say were tomatoes at Magner's Grocery! You might as well chew on an old sock.

"Oh, look at you two!" Two red rubies of tomatoes hung from a vine, just waiting to be my lunch. I looked at the sky and winked my thanks.

Back in the house I pulled a chipped plate from the cupboard, wiping the flowered border with a clean dish towel. That plate was from the first set of dishes Fred and I had. I'd saved Green Stamps for those plates. Or did we get them for a wedding gift? No matter. We'd had many good meals off those dishes.

I pulled the lid off the cottage cheese and sniffed at it. More than likely still good. I had a hard time remembering how long things were in the refridgerator, and my nose wasn't always the best detective. It seemed fine.

I sat alone at my table and bowed my head over my bounty. Two big spoonfuls of cottage cheese, fresh sliced tomatoes with a little sugar sprinkled on them, and a piece of bread with butter. *Use this food to feed my body. Use me to serve You. Amen.*

You would think a good meal would give me zip. Instead, I was sleepy. I looked at the large, black numbers on the clock. There would be time for a little nap, then I would go buy my lightbulb and have a cup of coffee at Vicky's. I yawned. *Catching flies?* I could almost hear Fred tease. I put up a hand, patting at my open mouth. Living alone for so many years was giving me bad manners.

How could a reclining chair feel so good when I'd hardly done anything today? I tugged the lever, pushed myself back, pulled an afghan over my chest, and closed my eyes. *The Lord is my shepherd; I shall not want. He maketh me to lie down in green pastures.* Or a recliner. I smiled with my eyes shut. *He leadeth me beside the still waters. He restoreth my soul...*

Oh, my! Oh, my! What? My eyes popped open. The phone was ringing. Oh! Oh! I pushed at the footrest of the recliner with my feet. Where was the strength of my youth? Why didn't it go down? Acht, the handle! Why did I always forget about the handle on the side of this contraption? My old hand fumbled for the lever. Why did they have to make these things so complicated?

My feet tangled in the afghan as I tried to hurry to the phone in the kitchen.

"Yah, hell-o." My breath was coming fast. So foolish to get so worked up over a ringing telephone.

"Aunt Ida? Are you okay?" Diane's clear young voice somehow settled me. My nephew, Kenny, was a bit of a goof-off, as Fred used to say about folks who put play before work, but he'd done a fine job of finding himself a wife with a good head.

"Acht, yah," I said, happy the person on the other end of the line wasn't some stranger trying to trick me out of my bank account number. "I was chust laying down until it vas time for coffee. I hadt a busy morning."

"We've had a busy time here, too," Diane said. Her voice got muffled. What was she saying? Oh, I hoped I didn't need hearing aids. They cost money I didn't have. "Ida? Sorry, I was talking to the kids. Are you still there?"

"I don't moof that fast." *Thank You, Lord.* My hearing was fine. I pulled out a kitchen chair and sat down. A little visit would be nice. "How iss everyone? The kidts ready for school?"

"They are," Diane said. "But something else has come up and I need a big favor from you. If you feel up to it."

I sat up straight, a queer excitement fluttering in my chest. It wasn't often an old woman was asked to do a favor. If it was in my power to help, the Lord knew I would. "Vhat iss it?"

"Kenny got hurt playing ball."

"He's like a kidt," I blurted. Sometimes the words wouldn't stay in my mouth.

"I'm glad someone besides me noticed." I didn't blame her for sounding a little disgusted. She sighed. "He's at the hospital in Carlton and I need to run over there. I'm hoping it's nothing serious and I can bring him home tonight. They were doing X-rays when Donny Klein called to tell me what happened. I called Cindy to see if she could watch the kids, but she's working. I'm hoping it's going to be just a couple hours. Renae can help watch Paige. And you know Billy. All he does is play with his cars. Like his dad."

"The kidts are alvays velcome here." My mind was racing. What would we do? What would I feed them for supper? "You bring dem right ohfer and don't tink one more time about it."

What had I been thinking? When Diane called to tell me Kenny needed surgery and that Ben could pick the kids up anytime if I was too tired, I'd offered to have them stay here. "They're tree liddle anchels," I'd said while they still were acting heavenly.

Now, Renae was on the floor trying to coax animal sounds out of Paige using the plastic farm animals I'd pulled from an old shoebox in the closet. Renae was prancing a cow around with one hand, turning pages of her book with the other. "Moo. Moo." Paige grabbed an old pig and threw it at Billy's lineup of race cars.

"Hey!" He threw a mean look at Paige, ready to throw the pig back at her. He looked at me. "Sorry." He put the pig back down. Paige made a dive for it, scattering his cars like dandelion fluff. "Argghh!" Billy threw back his head and screamed. Renae looked up from her book and then at me.

Lord, help me! "Who vouldt like to sing some songs?" I could only hope this sounded like fun to kids nowadays. I walked to the old radio cupboard Fred had hollowed out and made into shelves and pulled out my Autoharp. I sat down on the couch, fitted a pick on my thumb, and plucked at the strings. I closed my eyes and strummed a few chords, my fingers remembering how they went.

I opened my eyes. Renae had stuck her finger in her book to mark her place. Billy and Paige were staring at me. "That's a weird guitar," Billy said.

"Dis iss the kindt of guitar Dafid in the Bible might haff played." I stroked the strings as I spoke. "Remember Dafid? He vas the guy witt the slingshot and he—"

"Kaboom!" Billy whipped his arm in the air and shot off a pretend rock. "Knocked the giant flat."

"Yah, dat's the guy. Didt you know he also played a harp?"

"Ohhh." There was a kind of awe in his little-boy voice. "Can I play it?"

I patted the side of the couch by me, inviting him to snuggle in. "I'll push the chordts and you shtrum. Not too fast now."

Renae had taken her finger out of her book and pulled Paige onto her lap. "What kind of songs do you suppose David sang?"

Oh, my. These kids kept an old mind twirling. "The Bible tells us all kinds of the songs he sang in the Psalms. But here's a song I learnt as a little girl that I always thought Dafid sang vhen he knocked out that giant, Goliath."

I took over strumming from Billy, picking up the pace as fast as my old arm would move. My throat started humming all of its own. Renae clapped Paige's hands together in time to the beat. "I vill neffer ride in the calfvary, march in the infantry, shoot the artillery…" At least that was how I remembered the words. The kids tried to sing along as best they could with my wobbly voice. I taught them the actions. Pretending we were riding horses in the cavalry, marching our feet in the infantry, shooting a cannon with a clap of our hands. "For I'm in the Lordt's army-y-y-y!" We finished loud and strong, laughing hard at the three-person parade marching around my living room to my vigorous twanging.

"Do gan!" Paige cried.

So we did. Again and again. Adding more songs. "The B-I-B-L-E." "Jesus Loves Me." "I Will Make You Fishers of Men." Finally I threw my tired hands on the strings, sending an untuneful sound into the air. "My oldt arms are tuckered out."

Billy threw himself onto the sofa, spreading his arms wide. "That was fun!"

"It vas," I agreed, looking at my wristwatch. "Stars and garters, it's time for bedt!"

"Snack!" yelled Billy, jumping up as fast as he'd thrown himself down.

"Cookies." I pointed to the kitchen. They all knew where I kept them. I would wait here until the commotion in the kitchen died down. My saggy old bed was looking pretty good tonight.

⟞

I laid my head on the pillow. Ahh, did this feel good on old white hair. I pulled the covers up to my chin, remembering Paige's high-pitched prayer, "Tank You for songs. Tank You for marches. Tank You for Eye-da."

I shook my head against the pillow. Who would have ever guessed what this day would bring when I woke up so many hours ago?

"For I know the plans I have for you," declares the Lord, "plans to prosper you and not to harm you, plans to give you hope and a future."

Plans. He had my day all planned out before I even opened my eyes. I smiled at my bedroom ceiling. God could see, I knew.

I closed my eyes. I wondered what He had planned for tomorrow. *Maybe not so much, okay, Lord?*

My eyes popped open. I never did get that lightbulb.

Jan

"It's *how* much?" My mouth gaped open, an unbelieving fish. I could almost feel my mother nudging it shut. I'd never dreamed the few cosmetic procedures I'd hoped to have would cost as much as a new kitchen. Or a whole wardrobe of designer clothes.

Dr. Peters flashed me a practiced smile. "Yes, I understand. The price can be a shock." He semi-laughed, as if that would help ease the surprise. "I could tell you all the platitudes about beauty not being cheap, whatever..." He waved his long, elegant fingers through the air, dismissing the cliché. He grew serious. "I'm a board-certified surgeon, Mrs. Jordan. You can shop around. Maybe you'd find someone who would do the surgery for less money, but this isn't something you want to cut corners on. Surgery is serious business, no matter what kind of procedure you're having done." His smooth skin glowed under the fluorescent overhead light. He might not realize it, but he was a walking advertisement for his services. If he could look good under these kinds of lights, what woman wouldn't want what he offered?

I swallowed hard. "I just didn't realize it would be quite that much money." I didn't want to sound like a cheapskate, but my head was still reeling at the figures he'd tossed out. "What if we didn't do this?" I pointed to the "V" in the neck of the paper gown I had on. To the freckled skin I knew in a year or two would begin to sag like a stretched-out nylon. Already I hated the way it looked, but I could wear turtlenecks if I had to. "Or this?" I ran my fingers over the backs of my hands, pointing to the freckles that I suspected would be called ugly brown age spots in short order.

Dr. Peters' eyes followed my hand as I pointed. He nodded his understanding. "The areas you're referring to wouldn't be part of the operation you were talking about. Those are skin procedures that would be handled with laser resurfacing. I'm thinking I would refer you to my colleague, Dr. Mason, for those. She's an excellent dermatologist. With laser treatments she should be able to diminish the pigmented lesions on the surfaces of your neck and hands."

Pigmented lesions? I looked at the backs of my freckled hands. Light brown splotches, large and small, covered them. Ick. I tucked them under the sides of my legs.

Dr. Peters went on. "Frankly, you might want to consult with Dr. Mason before considering the surgical options." He made some sweeping motions with his hands around either side of my face, touching me only with the air that hung between his fingers and my skin. "I'm guessing your premature aging is mostly due to excessive sun exposure."

Premature aging?! I cringed. A vision of me slathering myself in baby oil while I lounged on a woven lawn chair in the backyard under the blazing summer sun appeared in my mind. How many summers had I done that? Too many, obviously. Why hadn't my mother warned me?

She did.

Suddenly I remembered. "Janine, you're going to wrinkle up like a raisin. Why don't you come inside for a while?" Instead, I flipped over where I couldn't see her, letting the scorching sun burn into my back. "Oh, Janine," my mother said two days later as she peeled long strips of shredded skin from my shoulders. "You have such beautiful skin, I wish you'd take better care of it." I remembered how I'd rolled my eyes up inside my sunburned eyelids, thinking my mother didn't have a clue how anemic she looked in her fair, pale skin. I was confident that the skin she didn't peel off my back would turn into a deep tan. If not, there was another layer underneath and I had all summer.

Now I shivered in the thin gown. I wished I had known about the words "premature aging" when I was fifteen. *You wouldn't have listened.* I was listening now. The words echoed in my mind as Dr. Peters went on.

"A chemical peel might do the trick. Along with collagen injections to fill in the deep furrow you have here." He pointed to the almost invisible line he had near his own left eyebrow. "Botox would help the wrinkles in your forehead." He sat back. "Of course, those are the simpler options. At some point you might want to consider a brow lift as opposed to the rhytidectomy. Face-lift," he translated quickly. "But, in your case, I honestly don't see the need for either just now."

Finally, one sentence that didn't make me feel as though I were falling apart. I tried to smile, but it was hard considering all he'd said about my deteriorating body.

"The only procedure I could see you benefiting from at this particular point in time is the mastopexy."

I couldn't help it, my eyebrows puzzled together in question.

"Breast lift," he replied to my unspoken query. "Gravity does its work over the years. Especially in large-breasted women like yourself."

Great. The one part of my body I'd thought was just fine. The gown I was wearing suddenly felt transparent. I felt my shoulders begin to slump inward, trying to hide the objects in question.

Dr. Peters pulled back the cuff of his French blue shirt, exposing the thin-faced wristwatch on his arm. He stood. "I've given you much to think about." He stuck out his hand and shook mine. "You'll want some time to talk this over with your family. If you decide to go ahead with any of the procedures we've discussed, you can call Nancy and set up an appointment. You might also want to have a consultation with Dr. Mason. I'll have Nancy give you her card. It's been a pleasure." With a quick nod he was gone.

But his words weren't. As I slipped into my clothes, a bad mix of vocabulary ran through my head. *Premature aging. Pigmented lesions. Excessive sun exposure. Botox. Chemical peel. Breast lift.*

I looked down at my chest. Dr. Peters was right; they did sag. Quickly I tugged my bra into place. I'd been so busy examining the wrinkles on my forehead, the crinkles around my eyes, and the fine lines that were beginning to surround my lips like exclamation points that I'd overlooked what drooped a foot below. Make that a foot and a half. I buttoned the red sleeveless blouse I'd worn today, noting for not the first time how the skin under my arms practically flapped as I worked the buttons.

Get a grip, Jan. Your skin is not flapping. Your arms are in great shape. You lift weights. You do push-ups.

They were too flapping. I could see the skin positively jiggling as I smoothed the hem of my blouse over the waistband of the black capris I was wearing. I wondered why Dr. Peters hadn't mentioned an underarm skin tuck...or whatever that operation was called.

Probably because your arms are perfectly toned.

They are not. A shake of my head flipped my hair over my shoulders and the thought away.

Yes, they are. Your arms are fine as they are. Just as you are.

An unexpected lump pushed its way into my throat. I was not fine. If I was so fine, then why had my first husband turned to another woman in place of me? I'd been in my early twenties then, no wrinkles and a figure that had other men constantly hinting at possibilities with the raise of an eyebrow. I ran my fingers through my hair, remembering the days when I'd taken my looks for granted. I should have appreciated what I had.

You should appreciate what you have now.

What I had now? What I had now was a body that was sagging and bagging. A knee that cracked every time I walked and a lower back that ached every morning. What was to appreciate about that?

You are as I made you.

I felt my eyebrows crinkle together. Where had that thought come from? *You are as I made you.* What was it supposed to mean? I slipped my feet into the red sandals I'd left on the floor. There wouldn't be too many sandal days left in North Dakota this year. My feet were the one part of my body age seemed to have left alone. I wiggled my red-polished toenails. Maybe they'd act as a decoy for all the parts of me that were falling apart.

You are as I made you.

I bent and then stood, swinging my knock-off designer purse onto my shoulder. I couldn't help but see again the way the skin under my arm jiggled in the process. It was embarrassing. This might be my last summer to wear sleeveless shirts. These arms might have seen their last bit of daylight.

Let My arms hold you.

An unfamiliar rush of comfort coursed through my body at the unexpected thought. What a reprieve it would be to let someone else hold me. Hold all these doubts and fears.

Would it matter if those arms were flabby? Wouldn't it be comforting if they were soft?

I had to admit, soft arms had their place if they were holding someone.

Your arms cradled Joey when he was born. Remember when he had bronchitis and the only thing that soothed him was lying in your arms? Those same arms held him tight when he fell down and knocked out his front tooth when he was four. Remember last night when you fell asleep? Your arms were holding Dan. He felt loved. Your arms have served you well.

Where were these tears coming from? I dabbed at the corners of each of my eyes with my index finger. My makeup was going to float away if I wasn't careful. Through watery eyes I looked again at my arms. Maybe they weren't so bad after all. Maybe I'd have to go home and think about the things Dr. Peters had said. Maybe if I stayed out of the sun, saw the dermatologist, and took her advice, maybe I wouldn't have to have surgery after all.

I blinked a few times to chase the redness from my eyes, then opened the door of the exam room and walked into the hallway. The mailman, who was handing a stack of mail to the receptionist, gave me an approving once-over. Smiled.

There. I took a deep breath, smiling back. He looked a lot like the boys basketball coach back when I was in high school. The coach who had put his arm around my shoulders and told me, "Jan, as long as you keep cheerleading, I'll keep coaching. Sometimes watching you is the only thing that gets me through a game."

These days his comment would be called inappropriate. At the time, the only way I knew to react was to say a self-conscious, "Thanks."

I stepped into the waiting area, feeling the postman's gaze warm on my backside. I'd long ago grown used to those sorts of stares. Unspoken compliments. Maybe things weren't as bad as I'd thought.

"Janine?" The woman's voice came from off to my left.

I stopped. Turned. One man sat staring at CNN on the waiting room television. An older woman was looking over the top of her magazine at me. I didn't know her. I kept walking.

"Janine Edwards?"

My maiden name. I stopped again.

The older woman was now walking my way. She held out both hands as if inviting me to take them in mine.

"I'm sorry," I said. "Do I know you?"

She smiled and pointed at herself. "Linda Kaleman. From high school."

Linda? Linda? I racked my brain trying to drum up an image. A face to go with a name. The one I came up with didn't come close to the one who was standing in front of me. Could this possibly be the Linda who'd sat in front of me in English class all through our senior year at Carlton High? Not this old woman. She had to be at least ten years older than me. Make that fifteen. Twenty.

I forced a smile onto my face as I took her hands in mine. "From English?" I guessed, hoping I didn't sound as astounded as I felt.

"I hardly recognized you, either," she said, squeezing before letting my hands go. "It's been *ages*." She lifted her head and looked toward the ceiling as if searching the heavens for the years that had passed.

In that upward lift of her head I caught a familiar angle. A glimpse of who she'd been. Her dark hair had faded to an unattractive shade best described by the word "mousy." If she'd seen a hairdresser since high school, it didn't show. I recognized her hairdo as the same style that had been popular when we graduated. What was it the magazines said about fashion? If you'd lived through a trend the first time, don't do it the second time. The way I figured it, Linda's style was on its third incarnation. Once was enough for her.

Her body was a plumped up version of the girl I remembered. I looked into her eyes. What I could see of them. Her eyelids drooped, large bluish bags hung beneath her small brown eyes. Her entire face looked as if it had somehow melted just a little. Time had not been good to her.

"Yes, it has been ages," I finally replied. My mind was doing backflips as I tried to put the image of the person I remembered from high school into some sort of context. Automatically I said, "You look—" I stopped myself. There was nothing positive I could say. "I mean…" I stumbled over my words. "What I meant to say—"

Linda interrupted me with a laugh. "I know exactly what you meant to say. I look old." I had to give her credit for not mincing her words. She laughed again. "I guess we both do. Look older, I mean." She shook her head, a twinkle in her puffy eyes. "Gosh, when *was* high school? My kids call it the olden days when I bring it up." Her shoulders shook.

For the life of me I couldn't understand what she found so funny.

"I imagine you're here for the same reasons I am," she said, reminding me why I had come here today.

A flash of horror swept over me. I couldn't possibly look as old as Linda. Could I?

She was talking, but her words were coming from another planet. "*Extreme Makeover.* That's what finally got me off the couch and into this office. Have you seen that show? It's on ABC, not cable."

As if that made it credible.

"Wow," she babbled. "I don't look half as bad as some of those women, and they end up drop-dead gorgeous. They take a person and do them over almost from the inside out," she explained. "They start with plastic surgery, whatever they need, and, believe me, some of them need a lot! Then they style their hair, get them new clothes, even whiten their teeth. It's amazing. I figure if I get the work done now, I'll show up at our thirty-year class reunion and no one will know me."

I stared at her. No one would know her now. If that was her goal she could save her money.

Linda lowered her voice. "So what are you going to have done?" She motioned for me to sit down, as if we were going to compare grocery lists.

I looked over my shoulder and then at my watch. I needed to get away. I couldn't look at her any longer. It was like looking into a fun house mirror...except this wasn't any fun. Her high school image was radically distorted, and I suddenly knew mine was, too. "I'm sorry, but I have to go," I stammered. "I have to be somewhere." I pulled my purse up farther on my shoulder. "Good to see you," I lied through my yellowing teeth.

"Good to see you, too," Linda said. "But it will be better to see you..." she paused, winked, and tossed her faded hair meaningfully towards the doctor's office, "later."

I knew what she meant. After our surgeries.

I hurried from the clinic. I thought I'd lied when I'd told her I needed to be somewhere, but I realized now I hadn't fibbed. I knew exactly where I was going. I slid into the car, shoved the key in the ignition, and started it up. I caught a glimpse of myself in the rearview mirror. If crow's feet could look panicked, mine did. Loose gravel spun under my wheels as I backed out of my parking spot.

I knew exactly where I was headed. I was going to find a job. I was going to earn whatever money it took to get "the works." Face it, I might *be* old, but I wasn't going to *look* old one minute longer than I had to.

I shifted into drive and headed toward the mall. Toward the only place I knew I'd be qualified to work. I'd never gone to college. I'd never had a career. The only thing I ever had going for me was the way I looked.

And, as usual, I was going to have to put it to good use now.

Kenny

"Dang!" The air compressor hose shot out of my left hand and slithered along the floor of the station garage like a slippery snake. For the second time in as many seconds I bent to pick it up. I thrust the nozzle onto the valve using my casted right arm as a backup against the pressure. Would I ever get this job done?

It had been three weeks since I'd slid into that base. Three itchy weeks of wearing this cast and trying to pretend I was still in charge of Kenny's SuperPumper. My other right hand, Mike Anderson, had left for college a week ago and it had been nothing but downhill from there.

Usually, come fall, nearly everyone in Brewster waited until a good hard freeze to start gearing up for winter. Not this year. No sir. This year every Tom, Dick, and Hulda wanted fuel oil in their furnaces and antifreeze in their radiators the second week of September. I wasn't complaining about the business; I needed every dime of it. I also needed a clone in order to get it all done. Already this morning there were two vehicles waiting for oil changes in the driveway near the alley. Normally an oil change would take me a half hour. Tops. But with this clumsy cast and my still-tender wrist, I was anticipating an hour apiece. If I ever got this job done.

The driveway bell sounded, letting me know someone had driven in for a fill. At least I hoped it was a fill-up. It was hardly worth wrestling down this air hose for anything under five dollars. I turned off the machine and hurried outside. It was cool out this morning. Automatically, I tried to rub my hands together. Something next to impossible with a cast on one of them. I could hear Diane telling me

97

I should have grabbed a jacket. Pneumonia was all I needed on top of my other troubles.

A woman I'd never seen before was getting out of her car. She wasn't from Brewster. I could tell by the way she was dressed and the fact that she was reaching for the gas hose.

"Hang on, I can do that for you." I slid my left hand under her outstretched arm and grabbed up the nozzle. "It's not self-serve," I explained as I held the nozzle under my right arm and turned the gas cap off with my left.

"Oh." She sounded confused. "Well, that's nice." She got back in her car and stared out the windshield.

Breathing in the familiar oily fumes, I got the gas started and then washed her windows with a squeegee and one hand. Someone from Brewster would have rolled down their window and kept me company.

"Check your oil?" I asked through the glass. Might as well give this stranger the full treatment. Maybe she drove through town often and would pull in again.

"Sure," she called back, bending to release the hood.

I was just lifting it as the phone inside the station office started ringing. The loud thunk of a valve closing told me the gas tank was full. Now what? I was waiting for a call from my bulk dealer. I needed to talk to him pronto. I'd had a run on diesel and needed another load now. A regular customer would understand if I suddenly ran off.

Quickly, I pushed up the hood until it stood open on its own and then ran toward the office. "The phone," I called over my shoulder, making answering motions with my hand, hoping the woman heard and didn't think I was simply nuts.

I grabbed up the receiver. "Hello!" I pulled in a lungful of air. Even with the extra effort of getting my regular jobs done these days, having this cast on my arm wasn't doing a thing to get me in better shape. "Kenny's," I added, just in case the caller didn't recognize my voice.

"Iss dis my faforite hendyman?"

I closed my eyes and ground my teeth together. The driveway bell dinged twice. I opened my eyes. One of the Brewster school buses had pulled in for a fill. "Aunt Ida, I've got to go. I'm busy."

"Acht, I'm sorry. I chust neffer know when iss a goot time to call." Her voice trembled, sounding flustered.

Well, good, so was I. I could see Marvin, the school bus driver climbing out from behind the wheel. That meant he wasn't in a hurry and had time to hang around. He was probably heading this way for a cup of coffee. I felt my jaw relax a bit. "What do you want, Aunt Ida?" I hoped she didn't notice the irritation in my voice and that she'd make it snappy.

"I vanted to remindt you that vhen the time changes next mont I vill neet dat kitchen clock changedt ant a new baddery for my shmoke alarm."

Good grief. She was worried about something almost two months away. "Yeah. Okay." I nodded at Marvin as he walked into the station. "We've got a little time for that. Gotta run." Someday maybe all I'd have to do would be to sit around and think about new batteries. I certainly didn't have time to think about them now. "Hey, Marv, pour yourself a cup of coffee while I go finish up outside."

We traded places as he grabbed the coffeepot near the phone and I hurried out to my waiting customer. She had her window rolled down a half inch and was holding her credit card out through the crack. My cue to get a move on.

"Sorry about that," I explained as I checked her oil, slammed the hood, and slid her credit card between the fingers sticking out from my cast. "It's a mom-and-pop operation around here and lately 'mom' hasn't been able to help out." The woman could see that Pop was half-crippled himself.

She forced up the corners of her mouth. It didn't take a rocket scientist to see she was just being polite. Okay, no chitchat.

"I'll run this for you." I held up the card and went back into the office. Normally, I would have started up the gas pump on the school bus first, but the woman made me feel as if I were already a shoddy one-man band.

I ran the credit card through the machine, waiting while it automatically dialed an authorization. Marv was grumbling about the kids on his bus route. The same story I'd heard since I'd bought the business. I tuned him out, mentally calculating the percentage of this gas sale that was going to the credit card company. Twenty-one cents just for the privilege of swiping the card, then almost two percent of the seventeen-dollar fill, and that didn't even count the ten-dollar monthly fee I had to pay to say, "Yes, I take credit cards."

I glanced outside. Curt Sayler was idling his pickup behind the woman's car. I snapped my fingers together, urging the machine to hurry up. It was turning into a busy day. This was a nickel-and-dime business, at best. No wonder the bigger towns had gone to self-service. Who could afford to have someone outside filling gas, someone else in the garage servicing vehicles, and one or two more people inside selling pop and candy and watching for shoplifters? I didn't know why I thought I could do it all by myself.

With Mike off to college, my days felt like a merry-go-round. Only there was no "merry" in the circle. I was more like a mindless gerbil, running on a wheel that went nowhere. Starting one task, getting interrupted. Going back to my first task until the phone rang or the driveway bell dinged, then off I'd go, running like a hungry dog, to answer the summons. Nothing was getting done, except for me wearing myself ragged.

At least when Diane had been able to fill in, I could stick to a job in the garage until it was finished. But these days Diane was having bouts of morning sickness that lasted all day. She was hardly able to stomach bringing me something to the station for lunch, much less the smell of gas, a constant perfume around here.

Finally the credit card machine spat out a receipt. I tore it off, grabbed a pen, and dashed outside. I waved to Curt that I'd be right with him. He lifted one finger in response. He understood.

While the woman signed her receipt, I stared up at the Kenny's SuperPumper sign that hung high above the street. My wrist throbbed in the cool morning air. I was going to need to climb the ladder and change prices when my next bulk load was delivered from the terminal. How would I ever manage that one-handed? The stations down the street sometimes liked to think we were big-town and pretend we were in a price war. Luckily, right now, neither of the other two station owners felt ornery. It didn't help any of us to sell gas below the price we bought it. But, that last load of gas I'd bought had been a high load. I'd had to pay good money to fill my bulk tanks, and then I had to raise my per-gallon price to cover it. In the meantime the bulk price had dropped and so had my competition's prices. They were selling gas a few cents cheaper than me while I was still trying to pay off the last load.

As the woman handed me her receipt and drove off, I saw Jerry Simon drive past on the highway, craning his neck to see my prices. He was one of those folks who would drive forty miles to save half a cent.

Good thing I had loyal customers like Curt. Some folks filled wherever the price was lowest…even if that meant filling out of town. I wondered what those same folks would say if they knew what it cost me to do business? What they'd say if all the service stations in Brewster closed and they had to drive to Carlton to get gas for even their lawn mowers? Maybe then they'd think paying an extra cent or two to buy locally wasn't so bad.

As Curt pulled up to the pump I got the gas going into the school bus. Poor Marv was in there drinking coffee by himself. Curt climbed out of his pickup. "Got time to change the oil in this thing today?"

I didn't, but I said, "Sure." Curt ambled toward the office while I fumbled with my left hand at the tight gas cap on his pickup. This one-handed stuff was getting old. The gas started flowing at the same time the phone rang in the office again. I could sure use Mike now. Maybe Marv would pick it up. It rang again. Or Curt.

Come on, guys. Can't you see I'm busy out here?

I left the gas cap hanging and jogged back to the office. Marv was pouring himself a second cup of coffee. He held out the pot and offered Curt a cup, too. As I snatched up the phone I hoped Curt would take up Marv's offer. I could use the time they'd spend jawing to finish up outside.

"Kenny's," I said. I didn't mean to sound as short as it came out. I apologized in my mind to whoever was on the other end of the line.

"You must be busy." Thank goodness Diane understood.

"Yeah," I said eyeing Jan Jordan's car as it pulled up behind Curt's pickup. Busy was good, but this was nuts. "What's up?"

"I'll make this quick. I've got good news and bad. Which do you want first?"

Oh, man, now what? "Give me the good first." I'd have plenty of time to stew over the bad news after I hung up.

"The good news is I'm sure this baby is a boy." Her voice lifted on the last word. She knew how much I was hoping for another boy. My heart did a funny little leap at her intuition-led prediction. "I'm feeling as sick as a dog. Exactly the way I felt when I was pregnant with Billy. And..." She grew quiet. I knew she was remembering our other little boy.

I drew in a deep breath. Suddenly her good news made me feel sad. Best to change the subject. "So is that the bad news, too? That you're feeling sick?"

"Sort of." I could hear her take a sip of something. Probably 7 UP. "I don't think I'm going to be able to make you a lunch and bring it over there today. I've been hanging over the toilet all morning. The thought of making a baloney sandwich—" She stopped talking. I didn't even want to imagine what was happening at the other end of the line.

"That's fine. Don't worry about it. I'll rustle up something off the shelves here." The truth was, I felt like gagging along with her. I was hardly able to stomach the thought of having beef jerky and Skittles for lunch again today. Time to change the subject again. Now that Billy and Renae had started back to school, Diane had her hands full keeping our toddler out of mischief. "How's Paige?"

"She's being a trooper. She was busy lining her stuffed animals up in the bathroom this morning as though there was a drive-in movie playing near the bathtub. I'm the featured attraction. I don't even want to think what *that* video would be called. Speaking of which..." Diane paused. "I'd better go see what our daughter is up to.

She's much too quiet. Paige?" she called out. "I've gotta run, Kenny. Sorry about lunch."

I was sorry, too. But I'd be fine. I didn't envy Diane one minute of her nausea. I'd had a couple hours of it when I was coming out of surgery and that was plenty. I just hoped she'd have enough energy to work on the station books. There were bills that needed paying, and with my right hand in a cast and as busy as I was, I didn't have the handwriting skills or the time to monkey with that stuff. The way the morning was shaping up I'd be lucky if I had time for lunch.

"Keys in your pickup, Curt?" If he was going to stand here and drink coffee with Marv, I was going to need to move his pickup so Jan Jordan could pull up to the pumps.

Curt patted at his pockets. "Guess I left 'em in there."

"No problem," I muttered as I dashed outside. I pulled the gas hose out of Curt's pickup and then climbed inside. I'd told Curt moving his pickup was no problem. Actually, it was. Trying to start a vehicle with a tender wrist and fingers that couldn't grip much more than a stick of beef jerky was impossible. Trying to start a pickup with my left hand wasn't much easier. Finally I managed, motioning over my shoulder for Jan to inch up to the pumps behind me.

"Hey, Kenny," she called as I walked back to her car. "Fill it up, please." She smiled. Man, the way she was looking at me… Reminded me of the way the girls used to look at me back in high school.

I pulled off my cap with the fingers of my right hand and ran my left hand through my hair. I tugged it back on and then hiked up my jeans. I couldn't help but grin back at her. She was a welcome sight for busy eyes like mine. I planned to consider the time I spent filling her car as my coffee break for the morning. At least a break for my eyes. Jan was a heck of a lot better to look at than Curt and Marv.

"Going somewhere?" I asked as I started to scrub her windshield, making conversation. She always dressed as though she were going someplace special, but today I could see her purse, an extra pair of shoes, a couple magazines, and a navy blue blazer on the seat beside her. I'd worked this job long enough to read the inside of a car like a detective.

"Off to my new job in Carlton," she answered. "Well," she put her elbow on the window ledge and ran her fingers through her hair. "It's not that new. I've been working almost two weeks now."

"Oh?" I said. There wasn't much that went on in our community that I didn't hear about. I was surprised I hadn't heard that Jan was working out of town. I wondered what Dan thought of that? He was on his second term as president of the Brewster Association of Commerce. One thing the association had spent money on was encouraging the local folks to spend their money locally. The way I figured, having his wife working out of town might not sit well with him. "Where're you working?" I asked, trying not to sound as nosy as my question felt.

Jan's grin grew even bigger. Man, her smile could be competition for a lightbulb. Mine might be, too, if I didn't wipe the silly grin off my face. I swiped at her outside mirror while I waited. At least I'd have something besides Marv's grumbling to tell Diane tonight. Jan shook her long blonde hair before she answered. If she told me she was modeling for some big-time hairdresser, it would seem perfectly logical, even though North Dakota didn't have any big-time hairdressers.

She gathered up her hair into a quick ponytail and then let it drop free. "I'm working at Elizabeth's."

I was surprised. The most exclusive store in Carlton. The one so expensive that Diane even gasped at their sale prices. Diane wouldn't be one bit surprised either when I told her this news. She'd always thought Jan Jordan was a little too stylish for our little town. "She dresses up to go to the grocery store," Diane had told me more than once. Well, it wouldn't hurt Diane to take a few lessons from Jan. I wasn't one bit into fashion, but I could tell the difference between the way Jan and Diane dressed without even breaking open a magazine. I doubted sweatshirts and jeans had ever been on the cover of…well, whatever the names were of the magazines that Jan Jordan read. And Diane didn't.

I suddenly realized Jan was staring at me. Expecting me to say something back to her instead of daydreaming the day away. Man, talk about acting like a kid in junior high. Quickly, I wiped the window on the backseat passenger side. "What're you doing there? At that store?"

"I'm working at the cosmetics counter." She gave me a look over the top of her sunglasses as if to say, "La-dee-da."

I was pretty sure that's what Diane would say when I told her, too.

"Like it?" I asked. I didn't know beans about makeup, but I did know I'd rather be talking to Jan than Marv and Curt. I could talk to them any day, and they weren't near the eye candy she was. I worked my way around her car windows as she spoke louder to make sure I heard every word.

"I love it!" she gushed. "It's as if this job were made for me." She reached into her purse and pulled out a tiny jar, holding it out the window so I could see it. "Would you believe this cream can prevent wrinkles from forming beside your eyes? I wish I would have known about it years ago. Well, of course, years ago I never could have afforded it, but with my discount and all." She pushed the small container back into her purse. "You should tell Diane to stop by when I'm working sometime. I could show her some products that would transform her skin. I just never knew there were so many breakthroughs in cosmetic technology. Why, we have a whole line of products specially formulated for men. You should stop by, too. There's this new..."

Oh, man, I prayed the gas would hurry into her gas tank. Why had I thought I'd rather listen to Jan than Curt and Marv? I didn't know a thing about women's cosmetics and I didn't *want* to know a thing about *men's*.

As she chattered on I pretended I was busy back by the gas tank. I'd heard about this new kind of guy she was jabbering about. The "metrosexual man" is what the gal on *Dateline* had called him. The kind of guy who would leave work early to get a manicure. I looked at the grease under my fingernails. He wasn't me. I wasn't him. Whatever. Other than Jacob, Brewster's one and only male hairdresser, I didn't think there was a single guy in Brewster who would come close to the man Jan was talking about. As I topped off her tank, I made a mental note to check out her husband a little more closely the next time he stopped by. If Dan started using that male facial crud Jan was babbling about, I wouldn't let him hear the end of it.

"Twenty-two." I stepped to Jan's open window and held out my hand. I wanted nothing more than to get back inside and tell Curt and Marv what we'd been missing. Facials and manicures…that would be the day.

Jan tapped my hand with her soft fingers. "Put it on our tab, okay? I've got to get moving."

I nodded as she drove off. Even though Diane had made a sign that hung in the station window saying "no credit," there were several people I just couldn't say no to. Dan Jordan was one of them. I knew I could count on him to write me a check the next time he stopped by. Most folks were a different story. Diane hounded me often to quit extending credit. She probably would again when she did the books this week. But she wasn't the one who had to stand here and explain why I couldn't charge a tank full of gas to a guy who'd stood beside me telling me how his crop had been hailed out, his best cow had been struck by lightning, and his wife was on the verge of packing up and moving to Carlton.

I'd heard it all at this station, and more. It was a wonder I didn't have an honorary degree in counseling by now. Or listening anyway. I mean, who else in Brewster was going to hear about men's facials today?

I chuckled as I walked back into the office, shaking my head.

"What?" Marv blew on his full-again coffee cup. Looked like it was time to make a new pot. Marv and Curt had pretty much emptied this one. Easy to do when it was free. "Are you smiling because Jan Jordan said something funny? Or just because she's so easy on the eyes?"

So he'd noticed, too. Wouldn't have thought it of old Marv. I grabbed up the pot to go fill it. "You're not gonna believe what we're missing, guys. Hang on while I get this coffee going."

As I headed outside to the bathroom to fill the coffeepot, I glanced out into the garage. I'd almost forgotten. There hung a pickup up on the hoist. The one I'd been working on forty-five minutes ago. The pickup that needed its tires rotated and oil changed. There were still two cars out by the alley waiting for similar work, plus the job Curt had asked me to do today, too.

Oh, well. Somehow it would get done. But first I had a good story to tell the guys.

⌒

I'd let Curt and Marv waste way too much of my morning. Make that all of my morning. By the time they'd left to grab some lunch at Vicky's, other than filling a couple tanks of gas while they drank my fresh coffee, I still had the same lineup of work I'd had when I came in this morning.

I tore open a stick of beef jerky. Maybe chomping on something would get rid of the pressure I was feeling to get something done today. I stood and chewed while the oil drained from the vehicle on the hoist. Finishing off a hunk of beef wasn't much, but it was more than I'd done all day. How could two guys who liked to gab put me so far behind?

You were busy gabbing, too. Putting fun ahead of work again.

I tore off another hunk of jerky with my teeth. I hoped Diane didn't find out how my morning had been spent. She told me often that I needed to tend more to my work and less to hanging out with my customers. But, heck, that was the fun about this job, talking to the people who stopped by. If I couldn't do that my days would get mighty long.

They might get even longer when you have to spend all night finishing those jobs. Look at the work you have lined up outside. If you would have worked while Curt and Marv talked, you could have a nice daily total to bring home to Diane.

I cringed at that thought. Diane knew exactly what the station bottom line averaged each day. What it took to break even, what it would take for us to get ahead. My broken wrist had her wringing her hands when she thought I wasn't looking. Even before my injury she'd chided me about becoming sidetracked by talking sports with the guys. She hadn't said anything, but she had to know that with this cast I wasn't keeping up with even my normal routine. I'd told her yesterday I had a couple jobs waiting for me this morning. If she asked and I didn't have them done...well, maybe I'd be having beef jerky for supper tonight, too.

$\sim$

I could set my watch by the late afternoon traffic on the highway past the station. I glanced at my wrist. Yup, three-thirty. The only time of day sleepy Brewster could be called "bustling." School was out, which meant the buses were running and parents were picking up kids. The ones who weren't getting picked up were riding their bikes or walking home. Kids who could drive and weren't in after-school sports were cruising Main. It seemed today that most of those folks, adults and kids, needed to stop at the station for something.

I hurried outside as two cars pulled up on either side of the pumps. Mark Bettenhausen, a freshman with a new driver's license, held up five fingers. That used to mean five gallons; these days it meant five dollars. I'd see what Marci Turner wanted first. If she asked for a fill I could get her tank going before I had to babysit the nozzle at Mark's Chevy.

I saw four junior high boys hightail it into the station. I hoped Mark wasn't here as a decoy so his buddies could run inside and swipe cigarettes. I wished I had a security camera inside...or another Mike. Someone who could help out. If I were lucky, Renae wouldn't have anything scheduled after school and might show up in a minute. But today Diane probably needed her at home as much as I needed her here.

Marci did want a fill. I got the gas going into her car, then started on Mark's five dollars worth of gas. I could see the kids inside the station pushing each other, as if daring someone to make the first move. Mark was just going to have to wait for his gas. I stopped the pump and jogged to the office. Justin Berg grabbed a bag of chips as

I walked in, quickly tossing the bag and a buck onto the counter. The other three boys darted out the door. I wasn't sure if they were pocketing what they'd come for or if I had diverted a crime spree.

"Find everything?" I asked Justin as I stepped behind the counter.

"Yeah." I could see his eyes darting to the cigarette rack that hung behind me. Justin was in Renae's eighth-grade class. He knew better than to push his luck and ask for smokes from me. I rang up his ninety-nine cent purchase. One good thing about living in a little town like Brewster was that I pretty much knew all the kids...and how old they were. If anyone was going to try to pretend they were old enough to buy nicotine legally, they were going to have to show me some ID. If it was fake, I'd know it. Then I'd call their folks. I wasn't about to take a chance on getting the five-hundred-dollar fine the state would levy for selling cigarettes to minors. Besides the fact they shouldn't be smoking, I didn't have five hundred extra dollars to take the risk. That, and the fact that Diane would kill me if she ever found out I let a kid ruin their lungs by a habit so stupid.

"Have a good one," I said to Justin's back.

Mark Bettenhausen was still waiting, my gas hose dangling from the side of his car. I didn't know him well enough to trust he wouldn't speed off with half my hose now that his friends had run off. I'd better hustle out there. I sidestepped around Justin, whipped open the door, and almost knocked Pete West over as he was about to come in.

"Whoa!" Pete said in surprise as I practically yanked him inside with the other side of the doorknob he was holding onto. "S'cuse me."

From what I knew of Pete, he wasn't in a hurry to get anywhere. Any parties that were going to happen around Brewster tonight wouldn't start until after dark...or until Pete showed up. He could wait a few minutes while I finished pumping gas outside. "Just be a sec," I said, giving him a pat on the back to let him know I appreciated his business, even if I was making him wait.

I took care of Mark's car, stuffed his five ones into my pocket, and then turned to finish Marci's fill. A car and a pickup were waiting for their turn at the pumps. I hadn't been this busy since Pumpkin Fest last year. From off in the distance I could hear the phone ringing in the office. One ring. Two. Marci was tearing a check out of her checkbook. *Hurry up!* I drummed the fingers of my left hand against my pants leg. The phone rang again. I grabbed the check and turned to run back to the office. Ah. The phone had quit ringing. Just as well. I had two more tanks to fill out here.

I got the gas going in each of the vehicles and then started washing the windshield of one. The phone started up again. Dang! My wrist was throbbing like a heart attack. I shoved the squeegee back into the water ready to dash inside. The phone quit ringing. If those calls were bulk delivery orders I was missing...man, I didn't want to know about it.

I took a check from one customer, a credit card from another. The traffic along Main Street had finally let up. Maybe I'd get a chance to get at Vince Bender's vehicle, rotate the tires, and be done. Well, not done for the day, but at least done with one of the chores that had been on my to-do list. I walked to the office to run the credit card.

Pete West was standing at the counter sipping a Mountain Dew, a dollar bill and some coins lying by his hand. "Busy place," he said.

I'd completely forgotten he was inside the office. My eyes did a quick survey. Knowing his reputation I wouldn't put it past Pete to help himself to something, but all seemed in order. "Yeah," I said as I swiped the credit card. I scooped his pop money into my hand, ringing it into the cash register. "Need anything else?"

He jerked his chin towards the cigarettes behind the counter. I knew his brand and grabbed a pack. He dug into the side pocket of his jeans and pulled out a ten. "Bad habit," he said as he handed over the bill.

I raised an eyebrow. Quite the admission for a punk like him. "I was thinking the same thing," I replied as I rang up his purchase. The credit card machine spit out a receipt and I grabbed it up. "I gotta take care of this." I held up the sales slip. "Anything else I can do for you?" I'd left him in here alone once today. I wasn't so sure I wanted to do it again.

He took a big swallow of his pop before shaking his head. "No, but here." He held out a piece of the notepaper I kept near the phone.

"You're supposed to deliver fuel out to the Wynn farm and your Aunt Ida called." When I didn't reach for the paper, he pushed it across the counter toward me. "I wrote it all down."

The person in the car outside tapped at their horn, my signal to get a move on. "Hang on," I said to Pete as I ran outside.

He's a punk.

Yes, but he answered the phone. It's more than Curt or Marv did for you. All they did was listen to the phone ring and drink your coffee.

He's screwed up more things than an electric drill.

He took messages.

From some place far off I watched as the woman in the car signed her charge slip. In my mind I was remembering the doctor appointment I'd had a month ago with Pete's mom, Dr. West. *He's got a knack for workings on motors,* she'd said. *He's between jobs.* Her words echoed as I automatically separated the two pieces of paper, handed one back to my customer, and watched her drive off.

You know Diane would tell you to take your time. To pray about what you're about to say.

I don't have time to pray. I need help. Now.

Lord, let this be the right thing to do. I hiked up my pants, took a deep breath, and then opened the door leading back into the station. I was going to have to go with my gut on this one…as out of shape as it was.

"Pete," I said, picking up the piece of paper he'd written neat messages on, "you working anyplace right now?"

He shrugged one shoulder. "Odd jobs," he said, taking a swig of his pop. "Why?"

Part of me screamed to shrug my shoulder back at him. Say, "Just wondering." Another part of me screamed louder. Spoke the words for real. "How'd you like a job?"

One corner of his mouth turned up the tiniest bit. One eye narrowed. "You offering?"

The geese that had been flapping their wings inside my stomach grew oddly quiet, as if waiting to hear if I really was going to do this. "Yeah, I am," I replied, as the flock of geese took flight and left completely. I was suddenly confident I was doing the right thing. "I am," I repeated.

"When do I start?"

I held up the paper of phone messages. "I think you already did."

"Have you seen this color? It's new!" I swiveled the lipstick out of the tube and into the perfumed air. "It's called…" I lowered my voice, making it sultry, "*Passionate* Plum." My customer giggled. Smiling along with her, I scribbled a line onto the side of my hand. "Personally, I think it has a more mauvey tone, not grape, but it would be wonderful with your coloring. Would you like to try it?"

The woman nodded and I reached for a Q-tip, swiping a gooey sample from the side of the waxy cylinder. As she preened into the countertop mirror, I snuck a little wave to Olivia. She was pretending to browse the eye shadows at the far end of my station until our lunch date at twelve-thirty. She'd driven to Carlton today to see me at my new job. I picked up a small white clock on the makeup counter, noting there were twenty minutes until my lunch break. I held the travel clock out to my customer in the palm of my manicured, well-lotioned hand. "If you purchase forty dollars worth of the SoNu cosmetic line, you'll receive this darling alarm clock as a free gift."

My customer eyed the clock. "I am taking a trip in a couple weeks." She leaned into the mirror again, inspecting her lips. "I do like the color. How much is this lipstick?"

"Seventeen ninety-five," I repeated from memory. It was surprising how quickly I'd learned the prices of the variety of makeup lines Elizabeth's carried. "The shade really does flatter your olive skin tones." I wasn't lying. I had an eye for this sort of thing. If she hadn't looked good in that color, there were at least ten other lipstick shades I could suggest.

"I'll take it," she decided. "That eye cream you showed me? It seemed kind of expensive. Does it work?"

I leaned toward her as if I had a secret to share. "I know it's a little pricey, but it's worth every penny. I've been using it for three weeks and already I can tell a difference." It was true, I could, but not enough to make me change my mind about the brow lift I planned to have early next year. I didn't tell her that part. Or about the tummy tuck.

"If I bought the eye cream too, is that enough to get the clock?"

"It is!" I said, feeling almost as delighted with her purchase as I hoped she would. I wrapped her two makeup items in filmy tissue and then used the time it took her credit card to run to show her a new line of perfume.

"I'll think about it," she said as I topped off her package with the small boxed clock.

"Have fun on your trip! Come back and tell me about it." I wiggled my fingers at her.

"You're good," Olivia said, slipping into the place where my customer had stood. "I think I might need some of that eye cream and lipstick."

"Oh, goodness." I put one finger on my chin, thinking. "Passionate Plum is *not* your color. I see you more in this." I pulled a tube of lipstick from the swivel stand near my elbow. "Raisin Rave. It would compliment your dark hair and be a nice contrast to your fair skin." I twisted the medium brown shade high enough so that it peeked out of the silver tube just so. I smiled at Olivia and then burst out laughing at the expression on her face. "You really weren't shopping for lipstick, were you?"

"No," she said, laughing along with me. "But I think I am now. Let me try that."

I dipped her a sample and waited while she wiped off her red-toned lipstick with a tissue. "Here." I handed her the Q-tip and watched as she spread the sample across her lips, smacked them together, and then looked into the mirror. "Can you see how it picks up the brown of your eyes? Rather than having your red lips scream," I made small quote marks in the air, "'*Look at us*,' this new shade freshens your face and sends the attention to your gorgeous eyes. Where it should be." The change in her face was so obvious. I only hoped she could see it as well as I could.

Olivia looked at me with a twinkle in her eye. "What else don't I know?"

I took a deep breath. I loved this part of my job. Opening a whole new world to women who needed my expertise. "Thank you for asking. I've got a couple foundations you might want to look at, but the one you're using matches your complexion quite nicely. Actually, what I would love to do with you is enhance your eyes. Can I?" I held up a cotton ball and some eye-makeup remover.

Olivia set her purse on the counter, lifted her hands in the air, and said, "Have at it."

Forty-five minutes later I was sitting in a booth at Café 58 across the table from my new-faced friend. She looked fabulous, if I did say so myself. I grinned at her.

"What?" asked Olivia, glancing up from her menu.

"You look great!"

She pulled a powder compact from her purse and looked into the small mirror, turning her head as she examined her Raisin Rave lips and her Brushed Brown shadowed lids. She lightly touched the deep brown liner I'd used on the rims of both her top and bottom lashes. "I do look different," she said, softly snapping the compact shut and putting it back into her purse. She studied the menu again.

"Don't you like the way you look?" Suddenly I felt uncomfortable. What if she'd bought almost a hundred dollars of makeup just to be nice? Just because she was my friend? Maybe I'd been too enthused and she had agreed to buy everything just to shut me up. "Libby." I put my elbows on the table and leaned forward. "If you really don't want that makeup, I'll return it for you. I wasn't trying to force anything on you. I was just trying to show you what's new. I know everyone isn't into this stuff like I am. Sometimes I get carried away." Slightly embarrassed, I looked down at the rings on my hands. I didn't understand how she could be so unconcerned about her appearance. I'd grown up knowing how I looked was the be-all and end-all.

Libby put her menu off to the side and took a sip of coffee from the thick, white mug before she spoke. "Don't apologize for loving what you do, Jan. You're a natural behind that counter, and while I might not have *needed* everything I bought, I can certainly put it to good use." She paused to take another sip of coffee. It seemed as if she might want to say something more but then changed her mind. She put down her cup and smiled. "I think Bob might enjoy my new purchases as much as I will." She winked one of her lined eyelids.

I relaxed at her assurance that I hadn't forced her to buy the products. "I know what you mean," I replied, winking back at her. "Every time I get home from work these days, Dan buries his head into my neck, sampling my fragrance-of-the-day with his nose. If I hadn't given up on that idea of having a baby..." I blinked at the sudden stinging in my eyes. I picked up my menu and looked down.

Libby reached a hand across the table. "Are you okay?"

I nodded but didn't look at her.

"Are you two ready to order?" The waiter had his timing down to perfection.

I jumped right in, anxious to forget the subject I'd so thoughtlessly brought up. "I'll have the Grilled Chicken Mandarin Salad. Dressing on the side, please. And no breadstick." I handed him my menu.

"I can't decide," Libby mumbled to herself, picking her menu back up.

This was another area where I could help. "You should have the Mandarin Salad, too. It's good and only has four hundred calories if you don't touch the dressing. They use three kinds of lettuce and two kinds of sprouts. That sort of stuff has all kinds of antioxidant vitamins in it. They keep you young." I paused a second. "At least I think I read that somewhere."

"That'll be fine." Libby closed her menu and handed it to the waiter. "Could you bring some extra dressing with mine? And I'd like the breadstick."

He nodded and left while I bit back the caution threatening to push its way out between my lips. Libby didn't need to watch her figure closely, yet she had to know menopause was just around the corner. A time when her metabolism would be changing. Big time. *Extra* dressing? A *bread*stick? Didn't she know preventative measures never hurt? I cleared my throat. It was hard not to warn her about what the extra calories and carbs could do to her figure. Not to mention the way the coffee she was drinking would stain her teeth over time. I needed to change the subject before I gave her a health lecture in addition to the makeup lesson.

As Libby sipped her coffee, I fingered the edge of the thick, white tablecloth. I probably should ask her how her writing was going these days, but I didn't want to spend my lunch break talking about books.

I took a sip of water and quickly debated whether I dared ask her how Emily was doing at college. She'd left for school a little over a month ago, leaving Libby in tears for a week. I wasn't so sure I wanted to bring up that subject, either. I was going to have to think of something.

Olivia beat me to it. "You sure seem to love your new job. What does Dan think about it?" She had no clue how loaded her question was.

I took a long sip of water through a straw, biding time while I thought. I'd been purposely *not* thinking about just what she'd asked. How much did I really want to share with her? To say the words out loud where even I could hear the thoughts I'd tried not to think? Carefully, I set the glass down on a napkin and twisted it around a couple times. I wasn't so sure this was something I wanted to talk about, either. Where was that waiter? Maybe I should try and change the subject. Answer her question with one of my own.

What are you hiding from?

I didn't mean a question like that!

Well…?

Hiding? I wasn't hiding. I squeezed the wedge of lemon into my glass, stirring the clear juice into my water. Some things were just easier to not talk about, not think about. Libby opened her mouth to speak and then closed it when the waiter came over to refill her coffee. I was going to have to leave this guy a big tip.

"So what does Dan think?" Libby prompted when the waiter had left.

Unexpectedly my throat closed. It was going to be hard to answer her question with a stone in my esophagus, much less eat a salad with no dressing. I waved my hand in the air. It was the best I could do at the moment.

"He's not crazy about you working?"

Again I tipped my hand back and forth, concentrating hard on the lemon seed floating in my water glass.

"Jan, would you please look at me?" Libby's firm words pulled my tear-filled eyes to hers. "You certainly aren't the first woman whose husband isn't thrilled with her job. If I told you all the times Bob has told me to quit writing, you'd flip over backward." She sat back as the waiter placed a basket of bread on the table.

"Bob has told you to stop writing?" I could hardly believe her darling husband would tell Libby something like that. It would be like asking her to cut off her arm.

She nodded, pulling one of the thick breadsticks from the basket, breaking off a third of it, and spreading it with a light coat of butter. She sprinkled the whole thing with salt, then held it in the air while she talked. "I used to get so mad. I'd stomp around the house half yelling. Didn't he think I was a good writer? Didn't he want me to do something besides—" she rolled her breadstick through the air, "oh, I don't know, stay home and bake cookies? I'd be furious."

She took a bite, chomping as if she might still be a bit upset with Bob. She swallowed and continued. "Until I finally realized that the reason he was telling me to quit writing was because I would get so bummed every time I received a rejection letter in the mail. I'd mope around the house for days. I'd complain to Bob about how hard it was to get published. '*Next to impossible,*' I'd say over and over. It finally occurred to me that he wasn't trying to take away what I loved doing…writing. What he was trying to do was take away the pain I was feeling." She pressed her lips into a thoughtful smile. "I could hardly be mad at him for that."

"No, I suppose not." I took my arms off the table as the waiter put our salads in front of us. He then set one tiny cup of dressing by my plate and a much larger cup by Libby's. For some reason her identical salad looked better than mine.

Could it be her attitude that looks so much better than yours?

Her attitude? I have a great attitude!

Then why are you so desperate to change yourself?

I'm not *desperate*. I just want— I picked up my knife and fork and started slashing through the chicken slices on the top of my salad. What I really wanted was to not think about this right now.

I could see Libby spooning most of her dressing onto her salad. How could she do that and not calculate the calories at the same time? I cringed as I took a bite of my dry lettuce. Libby took a bite of hers, closing her eyes for a moment, savoring the taste. "This *is* good," she said. "Thanks for recommending it." I nodded. Maybe just a smidgen of dressing wouldn't hurt.

Libby tossed her salad around with her fork. "Can you think of a reason why Dan might not want you to be working right now?"

I shook my water glass, trying to get the ice cubes to release the water I wanted to fill my mouth. Couldn't the woman ever just let something drop? It seemed as though she was always pushing and probing, trying to make me see some big *meaning* in even the simplest thing. Where was the waiter now? I didn't want to examine the argument Dan and I had had over my job. I wanted to forget it.

Libby filled the silence. "I'm thinking possibly Dan— Oh!" She interrupted herself. "There's Bob." She slid out of the booth. "I didn't expect to see him here. He must be having lunch with a client. I'm going to run over and say hi. Be right back." She brushed some bread-crumbs off her brown skirt as she stood and then tapped one finger near her shadowed eye. "I'll see if he notices the new me."

I watched as Libby approached Bob's table, waved back to Bob when Libby pointed my way, and then focused on my dry salad. I hoped they'd talk just long enough so that Libby would forget what we'd been talking about. Or what I'd been trying *not* to talk about.

I picked at my meal. Dry chicken and barely moist lettuce. Yippee. My thoughts felt as scrambled as the sprouts on my fork. As hard as I tried not to think about what Dan had said over the past couple weeks, I couldn't help but remember.

"You got a *job?* In Carlton?" As he dropped his hands into his lap, his arms loudly crumpled the weekly edition of the *Brewster*

Banner he'd been reading. "Don't you think we should have talked about this first? Where are you going to be working? What kind of schedule will you have? What about tax season? My tax work is going to start gearing up soon. You know how much you've helped me with that these past couple years."

I pressed my lips together and nodded. Dan had started a small tax preparation service as a sideline to his real estate business two years ago. My former job as a bookkeeper at a jewelry store had served us well when business started booming. It seemed that folks in Brewster were more than happy to let someone else do the calculations of what they owed the government. I'd ended up working side by side with Dan for almost four straight months last tax season.

His questions came faster than I could answer them. Questions I'd only started to think about as I drove home from my interview. From getting hired on the spot. I'd never dreamt when I'd walked into Elizabeth's after my appointment with Dr. Peters to ask for a job application that I'd be hired then and there. *"You have just the look we want for someone in the cosmetics department."* I'd had no trouble saying, "I'd love the job!" It looked as if I would have a harder time convincing Dan it was a good idea.

I opened my mouth and then closed it. I didn't know where to start. With my surgery consultation? I hadn't even told him about that. Maybe if I started by explaining how I'd felt running into my old classmate? How old I looked every time I gazed into the mirror?

Dan took a long, slow breath that he exhaled just as slowly. I'd learned it was a tactic he often used when he needed to calm himself. Needed patience. Uh-oh.

"My job will be good for us, Dan." I figured I'd better start explaining. "With Joey back in school, my days are as long and boring as...as C-Span." Not that I'd ever watched more than ten seconds of it, but that was my point. Boring. "He has football practice after school now, and he'll have basketball practice after that, then track."

Dan closed his eyes, opened them, folded the paper, and set it on the end table beside his chair. "I just wish you had talked about this with me before you did it." He sounded tired. Or exasperated.

"I know." *Now* I did. Too bad it hadn't occurred to me earlier.

Dan sighed. "It's not that I mind you having a job, Jan. It's just that I count on you for so many things."

A flush of discomfort flooded through me. What had I been thinking when I'd taken the job at Elizabeth's?

Obviously, you weren't…thinking, that is.

As with so much of my life. Barreling into my first two marriages with nothing but romance in my eyes. The reality of two divorces and single parenthood. It was all something I tried not to think about…even these days. When Dan had come along, he'd seemed an unlikely candidate for my list of husband-material requirements. Frankly, I hadn't paid attention to him.

He was nine years older than me. Thinning blond hair as opposed to the dark-haired guys I usually preferred. He was tall enough, but a couple extra inches wouldn't have hurt. And he'd never even heard of Counting Crows. "It's a band," I'd had to explain while he chuckled at himself, "not a drive in the country to count birds." His plaid shirt and khaki pants didn't help endear him, either.

What *did* help was his smile. And his eyes. The way they'd crinkle at the corners and twinkle in the centers every time our paths happened to cross in dinky little Brewster.

I'd moved here when Joey was five, wanting to live in a town small enough where he could ride his bike to and from school if I needed to be at work during those times. I wanted a place where neighbors might pitch in and keep an eye on him when I couldn't. Most of all, I'd wanted to create a new life for Joey and me. A new address. A new phone number. I was tired of the kind of guys I kept running into in Carlton. Long-divorced men with more baggage than me, or newly divorced men with nothing but a night of fun on their agenda. I'd said, "Heck with them," picked up Joey, and moved to Brewster.

The slow pace of life had almost been my undoing until I remembered that was the very reason I'd moved to Brewster. No longer was my meager bookkeeper's paycheck going to big monthly rental fees and babysitters. I kept my job in Carlton for a while, driving to work after Joey left for school and back home in Brewster minutes before he was. I'd found a two-bedroom home to live in for hardly anything. And babysitters were a thing of the past since there was nowhere to go at night in little Brewster…at least not anywhere I couldn't take Joey along. The good news was that Jacob, Brewster's best hairdresser, charged not quite half as much as my stylist in Carlton. Money was tight, but as long as Joey was in clean jeans and I could afford to keep my hair cut and colored and my nails manicured, life was good.

Then Dan came along and made it even better. At first it was funny the way my path kept crossing with this nice, but unremarkable, man. He just happened to be pouring coffee at the table Joey and I were sitting at for the Brewster Lions Club pancake breakfast one Sunday morning about a year after our move. That was the first time I officially met him. Then he was one bleacher behind me at the Brewster Badgers basketball game. Another day he asked, "Have you tried the grapes?" as I pushed my cart past the fruit section at Magner's grocery store. I was walking to Kenny's to pick up my car after an oil change one Saturday afternoon when Dan pulled up beside me and said, "Need a ride somewhere?" I didn't, but I said yes, anyway. Some adult conversation was a nice addition to a day I'd spent with a backyard full of seven-year-old boys. The day Dan showed up at Jacob's hair salon saying, "I thought it might be time to try something new," I figured something was up.

Call me stupid, but Dan didn't fit the mold I thought I'd been looking for. I wasn't madly in love when he proposed, but I was wildly in "like." "Comfortable" was a good word to describe our relationship, and after all I'd been through with lousy men, I was ready to relax into arms that were solidly around me instead of arms that groped for more than I wanted to give. Dan turned out to be my man after all.

Which was the main reason I was feeling so bad about taking a job and not talking to him about it first. "I'm sorry," I said again.

He pressed two fingers against the bridge of his nose. "I don't know what I'm going to do come tax season."

"Maybe I can arrange my schedule so I can still help you." I didn't like the way my suggestion came out sounding more like a question than an actual solution. "You really won't need me until end-of-the-year work in a couple of months. And then again in March and April. Maybe they'll let me work part-time in the spring. I mean, it doesn't matter if I wait a couple more months for my surgery."

The room filled with an odd silence.

"What did you say?" He cocked his head as though he hadn't heard me.

"I said," I repeated, "that it really doesn't matter if I have to wait a couple extra months for my surg—" And then I remembered. I hadn't told Dan about that, either. I'd been waiting for just the right moment…and this wasn't it.

He took his feet off the footstool in front of his chair and put them flat on the floor. "Did you say *surgery?*"

I gazed at his shoes and nodded.

"You're not sick, are you?" He sounded worried.

I shook my head.

"You'd tell me if you were, wouldn't you?"

Once again I nodded.

"Does this have anything to do with trying to have a baby?" Before I could deny it he went on. "Because if it does, you know I said from the start that if you wanted a baby it was fine with me, but that I love Joey like he was my own son. Well, he *is* my own son. I adopted him, remember?" It wasn't really a question. He talked on. "Just having Joey is enough for me. I spent all those years as a bachelor, pretending I liked living alone, going places by myself. It was all a sham. I didn't like it one bit. When you and Joey came into my life—" His voice cracked. He swallowed hard and went on. "I could have closed my eyes right then and died a happy man. But then, I wouldn't have had these past five years with you. With Jo-ey." Again, he choked up.

Except for the soft thump of music coming from our son's room down the hall, the house was quiet. I couldn't think of anything to say that would make this conversation go away.

Finally, he broke the silence between us. "What kind of surgery are you talking about?"

I checked my manicure. Tugged at my left earring. Rubbed my lipsticked lips together. "Cosmetic surgery," I almost whispered.

"Cosmetic surgery? You mean like plastic surgery?"

That *plastic* word made me cringe. I nodded anyway.

"And what exactly does that involve?" he asked.

I checked to see that the clasp on my necklace was in the back of my neck where it was supposed to be. If Dan had ever opened a magazine besides *U.S. News, Golf Digest,* or *Pheasants Forever,* this might not take so much explaining. "I was thinking about having some work done." It wasn't much of an explanation and I knew it.

"What kind of work?"

How to put this? Might as well just blurt it out. He was going to blow a gasket however I said it. "Well…I thought about having a facelift, a breast lift, and a tummy tuck. Maybe some liposuction." Now he knew it all.

Dan pressed his hands against his face for a second. "Jan, you look absolutely perfect. You are the best-looking woman in Brewster. In the state of North Dakota. Why on earth are you thinking about having *work* done?"

How would I ever get him to understand? All I could do was start talking. "You know how you like to trade in our car every few years? Get a newer model, one less likely to have problems?"

"I don't see what that has to do with this."

I was afraid of that. Oh! I had an idea. "Or, even better, think about your computer system at work. You know how you keep upgrading it so that it runs at top efficiency? Think of the procedures I want to have done as an upgrade. I want to look my best so I can be my best as long as possible." There. It would be hard to argue with that.

I could tell he was going to try. "But why would you want to put yourself through major surgery when you already look so perfect?"

Sweet, but not true. "Dan, you simply don't see me the way I really am."

The eyes of love don't lie. Try looking at yourself with My eyes.

My eyes examined every inch of me in the mirror every night. I knew exactly how I looked.

My eyes see deeper. Truer.

I hated to even contemplate what my eyes would see if I looked deeper.

I'm not talking about human eyes. I'm talking about Mine.

Suddenly I understood where these strange thoughts were coming from. I'd stopped going to church about the same time I'd been left pregnant and alone. If I was going to have to raise my baby by myself, I would. Without the help of any man…or even God.

My stubborn determination had stood me well for a time, but I'd found myself crying real tears for help more than once after Joey was born. Over the years God and I had developed a distant friendship. When I needed Him, He was there. And now it seemed, even when I didn't think I needed Him, He thought He should drop in and add His two cents. I wasn't so sure I wanted His opinion. I shook my head against the odd thoughts. I'd given this whole surgery business a lot of thought, and the only person I needed to convince now was Dan.

And you.

Me? I knew exactly what I wanted. Face-lift. Breast lift. Tummy tuck. So there.

You are as I made you.

"You are perfect the way you are." Dan's voice was so much like an echo it sent chills down my back.

I was getting tired of defending myself…to both voices in the room. "All I did was talk to the doctor. I haven't set a date or anything."

"So what does all this have to do with you getting a job?" He sounded tired, too.

"I thought I'd earn some money. To go towards the surgery," I lamely explained.

"How much is it?" Dan closed his eyes and waited.

I mumbled the price tag into the air.

His eyes popped open. "No way." I wasn't sure if he didn't believe the price or if he meant there was no way I was going to have the surgery. "No way," he said again.

A bubble of defensiveness pushed its way over my tongue. "It's my body and I can do what I want."

I could see the muscles in Dan's jaw working. He pushed his tongue into the side of his cheek. "I can live with the job thing, but not the reason for it." He put his hand on the arms of the chair and pushed himself out of it. "I can't talk about this anymore. Not tonight."

And we hadn't talked about it since.

I pushed chicken and lettuce around on my plate. Where was Libby? My thoughts were worse than trying to avoid her questions. I looked over my shoulder to see what was keeping her just as she slid into the booth.

"Sorry," she apologized. Instead of digging into her salad, she bobbed her fork in the air. Her voice was light. "That turned out to be an old college friend of Bob's. We haven't seen him in ages!"

I put down my fork. I was more than ready to hear how much this guy had changed. How old he looked. This might be exactly the opening I needed to explain the argument I'd had with Dan over my new job. The perfect time to get her support for my surgery.

"He hasn't changed a bit," Libby gushed. "He still has that silly little giggle. It makes me laugh to hear a big guy like that giggle. We used to tease him about it all the time." She laughed, remembering. "He's still so cute."

I didn't think he sounded one bit funny or looked one bit cute. I'd caught a glimpse of the guy. How could she not see his completely gray hair? He had a paunch on his stomach that I would have bet money wasn't there in college. I turned and looked over my shoulder. And jowls. The guy definitely had jowls on either side of his jaw line.

"And his eyes are the clearest blue I've ever seen." Libby finally took a bite of her salad. "And the best part is," she swallowed, "he still loves God. I didn't appreciate that about him back then, but it makes him even more appealing."

Appealing? It was a good thing I didn't have a mouthful of anything or I might have spewed it out. Olivia thought this saggy gray-haired guy was appealing? "You've got to be kidding," I blurted. I couldn't help myself.

"What do you mean?" Libby looked back at me as if she really didn't know.

I picked at my salad, trying to find the words to gently explain. "I don't mean to say something bad about your friend, but from what I can see of him...well, he just doesn't seem all that good-looking to me."

"Really?" She sounded genuinely surprised. Her eyes drifted over my shoulder to the spot where the two men were sitting. She stared a moment and then shrugged, turning her attention back to her salad. "I suppose just to look at him, he doesn't appear all that exciting. But if you'd talk to him, you'd see what I mean." She smiled as if she saw something I didn't.

Apparently so. I looked at the pressed-tin ceiling of the swanky café, trying to decide if I should say more. I had to. "Come on. You can't tell me you really find that guy attractive."

Once again Libby looked their way. "Yes, I do," she said. She sounded as if she meant it.

I chuckled. "I know you're trying to be nice." I grew serious. "But I want you to be honest."

She pushed what remained of her salad to the side of the table and pulled her coffee mug into the circle of her hands. She bit at her Raisin Rave lip. Uh-oh, I could read the signs. I pushed my half-eaten salad aside, too. Dry lettuce didn't go well with a sermon. Preemptive measures were in order. "Did Bob notice your new look?" Maybe now she'd forget what she had been about to say.

Slowly Libby closed her shadowed eyes, then opened them. She looked directly at me. "As a matter of fact, he didn't say a word. But then, I guess that's what happens when a person looks through love. You simply don't see what's only surface dressing.

"You know," she went on, "if Bob weren't sitting right over there, I don't think I could even tell you what he was wearing, even though I saw him get dressed this morning. It's not that I don't care. Sometimes I even have trouble remembering his eye color. It used to bother me until I realized it's because I don't see him like everyone else does. I look at him with my heart. It's a feeling more than anything. I sense his spirit, or something, instead of what he looks like. I look at most of my friends that way. You, too." She held out one of her hands as if she wanted me to put my fingers in hers.

I looked down at my own hands. With my thumb I touched the fingernail of my ring finger. The polish was chipped. *Kind of like your life. Your youth is dropping away like flecks of cheap paint.* Why couldn't anyone else see me the way I really was?

I do.

I knew where the thought came from. God was *supposed* to see me differently. That didn't mean humans did. Besides Libby.

"Jan, do you know what I mean?"

I didn't. How couldn't Libby see that Bob had thick brown hair with distinguished gray at the temples? And that it needed cutting? And she had to notice his large brown eyes. They matched hers. I had asked her to be honest with me; I'd offer her the same consideration. "Honestly Libby, I *don't* know what you mean. Take the way you described Bob's friend over there. It's not at all the way I see him. I don't know if it's my eyes or yours."

Libby sighed, ruffling her bangs with a quick breath of expelled air. "Jan, I really wish you'd stop focusing on your looks so much. My looks." She gestured toward the table where Bob was sitting with his college friend. "The way *everyone* looks. You know, even the Bible has something to say about that."

Why didn't it surprise me? I was sure she'd tell me. I sat back and waited.

Libby looked up, thinking. "I'm not the best at quoting Scripture."

I had no doubt she'd do it anyway.

"It's somewhere in the Old Testament, and it says something about not judging a person by their outward appearance because that's how humans judge people. But that God looks at our thoughts and intentions—our heart. I'm not saying I'm anything like God, but I'd have to say that's how I see Bob. My kids. Most of the time, anyway." She smiled, finally. "And you." This time she did reach out and take my cold fingers into her warm hand. Chipped polish and all. She looked into my eyes. "Everyone is beautiful when you take the time to *really* look."

If that's how she saw things, Libby would never understand why I needed this job or my surgery. I slipped my hand out of hers, purposely making a point of looking at my watch. "Oh, my, look at the time. I've got to get back to work." I dug in my purse and pulled out a ten-dollar bill.

Libby waved it away. "Bob said he'd get our lunch." She laughed as she reapplied her new lipstick. "Maybe he noticed my new look after all." She winked.

I gave her a quick hug as we parted by the door of the café. I then hurried through the mall, gazing into the windows of the stores that lined the corridor, eyeing the people walking my way. So many pretty things. So many out-of-shape, out-of-style people. Couldn't they see how unattractive they were? Why didn't they do something about it?

The eyes of love don't lie. Try looking at them, at yourself, with My eyes.

I twirled the echoed thought around in my mind. *The eyes of love don't lie.* Words that had argued with me minutes ago took on new meaning now. That was the way Dan looked at me. With eyes of love. No wonder he didn't see the need for my surgery.

As I took up my place behind the cosmetics counter at Elizabeth's I realized I had a project ahead of me. I was going to have to get Dan to see me the way everyone else did.

Then he'd be behind this surgery of mine.

One hundred percent.

Kenny

I had to admit it was nice having a couple extra hands around the place, even if I wasn't so sure I trusted either one of them. Left or right.

"I'm gonna run to get the mail, Pete. Think you can hold down the fort for a few minutes?" I watched him carefully. If his eyes even flicked to the cash register I planned to change my plans.

"No problem," he said, not even bothering to look at me over his shoulder. He continued to load plastic bottles of Coke, Pepsi, and Mountain Dew into the small cooler. He could fill the shelves three times faster than I could with this thick cast still on my arm. I was getting it off tomorrow. Good riddance.

"Okay, then. I'm going now." I walked out the door of the station, purposely leaving the stack of bills I planned to mail on the counter. It was my lame plan to give me an excuse to check if he would keep working after I left or head out back for one of his many smoke breaks. I walked out to the pumps, pretending to check the fluid in the squeegee bins, a task I did every morning before I even unlocked the front door. Then, in case Pete was watching, I thumped myself on the side of my head, pretending I was dumber than a doorknob, and went back into the station. "Forgot the mail," I said, quickly casing the joint with my shifty eyes. In the minute I'd been out he'd finished loading the cooler and was now unpacking Snickers and Salted Nut Rolls onto the narrow candy shelf. Suddenly I did feel dumber than a doorknob. "I might stop by Vicky's and have a cup of coffee if you think you've got things under control."

He looked up and then back at the candy. "Go for it, man."

That was exactly the kind of talk that made me suspicious. Was he trying to make sure I stayed away longer so he could...? "Maybe I won't," I added. "I'm not sure." There. That would keep him on his toes.

"Whatever floats your boat." Pete tore open a box of Skittles and began stacking them beside the M&M's as if he'd been doing it for years.

I grabbed the stack of envelopes and left, cutting through the alley so I could swing by Vicky's café first. I needed advice with my cup of coffee this morning.

"Long time no see." I slid into an empty chair at a table already surrounded by businessmen. Ten o'clock was coffee time in Brewster, and attendance was required at least now and then if a person wanted to stay in the loop. The last time I'd been here was weeks ago when Mike was still helping at the station. Big cities had their country clubs; Brewster had Vicky's. I nodded at Dan Jordan, the town's only Realtor; Paul Bennett, the bank president; and Jim Magner, owner of our one and only grocery store. If Brewster had heavy hitters, I was sitting with them. "What's up?"

"Not the market." Paul took a sip of his coffee. So did the other two. It was as if I'd never been gone.

I held up one finger, letting Vicky know I would take a cup. "I wouldn't know about that," I said. "I gamble enough just opening the station doors every morning. If I had any extra money, I'd take the kids to Disney World before I'd put it in the stock market."

You would, wouldn't you. Diane didn't even have to be near and I knew what she'd say. I took a sip of my coffee as the other men speculated about their investments. Ha! Investments. The station was my one and only investment, and that was barely making it. Just last night Diane had asked me again what kind of savings plan we had for the kids for college.

"Plan?" I'd answered, grudgingly pushing the mute button on the remote. I really wanted to see this next play. It was third and seven for a Vikings touchdown. I pulled my eyes away from the TV. Diane was always jumping me about all the sports I watched. I'd learned the quickest defense was to answer her question. "The plan is for all that reading Renae does to win her a scholarship. Billy can get a football scholarship, and—"

Diane started laughing. Not a funny kind of laugh. "Billy is six, and you're planning on him getting through college on a football scholarship?" I didn't like the way her voice was getting louder.

I glanced away from the game. "Uh, sure." Man, fourth down and inches. Ah, time-out. I looked back at her.

"What about Paige? I suppose she's supposed to get a football scholarship, too?" Diane's eyes were beginning to glisten. Not a good sign. "And what about this baby? What about him? Her?" She held her stomach in both hands.

Uh-oh. Hormones. "It's a him," I said, then added, "Honey, can we have this conversation sometime when you're not so…so…emotional?" The huddle was breaking up. This was it. The Vikings could win the game with this play.

"*Emotional!*" She grabbed the remote from my hand, turned off the TV as she fumbled with the control, removed the two batteries, and stormed from the room.

"Hey, who won the game last night?" I sipped at my coffee. I knew I'd stopped at Vicky's for a reason.

"Packers," Dan and Jim said in unison, pushing their cups to the edge of the table so Vicky could refill them.

I was kinda glad I'd missed the bitter end, but I'd never admit it to my wife. Well, at least not until we started talking again. I took another swallow and let Vicky top mine off.

Jim leaned back in his chair to talk to someone at the table behind him. Perfect. I quickly grabbed the saltshaker and twisted off the top, letting the buildup of hard crystals fall into Jim's coffee cup. I nodded at Paul and Dave to keep mum. Both of them grinned and sipped quietly. This old trick would work again.

Jim turned back to the table and picked up his cup. I waited, innocently sipping.

"Phhhttt!" Jim spit his coffee back into the cup.

I tried not to laugh, but it didn't work. "Gotcha!"

Jim shot me an annoyed look before flagging Vicky down. She didn't look too pleased about wasting a good cup of coffee. Could I help it if they didn't have a sense of humor?

Life was too short to be so serious, but even I knew sometimes there was work to do. I'd better get to the point and get back to the station. I put down my cup. "I got a question for you guys. You hear anything about the station? About, you know, Pete West working for me?" All I'd need was for business to slack off because I had employed half a criminal. That kid had a rap sheet a mile long. At least according to the local rumor mill.

"Nah," Jim Magner shook his head. He'd already forgotten my joke. "I haven't heard anything, but then I'm usually so busy at the store I don't have time to listen to gossip."

Dan stirred sugar into his brew. "The only thing I've heard is from Jan. She said Olivia Marsden told her that Ellen West was glad you gave the kid a chance." He laid his spoon on a napkin and started grinning. "Oh, and she also said she thought Pete looked a little like I must have back in the seventies. You know, buff. Long hair and all." We laughed out loud. "Hey!" he countered. "Don't laugh. I used to have a full head of hair. Really. I have pictures to prove it."

"Those I'd have to see to believe," Jim Magner joked, although we all knew he and Dan had been friends since high school. A time when they'd both probably had long hair. And been buff. I looked down at my stomach. Come to think of it, I didn't have much to laugh about.

Leave it to Paul to get back to the point. "How's Pete been working out for you?"

I tilted a hand from side to side, then picked up my coffee cup. "You know, he's been an okay worker but, I don't know why, I keep waiting for him to screw up. I mean, I've heard so much bad stuff about him it's hard to believe he's going to stick with the job. Half the time I'm wanting to ask him to do more, but then I figure what's the use in teaching him stuff if he's just gonna be out the door? I guess I was hoping you guys could give me some advice."

"Not me." Jim said flatly. "Been there, done that with my own kids and, believe me, I'm glad they're out on their own. I've got enough problems keeping my baggers and stock boys in line."

"That's why I thought you could help me. You work with kids all the time."

Jim rubbed the back of his neck. "To tell you the truth, I never have much trouble with 'em. I've been lucky. I've always had good kids working for me."

Dan chimed in. "Don't look at me. I never had a kid until I married Jan. And Joey's only in eighth grade. I'll be asking you for advice before long."

I knew better than to look to Paul. His two little girls were barely out of diapers.

"Well, what do you think?" I asked all of them, "Do you think I should trust the kid?"

"Has he given you any reason not to trust him?" Paul asked quietly.

I thought about Pete's first day on the job. How he literally ran outside to the pumps every time the driveway bell sounded. His eagerness to try out the hoist and the tire machine. He also had a little scrap of paper by the cash register where he kept a running tally of the snacks he grabbed from the station shelves, even though I'd said he could have a couple treats a day on the house. "You can take those out of my paycheck, Mr. Pearson," he'd told me.

Mr. Pearson. As though I were a schoolteacher or something. "Call me Kenny," I'd said, as if this young punk might be my friend.

"No," I finally answered Paul, "he hasn't given me a reason to not trust him. But I've heard so much bad talk about him and that crowd he runs with that I'm afraid if I turn my back he'll rip me off. Speaking of which," I pushed back my chair, "I'd better pick up the mail and head over to the station. I just hope it's still there when I get back."

Dan and Jim laughed as Paul also pushed away from the table. "I'd better get back to work, too. I'll walk with you across the street." He tossed a five-dollar bill on the table. "My treat today, guys. Come on, Kenny. Let's get before they order caramel rolls and expect me to pay for them."

"Just a minute, guys." Jim called us back to the table. "Can I count on you two to help get things set up at the old gym for Pumpkin Fest?"

"Pumpkin Fest?" I asked. It couldn't be that time of year. "Already?"

Jim leaned his head toward the large calendar hanging on the café wall. "It's in three weeks. Last Friday in October, like always. Gotta line things up. I'm in charge of setup."

"Sure," Paul offered. "Count me in."

"Yeah, me, too." What could I say? Pumpkin Fest was supposed to be a "thank you" from the local businesses to our customers, but it was another evening I'd have to close the station early in order to help out. If I had those new credit card pumps, it might not be so bad, but with the station locked up tight I wouldn't sell a thing. Unless I left Pete in charge.

Sure. Then instead of selling nothing, he could steal the little you do have.

I nodded halfheartedly at Jim. I'd just have to close early. I was already hearing what Diane would have to say about that. Maybe I could still get out of it. I held up my weak right arm. "I might not be much help."

"One arm is better than none," was Jim's response.

Okay. That plan hadn't worked.

Paul held open the café door to let me walk out in front of him. Then he fell into step beside me. "It's called 'faith,' Kenny," he said thoughtfully, putting one hand on my shoulder as we walked.

"Huh?" Where'd that comment come from? I stopped at the curb and Paul turned to face me.

"What you asked. If you should trust Pete? You said you've heard bad things about him, but he hasn't done anything to make you *not* trust him. That's what faith is. Trusting without evidence." He began walking across the street and I followed. "We could hardly live our lives if we didn't take a chance and trust people. For instance, when my brother-in-law, Dave, tells me I need to upgrade my insurance coverage, I trust his word because that's his expertise and he's never given me reason to doubt him. When my wife, Ruthie, says, 'You need a haircut. Trust me.' I've learned she's right. I can't see that my hair looks all that bad, but when I get it cut, even I can tell it needed it." He stopped now by the side door leading into the bank. He looked down at the sidewalk for a moment and then back at me. "From what I've heard, I think Pete could use a good role model. A family guy like you."

Like me? I was nothing but a grease monkey. And Paul should talk to Diane about how much time I spent with my family. He might change his tune.

"If I remember rightly," Paul continued, "Pete's dad left the family when Pete was just a kid. Who knows what something like that does to a young boy? I think he might need exactly what you can give him, Kenny. A place to keep his hands busy. Work he likes. Some older guys to hang around with during the day to let him know life can be good with responsibilities."

I looked at Paul sideways. "You calling me old?"

He laughed. "Yeah, I am. Older than Pete." Paul put his hand on my forearm, suddenly serious. "He needs a mentor like you, Kenny." He let himself into the side door of the bank, pausing a moment. "No matter what you think people are saying, I think you've done a fine thing in hiring Pete. I'm going to put him and you on my prayer list, if you don't mind."

Mind? Nah, I didn't mind. I could use all the help I could get with that kid. I walked down the sidewalk, kicking a rock as I went. Leave it to Paul to use a word like "mentor." I wasn't even sure what it meant exactly. But I did know what "fine" meant. *You've done a fine thing.* Huh, go figure. A fine thing.

Maybe I could at least give the kid a chance. Maybe after I picked up the mail I'd take an extra minute and make a swing past my house. Give Diane a kiss and see if she'd start talking to me. Show her that I was trying to be what Paul thought I was. A family kind of guy.

I liked the sound of that.

As I headed for the post office, I gave the rock a final kick into the brown weeds near the curb. *You've done a fine thing.*

A tiny muscle tickled inside my chest, somewhere near my heart. Like a balloon that could hardly hold one more breath of air or it would burst from being too full.

Ida

If I weren't so flabbergasted trying to cut pumpkin pie slices faster than people could stick a fork in them, I would try and remember just how many Pumpkin Fests I'd been at. I stood up straight for just a second, letting my ears listen past the hubbub of people talking to hear the good accordion music coming from the front of the old gymnasium. I remembered the Pumpkin Fest when Fred grabbed me in his arms right in front of the lumberyard booth and twirled me around to the "Farmer's Polka" in the middle of the crowd. I'd swatted him when the music stopped, but I also clapped and laughed just like the folks around us were doing. Those were fun times, those were.

"Ida? Do you have that pie ready to go?" Ruthie Bennett put one hand on my shoulder, her other hand ready to grab the pie tin out from under my knife. "I can't believe how many people are still in line. Usually by this time of night the crowd thins out a little. I'm afraid we might run out of pie."

My eyes quickly counted the number of full tins left. Three. Twenty-four slices left in this busy night, and I hadn't even had a taste yet. "Oh, vell," I said as I began cutting again, "it vouldn't be the first times ve ran out. They can chust come to Wicky's tomorrow and get a schlice."

"That's true. It's back at it again in the morning," Ruthie said, laughing. "I'm not so sure I needed to be reminded of that right now." She brushed her hair off her forehead with the back of her hand. "I think I'll sleep well tonight." She picked up the sliced pie. "Are you sure you're okay?"

"Go on." I scooted my fingers at her, telling her to get.

Ruthie stood right there. "If you need a rest you tell us, okay?"

I waved my knife at her. "I vorked harder than this in my life. Cutting pies iss a piece of butter comparedt to the vork I used to do on the farm." I tossed my chin at her. "Now you get out dare witt that pie. No vun iss going to eat it back here."

Ruthie left, leaving me with the remaining pies, a sore wrist, and a throbbing hip. I knew if I said anything she would take away my knife. Arthritis was arthritis whether I was using my joints or not. I'd just as soon be busy.

I finished the next pie and then put my knife down on the counter, flexing my stiff fingers just to make sure they could still make a shape other than curled. With the thick part of my palm I rubbed at my hip. That tumble I'd taken earlier was showing up now, and a day of standing on this hard cement floor hadn't done any good for old "Art," who lived in my hip joint. It seemed he had lots of relatives, and they'd taken up living in just about every nook and cranny of my bones. They were having a family reunion tonight. Ah, well, complaining never made things any better, but staying busy kept my mind off it. I picked up the knife again. *Thank You, Lord, for things to do.*

I pulled the next to the last pie tin toward me. It was hard to believe how fast time could move when a person stayed busy. This morning I had gone to the café to help Vicky and Ruthie pack up the pies to bring to Pumpkin Fest. I had to chuckle to myself at how those two sisters looked after me as though I were related to them.

"Ida," Vicky had scolded when I poked my head in the back door of the café early this morning, "you weren't supposed to come here. You were supposed to meet us at the gym."

I untied the scarf that covered my ears and tucked it into the sleeve of my old wool coat as I hung it on the coatrack by the door. It would do no good to argue with them about what I was supposed to or *not* supposed to do. I didn't get to be past eighty by sitting around avoiding hard work. "It's going to shnow outside," I told the girls, changing the subject.

"Oh, no," Vicky said. "I hope that doesn't keep people away today. What would I do with seventy pumpkin pies?"

"Freeze them," I said. I shook my head as I tied an apron around my waist. Sometimes these young people had no common sense. "Dis iss North Dakota. If a little shnow iss going to keep peoples avay, they've got a long vinter aheadt of dem."

Ruthie looked out the back window. "It doesn't look like snow to me."

"Tell dat to my tricky knee," I told her. "Now vhat shouldt I do?"

By the time we had the pies put in large flat boxes, Dave and Paul, the girls' husbands, had showed up to help carry things to the car.

"Did you see?" Paul Bennett said as he hurried in the back door, brushing at his shoulders. "It's starting to snow."

"You're too smart, Ida." Vicky winked at me. "Or, I guess it's your knee that's so intelligent."

"At least it's goot for somethings." I tried to wink back. Both my eyes blinked. It seemed nothing worked right anymore.

"Here, Ida," Ruthie said. "You carry the cups." She handed me an armful of Styrofoam cups that were light as feathers. Those girls babysitted me as if I were an infant. Oh, well, it was good to know they had respect for us older ones.

I stepped outside the café, noticing that the slippery plastic around the cups wasn't making my easy job as easy as I thought. The thin new snow underfoot was another thing my mind had to account for. I wished I had my galoshes on. I juggled one row of cups back in line with my elbow, sending another row spilling off the other side. Without thinking, I tried to grab it before it fell to the ground and sent the whole stack tumbling. Before I could stop my feet, one foot stepped on the round row of cups, and the next thing I knew I was on the ground.

"Ida!" Four voices like a choir called out my name. "Are you okay? Are you hurt? What happened? Is anything broken?" They each had questions I couldn't answer till I took stock.

"Land sakes," I finally said, "if anytings broke it's the cups I'm sitting on." I could feel a hot flush rising in my cheeks. It was embarrassing sitting in the snow like a helpless old woman.

Before I could ask for help, Dave and Paul lifted me to my feet as if I were a little bird.

Vicky brushed at my backside. "I want you to go home and get in a hot bathtub and soak for a while."

I pushed her hand away and bent to pick up the row of smashed cups. "Den I'd miss the festival."

"It would go on without you, you know." Ruthie took the ruined cups from my hands. "You need to take care of yourself. At least drive home and rest for a little while before—" She looked around. "Where's your car?"

"I valked."

"You walked? It's five blocks from your house to here and another two to the gym. And you already told us you knew it was going to snow. Ida." She put her hands on her hips. "What are we going to do with you?"

I couldn't help it, one side of my mouth went up, then the other. I knew the answer to her question. "Giff me a ridt to Pumpkin Fest." Now it was settled. If I went home all I'd do was sit in my chair and feel my muscles gripping up. Staying on my feet was the best remedy I knew. For my muscles and my mind.

And here it was, almost the end of the day already. I pushed the last of the pumpkin pie to the side just as Ruthie came to get it. She had a plastic fork in one hand, a paper plate in the other. Without saying a word she scooped one slice onto the plate and handed it to me with the fork. "Now you grab a cup of coffee and go *sit down*." She looked at me sternly.

I knew better than to fight her. Besides, I'd done all the work that was left in here until it came time to load the empty pie tins. But then, I already had most of them stacked in their boxes for the ride back to the café.

"Yah, yah," I said to Ruthie. "Vill you and Wicky come sit witt me? You twos haff been vorking hardter than me."

Ruthie laughed. "If I have half your energy when I'm your age, I will be thanking the good Lord."

"Vell, you shouldt be tanking Him already."

Ruthie put her arm around my shoulders and gave me a fast hug. "I already do thank Him, Ida. Every day. Now," she released me with a gentle push, "go *sit*."

My goodness, it did feel good to get off my feet. I blew on the top of my coffee and took a hot sip. I didn't realize how dry my throat was until I swallowed. *Thank You, God, for coffee. And pie. And sitting.*

I took a bite of the spicy pie. Yah, that Vicky could make piecrusts as good as us old timers. Of course, she should. I taught her. A little feeling of pride beat through my chest. It felt good to know some things would stay the same as they used to.

I cut another bite of pie, letting the creamy filling coat my tongue. It wasn't until I started eating that I realized how hungry I was. Quickly I swallowed and sent another bite into my empty stomach. I'd had a hot dog from the Magner's Grocery booth for lunch and I'd been slicing pies ever since. I had a feeling Dr. West wouldn't be too happy if she knew I'd missed taking my pills this afternoon. Well, sometimes getting out of the house all day was better than medicine. Other than my aching joints, I felt like a silver dollar. Not bad for eighty-two. The Lord had been good.

I took another sip of my coffee. Oh my sakes, there was that Jan Jordan prancing around the gymnasium, dressed as though this were a highfalutin party in Carlton. I wondered how she could walk in high heels so big? She looked like a glamour model compared to the rest of the folks crowding the fest. My eyes couldn't help but see how short her skirt was. If she weren't careful, her knees would get arthritis before long, sticking out in the cold weather the way they were.

Oh, my. It was hard not to stare at her. Even the old men were turning their stiff necks as she sashayed by. I wondered if there was a special way she made her long blonde hair bounce up and down in time with her walking. Even in my young days I'd never looked pretty like her. And my hair never bounced a day in its life without the help of a Toni home permanent. But Fred had loved me anyway.

I put a bite of pie into my mouth as Jan's wide eyes landed on my wrinkled ones. And then she quickly looked away. It wasn't hard to tell what she thought of my old wrinkled face. Oh, well, I didn't care what *she* thought…only God. The wrinkles were the places where Jesus had traced His fingers over my worries. I felt sorry that Jan couldn't see that. I'd bumped into her lots of times around town…the grocery store, the post office, even at my nephew Kenny's gas station last week when I'd dropped in to remind him that Daylight Savings time was coming and that my old kitchen clock, high above the sink, would need turning back. Jan hadn't even nodded at me as she whirled in the door to grab a bottle of Diet Coke from the cooler. I tried not to fault her. She hadn't lived in Brewster her whole life like me. People who grew up in bigger towns didn't know about things like saying hello even if you didn't know someone by their front name. I guessed to her I was just one of the many old ladies in town. We probably all looked alike to someone like Mrs. Jordan. Our white hair curled close to our heads and our wrinkles scared away the eyes of someone so young and pretty. I sipped my coffee as she danced on by. Her time would come soon enough, as it did for everyone. *Lord,* I prayed inside, *help her to know the beauty that comes from knowing You.* There, that was all I could do for her.

I forked the last bite of pie into my mouth. Ah, such sweetness. I lifted my coffee to my lips and then looked into the cup. Nothing but a brown ring at the bottom. How could a cup full of coffee disappear so fast? I pushed myself to my feet. Hoo, I should never have sat down; my hip had stiffened up something good. Or bad, I guess. Slowly I limped toward the coffeepot. Ah, there, my hip was loosening up now. I filled my cup from the spigot and then made my way around the makeshift café to help the girls clean up. As usual, I knew the best medicine was to keep busy. If the good Lord was willing, this wouldn't be my last Pumpkin Fest.

"Any pie left?"

I turned to look behind me. Sure enough, my ears were two things that were still working; I had recognized my nephew's voice, all right. Leave it to Kenny to show up when everything was being put away.

"I tink all the pie is in stomachs," I told him. "Unless you're a bird." I brushed pie crust crumbs off the tabletop into my open hand.

"Shoot." Kenny snapped his fingers. "I just closed the station. It's been busy. Are you sure there's no pie left?" He looked over my shoulder into the kitchen.

I knew two slices were hidden under a hand towel in a corner of the countertop, but those were saved for Vicky and her husband to eat later. A latecomer like Kenny wouldn't weasel those pieces out of me. Besides, to look at him, it wouldn't hurt him one bit to miss a meal, or a treat, now and then. If he couldn't get here on time to eat pie, it was maybe for the best. I started folding up the thin, white-plastic covering that had made the tables look nice. "You shouldt haff come earlier. I taut you hadt dat new kidt vorking for you now?"

"Pete? Yeah, he's working for me. But, well…" Kenny paused, shuffling his feet as though he were wiping mud off them. "Let's just say I'm not ready to let him close up quite yet."

Vicky came out from the kitchen and started crumpling up the plastic covering on the table next to where I was working.

"Vhat are you doing?" She would ruin the thin table covering if she yanked at it like that.

Her eyes landed on the neat square I had folded over my arm. "Oh, Ida, we just throw this away. You didn't have to work so hard to fold it up."

"Trow it avay? It's still got good in it." I could think of all kinds of ways that plastic could be put to good use. Cover tomato sprigs in the garden next spring. A floor covering if there was any painting to do. "Vhy, I bet Kenny couldt use it at his garage to keep a clean shpot on the floor vhen his new baby comes to wisit him at vork." That was a good idea if I had to say so myself. I handed my neatly folded plastic to Kenny. "There you go. No pie, but maybe something you neet better." I tried to keep my eyes away from his big stomach. "Ant it's free."

"Gee, thanks." Kenny tucked the plastic under his arm.

"Giff yours to Kenny, too." I motioned with my chin to Vicky. Kenny smiled goofy-like when Vicky handed him her quickly folded square. So what if they thought I was a penny-pinching old woman. If someone didn't teach these kids that everything wasn't made to use once and throw away…well, what would this world come to?

Vicky scooted back into the kitchen as Kenny turned to walk away. I wasn't about to let him get away so fast. "Do you remember about my clock?" Daylight Savings time had been here one week already. It was getting confusing to walk from my bedroom into my kitchen and think I had missed a whole hour while I'd poked down the short hallway. "You saidt you'd come climb up and turn it back for me."

He closed his eyes and breathed in deep. "Yes, Aunt Ida," he said opening his eyes, "I remember. I've been really busy. I don't like to leave Pete alone at the station much, and even though I got my cast off, my arm is still stiff, so everything takes longer to do."

I was tired of his feeble excuses. "Vell, changing that clock vouldn't take but one minute."

He closed his eyes for a long second again. "I'll tell you what. I'm going to take Billy and Paige trick-or-treating tomorrow night. When we get to your house, I'll come in and change it. Okay?"

I didn't like the way he put everything off till tomorrow. My way was to do something the first time it came into my brain and then I could quit thinking about it. But after a week of having my kitchen in a different time zone altogether, one more day wouldn't matter. Besides, beggars couldn't be choosers. "Dat vill vork out goot," was all I said as a little stab of anger at his too-busyness jumped around in my heart. I would have some hard praying to do tonight to get my heart soft again.

～

"Goot night." I said as I opened the rear passenger door of the car and stuck one foot into the air.

"Here, let me help you." Paul, Ruthie's husband, had somehow jumped out of the driver's seat and lickity-split run around the back end of the car. He held out his hand. Any other night I would have swatted it away; I liked doing things myself. But it had been a long day on my sore feet, and a little boost would be nice.

I handed him my lumpy purse first. He tossed it on his shoulder as if he carried a purse to work every day, then took my gloved hand in his. "Here we go." He tugged at my arm. My tired behind lifted from the seat and then fell back as if it wanted to stay right there and go to sleep.

"Chust a minute," I said, scooting myself closer to the edge of the seat and the outside. A sharp edge of frustration nicked at my chest. I didn't especially like to be reminded that I didn't have the strength to step out of the car without making a production of it. "Okay, let's giff it another try."

In a blink I was standing on the curb, Paul's arm holding mine. "Let me walk you up the steps," he said. "That snow we got this morning stuck around all day. Your steps could be slippery. I'll sweep them off for you."

Taking my purse out of his hand, I pushed his arm away. "I've valked up those shteps for more than fifty years by myself. You get that vife of yours home. She looks like she's ashleep sitting up."

Paul peered into the car. "I think she *is* sleeping."

"Yah," I said, "vhere ve all shouldt be. I'm going to get my beauty shleep. You better, too."

"Ida," he chuckled back at me. "There aren't enough hours of sleep in a day to make me beautiful."

I knew he was joking, but I answered anyway. "Everyone is beautiful in God's eyes. Even wrinkled oldt vomen like me."

He pulled me close under his arm, squeezing tight. "Especially women like you."

The warmth of his hug stayed with me as I shuffled my way up the walk. I could hear the soft rumble of Paul's car as he waited at the curb to make sure I got inside okay. It made me mad to think he had to watch me as though I were a stumbled-footed mule. I put my foot on the first step and then turned to wave him off. Even though I had never had children of my own, I knew both he and Ruthie would be up early with their two little girls. Two children a year apart didn't give parents any extra shut-eye time. I imagined their Grandma Bennett, who had watched the kids all evening, would be gratefully sleeping in tomorrow morning.

Carefully, I climbed up the four steps to my small porch, grabbed the broom I kept tilted in the corner, and began to sweep. With a light beep of his horn, Paul drove off. The snow flew like dandelion fluff as I swished at it, my thoughts whirling along with the snow.

Some days this getting-old business was fine and dandy, one step closer to my permanent home in God's perfect world. But when people treated me like cut glass and acted as though I were ready to be put out to pasture with the glue horses, it made me so mad. Just thinking about it made me angry at no one in particular and the world in general. I attacked the last step with a gusto I hadn't felt when I walked out of the Pumpkin Fest hall minutes ago. Surprising how a little heat under the collar could make a person feel invigorated.

I set the broom into the corner, stomped snow off my shoes, and went into my house. As I often did, I said a small prayer for a furnace that worked at the click of a dial. I remembered the messy coal stove of my youth and the way we had to scrub a greasy film from the walls come spring. Good riddance to that. I'd left the dial at sixty-two for the day. There was no sense heating the house when I'd be at Pumpkin Fest. And now I'd be climbing under my warm covers soon enough, so there was no sense to heat the air I wasn't going to be sitting in. I turned the furnace dial down a couple more notches before hanging my coat in the closet. Then I walked into the kitchen. A small glass of warm milk would put me right to sleep.

I turned on the stove, poured milk into a glass straight to the top, and then poured it into the small pan I always kept on the burner. None of that microwave business for my kitchen. Sometimes old-fashioned ways were better. Young people nowadays had no idea how good they had it. I recalled the feeble excuses Kenny gave for not changing my clock. Always complaining how busy he was in the same breath he talked about how he wanted more business. Busy. Busy. That's all people were these days. I wondered what Kenny would think busy was if he had to *milk* the cow to get the milk his kids drank every day? I'd be willing to bet that young man didn't even know what a separator was, much less how much time it took to wash one. And let him just try to find time in his busy day to churn the cream into butter for Billy's toast. Or make the bread to begin with! I turned off the burner as small bubbles formed along the side of the pan. Why, that Kenny could use a good kick from a mule some days to knock some sense into him. He didn't know what busy was.

I poured the milk into my glass and wrapped a napkin around the sides to keep the heat from burning my fingers. I blew over the top of the steaming milk, pulling the foamy bubbles along the rim into my mouth. Ah. Good. As soon as I finished this milk my head would be on my pillow. What time was it, anyway? It had to be long past my usual bedtime of nine-thirty. I tilted my head and looked up at the clock. Midnight?! Stars and garters, you'd think it was New Year's Eve and I was twenty again. I'd let this milk cool a little while I washed up and put on my nightgown.

I hurried toward my bedroom, unbuttoning my smock as I scurried down the hall. Sitting on the bed, I bent over and untied my thick-soled beige shoes, pulling each shoe off each swollen foot as if it were being yanked out of spring mud. I tugged off my stockings and pushed my feet into my fluffy scuffs. *Thank You Lord, for terry cloth slippers.* I wiggled my happy toes. If I didn't get to bed quickly, tomorrow would be nothing but fog. It seemed no matter what time my head hit the pillow, my eyes flew open at four o'clock, then five, five-thirty. After that I might as well get up for all the shut-eye I'd find tossing and turning.

I quickly calculated. Four hours of sleep. Oh, dear. And tomorrow morning I had to get to Magner's to buy Halloween candy for the popcorn balls I'd forgotten to make. Acht, getting old was having Swiss cheese for a brain. I'd need a nap, for sure, if my doorbell would be ringing half the night. I yawned as if tomorrow were already here. I slipped my nightgown over my head, then slid my Timex off my wrist and laid it on my bedside table. What? My eyes stopped on the hands of the clock by my bed. It wasn't midnight! It was a little after eleven. Still late, but not Cinderella-kind of late.

A small burn began inside my chest as I scuffed out to the kitchen. That Kenny. Always too busy. Too busy to take one minute to turn my kitchen clock back to the right time. Too busy to lend a quick hand to his old aunt. It was Diane and Vicky and Ruthie who kept giving me cautions about my old age. Saying I had to be careful. To wait and let someone else do a job for me. Well, I had done things for myself my whole life. I could do this, too.

I pulled a kitchen chair over to the edge of the counter, directly under the clock. There it hung, ticking away, as if it didn't have any idea it was telling the wrong time. I'd change that in short order. Lifting my nightgown out of the way, I put one slippered foot on the yellow vinyl seat. Holding tight onto the backside of the chair, I lifted my other foot up. The hip that had been hollering at me all day screamed now. I gave it a little rub with the heel of my hand. *There, there.* Sometimes a body needed tending like a baby. The spasm settled soon enough. I reached up to the clock. Oh! I could lay a measuring cup on its side and my short fingers were just that far away. I debated about pulling my tall kitchen stool over instead, but its wobbly legs were another thing Kenny never got around to fixing. If I could just scootch myself up an inch more…

I stretched, wishing God had given me piano-playing fingers instead of stubby lead pencils. No, I still couldn't reach. I stood on the chair, in my flannel nightgown and slippers, surveying the situation. God had given me knees for a reason.

I folded the hand towel lying at the edge of the sink and draped it over the counter, thinking carefully about the trick I needed to perform. I lifted my left knee and rested it carefully on the cloth, then I grabbed an upper cabinet knob with my left hand and put my right hand on the edge of the counter. With a deep breath and a quick prayer, *Help, Lord!* I launched myself up.

Up. *Up.* In my imagination I moved much faster than this. Higher than this. Dear, oh dear! I felt myself falling backward. My slippery grip on the cabinet knob was a thing of the past. The towel slid out from under my left knee, while my right leg caught on the edge of the chair as I fell past it. My careful planning had forgotten to take into account my flannel nightgown. The way it would pull tight under my knee as I hoisted myself up. The way it would stretch just a tiny bit and then pull me back down. Down. Down. How could it take so long to get to where I knew I was headed?

The floor. Ouch! There it was. Hard. So hard.

Like your head!

As I thudded into a heap I heard, or felt something crack inside me. My pride? My leg? My hip? *Oh, dear Lord. No. Please, no.*

As fast as I'd fallen, I remembered the several friends I'd known who had broken their hips. The injury had quickly taken the life of one friend. Sent another to the Brewster Nursing Home in a wheelchair for good. And another to live with her daughter in another state. *No, dear Lord. No!* My heart banged in my chest as I closed my eyes.

Quit laying here you stubborn old woman. Get up!

The anger that had fueled my harebrain idea had vanished.

Pride goes before destruction and haughtiness before a fall. The proverb mocked me. Me and my stubborn pride. I knew that Bible verse by heart and yet look where it had gotten me. In a heap on the floor. I should have listened. *Forgive me, Lord God.*

Get up!

Weakly, I pushed at the beige linoleum where I lay. My arms were as useful as cooked spaghetti noodles. I fell back against the floor. A dull ache thrummed through my pelvis. A different kind of tiredness than the one I'd felt earlier crept over me.

You can't just lay here. You have to try to get up. Get help.

Once again I pressed against the clean vinyl I used to call my floor. My arms held no strength. My legs were useless. Maybe tonight my floor would become my deathbed.

You can't give up, woman.

How long would it take? Who would find me?

I lay on my side, staring at the phone that hung on the wall, much too far away to even try and reach. My eyes fluttered shut. I tried to open them. Eyelids heavy as horseshoes. Might as well leave them closed. Think. What could I do?

Pray.

Ah, so this was it. All I had left. Just me and my God.

Pray.

My heavy heart clung to the Word. *The Lord is my shepherd; I shall not want...*

Only me.

Only my God.

Forever and ever...

Kenny

Another day, another fifty cents. It was quiet on Main Street this morning as I cruised the few blocks between my house and the station in my old pickup. But then it usually was quiet this early in the morning—especially a Saturday morning. Good thing, too. I'd overslept and run out of the house without breakfast. It might have to be Cheetoes today.

I opened the front door of the station, switching on lights as I made my daily walk through the garage. The oily smell was as familiar to me as the coffee I'd get brewing in a second. I reached my arm around the cement doorframe at the rear of the garage, flipping the switch that would turn on the gas pumps outside. Suckers! My right wrist was throbbing like a basketball during a fast break down the court. Yesterday's first snowfall had turned my broken joint into a weather-predicting device. I massaged my forearm with my left hand as I made my way back into the station. Helping tear down the booths after Pumpkin Fest must have put a strain on my still-tender muscles. It had been after one o'clock before I crawled into bed beside Diane last night.

"It's late," she'd murmured, half asleep as I curled myself around her in a backward hug. I curved my hand around her abdomen, holding her gently protruding tummy tight. After three pregnancies and two miscarriages, it hadn't taken long for the little guy she was carrying to show us he was in there. At least I liked to imagine it was a little guy in there. It would do Billy good to have a brother to play with instead of sisters who had him playing things like house, dolls, and dress-up. I could already see the three of us,

Billy, me, and Kenny Jr., piling into my pickup to go hunting or fishing or to a ball game of any sort. I'd teach both of them, side-by-side, how to fillet a fish, breast out a pheasant, or slide into a base when they were caught in a squeeze play. All the things Renae said were, "Ooo-kie." A girl-word if I ever heard one.

The driveway bell outside the station yanked my mind out of my daydream. I glanced at the empty coffeepot as I hurried outside. I hoped whoever was out there wasn't planning on a hot cup quite yet. Man, a guy couldn't even oversleep ten minutes without someone in Brewster knowing about it.

I nodded to the stranger sitting huddled behind the wheel of the rusted Malibu by the pump. Obviously he hadn't been up too long, either; there was still a thick coat of frost on his windshield. Either that or, from the looks of him, he was just heading home from a long night somewhere other than home. It certainly didn't look as though he'd shaved or combed his straggly hair. Maybe he was getting a head start on his Halloween costume for tonight. He gave a thumbs-up without looking at me. Fill 'er up.

Okay. I stuck the hose into the tank, hoping this fill would be from the bottom up and not just a top-off. Now that I had Pete working for me, every extra dollar helped pay his salary...and then mine. He'd be coming in later so I could take a lunch break for a change...and maybe a nap. It would be the longest time I'd left him alone at the station since he'd started working six weeks ago. I figured he couldn't do too much damage alone for an hour. The kid knew his stuff about cars, that was for sure, but I wasn't so sure I trusted him with the cash. Or the cigarettes. The guy had a two-pack-a-day habit that must be hard to keep up since I didn't let him smoke in the shop.

I shoved my hands into my pockets, trying to keep them warm. It didn't pay to clean a frosty windshield, and the strange guy wasn't rolling down his window to make conversation. Fine by me. My mind started thinking about the day ahead.

Make coffee. That was the first thing I had to do. It was a Saturday, which meant Marv would be stopping in this morning without his school bus.

The gas hose clicked itself off, and I quickly rounded the fill to the nearest quarter dollar. Yup, before long I'd be teaching my two boys how to run the station, and then I wouldn't have to worry about hiring an extra pair of hands.

With a knuckle I knocked on the side window of the Chevy. "Twelve-fifty," I called through the frost.

The car door flew open, causing me to jump out of the way. "Gotta go," the guy said, sliding out of the car.

Fine time to decide to use the bathroom. I followed him back into the shop and handed him the key. "They're outside," I explained when he didn't head straight for the door.

"Huh?" he said. His eyes darted everywhere but at me.

"The bathrooms," I said loudly, as if he were deaf. "They're outside. Around the corner." I motioned with my chin.

He shuffled outside. I should know on Halloween I'd get a crazy person right off the bat. Figured. The guy had to be on something. The sooner he left, the better. He was starting to give me the creeps. If I were lucky, Eddie, Brewster's cop, would swing by on his morning route. I looked at the oil company clock hanging on the wall. No, even Eddie wouldn't be out this early. Might as well load the coffee grounds while I waited for Weirdo to get out of the bathroom and pay for his gas. I flipped open the coffee filter basket. What the heck? For a second I thought I'd left the used grounds in the filter from yesterday, but no, these were dry. I didn't remember filling the basket, but it wouldn't be the first time I'd forgotten. I must have really been in a hurry to get to Pumpkin Fest last night. I chuckled to myself as I lifted the pot. It was strangely heavy. Go figure, I'd even filled it with water last night. Huh. I didn't know whether to be worried or proud of myself. I poured the water into the reservoir and pushed the start button. I'd be ready for Marv in less than two minutes.

I turned as the door to the station opened. The weird guy walked in, bathroom key hanging from his hand. "Is Pete working?" he asked, his voice nervous, eyes darting.

Oh, so that was it. The guy was looking for a fix from Pete. Great, just great. Selling gas was one thing, drugs another. I stared into his shifting eyes. "No," I said, "he's not." I wasn't about to tell him Pete would be here in a few hours. And gone. If Pete was dealing from the station, today would be his last day. "It's twelve-fifty," I reminded. Pay up and get out.

The guy dug in his pocket and pulled out what looked like a jack-knife. The kind Ben and I used to play with in the backyard when Mom wasn't watching. Small but sharp. He pulled it open and held it near his hip. "Why don't you pay me?" he sneered.

A cold shot of fear zinged through my arms, settling in my stomach. Diane! The kids! My new baby!

Adrenaline surged. This kid wasn't going to knife me. He wasn't going to take money I'd worked darn hard to earn. I wouldn't let him. My mind raced. If I wasn't so heavy I might be able to leap the counter and tackle the scrawny guy. He looked to be in enough of a fog that I could take him by surprise. But my stomach was big, my courage was small, and my right arm, the one I'd slug him with, was too weak. Ducking down and hiding wasn't an option. All the kid would have to do was walk around the counter and slice me.

"Quit stalling," he said, jabbing the knife my way. "Open the cash register."

Stay calm. From a place I didn't know, the words quieted me. "Listen, kid, you don't want to do this." I patted the air with my hand. "You can have your gas. Just get in your car and we'll call it good."

"What would be good is if you'd open that cash drawer." One eye narrowed. "Come on." He shifted from foot to foot as if getting ready to run...or attack.

I looked down at the register keys, my mind blank. *Open it.* Which key opened the drawer? It was as though I'd never seen a cash register before.

"Now!"

Oh, man. I closed my eyes and poked. The drawer flew open.

"That's more like it." The kid transferred his knife into his left hand and reached around the register into the drawer. "What the—"

I looked down. Of course, the drawer was empty. I hadn't taken the money out of the safe yet this morning. A quick flash of relief was followed by a greater one of fear as the guy pushed the knife close to my stomach. "Where is it?"

"It's, ah—" I had to stop and clear my throat. "It's in the safe." So much for not giving him the cash. All I cared about now was my skin. "In back."

The kid looked over his shoulder out the window, casing the quiet outside. He had time. "Let's get it." He nudged my jacket with the knife point.

I took a step forward as the coffeepot hissed. Without stopping to think, I grabbed the pot and threw ten cups of Folgers Classic Roast at the guy's face. He screamed, dropped the knife, and took off running, slipping on his way to the door. Swear words filled the air and then he was gone. Other than a floor full of coffee, it looked like just another ordinary day.

I grabbed the mop that always rested around the corner in the garage and began to clean up the brew. It was then that my hands began to shake. Jell-O. That's what they were. Pure Jell-O. Whoo-boy. I wiped up the last of the coffee and took a deep breath. Calling 911 might be a good next step. I picked up the phone and looked at the clock. Ten minutes? Only ten minutes had passed since the guy had pulled his knife? It felt like half a lifetime. I put my finger on the nine as the driveway bell signaled a customer. As if I'd already made the call, Eddie pulled his cruiser up to the pump. His cop car had never looked so welcome.

I hurried outside to meet him, wondering where to begin my story. Holdups weren't everyday stuff in a small town like Brewster. As he always did, Eddie slowly climbed out of the car, ready to saunter inside and have a cup of joe while I filled his tank.

I stopped in my tracks. "He went thataway!" I pointed east, as if Eddie would know exactly what I was hyperventilating about.

Eddie laughed. "Yeah, and Ossama's in the back room. Fill 'er up, Kenny."

Suddenly I realized that he thought I was making one of the many wisecracks I'd pulled on him over the years. "No, really." I hiked up my pants. "A guy just tried to hold me up."

Eddie must have read the look on my face and decided this time I might be serious. "Is that so?" he asked.

"Yeah. He pulled a knife and I…" I realized how stupid this was going to sound. I pulled off my cap and raced my fingers through my hair. "I threw coffee at him."

"Uh-*huh*." Eddie nodded as if now he'd heard 'em all. "And you expect me to believe that. Good try, Kenny. It's Halloween, not April Fool's Day." He started for the office.

Okay. Good. He could see for himself what had happened. I followed him inside. The mop and bucket stood in the middle of the floor. "See." I pointed to the damp floor as if he couldn't see the evidence for himself. Well, maybe he couldn't since I'd wiped it up. I started explaining. "The guy pulled up and told me to fill his car, so I did. Then he said he had to use the bathroom, so I gave him the key and started making coffee." I stopped for a breath. "When he came back he pulled a knife and told me to open the cash drawer—" I stopped and pointed to the open drawer.

Eddie walked over and peered in at the empty slots. "He got it all?"

"Well, no, actually he didn't get anything." I pushed the mop and bucket toward the wall. "You see I overslept this morning, only ten minutes, but I was hurrying to get the pumps turned on and coffee going, so I forgot to take the money out of the safe and put it in the drawer."

"Did you check the safe? The money's all there?"

Was the guy dense? "I told you, Eddie, the money wasn't in…" The words trailed away as a dim memory from last night took their place.

"I'm gonna head over to Pumpkin Fest," I'd told Pete. I had nothing but a piece of Vicky's pumpkin pie on my mind. It was getting late, and she'd been known to run out. The station was only scheduled to be open for ten more minutes. I would bundle up the cash, put it in the safe, and head out. "If anyone comes after I leave," I'd told Pete, "just leave the money in the cash drawer. That little bit won't hurt if it sits in the drawer overnight." I'd reached for the register just as my brother, Ben, pulled up outside. "I'll get him," I told Pete. Ben kept a running tab that he always paid in full at the end of the month. "I'll leave as soon as I fill him."

And, it suddenly occurred to me, I had left.

Leaving the money in the drawer.

All of it.

"Man!" I laid my head on top of the register. "I am so stupid." I stood up. "I never put the money in the safe." I gestured at the empty drawer. "It was all in here." I could feel my heart somewhere around my knees. It was too bad Weirdo hadn't killed me. Now Diane would have to do it.

"So," Eddie said, "the guy *did* get the money?"

I shook my head. No wonder he couldn't follow my story. Even I was still piecing it together. "No, he didn't take anything."

"Well, then, where's the money?"

I shrugged my shoulders, hating to say out loud that the guy I'd hired had stolen me blind. That I'd practically handed him the cash and said, "*Here.*" I'd fess up soon enough. In the meantime, as I kicked at the floor in frustration over my stupidity, the edge of my shoe sent something shooting across the floor towards Eddie.

He nudged it with his boot. "This the weapon?" He pulled a winter glove from his pocket and bent to pick up the knife. He held it high. It looked a lot smaller now.

"Yeah," I said, feeling like a wimp as I looked at the two-inch blade. The fear I'd felt earlier felt more like embarrassment now. This whole thing might have been a setup. Throw suspicion off Pete somehow. I wished I'd stayed awake through more *Columbo* reruns. Maybe then this would all make more sense.

"Tell you what," Eddie said, taking charge, "why don't you go check the safe? Sometimes a guy forgets things he does every darn day."

He followed me out into the garage to the small safe I'd cemented into the corner near the furnace. It wasn't hard to see it was empty. The door stood partially open, the way I always left it when I took the cash out in the morning. Make that yesterday morning.

"It's gone." I said it. It was official. Stupid! Me and my big stomach. I was never going to eat another piece of pumpkin pie again.

"Let's go inside," Eddie directed. "We'll start from the top."

Head down, I followed him back into the station.

"Hey, there you are." Pete West was standing with his hands in the till.

Had he come back for more? He didn't even flinch when Eddie and I walked in on him. I had to hand it to Pete; he was one cool customer. Or as dumb as a stump. Did he think the little trick his friend had played on me would cover his tracks? All my suspicions of the past weeks had finally been confirmed. So much for the *fine thing* Paul had thought I'd done. I'd hired a thief. The next job he'd have would be making license plates at the state pen. "What are you doing here?" I asked. My voice was pure gravel.

"You said to come in before lunch. I know it's way early, but I wanted to work on the Weber transmission before it gets busy over noon and you're not here."

The fake diamond in his left earlobe glinted. Or maybe it was real. Bought with stolen money. I glared at him.

"You're still planning on taking a couple hours off this afternoon, right?" He hadn't moved his hands from the empty slots in the cash drawer.

He stared at me. I stared back.

"What?" he said then, sounding defensive.

"What?" I replied, my voice rising. "You have the nerve to walk in here and say '*What?*' as though nothing happened. Do you think I'm a fence post? Eddie, guard the door." I tilted my head toward my backup. He didn't move a muscle. My tax dollars at work. I was going to have to do this by myself. "My money is missing, that's *what.*"

I was ready for him to run. I'd wimped out once today, but it wasn't going to happen again. If I had to tackle Pete, I would. I only hoped if I missed, Eddie was ready to get run down.

"It's not here?" Pete sounded genuinely surprised.

He didn't flinch. Not even an eyelid.

"No, it's not here." Suddenly, I was fed up with his act. "Where is it, Pete? Where'd you put the money?"

"It's supposed to be right here." As if he were a magician, he pulled the plastic liner from the drawer. The bills—ones, fives, tens and twenties—were lined up underneath like a well-played Monopoly game. "You left last night without putting the money in the safe. I didn't think you'd want to leave it set out, so I put it under here." He pointed at the cash and checks. "I thought for sure you'd find it."

Relief flooded me like a warm shower. Shame, too. The words Paul Bennett said a few weeks ago haunted me now. *You said you've heard bad things about him, but he hasn't done anything to make you not trust him. That's what faith is. Trusting without evidence.*

I'd accused Pete on no evidence, only rumors. Maybe now it was time to trust him on his actions.

And on faith.

Yeah, and on faith.

I reached my right hand out to him. When he took it I pulled him toward me, giving him a quick, grateful hug, thumping his back as if he needed burping. "Sorry. And thanks," I mumbled, stepping back. "It's been quite a morning. I think I need some coffee. Strong coffee."

"Hey," Pete said, "did you see I got that ready to go last night?" Almost as an afterthought he shrugged one shoulder as if he didn't really care whether I'd noticed or not.

"You did that?" So I hadn't done it and simply forgotten. I couldn't help but laugh out loud. I'd blamed Pete for everything, and his advance planning might have saved my life. Go figure.

"So," Eddie said when the second pot of the morning was brewing, "I'm going to need a description of the guy who tried to hold you up."

The whole force of the incident suddenly hit me. What *could* have happened. Even though the jackknife looked miniature when Eddie held it up, I knew it was long enough, sharp enough, to slice through the thick vein that always throbbed along the side of my neck when I was upset. I could be lying in the back room right now, Diane a widow, my kids without a dad. I shoved my hands into my pockets so Eddie and Pete wouldn't see them shaking.

"Can you remember the make of the car?" Eddie asked. "What about the guy? What did he look like?"

I closed my eyes, racking my brain. "Wet," was all I could think to answer. Finally I remembered more. "He asked for Pete."

"You said the guy knew my name?" All of a sudden Pete was turning into Eddie's sidekick. "I must know him. Or…" His words trailed off. He eyed Eddie, me, and looked away. "Or someone told him to ask for me," he said to the floor. Quickly, he held up a hand. "I'm clean. I swear. I'm not doing that stuff anymore. Not since I started working here. I like this job. Working with engines and stuff."

Once again Paul's words echoed in my head. *I think he might need exactly what you can give him, Kenny. A place to keep his hands busy. Work that he likes. Some older guys to hang around with during the day to let him know life can be good with responsibilities.*

I had looked up that word Paul had used about me and Pete. *Mentor.* I'd paged through the thick dictionary Renae had at the top of her birthday list the year she turned ten. A dictionary of all things! What kid ever *wanted* a dictionary for a present? Hardly seemed that girl of mine could come from my genes, or chromosomes, or whatever decided those sorts of traits. Either way, I was glad she kept the dictionary by the television.

The word was spelled just like it sounded, thank goodness.

Men-tor (men'ter) Mentor, friend of Odysseus 1. a wise advisor 2. a teacher or coach.

I didn't have a clue who Odysseus was, but with a name like that he had to be someone significant. To be in the dictionary and all. So whatever a mentor was, it had to be important. I did know what a wise advisor was…even though I'd never had one.

I can be that person for you.

Weird. I was starting to recognize that still, small voice. I tucked the sentence away to think about later. Man, this day was turning out to be…well, something.

It was hard to believe that I would ever be considered something like a wise advisor, but I supposed I could be sort of a teacher to Pete. Show him how to do stuff around the shop. And I kind of liked the idea of being a coach. If I ever had the chance to do things over, my dream would be to be a coach. I knew I could be good at that. If I couldn't do it on a field or a court, maybe I could do it around the station.

A sudden lump formed in my throat. I pushed the words past it. "You've been doing a good job around here, Pete. A fine job."

There. Again. Paul's words echoed. *I'm going to put him and you on my prayer list.*

If the way this day was turning out were the results of Paul's prayers, I might have to take up the hobby, too.

Wouldn't hurt.

I sucked in a smile. Who knew that God had a sense of humor?

"I think we're going to make a good team," I said aloud to Pete. I wasn't sure, but just maybe, I was saying those words to Someone else, too.

⌒

"Trick-or-treat!" Billy shouted the words at the top of his lungs and held out his half-filled sack, accepting what had to be his hundredth Snickers bar from Donny Klein's wife. My softball buddy pulled himself off the couch and came to the door.

"Nice costume," he said.

"Thanks!" Billy beamed, puffing out his parka-padded chest. "I'm Kung Fu Fighter." He chopped a hand through the air.

"I meant your dad." Donny winked.

"Hilarious." I couldn't help but smile in my parka and Ducks Unlimited cap. A cap I'd paid good money for at a fundraising auction last year. "Just for that you'd better give me a Snickers. Make that two." I held out my hand while Donny put two miniature bars in my hand.

His wife handed Donny the basket of treats. "If you guys are going to visit, either come in or out. It's too cold to stand here with the door open."

Donny stepped outside, partially closing the door behind him. He watched as I tore open one of the candy bars. "So, you gonna play softball next summer?"

I chomped and swallowed. "Why not?"

His eyes grazed my wrist.

"Oh, that." I twisted my wrist back and forth, around in a circle so he could see for himself. "Sure. No problem."

"The guys said you busted it something good."

"Hey," I nudged his arm with the back of my hand. "I'm tough."

"Da-ad." Billy pushed a shoulder into my hip.

"Gotta get," I said, secretly rubbing my wrist under the cover of my jacket sleeve. After my show-off maneuver for Donny, my joint was pulsing as if it had a life all its own. But then I'd only had my cast off a few weeks. Not to worry. I'd be full strength by spring.

Billy hopped into the pickup. "Where to next? We have to go to my teacher's house. And don't forget my Sunday school teacher. And Mom said we should be sure and go to..." Billy babbled on as I started the pickup. I could swear we'd been to all those places already. A few random flakes of snow fell as I pulled out into the street. How much candy did a kid need?

We'd started our annual rounds at the Brewster Nursing Home, where all the kids had been instructed to "Talk *loud*. Many of the older residents don't hear well." Billy hadn't forgotten, even though we'd left there a half hour ago. He'd been screaming his greeting at every door we'd knocked on.

I'd taken Paige along on the first swing of the evening. The old folks seemed to enjoy little costumed kittens like Paige. They shook her chubby little hand and squeezed her eye-liner-whiskered cheek hard enough to widen her eyes but not make her cry. Then they'd tug at the stuffed nylon that was supposed to be her tail. She was a trooper, all right. Even if all she could say was, "Twick," her candy sack filled up as fast as her brother's.

Diane asked me to drop Paige back at home before hitting the streets of Brewster with Billy. "It's too cold for her to be outside so long." As an eighth grader, Renae was happy to stay home and read in between answering the doorbell while Diane scrubbed whiskers off of Paige.

So it was just the Pearson men the rest of the night. Uh, boys. Well, one of each. By next year this time there would be one more Pearson boy in the family. I was beginning to like the sound of that.

Tonight Billy was dressed as some sort of miniature kung-fu kid. He had a thin, white coat that look suspiciously like an old bathrobe of Diane's wrapped over a thick parka. A torn strip of a cotton dishtowel Aunt Ida had given Diane when we got married was tied around Billy's forehead. He looked more like a chubby, deranged hospital patient with a tourniquet around his head. Halloween in snowy North Dakota left a lot to the imagination.

I hadn't forgotten that I'd promised Aunt Ida I would stop by tonight and change her clock for her. Finally get her off my back about it. I was surprised she hadn't called to remind me. Best to leave her for last. She'd more than likely have a list of other odd jobs that would take up a good portion of Billy's trick-or-treating time if I stopped there now. How one woman could accumulate so many requests from week to week boggled my mind.

I swung my pickup down Seventh Street and pulled to the curb. "Okay, Billy, you run to the Jordans' and the Millers', then we'll swing by the station and see how Pete's doing."

"Again?" My kung-fu kid rolled his eyes as if we'd spent the entire evening stopping at the station.

"I gotta check on him," I explained. "He's never run the place all night by himself." At about every other street tonight I had taken a swing by the station to make sure Pete was doing okay on his own. So far, it didn't look as though he needed me much. "Well, then," I said, changing my plan, "after this block we'll go to the Johnsons', then swing by Vetters' and Pastor Ammon's. After that we'll head over to the Marsdens'. They live right across the street from Aunt Ida. You can trick-or-treat at their house and then meet me at Aunt Ida's. I have to go in and do a couple things for her." I only hoped it was a *couple* things.

"I hope she has popcorn balls," Billy said, sagging against the door of the pickup. His eyes closed. Fluttered open. "They're good," he said, already half asleep.

I looked at his bulging sack of candy. Cavities in a bag. I reached out and ruffled his spiked hair. "You're right, kiddo. Aunt Ida's popcorn balls are good. How 'bout we go straight to her house?" Billy didn't even bother to open his eyes, but he did manage a smile with his nod.

I pushed down my blinker and drove the few blocks to Aunt Ida's house. Funny, her porch light wasn't on. Her house was dark except for a dim light in the kitchen. That was strange. Aunt Ida looked forward to Halloween. She was known for her homemade popcorn balls and loved handing them out to, as she called them, "da little gopplins," as much as the goblins enjoyed eating them. She always gave us extra. It couldn't be so late that she'd given up on us, could it?

I held my wrist up to catch a glimpse of my watch from the dashboard lights. It was nearing eight-thirty. Nine o'clock was the unwritten time limit for trick-or-treating in Brewster. I felt a twinge of guilt as I remembered the long day Ida had put in at Pumpkin Fest yesterday. Maybe she was exhausted. Asleep in her chair. Well, if that were the case, it would be just as well I woke her up so she could climb into a comfortable bed.

I looked over at Billy and thought about changing my mind. It was be easy to skip Ida's house altogether. Let both of them catch up on the sheep they were counting. I could change that clock of hers any time.

Go in.

An odd urge prodded my conscience. I'd put Ida off enough times as it was. If I didn't change her clock tonight, it wasn't going to be more convenient any other time. All I'd get for procrastination would be more of her nagging.

Go in.

All right, already. I reached for the door, half-hoping Billy would simply sleep through this stop. I could get in and out of Ida's a lot faster if Billy didn't come along for her to fuss over. No such luck. The interior light in the pickup went on. Billy's eyes popped open.

"Aunt Ida's!" Billy sat up as if he'd been kicked by one of his kung-fu pals.

"Last stop, buddy," I said as I put one foot out of the pickup. "Let's rumble."

"Yeah," Billy called, acting as if his sixty-second nap had been a full eight hours. "Let's rumble." He roared like a bull on steroids as he raced up the sidewalk.

"Don't run right in!" I shook my head as Billy bypassed the doorbell, or even a knock, and ran straight into the house. Maybe now Ida would listen to me when I'd tell her for the millionth time, "Lock your door. Just because this is Brewster doesn't mean you can let anyone in." Billy included.

Bursting through the door, he screamed as he'd been doing all night, "Trick-or-treat! Popcorn balls!" He stopped inside the dark entry way, his voice quickly losing enthusiasm. "Yippee." As I stepped in behind him, he turned. "Dad?"

Even a six-year-old could sense something wasn't right.

I called into what felt like nothing. "Ida?" I took a step around Billy. "Aunt Ida?" The house felt cold and empty. As if even if Aunt Ida was in here somewhere, she wasn't here. "Billy, go wait in the pickup."

He grabbed the hem of my jacket in his hand. "I'm scared."

"Ida," I called again, flicking on the light switch near my arm and glancing into the living room on my left. She wasn't asleep in her chair. "Are you home?" Maybe she'd gone over to a friend's house for a visit. Even as I thought it, I knew it was unlikely. Ida always liked to be home before dark if she could help it.

I took two tentative steps into the room, Billy trailing behind like an oversized kite tail. She could be asleep in her bedroom. Did I dare go check and possibly give her a heart attack to see a big lug like me hovering over her bed in the dark?

I didn't dare not check.

"Wait here," I told Billy, easing the edge of my coat out from inside his clammy hand.

He took two steps to follow but stopped when I gave him a stern look. "I'm going to go see if Aunt Ida's in her bedroom." I tried not to sound worried, but I didn't do a very good job. "I'll be back in a second."

An ominous hand pressed against my chest as I started for the bedroom. Suddenly Halloween didn't seem one bit fun.

"Dad!" Billy's voice had raised at least a half-octave. It was more squeak than tone.

I looked back over my shoulder. Billy was pointing to his right, into the kitchen, a look that said "*scared*" plastered across his face. His candy sack dropped with a thump to the floor, sending me into motion.

"Ida! Oh, *God*." It was a prayer.

She was lying in a crumpled heap on the floor, her right leg twisted beneath her as if it had a completely different notion than the rest of her body. A kitchen chair was tipped on its side next to her. I ran to her motionless body and knelt beside it. It didn't take a rocket scientist to imagine what had happened. Her large kitchen clock hung above my head, ticking away. An hour ahead.

I brushed the side of her wrinkled cheek with my hand.

"Fred?" she murmured, her voice barely a whisper. "*Liebe?*"

She was calling for her husband. Her dead husband. Her love. I wasn't sure if that was a good sign or a bad one.

"Billy," I yelled, even though he was standing right next to me, "call 911. Now!"

His feet scurried as he scrambled for the phone hanging on the kitchen wall.

As Billy waited for someone to answer his call, my EMT training kicked in. The training my hospital-administrator brother, Ben, had practically forced me to take two years ago when Brewster's volunteer ambulance squad needed extra bodies. The training I thanked God for now. I hadn't prayed as much all of last year as I was praying today.

Lord, help me. Help her.

Ida's skin had a blue tinge and she was cold to the touch. Quickly I unzipped my jacket and put it over her upper body. I grabbed a small thick towel that was crumpled on the floor near her, folded it, and put it under her head. Anything to make her twisted body more comfortable.

"Dad, what's the address here?" I hadn't even heard Billy talk to the dispatcher.

Oh, man. No one in Brewster used addresses. You just *knew* where everybody lived. I closed my eyes. Think. Think.

"Ninth Street," I said to Billy. "Tell them Ida Bauer's house. In Brewster. On Ninth Street. The ambulance crew will know."

I listened as Billy repeated my instructions into the phone. He had barely hung up the phone when he appeared at my side asking, "Why aren't they here yet?"

Stupidly, I was wondering the same thing, even though I was well aware of the drill. Billy's call was now being patched through from the county sheriff's office to the local police and Brewster's small hospital. From there beepers would start buzzing in the pockets and bedsides of the few volunteers who were on call tonight. They'd hightail it to the hospital, find out the location, start up the ambulance, and, finally, head this way.

If everything worked the way it was supposed to.

I took off my cap and ran sweaty fingers through my hair. I knew all too well the times a volunteer was slow answering the call. They might have walked to a ball game and need to run home to get their car. They might be in the shower or…who knew? This was taking forever.

Billy knelt beside me, staring at Ida's closed eyes, her unmoving body. "I think Mom would tell us to pray," he said, his voice pure quiver.

"I think you're right." I bowed my head and silently started sending my petition.

At my elbow Billy spoke out loud. "Dear God, You've just got to make Aunt Ida better." I'd never heard such sincerity, even from a pulpit.

"She makes the best popcorn balls and cookies." He took in a deep breath and blew it out. "She loves us and we love her." One more deep breath, then silence.

I waited for an *"Amen."* A *"that's it."* Something. I opened one eye and looked down at Billy. He was looking up at me.

"Your turn," he said.

Oh, man. I wasn't the kind of guy who prayed out loud. My heart started thumping again. Cold sweat on my upper lip.

"Dad?"

What could I do? He was my son.

Just as you are My child.

If Billy thought I could do this, I'd die trying.

Just as I did to save you.

Goose bumps crowded my forearms. The whole day had been like this. I took a deep breath of my own, talking much too loud in the still kitchen. I had a feeling it didn't matter how loud I spoke, just that I said the words. "Lord, we're scared," I started. "I'm scared." Feeble, but honest.

"Me, too," Billy chimed in as if we were a praying tag team.

"Aunt Ida has done nothing but love us. She doesn't deserve to be—" My throat closed. I cleared it and tried again. "She needs Your help, Lord." In my heart I added, *I need Your help.* The impact of what I'd done, make that *hadn't* done, weighed heavily on my shoulders. "Bring help quickly." For Ida. And me. I was out of words. "Amen," I said.

"Amen," said Billy, as confidently as any preacher I'd ever heard. Not that I'd heard that many.

A calm silence covered the three of us. Billy stood by the window, watching for the ambulance. I brushed Ida's hair away from her face and felt her faint pulse.

Silently I prayed that the next hour, the hour the clock showed had already passed, would be merciful to my aunt. And that in that same amount of time, if it were ever possible, I prayed that God would forgive me for being the cause of this awful accident.

"I listed Ida Bauer's house today." Dan set his briefcase next to the front door and walked over to the couch to give me a kiss. His face was red from the February wind. We'd had a cold snap ever since the holidays. I cupped my hands around his icy cheeks and kissed him back.

"Mmm," I said, closing my eyes, "that's nice."

Dan sat down beside me, throwing his arm over the back of the couch. "What's nice? The kiss or the listing?"

I laughed, closing the *InStyle* magazine I'd been studying ever since I got home from work. "Well, I meant the kiss, but the listing is good, too." I was glad that after weeks of strain between us this fall, Dan had finally come around and given his stamp of approval to my job...and my surgery. I knew the few hours a week I was trying to help with his tax work wouldn't be nearly enough in the coming weeks. We still hadn't talked about a compromise. But I didn't want to bring that up now. "Is the house nice?"

"For a little house it has amazing features." As usual, Dan added his real estate lingo to brag it up. I'd seen many of the *amazing* houses he'd listed before. I knew Brewster really didn't have any amazing houses on any of its quiet streets. I listened with half an ear as he went on. "I can't believe I've never been in it before."

"Ida Bauer," I said, wondering aloud, "which one is she?" For the life of me I didn't think I'd ever get the many old women of Brewster straight. They all looked as though they'd been cloned from the same beauty shop. Tight, permed, white curls that had been ratted, sprayed, and backcombed into a helmet they called hair. It was scary how alike they all looked. I'd already vowed I'd never come close.

"You know Ida," Dan said. "She lives right across the street from Libby and Bob's house. In the yellow stucco?"

I felt my eyebrows head together. For once it didn't matter. I was going to be having surgery in a couple of months. Let my brows wrinkle all they wanted, give the doctor something to work on. "I can picture the house, but I just can't think who Ida is."

"Oh, you have to know her. She used to be in Vicky's café almost every day having coffee. She's the one who helped bake all those pies for Pumpkin Fest every year."

"Oh," I said, finally remembering Ida out sweeping her sidewalk across the street from Libby's. "I know who she is." I was pretty sure I had the right woman in mind. Dan never could understand why I didn't know everyone in town the way he did. I opened my magazine and continued to page through it. "Look at this." I held the oversized page up for Dan to see. "I'll bet you anything she's had work done." A porcelain-faced model stared at the two of us. "Look at the space between her eyebrows. Botox, for sure. Brow lift? Maybe."

Dan lifted the magazine out of my hand and set it on the coffee table in front of the couch. He took his thumb and rubbed it gently between my brows. Smoothing. Soothing. "I like a woman with some character in her face."

I rolled my eyes. We'd been through this before. "There's a big difference between 'character' and 'old hag.'"

Dan chuckled, sliding over on the couch, putting a pillow on his lap, and then easing my head onto the pillow. I smiled up at him. Lightly he ran his fingers across my face, threading them gently through my hair. Other than picking Joey up from basketball practice in a half hour, I didn't have anywhere to be tonight. Dan could mess my hair and makeup all he wanted. I closed my eyes, relaxing.

"Did you hear Ed Brinkman died today?" Dan spoke softly as he lightly tickled my face.

"Which one is he?" I asked.

"He's the man who used to own the farm that Paul and Ruthie Bennett live on. Out by Brush Lake."

"Oh, okay." I didn't have a clue.

"It's really sad to see so many of the old people in town dying. It's like a changing of the old guard. I know it's inevitable, but that's one thing I don't like about living in a small town. When someone dies, you know them."

"Um-mmm," I murmured. "Do you think you'll have any trouble selling that Bauer lady's house? She didn't die, too, did she?" I was pretty sure Libby would have mentioned something.

"No," he said. "She didn't die. She's moved to the nursing home. Kenny Pearson—Ida's nephew—has been helping her line up the sale of her house. "He told me they'd hoped Ida's hip would heal well enough so she'd be able to return home, but that's not going to happen. She fell back in October. Between her time in the hospital in Carlton where she had her hip repaired, and the swing bed at the hospital here, she maxed out the time Medicare allows for that kind of thing. Kenny said they had to face it; she was not going to be able to live on her own again. She moved into the nursing home last month."

"That's too bad," I mumbled, half dozing while Dan rambled.

"Last week when Kenny checked on her house there were some problems with the furnace. When he told Ida about it, I guess she said, "Sell the house to someone who can be happy in it." Dan's fingers lingered briefly on my jaw line, then continued moving across my face. "I stopped by the nursing home today to have Ida sign some papers. Do you know what she told me?" He paused, smiling slightly. "She said, 'I've got a better home waiting for me anyway.' She's a feisty gal." He chuckled.

"What did she mean by that? A better home? The nursing home isn't that nice." At least I didn't think it was. I'd never set foot in it myself.

Dan laughed. "You have to know Ida. She and God are like this." He stopped stroking my face and crossed his fingers. "She meant her home in heaven."

"Oh." If the thought made an old woman feel better, let her think it. "I can't imagine that little house of hers will bring much." Cracker box might not be the term Dan would use to describe it, but any woman in her right mind would see it immediately.

"You might be surprised," Dan said. "It has a nice-sized master bedroom."

"Just one bedroom?"

"Well, there's another small room down the hall. Ida had a twin bed in it, but I'll probably call it an office. The unique thing about the house is that the living room walls were hand painted back in, I don't know, maybe the twenties, by an artist from Europe. They've got these great vines that trail around the edges of the walls. I can't believe someone hasn't painted over them."

"Vines?"

"Yeah, like grape vines or something. Leaves. Branches. They're subtle, but great."

"Sounds...well, different." I was trying to be nice. Dan had to sell the house, after all. But vines painted all over the walls? Not in any house I'd ever buy.

"They *are* different. Really exceptional. They add a lot of character to an otherwise standard house."

Of course real estate agents were used to putting a positive spin on any listing. I could only imagine.

He went on. "The master bedroom has a large closet and a bathroom off of the bedroom. You don't see that in a lot of these smaller older homes." For a small home he was certainly finding enough to say about it.

"A starter home then." Might as well tell it like it was going to be.

"Or a nice home for an older couple wanting to downsize."

Goodness, Brewster certainly had enough of those. "An ending home, then."

Dan tapped my nose with the tip of his finger. "Remind me to never let you write my ad copy." He checked his watch. "Something smells good. What's for supper?"

"I've got Rosemary Beef in the Crock-Pot. Joey's favorite."

"Mine, too," he said.

I sat up, smoothing my hair with my hands. "Which reminds me, I'd better get over to the school and pick up Joey."

"Want me to go?"

I shook my head. "What you could do is set the table. Libby had me bring some foundation home from Elizabeth's for her today. I told her I'd drop it off when I picked up Joey. I can check out that lady's house when I swing by."

"Well," Dan said, walking with me through the kitchen and pausing by the door as I buttoned up my bright red wool coat, "the outside doesn't look nearly as appealing as the inside. I'll have to show it to you sometime."

"Um-hmm," I purred, noncommittally. If he forgot, it would be okay with me.

~

I backed the car out of the driveway. An icy February wind pushed at the side of the car. I should have let Dan run this errand. It was too cold.

I wove through the side streets of Brewster, humming along to the radio. It was good to be back in town after spending the day at work in Carlton. The hours behind the makeup counter weren't flying by quite as quickly as they had during the busy holiday season.

I'd been the top cosmetics salesperson in December and January, but February was proving to be slow for all the stores in the mall. There had even been talk in the coffee room that Elizabeth's was thinking of laying some people off. I hoped I wasn't one of them. I knew I'd never save the amount of money I needed for my surgery by next month. Not even close. But Dan had agreed to take out a loan for the procedure and let me pay it off with the paycheck from my job. In order to keep up my end of the bargain, I needed to keep my position behind the makeup counter.

That's why I'd started calling friends like Libby to see if they needed anything from my department. I figured if I could keep my sales figures up, the management at Elizabeth's would have no choice but to keep me employed. The extra work it took to deliver the merchandise when I got back to Brewster was worth it.

I pulled up to Libby's house and glanced into the rearview mirror. What had I been thinking? I'd left the house without checking my face! My eyeliner was smeared, and it looked as if the last time I'd applied lipstick was before it had been invented. *Janine!* I could hear my mother's voice as if she were sitting beside me. *You can't go out looking like that! What will people think?* I quickly dug into my purse and pulled out a tissue, wiping carefully at the smudges below my right eye. There was a huge difference between sexy-smudged eyeliner and what had happened to my eyes. I swiped Real Red across my lips and smacked them on the tissue. There. Thank goodness I hadn't gone up to Libby's door looking like a *before* photo.

"Jan, come in." Libby held the door wide, cold air rushing in behind me.

"I can't stay long," I said, gently tapping snow from the toes of my new, two-inch heeled, brown leather boots onto Libby's entry rug. "I'm on my way to the school to pick up Joey from basketball practice. Besides, I don't want to interrupt your dinner."

Libby waved a hand through the air. "Bob has a meeting tonight, so I didn't even make supper. To tell you the truth, I was planning on curling up on the couch with a good book and a big bowl of popcorn." She laughed. "Probably not the most nutritional supper, but it doesn't hurt once in a blue moon, right?"

I smiled back at her, noncommittally, biting my tongue to keep from asking if it was air-popped popcorn or if she planned to douse it in butter. I held out the light aqua bag that was Elizabeth's trademark color. "Your goodies," I said, handing it to her. "I threw in a few samples just for fun." I'd learned that being generous with samples often led to a customer coming back to me to make a purchase later on. Not that I was worried about who Libby would buy from, but it didn't hurt to treat her the way I did my other best customers.

Libby peeked into the bag. "Oh, fun! Thanks. This saves me a trip to Carlton. Sometimes I get so tired of making that drive for every little thing." She set the goodie-filled bag on the side table by the door. "Are you getting tired of driving there so many times a week?"

I didn't hesitate. "Not a bit. I love this job. I think it was created just for me."

"Goodness," Libby laughed. "I guess I didn't realize you liked selling makeup quite that much. But then, God has a plan for everyone. I'm glad you've found yours. Do you have time to sit down?"

I quickly glanced at the Anne Klein watch I'd purchased with my discount last week. Joey's coach was a stickler for time. Practice never was over a minute early. Or went a minute late. "I can stay five minutes."

"We'll just have to talk fast," Libby said, leading the way to her comfy couch.

I unbuttoned my DKNY coat and sank into a corner of the soft sofa, running my fingers over the textured fabric. Nice. I knew the cushions had to be down-filled.

"So," Libby said, curling her feet under herself on the other end of the couch, "you look fabulous. This job must agree with you, but I have to tell you…" she paused, tilting her head a bit as she looked at me, "I miss the times we used to get together for coffee. I hardly see you anymore."

It was true. This new job had pretty much taken over my life. I'd been scheduled full-time over the holidays and, while my hours had been cut back a little since the middle of January, any extra time I had had simply disappeared. I often found myself driving to Carlton early and spending an hour or so browsing the mall. Since I was saving as much as I could for my surgery, window-shopping was my specialty. Well, except for bargains I couldn't pass up, like my new boots and watch and the red coat I was wearing. What Libby had said was true. I couldn't remember the last time I'd had a long chat with any of my friends. I suddenly felt a flash of guilt for the way I'd ignored Libby. Without thinking I blurted, "Just wait until next month. I'll have all kinds of time to visit."

"Why? What's next month?" Libby asked.

"I'm having my surgery March seventh," I said without thinking. "I'm taking six weeks off work." I only hoped six weeks was enough for me to heal up so that my customers wouldn't suspect a thing…except that I looked amazing.

"Surgery?" Libby brushed her hair behind one ear and leaned forward. "Is something wrong?"

Me and my big mouth. Now I'd done it. Mentioned the one thing I hadn't planned to tell anyone beside Dan…and my doctor, of course. I could feel a flush of heat rise through my chest and fill my face. I lifted my sagging chin. "Okay, here's the deal." I leaned towards Libby. "You have to promise to keep this a secret."

She nodded. "Scout's honor."

"I'm having my face done."

Libby's eyebrows puzzled together. "Your face done? What do you mean? Like a makeover? Why would that take surgery?" Her eyebrows lifted as my meaning sunk in. "Oh-hh."

I nodded. "I'm having a face-lift in three weeks."

"*You?* What's there to lift?"

Okay, so she was trying to be nice. I held a hand on either side of my face and pressed the skin gently toward my ears. "See?" I said, knowing exactly how much better I looked with that tiny bit of lift. I should know, I practiced looking at the new me in the mirror every day. Make that several times a day.

"No," Libby said, squinting her eyes at me, "I don't see."

Well, then, she had to be blind. "Look." I leaned in close and pointed to the crinkles beside my eyes. I ran a finger over the deep crease that ran along both sides of my nose and my mouth. Then I pressed the back of my hand against the loose skin below my chin. "I'm getting it all done. That's why I've been working so hard at my job. I'm saving money to help pay for the operation."

"Oh, Jan," she said slowly, as if she somehow felt sorry for me.

Libby was a natural beauty. Of course she could see that I wasn't. At least, not anymore. I crossed my arms, bracing myself for what was coming.

"You are so beautiful." Libby's face glowed as she said the words.

Not what I expected to hear. A lump pushed its way into my throat.

She went on. "God gave you that face. It's stunning, and you don't need to do a thing to it." She bit at a corner of her lip and then spoke again. "But I hope you know that no matter what you do, how you look on the outside means nothing."

"Nothing?" I said. "It means *everything*." If anyone was going to understand, I thought, for sure it would have been Libby. But then, why would she? She was flat-out gorgeous. That God she talked about had given her nothing to worry about. Unlike me with a face and body that were melting like a slow spring thaw. I stood and started buttoning my coat. "I need to get to the school and pick up Joey."

"Jan." Libby laid her hand on my coat sleeve. "Don't be mad. I was giving you a compliment."

"I'm not mad," I said, my teeth barely separating as I spoke.

"It sure seems like it."

The words fell from my mouth. "I *hate* the way I look. Why can't anyone see me the way I do?" I could feel tears sting my eyes.

Libby pulled my stiff body into a hug. "It doesn't matter how anyone sees you," she said into my ear. "It only matters how God sees you." She kept her arms on my shoulders and leaned back to look me in the eye. "And He thinks you're beautiful just the way you are."

I rolled my wet eyes. What she'd said were words a mom would say trying to comfort an upset kid. *You're beautiful just the way you are.* Words my mom had never uttered. At least I had to give my mom credit for being honest. She'd replaced empty words with beauty tips.

I knew Libby's words were meant to console. Much like that Mr. Rogers guy on the show Joey used to watch when he was little. Platitudes all around. Her words were no different. She was only trying to make me feel better. Yet the only thing that would make me feel better was to get my surgery over with. Then maybe everyone would be able to see just what I was talking about. "I've really got to get going."

"I don't want you to leave upset." Libby squeezed my hand. "Can you stop back after supper? Or, are you off tomorrow? Maybe we could meet for coffee."

"I'm scheduled to work," I said, relieved to have the out. I really did not want to talk about this one second more. No wonder I'd kept the whole thing a secret.

Libby trailed me to the door. "Jan," she said as I put my hand on the doorknob.

I turned. Once again I could feel a furrow across my face.

Libby stood calmly, her usual collected self. "I want to tell you one more thing before you go."

"What?" I couldn't help the way the word came out with a snap.

If Libby noticed, she ignored my rudeness. "There's a verse in the Bible that tells us to not be one bit concerned about what we look like on the outside. If you stay a minute I'll find it and write it down for you."

Oh, great. More platitudes. I closed my eyes for a long second while I told myself she was just trying to help. "You know, Libby, I'm really not feeling that well. Maybe some other time, okay?"

"Sure," she said, as if I'd just patted her hand with my own platitude.

~

As I pulled away from Libby's house, I remembered to look at the darkened, empty house across the street. Dan had already put a For Sale sign in the snowy front yard. The house looked old. It could use some work. Just another reminder of how I'd look if I didn't follow through with my plans. I was tired of looking faded and worn, like an old house that had seen better days. Well, in three weeks I'd be close to new again. *March seventh. March seventh.* I repeated the words as though they were a good luck charm.

I drove the few blocks to school under cover of early evening darkness. As I pulled to the curb, Joey came shuffling his way down the long walk that led from the school gym. For once I was glad for a North Dakota February where a cloud-filled night blocked out any light.

"Hi, Mom." Joey opened the back door of the car and threw his large duffel bag onto the backseat. I closed my eyes as the overhead light came on. For some weird reason I didn't care to get even a glimpse of myself in a mirror just now. He slammed the door and slid onto the front seat.

"Buckle your seat belt," I automatically reminded.

As I put the car into drive Joey leaned forward, crossing his arms over his legs. "My stomach hurts."

I glanced over at him. The kid was a bottomless pit these days. "Maybe you're hungry."

"It doesn't feel like that. I think I'm sick. Jeff threw up a little while ago."

Oh, so that was it. Teamwork of a different sort. "Did you have a hard practice?" It wouldn't be the first time the coach had run them to the point of retching.

Joey shook his head. "A bunch of kids were gone from school today."

"Is that so?" All of a sudden the Rosemary Beef I had simmering at home didn't sound all that appealing. It was turning out what I'd said to Libby about not feeling well was true. "I hope it's not the flu."

"I hope not, too." As I pulled into the driveway he threw open the door and bolted toward the house.

Not a good sign.

~

"Are you sure you're going to be okay?" Dan was standing at the end of our bed, ready to go off to work.

I barely nodded. Afraid to move my head for fear of setting off another bout of nausea. Joey's flu bug had run its course during the early evening and had left him pale but off to school this morning. Unfortunately, the bug had decided to run on over to me in the middle of the night. "I'm fine," I croaked. "Did you call Elizabeth's and tell them I won't be in?"

"Already done," Dan said. "Can I get you anything before I leave?"

I closed my eyes and shook my head a mere millimeter. "This tea is fine." I moved my eyes in the direction of the bed stand where a steaming mug stood. I already knew it would be ice cold before I had the stomach to taste it. "I just need to sleep," I said to Dan, inching the covers up to my chin.

"Okay," he said. "I'm going in to the office now. I'll check on you in a couple hours."

"Don't call," I cautioned. All I needed was a ringing phone to wake me from a deep sleep. And sleep was the only thing that sounded good right now. "Bye," I murmured as he gently squeezed my shoulder.

I heard the garage door open and then close. Very slowly I turned onto my side. I'd been up and down almost all night, running to the bathroom, dozing a bit, then running again. All I wanted to do this morning was sleep. I pushed my cheek deep into the pillow, remembering the time when Joey was in grade school and just beginning to learn about things like measurements and yardsticks. He'd once said, after a bad sore throat, "I think I'm one foot better."

If my condition could be measured, I was guessing I was one inch improved. Not much, compared to last night, but I had to take what I could get. I let my eyes drift shut, trying to focus not on my stomach, but on how I'd look and feel after my face-lift.

⌒

What time was it? My eyes were still closed, but I could sense by the way light from the window fell across my face that it had to be late afternoon. Had I really slept that long? Had Dan come and gone…or forgotten to check on me altogether?

I peeked at the bedside clock through half-open slits. A note was propped against the face of the clock. Dan's scrawl in heavy black ink. I could read it from where I lay.

Sleeping Beauty, I didn't want to wake you. Have a lunch meeting and two appointments this afternoon. I'll stop by after that. Call if you need anything. Love, Dan. AKA: Prince Charming

I closed my eyes and smiled to myself, feeling an odd tug on the right side of my mouth, the side pushed into the pillow. I brushed the side of my face with my hand. Goodness, I was drooling like a teething baby. How embarrassing. Even the pillowcase was wet. I must have slept like a boulder.

I turned onto my back, carefully scrutinizing the move to see if nausea was going to rear its ugly head. All was well except for the strange weight that seemed to be bearing down on the right side of my face. It felt as if it were still asleep. I must have lain on it too long and too hard. This was a first. My feet had fallen asleep many times, my arms, too, when I'd slept on one of them weird, but never my face. I relaxed under the covers, waiting for the familiar pins-and-needles prick that would indicate it was waking up to join the rest of my body.

While I waited I rubbed my hand against my cheek, hoping to massage feeling back into it. If I didn't know better, I'd swear I'd been to the dentist while I'd been sleeping and had an overdose of Novocain. A thin line of tears ran from the corner of my eye, wetting my fingers as they brushed by. This was so strange.

I adjusted the pillows so that I could partially sit up while I waited for normality to return. My eyelids flickered as the thin afternoon sunlight hit my face. My left eye automatically shut against the brightness, my right eye allowed a small sliver of light to blind me. I raised my hand to cover my eye, using my fingers to close the lid as though it were a small door that needed help to close completely. Bizarre.

Oh. I must have dozed. The phone was ringing. I leaned over toward Dan's side of the bed, propping myself on my left elbow, reaching for the receiver with my right hand. I fumbled with the handset, afraid I might hang up on the person before I got a grip on the phone. There.

"Hell-wo," I said, my voice froggy. I cleared my throat and tried again. "Hell-wo."

"Jan?" It was Libby. "Is that you?"

"Yes-shh. I-It ishh," My words were oddly slurred. A chill ran up my back and seemed to settle in my ears, turning them into two blocks of ice.

"I ran into Dan at Vicky's this afternoon," she said. "He told me you weren't feeling well."

I hoped she noticed that I hadn't lied to her last night. I really had been coming down with a bug.

"The flu?"

"I fink sho." What was wrong with my lips?

"Are you okay? You don't sound all that great."

So, it wasn't just me. Libby could hear it, too. My heart started a heavy drumming inside my chest. I breathed thickly into the phone.

"Do you want me to come over?"

"No. I'mmm okaaay."

I hung up the phone after promising Libby I'd call if I needed anything. I slumped back against the bed. The numbness in my face wasn't any better. There weren't any pins and needles. What there was, was nothing. I wasn't "okay." Something was wrong. Terribly wrong.

I pushed myself out of bed and made my way to the bathroom. My right leg felt weak and wobbly, as if it might decide to collapse under me at any time. I grabbed onto the doorframe just in case, standing there for a moment to steady myself. Okay. I put one hand on the vanity countertop as though I were a toddler making my first foray through an obstacle course. I stepped into the bathroom, preparing myself to look at my face. My face without makeup was never a pretty sight. Add a night of vomiting and no sleep…I could only imagine. I stepped in front of the mirror with half-closed eyes, took a breath, then opened them.

The face looking back at me was not mine. My right eye drooped as if a small child were tugging at my eyelashes. The same side of my mouth hung down and open as though the small child was hanging from my lower lip. Even my nose seemed somehow stretched and distorted. A thin line of saliva hung like a bungee cord from my chin.

I tried to move my lips. My eye. Nothing. No movement. A freak in the mirror stared back at me.

From where I stood I heard an unearthly sound. It was coming from me. From my mouth. Or what used to be my mouth. "Aaaa-oooo-wwwww-aaaaahhh."

From somewhere inside, my heart screamed. *Oh, God!! Please help me!*

Ida

I tried to scoot myself up higher in the sagging seat of my wheel-chair, but my scrawny arms, arms that used to hoist such things as large rocks and hay bales out on the farm, were about as helpful as the tines of an old pitchfork. Rusty from not being used.

I dropped right back to where I'd been slumping. A little flash of anger burned in my chest. How much longer was I going to have to sit here looking like an old rag doll?

"Ida, Ida!" That assistant girl, Wendy, screamed at me in her always too-loud voice. "You shouldn't sit like that. You're going to put too much pressure on your hip! Here, let me help you!"

Did she think I was deaf?

Most of the people here are hard of hearing. Count your blessings, My child.

It wasn't the first time the Lord had told me to be thankful for something others didn't have. I tried to apologize for my rude thought with a smile, but it was hard to catch Wendy's eye when she had her arms wrapped around me and was tugging at my body like a bird after a fat morning worm. Sometimes it felt as if the aides would yank me in two before they got me where I was supposed to be sitting.

"There! Is that better, Ida?" Wendy squatted beside my chair and patted my hand, yelling again. "How are you doing today, Ida?!"

Why did she keep repeating my name? Did she think I was going to forget it between her short sentences?

Many people here don't know their names anymore. Count your blessings…Ida.

God, again. He had a way of talking to me that could calm me right down. And make me smile to boot.

"I'm doing goot, Vendy." I didn't tell her about my restless night. How my legs thrashed around under the covers as if they were two donkeys trying to kick horseshoes off their stubborn feet. I thanked the Lord when my favorite nurse, Julie, came in to check on my roommate and me in the middle of the night and offered to rub lotion on my knees and restless calves.

She rubbed the smooth lotion on the thin skin on my legs and whispered to me at the same time. "Were you having a bad dream?" She sounded as if I were a young one who needed soothing.

"Nah," I said. Then I remembered, *Thou shalt not bear false witness.* "Vell, maybe a little vun."

It wasn't so much that the dream was bad, but it reminded me of how life had been so much different than it was now. It was the same dream I'd had many times since I'd moved to the nursing home. I was back on the farm in the early days with Fred. We were having a picnic in the middle of the cow pasture. Lemonade in pints jars. Cold fried chicken and tiny sweet carrots from our garden. Potato salad, too. Fat oatmeal cookies for the end. The sun was warm on my back, shinning so hot Fred's face looked as if it were glowing around the edges. We'd gathered up the leftovers and were walking back to the house when I'd started running and called over my shoulder, "First vun home gets a prize!" I didn't know what the prize would be, but it didn't matter. I just felt like running for the happiness that was inside me.

Then I woke up. My legs still running, my eyes taking in the yellow walls of the nursing home around me. The shadowed drapery on the window that opened during the day, not to big pastures, but to a small courtyard that no one ever sat in and the brick side of another wing of the home. My mind knew where it was, but my legs kept trying to get me away. Back to my first home with Fred on the farm. Back to my little home on Ninth Street in Brewster. Anywhere but here. This was not my home.

Of course it isn't. None of those places were your true home. I am busy preparing a place for you as you sleep. As you wake. Soon. Very soon.

"Tank you, Chulie," I'd whispered, as she tucked my flannel nightgown around my relaxed legs. It was comforting to have someone touch me. A balm to know a better home waited for me. I closed my eyes as Julie went back to her rounds.

If I were back in my little house on Ninth Street, I might crawl out of bed and fix myself a glass of warm milk. Read my Bible while I waited for sleep to find my eyes. Instead, all I could do was lie here, listening to my roommate, Verna Stolz, rumble her way through the night.

I hated the long, dark hours when the bustle of the day gave way to the dead of the midnight hours. A time when dreams of old times were called out with loud tears from several rooms that lined these halls. It seemed we all had nights in which we wished for earlier times when our legs could run and our arms could wrap themselves around folks we loved whenever we wished. Oh, the ache in my heart when I remembered too much.

Out of habit I tried to push myself upright in the darned contraption they called a wheelchair around here. A prison-with-wheels was my nickname for it.

Ida. Ida. Be thankful you can sit up. There are many here who spend their days, all their days, in bed.

When would I learn? As my mother used to say, "Thank the Lord for small favors." I closed my eyes and breathed a small prayer. *Thank You, Lord, for sitting.* A small favor, true, but better than the substitute. Flat on my back with nothing but a beige ceiling to stare at.

"Ida!" Loud Wendy, again. "Do you want to come to the morning discussion?!" She started pushing my chair before I had time to nod my gray head. "Discussion" they called the morning hour when the activities director talked about the old times and we were supposed to chime in with our memories.

Wendy pushed my chair into the ragged circle of residents and locked my wheels, as if I would escape with a backward push of my rubbery legs if she didn't put the brakes on. Looking around at this sad group, I doubted there were more than three whole brains among the lot of us.

Be glad you are one of the folks who do have a whole mind.

If God would take a break from all of His reminders to me, I could enjoy feeling sorry for myself. I rested my elbow on the arm of my prison. The old hymn that talked about what a Friend we have in Jesus left out the part about how He could nag like an old washer-woman when He had a mind to.

Or a reason to.

I smiled inside. He was a good Friend. Never leaving me alone, even when I was lying on my kitchen floor all those hours. Even when I would rather take a bath in my sorrows instead of count my bless-ings. He was a good rememberer.

"I think we're ready to start! My name is Dorothy! Today we are going to talk about the blizzards you remember!"

There were times when I wished for bad hearing. Times like now when I could reach up and turn down the volume on a hearing aide. Or turn it off altogether. I didn't want to relive the past every day. It reminded me too much of what no longer was.

Edgar Delzer raised a thick finger. "The blizzard of sixty-six," he said, apparently not minding one bit having to relive feeding freezing cattle in the storm of the decade.

I looked down into my lap and then let my eyes drift to a leafless tree outside the window. It was times when I tried *not* to think about earlier days that I found my mind repeating the closer days that had brought me here. I didn't want to think over that time, either, but since when did I ever tell my mind where to wander?

Lying on that floor had been a tunnel. The longest tunnel I'd ever been in. The voice of a child calling me. Was it the baby Fred and I lost in stillbirth? Then it was Billy, calling out my name. *Ida! Aunt Ida. I love you.* He sounded scared.

Don't be scared, I remember thinking. I wasn't sure if I was trying to tell the words to Billy, or if God was saying them to me. It didn't matter. They were assuring words however they were meant.

I only had bits and pieces of the next hours. The ambulance men—or was it a lady and a man?—counting in my kitchen, "One, two, three," and then lifting me into the air. Kenny calling loudly, "Be careful! Be careful." I remembered moaning. Trying to talk. Trying to thank Kenny and Billy for finding me. Then I was coming out of surgery. The doctor in Carlton explaining the pin they'd put in my hip. I imagined a big safety pin holding my broken bones together. And then I was in a hospital room, a bouquet of daisies—imagine, daisies in October—by my bedside. Or was it already November?

I was confused but not lonely. Kenny and Diane took turns by my bed. One time I opened my sleepy eyes and there sat Renae, reading a fat book. Before I could rummage through my brain to find her name, I was back asleep, opening my eyes to see Billy's staring into mine.

I croaked the first word that came to mind. The first word I could remember saying in days. "Boo." The last time I'd seen Billy, he'd been dressed for Halloween.

"Boo," he whispered back, as if it was a secret between us. He put his head on the bed beside me, standing there, head cockeyed, as if he had nothing better in the world to do right then.

I fell asleep as he stared into my eyes.

Not alone. Never alone.

It had been hard to keep track of the days. And the nights. Looking back over them now, they appeared as though they were part of a different calendar. Just when I thought I was making progress, my hip beginning to mend, the hospital staff shuffling alongside my walker as if I was a turtle that needed a babysitter, the pneumonia set in. I coughed like a cat with a bad case of hairball until I was too weak to cough. Too weak to do anything but lie on my back and try to pray.

"Is she going to make it?" Kenny's worried voice filtered through my closed eyes. Through my brain, fogged with sickness and medicine.

I didn't hear the answer, but by then it didn't matter. I was so sick the words *heaven* and *hospital* both meant a cure for what I had.

And then there was the blood clot in my calf. More medicine. More doctors. More time in the hospital. One more fall that broke nothing but my independent streak. Until then I'd held out hope of returning to my little house on Ninth Street. But the fact was, I was an old woman. A weak old woman. Eighty-two and not getting any younger. Even if God never left my side, He couldn't carry my laundry down the narrow basement stairs for me. Or back up. He couldn't stand at the stove and stir together a pot of hot soup. I couldn't, either.

"Sell the howse," I told Kenny one night when he came by the hospital on his nightly visit. By then I'd been transferred to the Brewster hospital, into a swing bed on the far end of the short wing. I'd already overstayed my welcome, according to Medicare.

"Aunt Ida, no." Kenny was shaking his head. "Diane and I will help you. Diane can help you with housework and stuff. Renae, too. I'll fix anything that needs fixing."

Fred and I had a dog on the farm that wasn't half as eager as Kenny.

"You haff your own family to take care uff." I shook my head back at him. "I'vff mate up my mindt. I'm moofing to the nursing home."

The deal was done. No matter that Kenny kept shaking his head. Kept trying to get me to change my mind. I could out-stubborn that young pup any day.

So, here I was. Sitting in a wheelchair in the Brewster Nursing Home, smelling disinfectant and old people. It was hard not to think about better times.

"Do you want me to push you to therapy?!" Wendy was screaming again. Would her shift never be over? She was glued to me today like a spoon handle with syrup on it. As usual she launched off with me like a rocket, not waiting to see whether I minded where we were going or not.

Oh, well, what else did I have to do but keep these young people busy just by sitting in my chair?

Wendy pushed me down the long hall. Past the big bulletin board that posted the meals for the day in letters so small a person would have to be an eagle to read them. They should print the menu the way Wendy talked. Then we'd all know what to expect for supper. Give us all something to talk about to fill the hours until dinnertime. But then again, when I wasn't the one doing the cooking, it wouldn't do to complain about what was on the table no matter what was being served.

Wendy suddenly stopped my chair in the middle of the hall. "Shari, I haven't seen you in ages," she said to the young woman who stood facing the both of us. Somehow Wendy knew enough not to scream her words this go-round.

The young woman pulled gloves from her hands. "I know. It's been like...forever." Her eyes sparkled as they spoke to Wendy but grew dull as old tinfoil when they fell on my face. She quickly moved her eyes back to her friend. "I'm here to visit my grandma." She babbled away, neither of the young girls seeming to have one concern that I wasn't part of their hallway coffee party.

I looked up at the blue eyes of Wendy's friend. It wasn't hard to see myself through this stranger's eyes. Through the eyes of most of the visitors who walked down these hallways every day. It wasn't much of a secret what they were thinking. Thanking their lucky stars they weren't the ones confined to a place like this.

I could tell plain as day that Wendy's friend, Shari, saw nothing but a decrepit old lady sitting slumped in a wheelchair. An old woman dressed in nondescript gray clothes, her ankles swollen over the tops of orthopedic shoes. I'd bet money on the fact that she didn't even see the rhinestone pin on my white cardigan. The pin Fred had given me for our tenth anniversary. Earrings to match. Antiques now. I touched them with my fingers to remind myself that I had been the apple of somebody's eye...even if it was a long time ago.

Shari jabbered away, her eyes drifting again to mine. They looked right through me, as blank as a chalkboard that had been wiped clean. If I could have, I would have stood up then. Stood nose-to-nose with the healthy young woman just to show her that she didn't have the corner on the staring market. Or the standing market. But the fact was, she did.

Still, I wished I could show her my face close up, wrinkles and all, and let her know some things about me that she couldn't tell just by grazing at me with her eyes.

I sat in my chair, thinking of what I would tell her if I had the chance. "You don't know me," I'd start out by saying softly. "But I used to play the organ back vhen I vas your age. Vhen my eyes vas shtill goodt I readt the dictionary for fun."

Oh, I remembered how I'd try out my new words on Fred. "How *magnanimous* of you," I said the night I singed the pork chops and he said he liked them blackened on the edges just that very way.

I looked up at that Shari person. Who did she think she was, dismissing me with not so much as a glance?

Face it, you are nothing but an old woman with nothing left to offer.

I'm Ida Bauer! I wanted to holler my name as loud as Wendy talked. I was a wife. I was a good friend to many people. I'm still an aunt. I am somebody living, not somebody almost dead. I'm sitting right here in front of you. Look at me. See me!

But she didn't. She laughed with Wendy. Said, "Hi!" to other nurses as they waltzed by, and continued to take in her world that included everyone under the age of forty.

Just an old woman you are. Useless as a sock with a big hole in the heel.

I felt my heart lying in the bottom of my stomach. Suddenly sad that my young days were past. Sorrowful over the way I had taken so many of those days for granted. What good was an old woman, anyway? What did I have to look forward to? I closed my eyes against the gloomy idea, letting my chin fall onto my chest.

There was no one I could tell these thoughts to. Fred was gone. My two best friends, Joyce and Lillian, dead and buried along with all the heartaches we'd shared. The laughter, too.

Who cares about an old woman who can do nothing but sit?

I watched as my crinkled fingers folded together as they had so many times during my lifetime. All I could do was wait. Eat when they told me. Take a bath when it was convenient for someone else. My job was to sit here. I was on Wendy's schedule now. Not mine.

No, Ida. You are on My schedule.

There He was again. Just when I thought I was all alone. There He was.

I have a plan for you. Talk to Me. Tell Me what's in your heart. On your mind. I'll listen to every word. I haven't forgotten you. Remember, I had a plan for you even before you were born. You are still part of My plan. Still part...

As Wendy and Shari continued to talk, the silent words in my heart filled me up. His words. The one Friend who had never left. Never refused to listen. My eyes filled with tears.

Oh, Lord, what good am I now?

Wait...

One word is all He gave me. One word I didn't have any choice about anyway. *Wait.* It was all I could do.

I crossed my hands in my lap. There were many ways to do what God had told me. Patiently. Impatiently. I knew them all. I sighed, filling my lungs full of air the good Lord had given me to breathe.

I would wait. But some days all I wanted was to go Home.

Kenny

The Millers' lube job could wait. "I'm going to run by Ida's house and check the furnace." I pulled my jacket off the chair behind the cash register and stuffed my arm into a sleeve.

Pete nodded. He knew the drill. It was ten forty-five, time for me to make what had become my daily rounds. "You gonna stop by the home and visit her, too?"

As if he had to ask. I pulled the keys to my pickup out of my pocket and tossed them in the air, catching them as smoothly as a well-tossed baseball. "Yup. I'll be back before noon."

I left the grease and gas behind as I maneuvered my old pickup through the streets toward Ida's. Before her fall I'd found every excuse in the book to put off going over to her house to check on things. Now I couldn't keep myself away.

Lot of good it does.

I tapped the heel of my hand against the steering wheel. Yeah, as usual I was a dollar short on trying to make up for something I couldn't change. But it made me feel better to at least try.

I pulled the truck into Ida's driveway, noting the thin puff of smoke coming from the chimney. I'd filled the fuel tank last week, flushed the toilet, and ran water into the sink trap yesterday. I should really just drain the pipes, but then what would I have to do when I stopped by?

I turned the key and stepped into the house. The fifty-five degree air didn't feel a whole lot warmer than outside. I walked into the kitchen. Nothing had changed since yesterday. Even the clock hands above the kitchen sink, long since turned an hour back, seemed to be in the same spot as the day before. I looked at the bank calendar hanging on the wall. March. Practically time to set the clock ahead again.

I walked into the living room. Oh, I corrected myself, the *front* room, as Ida would say about her small living space. To feel useful, I pulled open the drapes. Light streamed through the winter-dirty window. As soon as all the snow melted, I planned to grab a ladder out of the single-stall garage out back and clean all the windows.

You should take such good care of our house.

Diane didn't even have to be near me and I could hear what she'd say. She'd be right, as usual. But she didn't have to live each day with the picture in her mind of Aunt Ida lying stock-still on her kitchen floor. I thought she was dead. For sure.

It wasn't a night I liked to remember, but I kept thinking about it anyway as I settled myself into the lumpy stuffed chair Ida kept by her front window. This wasn't the first time I'd taken the time to see what Ida was missing out on her street while I remembered that night. Not counting funerals, I'd seen two dead people close-up, on two different nights when I'd been on volunteer ambulance calls. One old man, one old lady, both of them nearly dead at the nursing home. All they needed was a ride to the hospital to make it official. Ida had been a dead ringer for the way they looked.

Kenny! Dead ringer?

I didn't mean it like that. Not funny-like. I was just trying to put what happened into words. I—

Good grief. What was I doing? Explaining myself to…well, myself.

You shouldt haff your headt examined.

I shook my thick head now. Ida didn't even have to be in her house to give me advice. The truth was, I'd wondered the same thing myself. Would talking about how I felt inside take away any of the guilt that rode on my heavy shoulders? I knew darn well that if I had stopped by here as many times a week as I did now, Ida wouldn't be sitting in that steel-wheeled chair at the home today. I pressed a knuckle against the bridge of my nose. Hard. It was all my fault, and I didn't know how to make it better.

I'd thought about stopping by our church. Talking to Pastor Ammon. But the last time I'd been in church we'd been singing Christmas carols. He'd probably say something about not seeing me in church for so long.

Kenny, that's not true. Pastor Ammon stops by the station practically every week—and he's never said anything of the kind.

But what would I say to him? I mean the guy'd been to umpteen years of college and I had, what? Eighteen months of grease monkey school? How would a guy like me talk to a guy like him?

Say the same stuff you say to Me.

Hey, you gotta know I don't talk to You all that much, either.

You're talking to Me now, aren't you?

Oh, man. I looked around Ida's small front room. Maybe it was the house. This was weird. Aunt Ida talked to God as though He was her best friend, and now I was doing it, too.

I am.

Huh?

I am her best friend. I can be yours, too. Talk to Me.

I can't do that.

You already are.

It was true. Wanting to or not, I was talking to Him. To Someone. I held my head steady and roamed my eyes around the room. Looking for? For what? Maybe I *was* losing it. Maybe the pressure of everything had finally gotten to me.

What pressure?

The long hours I have to put in at the station. The measly income I make. Wondering whether I really can trust Pete alone at the station. Wondering how I will feed my kids. Send them to college. If they'll be smart enough to go to college.

Thoughts poured out of my heart like a gas hose stuck on "fill." Got another kid due any day, you know.

I know.

One corner of my mouth turned up. Just a little. Whoever I was talking to seemed as though He were smiling. As if He really did *know* how I felt. Did I dare tell the rest?

My eyes stared out the filmy window at the For Sale sign pushed into the frozen grass out front. I'd already tried telling myself all the excuses I could think of that might make me feel better. *Aunt Ida was old. She could have tripped on her bathroom rug just as well as off the chair. It was time she started taking it easy. Let trained nurses and aides watch out for her. Let someone else do her cooking and laundry. She deserves to be waited on.*

And on it went. Every excuse in the book and then some. None of them did the trick. The trick of turning a screwup like me into someone responsible. Respectable. I slid my elbows onto my knees and put my face into my hands, scrubbing at it hard. Everything I did seemed to go wrong.

Marrying Diane?

Okay, so I'd done one thing right.

Renae? Billy? Paige?

Three more, then.

Your new baby?

Well, yeah, him, too. About the only thing I could get excited about these days was the baby Diane was about to deliver.

Kenny Jr. we had agreed, if it, *he*, was a boy. Kendra for a girl. But it wasn't going to be a girl. I just knew it. Diane had told the doctor that, unless he felt it was necessary, she didn't need an ultrasound since her husband was already convinced the baby was a *him*. The doctor agreed that since Diane had been feeling fine, the test was unnecessary. I felt a small swell of pride fill my chest. Another boy. Cool. Very cool. Man, I loved my kids.

I love My children, too.

As if someone pushed me firmly with a finger to my breastbone, I sat back in my chair. Was that how God felt about me? The same way I felt about my kids? I let the new thought simmer, a place in my heart gurgling with the idea. Air bubbles in a fish tank. I'd never thought about God that way. Awesome, as Renae would say.

The sound of a car driving past out front brought me back to Ida's front room. I watched as Olivia Marsden waited for the car to pass before backing her car out of the driveway across the street and driving off. With the back of my hand I brushed the tip of my nose. Sheesh, it felt like a dog's nose. Cold and a little damp. About right. If I didn't get a move on I'd be in the doghouse with a lot of people.

I pushed myself out of the chair, feeling the cold denim of my jeans press against my legs. *Better double-check the furnace.* Just as I thought the thought, the furnace kicked in, sending warm-tinged air out of the vent near my feet. I walked to the front door, stopping with one hand on the cold doorknob. I turned and looked back over my shoulder at the cabin-like quiet.

I wasn't a guy for fancy words, but the word "refuge" poked at my brain, a hunting dog flushing birds that were trying to stay hidden. It didn't make sense that Ida's ridiculously green couch could make me feel like that. Or her lumpy chair where I'd just sat. I stared at the cross made out of wooden matches and glitter that hung above her television. If I remembered right, Renae had made that in Vacation Bible School a long time ago. Next to the TV stood Ida's dark wood bookshelf filled with knickknacks, her autoharp, and a Bible. I walked over to the shelf and picked up the harp. Ida might like to pass some time by playing it in her room. I turned away, then back. Her Bible. I'd forgotten! She'd asked me to bring it and I'd forgotten. But then, she practically knew the whole thing by heart. I picked up the old Book. I'd take both of these things to her right now.

As I stepped out of the house I pulled the door closed behind me, twisting the knob to make sure it had locked. The strings of the autoharp tucked under my arm softly chummed. A chord that lingered in the cold morning air.

As if I was leaving church or something.

"Bye," I found myself muttering under my breath as I took the three steps to the sidewalk.

Bye?

As if I'd really been talking to someone.

And beauty is fleeting...

Ian

"I've ruled out a stroke." The doctor's words filtered through the thin veil of sleep I was trying to lose myself in.

"That's good." Dan sounded relieved.

I turned my head away from the both of them, lifted my knees from the hospital bedsheets, and turned onto my side. All I wanted to do was to curl into a ball and go to sleep. Or die.

I blocked out their voices as the image of my grotesque face loomed in my memory.

Ugly.

Horrible

Freak.

It wasn't hard to think of words to describe how I looked. Especially when I was trying to avoid the words that described how I felt.

Hollow.

Empty.

Terrified.

I pulled the thin, white bedsheet over my ear, as if that could block out my thoughts. It was as though the reflection of my distorted features had been seared into my mind with that one shocking look into the mirror. As I tucked my hand beneath my unfeeling right cheek, a sticky line of saliva smeared across my fingers. Gross. I wiped my hand against the pillowcase and tried to block out Dan and the doctor's conversation.

"...Bell's palsy," the doctor said. Out of the corner of my eye I could see him thread his stethoscope off his neck and place it on the rolling tray table near my bed.

"*What?*" Dan sounded as if the doctor had spoken a foreign language.

I didn't want to hear whatever was coming next, but in a hospital room the size of our bathroom at home, it was hard not to hear.

"We're not exactly sure what causes the disorder, but it seems to be linked to some sort of virus. You said your wife had the flu the past two days. Correct?"

I found myself nodding into the pillow. So much for not listening.

"Sometimes a viral infection will cause swelling of the facial nerves. There isn't a lot of room for expansion in the boney, cranial space, so sometimes these nerves will become compressed, resulting in a paralysis, or palsy, on one side of the face."

"I'm paralyzed?" Odd how clearly I could pronounce that particular, *awful* word, when most everything else came out sounding as though half my tongue had been glued to the bottom of my mouth.

Doctor Kuhn stepped to the side so I could see his face as he spoke to Dan and me. "In most cases the palsy is a temporary condition. It can last anywhere from a couple weeks to a few months. I—"

"Mmmost cay-shes?" My heart pounded inside my chest. I couldn't look like this for weeks or *months*. Like some...some... Thankfully, Dr. Kuhn didn't give me time to complete my thought.

"I suspect," he said, ignoring my interruption as if he couldn't hear the pounding coming from the drum inside me, "that we'll see some improvement in a couple of weeks. There's always the outside chance that some of the residual effects could be permanent but..." He paused to pick up his stethoscope. "Well, that's highly unlikely. Let's hope that's not the case here."

Hope not? Hope not!! I would rather die than walk around looking as if half my face had melted like a cheap candle. That's what I looked like. Melted wax.

"So what can we expect?" Leave it to Dan to get to the point.

Dr. Kuhn pulled a pen from his lab coat pocket. "Since we've ruled out anything more serious, I'll be discharging your wife today." He scribbled something on the clipboard lying on the tray table. "I'm going to want to patch her right eye until she regains better use of the muscles. It's quite common with this condition for the affected eye to only partially close until muscle function returns. We don't want it drying out. Cornea damage," he added, as though we knew all about these sorts of things. "I'm going to prescribe some steroid medication. That should help reduce the swelling of the facial nerves. Physical therapy should help with any residual effects." He clicked his pen. He'd said it all.

As he spoke I felt myself curling ever tighter into a fetal ball. I hoped Dan was listening closely because all I was hearing were giant words that were hitting the sides of my head like boulders falling from above.

Patch her eye. A patch? Over one eye? I'd rather have both my eyes completely covered than walk around looking like some deformed pirate. Before I had time to conjure up an image of myself, Dr. Kuhn had dropped the next rock.

Steroid medication. Steroids? Only athletes who had something to prove took those. Or people with odd diseases. The only thing I knew for a fact about steroids was that they made a person look puffed up. Balloonlike. No way! No way was I going to look like this…only worse. A fat pirate with a melted face. *No. No. No!* But even my internal screaming couldn't stop the good doctor.

Physical therapy, he said next. Only people who'd been in accidents or had surgery needed physical therapy. Not someone like… like…

It was starting to feel as though my heart was going to simply thump itself out of my chest. I took a deep breath. Gathering up my idea. Another breath. "What abow shurr-gery?"

Dr. Kuhn placated me with a smile and a slight shake of his head. "Only in rare cases is a surgical option considered for Bell's palsy patients. Typically these cases clear up on their own once the viral swelling subsides. As I said, there may be some lingering affect, but…" Another head shake. "You need to be patient, Jan." He might as well have reached out and patted my hand.

I turned onto my back so I could look him in both eyes. Even if my right eyelid was drooping like a cheap nylon I stared at him. I spoke slowly, carefully enunciating through the half of my mouth that wasn't paralyzed. "You don't undershtand. I already have an appoiyyment. For shurgery. I was going to have a face-lift. Next week. I can shtill have it. It will fix thishh."

Dr. Kuhn was nodding his head. Up. Down. Left. Right. Agreeing. Disagreeing. It was hard to tell.

I shot my eyes over to Dan. "Tell him," I said.

The same half smile from my husband.

He knew how hard I'd worked for that surgery. How badly I wanted it. Maybe now the surgery would be covered by insurance. Maybe this wasn't all bad. "Tell him!"

Dan glanced at the doctor, then back to me, and said, "She's scheduled for plastic surgery on the seventh."

"Coshmetic surgery," I inserted as firmly as I knew how to under the circumstances.

"She was going to have a face-lift." Dan's eyes were tap-dancing between Dr. Kuhn and me. "I'd taken out a loan. If surgery can help, we can afford it…" His voice trailed off into nothing as Dr. Kuhn held up a hand.

"This condition involves the underlying muscular structure of the face. I'm afraid a cosmetic procedure at this time is not an option. I think if you—"

"Bu—" I tried to interrupt.

Dr. Kuhn stopped me with a lifted finger. "I think if you give this time you will be surprised at the recovery process of the human body." He paused as if waiting for my rebuttal, and then he said, "I'll write up orders for you to begin physical therapy. I'm assuming you'll want to do that in Brewster?"

When I didn't move, Dan nodded his head for me.

"Okay, then." Dr. Kuhn shook Dan's hand and then, when I didn't offer my hand, gave my shoulder a gentle squeeze. "Give it time," he said again.

Time! Ha! Some doctor. I didn't have time to look ugly. Disfigured.

"I'll send in the nurse so she can get you ready for discharge." I heard the word too late. Dr. Kuhn was gone. "Dishcharge?" I said to Dan. "I can't go outshide looking like thish." I could feel my left eye open wide, my right eye still half shut. I brushed my hand against my face as though my touch could make my eye open normally. All I got for my effort was a wet finger as a line of tears dripped from my half-closed, drooling right eye.

"Someone gets to go home today!" A nurse I hadn't seen in the day since I'd been admitted to the Carlton hospital entered the room. "I'll go over the doctor's instructions with you and you'll be all set."

I listened dumbly as she pressed a small, plastic bottle of eye drops into my hand. "Use these during the day to make sure your eye stays lubricated. A couple drops before bed and then place this covering over the eye." She laid a curved, cookie-sized dome on the sheet covering my lap. Gauze and tape followed. "This will protect your eye from drying out during the night." She blabbered on. I only hoped Dan was listening. I planned to have nothing to do with any of this.

"Thank you," I mumbled automatically as the nurse wheeled me out of the hospital toward our idling car. I ducked my head as an older couple headed my direction on the sidewalk. I didn't want anyone to see me this way, even if I didn't know them. Even if they were old and saggy themselves. More importantly, I didn't want to see what their faces might look like if they got a glimpse of me.

"I know how anxious you were to have your cosmetic procedure done." Dr. Peters pressed his lips together into a thin line. "But I'm afraid the surgery I had planned isn't possible until your underlying condition improves."

I kept my face at a downward angle, tilting my head so that my long hair fell across the right side of my face as if it were a veil. It had taken all the nerve I could muster to come to this impromptu appointment in the first place. It was two days before my face-lift was to have taken place, and here I sat, needing the work done more than ever, as Dr. Peters told me he couldn't do it. Wouldn't do it.

I lifted my head to look at him, holding my hand over the right side of my melted face. Even as I began to speak I could feel the tug of muscles on the good side of my face as they tried to accommodate for the side of my face that had given up. "But, there has to be someshing you can do."

Dr. Peters ran a hand across the back of his neck. "What I recommend is that you follow through with the therapy and medication Dr. Kuhn prescribed. Eventually your facial muscles should rebound. I would expect a good outcome given the statistics for this disorder. Then we can take another look at the cosmetic work you wanted done."

My half-open right eye was already watering. Now tears started falling from my left eye as well. Suddenly, the face-lift I'd been dreaming of seemed as sugary as frosting. I *needed* this surgery for another reason altogether. My lips tugged and distorted as I forced the words out of my tear-clogged throat. "All I want is to look normal again."

This time the doctor really did reach over and pat my hand. "Best of luck to you Mrs. Jordan," he said. "Come and see me again when your condition improves. We'll see what we can do." Practiced words if I'd ever heard them.

I drew my hand out of his grasp. There were words elbowing for position on the tip of my sluggish tongue. I bit them back. "Than-nk you." I should have known better than to try and smile. I could feel the lopsided scrawl that pulled my lips into a shape I didn't want to try and imagine. I bowed my head, letting my hair do its magic trick across my face and make it disappear. I hoped that by the time I picked up my purse and had to lift my face the doctor would be long gone.

"Jan, you can't just sit here forever!" Dan paced in front of me while I sat in a corner of the couch. The same place I'd been sitting for the past three days. When I wasn't curled up in bed, that is. "You have to do something. You have a life to live."

"No, I don't." My voice was flat. I would never go out in public looking like this. He had to know that.

"What? You're going to sit on the couch for the rest of your life? What about Joey? You don't plan to go to any of his ball games? His teacher's conferences?"

Not if I looked like this.

"I'm going to have to hire someone to help me prepare taxes. Couldn't you at least do that?"

Weakly I shrugged my shoulders and hung my head.

"What about your friends? Libby called again. What's that... three times now? And you still won't talk to her."

I looked up sharply. "You diwdn't tell her? Diwd you?"

"Of course I told her. She's one of your best friends. How long do you think she'll keep trying?"

I stubbornly shook my disfigured face. Who would want to be friends with someone who looked like me?

Dan held his hands in midair, lifting the air as though sifting for words. Finally, he let his arms drop to his sides. "I don't know what to do."

I didn't either.

～

"Mom?" Joey was standing by the couch with his backpack on his shoulder.

I roused myself from the dream I'd been having. I wasn't sure if he was home from school or just leaving. It was difficult to climb out from the dreamworld I'd been living in for the past week. The perfect world where I was young again. Pretty again. "What?" I asked, my voice a croak.

"I'm going to school now." So it was morning. Another day to crawl through.

"Okay," I said, anxious only to have him go so I could get back to dreamland.

"Uh." He tapped one tennis shoe against the fabric of the couch until I looked up at him. He didn't cringe when he met my eyes. How could he stand it? To look right at me like that? Either he was a good actor or someone had done a good job raising my kid. "Dad said to tell you that you have a physical therapy appointment at the nursing home at ten-thirty."

"What?" My throat was clearer now, filled with a combination of wonder and fear at the two things I'd just heard Joey say. I wasn't sure how to respond. Surprise at how easily Joey had called Dan *"Dad"* after the past years of calling him "Dan." As if suddenly the two of them were in this together. Without me. The first bit of emotion I'd felt in a week, a lonely throb, tugged somewhere near my heart.

But even more surprising was how Joey had the nerve to tell me about the therapy appointment Dan must have arranged behind my back. The chicken. A flash of anger zapped at my stomach.

"Tell Dad I won't be going."

"He said to tell you that Olivia Marsden will pick you up at a quarter after. I gotta go now or I'm gonna be late for school."

The door slammed behind him before I had a chance to say, "Tell Dad to tell Olivia not to come."

Now what? Refusing to go and throwing a fit in front of Dan was one thing. It was something else entirely when it came to my friend. I could feel my one good eye narrow. My husband had pulled a sly trick.

I threw back the cotton blanket that had been my cocoon these past few days and sat up. A wave of dizziness tilted me sideways. Other than trips to the bathroom, where I avoided the mirror like the plague, and the couple nights I'd slept in bed with Dan, the couch had become my home. I waited while the lightheaded feeling passed, watching the coffee table as a dried piece of cheddar cheese and a brown apple slice did a woozy dance in front of my eyes. A mug of cold tea bounced along. So, I had eaten. I hardly remembered.

I put my elbows on my knees and rested my head in my cupped hands, wondering if it was safe for me to stand up. The right side of my face felt crusty and damp. Old tears and new clumped together, a reminder of the hell I was still living in.

It would only get worse if Libby saw me like this, the right side of my face a misshapen shell of who I'd been. I had to either call her or call Dan. Somehow I had to let her know not to come over.

I reached forward, steadying my hand on the littered coffee table. A box of Kleenex. My eye patch and gauze. The drops I'd forced myself to use only because my eye felt lined with sandpaper if I didn't. A stack of mail-order catalogs and the latest *InStyle* magazine. Bits of old food on my favorite antique-pink plate. Three white carnations in a narrow vase. Dan had tried to make this as palatable as he could.

Once again a bit of emotion tugged at me. *No!* I swallowed, trying to push it away. I didn't want to *feel* anything.

My eyes fell on an envelope propped against the side of the tissue box. I had a vague recollection of Dan telling me I had mail. Me mumbling, "I don't care." He must have left it there.

I picked it up, recognizing Olivia's handwriting from recipes we'd exchanged in times past. I slid my thumb along the top crease of the thick, cream-colored envelope. She was a writer. I should have expected she'd have something to say when I refused to take her phone calls. As I drew the blue-outlined correspondence card from the envelope, I closed my eyes, well, as much as I could close the misshapen right one, and braced myself for what Libby might write.

I read:

Dear Jan—

I found the Bible verse we talked about last week when you stopped by. I guess there was a reason God waited until now for me to find it. I hope it's helpful for you.

"Don't be concerned about the outward beauty that depends on fancy hairstyles, expensive jewelry, or beautiful clothes. You should be known for the beauty that comes from within, the unfading beauty of a gentle and quiet spirit, which is so precious to God." 1 Peter 3:3-4.

I'm praying for you. I'll call soon. Feel better.

Libby

Feel better? Ha! This had nothing to do with how I *felt*. Everything to do with how I *looked*. Awful. Ugly. A creature, not a person.

I felt like ripping the card into a million pieces. Instead, I fingered the finely woven card as my eyes drifted back over the words Libby had so carefully copied. *Don't be concerned with outward beauty...*

How could I *not* be concerned when I looked so awful?

You should be known for the beauty that comes from within...

What was *inside* me was causing all this. A virus. A disorder. Muscles that refused to do what they were supposed to. I might be misshapen for the rest of my life...

...the unfading beauty of a gentle and quiet spirit...

Unfading?

My eyes lingered on that one word. Unfading. Two words. Unfading beauty. Two words I hadn't thought to string together before.

How could beauty be unfading? Didn't everyone grow old? Everyone, everything, wrinkle and sag? Pale? That was the nature of things. Even the carnations Dan had placed on the coffee table a few days ago were beginning to wilt. Die. Fade.

Curious, how soft that phrase sounded. I whispered it out loud, "Unfading beauty." Odd comfort, as nothing else had been this past week.

⁓

As I stepped out of the shower, I made sure my eyes stayed far away from the steamy mirror. I had decided I would take the time under the water to think of a good excuse why I couldn't go to the therapy appointment with Libby. As I toweled myself off, I now knew how the crazy people on *Survivor* must feel after their first hot shower in weeks. I shuddered to think that it had been possibly five days since I'd last been this clean. I was surprised Dan and Joey hadn't simply picked me up off the couch by my wrists and ankles and tossed me into a full tub, nightgown and all.

I hung the towel over a rack and slipped into a silky robe, feeling almost human again. Did I dare look into the mirror? I wasn't naïve enough to think the hot water had washed away my palsy. I could feel by a simple twitch of my lips that the right side of my face was still uncooperative. Through my right eye I could see the blur of my eyelashes as they perched on the edge of my drooping eyelid. Did I dare look? How would I put on makeup if I didn't?

I closed my eyes and took a deep breath, squaring myself in front of the counter as I'd done hundreds of mornings before. I found myself repeating the words from Libby's card. *Don't be concerned with outward beauty. Don't be concerned with outward beauty.* Whatever I looked like when I opened my eyes, I wasn't going to scream. I was going to…

Well, I didn't know what I was going to do, but I'd soon find out. One more deep breath. A slow exhale. I lifted my lids just a little. My face was a blur. Soft. A dreamy view of reality. Vision through a kind camera. A loving director.

That's how Dan sees you. How I see you. Don't be concerned about outward beauty.

I opened my eyes a bit more. My right eye wouldn't lift any further. My left eyelid hovered a bit, as if it didn't want to do more than its companion, then it opened fully. There I was. Staring back at myself. The memory of what I *had* looked like was facing the reality of who I was now.

My heart thumped in my chest. As if I was meeting a new, nervous version of myself.

Remember, you don't have any makeup on.

As if that would hide what I was seeing.

I examined the left side of my face. It was pale, my eye slightly swollen from days of lying on the couch with my head against a pillow. A dark circle hung below my eye. Concealer would take care of that and the redness around my nose. Foundation to cover it all. Crying had never been good for my complexion.

I turned my eyes to the right, steeling myself for the worst. My face wasn't nearly as grotesque as my mind had remembered. My right eyelid hung at half-mast, a sleepy me. The nostril of my nose had a slight skew to it, hardly noticeable unless you were inspecting. It was my mouth where the real damage showed, my lips looking as if a little kid had been trying to draw a smile with a pale, maroon Crayon and had tired of the effort halfway through. An upward curve on the left, a downward scrawl on the right. No amount of concealer or lipstick could ever hide that.

Don't be concerned with outward beauty.

I closed my eyes against the image in the mirror. *You're the pretty one.* One look at my mother's face when she'd come to see me in the hospital told me that wasn't true anymore. What else was there if I didn't have my looks? I'd depended on my long blonde hair, my big brown eyes, and my brilliant smile my whole life. More than a few times that combination had gotten me my way…or a guy. Or both. All I had left was my long hair and even that wasn't completely natural anymore.

You should be known for beauty that comes from inside.

I looked intently into the mirror. Leaned close. Tried to look past the surface. Past the crinkles at the corners of my eyes. Past the wilt that was now the right side of my face. What was inside of all that?

The unfading beauty of a gentle and quiet spirit.

My breath fogged the mirror as a sigh escaped the jagged line that was now my lips. Amazing the way the words Libby had written had embedded themselves into my mind. Me, who kept a stack of Happy Belated Birthday cards on standby, was suddenly remembering a Bible verse.

I pulled open the drawer that housed my stash of makeup. If Libby had penned the words, it was just possible that she believed them as well. If I was going to chance letting anyone see me like this, it would be her. But first I'd do my best to camouflage what was left of my face. The expensive products I'd bought with my discount at Elizabeth's had better do the trick now.

Fifteen minutes later I gazed into the mirror a final time.

A mask.

That's what my face looked like. A mask. As if I were trying, desperately, to hide something that couldn't be concealed even by the best magician. Or makeup.

I turned the water faucet on high and hot, wetting a bar of glycerin soap under the fast-moving stream. When my hands were covered with foamy lather I rubbed them into my face, scrubbing hard. Washing pricey makeup down the drain along with my hope that makeup might fool any eyes that happened my way.

I splashed steaming water across my face, over and over and over again. If Libby wanted to see beauty that came from within, she would. Because that's all I had left.

If there was any there to begin with.

Ida

"Goood, Ida. That's good. Now let's do it again."

I touched the tip of my thick-soled beige shoe to the floor and pressed down. I held it there, watching for Jodi's nod to tell me I could lift it up. The physical therapy I was doing wasn't my favorite activity. It was hard work for an old glue horse like me. But working with Jodi was better than having Wendy screaming in my ears.

"Good girl!" Jodi flashed me a smile as her eyes drifted toward the doorway. Maybe my old-lady babbling wasn't interesting enough for her. "Do it again." Her eyes bounced to the door a second time. "We'll get you out of that wheelchair and using a walker in no time if you keep this up."

"Acht, dat vouldt be goot." I had a notion she said that to all the people here, but I pushed my foot down onto the floor one more time anyway. It would be good to be able to walk on my own two feet again. Between the pin in my hip, the pneumonia, and the blood clot, I'd experienced setbacks on the path to my feet. Jodi had told me I should have been up and walking months ago. Easy for her to say with her skinny, strong body as a backup plan. I wasn't so sure I trusted my legs enough to put them under me just yet. Especially when ten times of pushing my left foot and then my right foot onto the floor left me in a huff for air. I could think of all kinds of things Fred would have said about a weakling like me.

"That's good for today." Jodi released me from the foot exercise with a nod. "Let's move you over to the wall and we'll have you do some upper extremity exercises." She twirled my wheelchair as if it were a child's top and pushed me toward the handles that hung from thin ropes on the white, block wall. "It's not all about your feet. We have to get your arms in shape to use that walker, too, you know." Again, she spun me around so that the back of my chair was against the wall. "Left hand," she said absently, putting a hand grip attached to a rope into my left hand. "Right hand. There." Her eyes darted to the clock on the wall. "We'll get you going on this before my next client shows up."

"Here you are!" Kenny poked his head into the therapy room. "I've been looking all over for you."

"Ah, yes," Jodi sighed, "you and all the other handsome men in town." She wiggled her ringless left hand at him.

"Jodi, Jodi," Kenny said as he walked into the room hiking at his waistband. "One of these days I'll let you get your lucky hands on me. You just about had a chance with this wrist of mine." He held up his right arm. "But I toughed it out on my own."

"What a *man*." Jodi winked at me.

"Tell that to Diane." He tugged at his belt again, then put a warm hand on my shoulder. "This is the gal I'm looking for." He squatted down beside my chair. "I looked in your room but you weren't there. Or in the activities room. I thought maybe you ran off with one of those good-looking guys around here."

Kenny was always teasing. "You didn't giff me enough uff a headt start iff we're playing hidt-andt-seek." It was good to see his face.

"Tell you what," Jodi said. "My next appointment will be here soon. I'm going to run to the little girl's room while you two visit. Ida—" She pointed at me. "You keep those arms moving while you talk. Kenny—" She pointed a finger at my nephew. "You're in charge of making sure she does her exercises."

"Yes, ma'am." As Jodi left, Kenny saluted as if he'd been in the army.

I tugged at the handles that were in my hands. First one, then the other. "You're early dis morning."

"Yeah," he said, standing now. "Diane has a doctor appointment over in Carlton close to noon and I have to drive her. I left Pete in charge at the station." He held up two crossed fingers. "I hope everything goes okay."

"You shouldt pray insteadt of vishing."

"Well…" He shuffled his feet against the floor. "I've been doing some of that, too." He pulled a chair near to my wheelchair and sat down backward on it. His hands rested across the backrest, his legs straddled the seat as if he was sitting on an orange vinyl horse. "Everything looks good over at your house. That For Sale sign is still in the front yard. No lookers yet."

"In Got's goot time," I said, pulling the weight in my right hand forward. I didn't like to think much about my cozy house sitting all empty. "How iss Diane feeling?"

He lifted his eyebrows and chuckled. "Big."

"So you'ff gott a shtubborn baby. Chust like Daddy. A baby dat hass a mindt of its own already."

"Yeah. Diane wishes he would make up his mind to join us."

"*He?* Iss it a him? Do you already know that?"

"Diane isn't convinced, but I am. I've just got a hunch that it's a boy." His face was covered with a silly grin. "Guess what we're going to name him?"

"Acht." I swung my left arm forward, swatting at the air at the same time I was doing my exercise. "The names nowadays are so strange to me, I don't effen vant to take a chance. You chust tell me."

Kenny sat tall in his saddle. "Kenny Jr."

It wasn't hard to figure how much my nephew was looking forward to this new little guy. I felt a tingle in my arms. Goose bumps running up and down. "A goot name," I said, smiling back at him. I well remembered the little boy they lost too early. I knew that feeling from my own time of sorrow. It was good to know this baby would be born into arms that were ready to hold him. "So you're going to be a papa again. You're going to haff a lot of moutt's to feedt around your table."

"I know." Kenny glanced at the floor, nodding his head. With a slight shake he lifted it. "I wish the station were doing better." He heaved a sigh. "And I imagine Diane will have her hands full when she gets home from the hospital. I just hope she has enough time to keep doing the books. I'm a *dummkopf* when it comes to that."

It had been ages since I'd heard that old German word. I laughed. "Even dumbheadts can learn new tings iff they haff to."

He knocked at the side of his head. "I might have to. But let's pray I don't."

I continued to swing my arms up and down on the handles. "Dat's about the only ting that's left for me."

Kenny tilted his head. "What's left for you?"

"Praying," I answered. "I'm goot for not much else these days. But I can shtill pray." I rolled my eyes heavenward. "Tank the Lordt for small tings. Iss there anyting special I could pray about for you, Kenny? I'vff got all da time in the vorldt."

He was silent a minute, and then, just as he started to speak, Jodi hurried back into the therapy room. "You two still at it? Ida, you're going to be able to compete in a bodybuilding contest if you keep working like that. I think you've done enough for today. Kenny must be a good coach for you to keep working all this time."

Kenny bit back whatever he had been about to say and instead said, "Hey, what can I tell you? It's my natural charm."

Jodi laughed. "I don't think they call it *charm* down at the café." Jodi unlocked the brakes of my wheelchair. "You worked hard for me today, Ida. Thank you."

It was my turn to look at the floor. It had been a long time since I'd been praised for much of anything. This time goose bumps ran across my shoulders.

Jodi pulled my chair away from the wall and turned the back of it toward Kenny. "Would you mind pushing Ida back to her room? My next client is on her way."

"No problem," Kenny said, grabbing the yellowed plastic handles and turning me toward the doorway.

"How's Diane?" Jodi asked before he had a chance to start pushing my chair. "Isn't she about due?"

"She was due three days ago," Kenny stated. I stared in the opposite direction as he turned back to Jodi, resting his beefy hand on my shoulder. "We're heading to Carlton in about an hour. The doctor's going to see about inducing her. Maybe tomorrow. We're going to have Ben and Cindy watch the kids overnight."

My other nephew, Kenny's twin brother Ben.... A young man with a big-shot job. Administrator of Brewster's small hospital. And no time to spare to visit an old aunt like me. His wife, Cindy, was the director of nurses here at the home. At least she had a minute now and then to walk down the hall and squeeze my wrinkled hand. But it was Kenny, with his big stomach and bigger heart, who was my favorite. Even if he did act like a big Dennis the Menace most of the time, a person couldn't help but have a soft spot for his teasing and the time he took to visit an old woman like me. I reached my hand back to my shoulder and found his hand resting there. I put my hand on top of his and let it relax.

"Good luck," Jodi said as Kenny slid his hand from under mine.

"Thanks," he said as he began to push my chair forward.

He must have had his head turned back toward Jodi. Must not have even glanced where we were going. "Kenn—!" The partial word came out too late. My two beige shoes and the metal footrests of my chair rammed into the shins of a woman who had just stepped into the doorway.

"Owwch!" she said as her lopsided mouth twisted at the garbled word. She did a quick dance backward, turning her face away from us.

"Oh, man! Sorry!" Kenny yanked me away from her. If he wasn't careful, I'd be in therapy for whiplash. "Are you okay?"

The woman nodded. Her long blonde hair was waving like a surrender flag, her face completely hidden. Another woman stepped in front of her saying, "I think she'll be fine."

It was my across-the-street neighbor Olivia Marsden! I held out a hand. "Oliffia!" What a good feeling to see her. As if we were out on our sidewalks waving hello on a warm spring morning.

"Ida!" She took my hand in both of hers, rubbing it gently between her palms. "I've been meaning to get over here and see you. I miss having you across the street."

"Yah, I miss it, too. But dis iss my home now. It's not so badt." Jodi had stepped into our small circle and I caught her eye. "Except for the slavffe driffers like dis one." I pointed a finger at Jodi.

Olivia laughed and then said, "I see your house is for sale. I can't imagine who will ever be a better neighbor than you. I know no one else will ever bring me kuchen like you make."

A proud feeling throbbed behind my breastbone. I waved a hand at her good words. It wouldn't do to get a big head over baking I couldn't do anymore.

"Has there been any interest in the house?" Olivia was looking at Kenny.

"Not yet," he said. "If you know of someone looking, send them my way." He rolled my wheelchair back and forth, as if waiting for a starting gun. "I'd better be off. I have to get Diane over to Carlton yet this morning."

"Then you'd better go," Olivia said. While we had been talking, the other woman with Olivia somehow slipped around us into the therapy room. Olivia reached down and squeezed my hand. "I promise I'll come have a real visit with you soon, Ida."

"You do dat." I squeezed her hand back. It felt good to have company to look forward to.

Kenny pushed me through the doorway, pausing only slightly as he called back over his shoulder to the silent woman, "Sorry again." He wheeled me a few steps down the hall, then leaned forward as he walked and whispered near my ear. "Do you know who that other lady was? The one I bumped you into?"

In my mind I saw her long hair, her twisted mouth. A brief glimpse of brown eyes that looked plain. And sad. Nothing familiar except for the sad part. I recognized that feeling all too well these days. "No." I found myself shaking my head and saying back to Kenny, "I don't know her."

"Sure you do," he said, speaking just a little louder now, but still bent near my ear, as though this was an important, secret person he was telling me about. "That was Jan Jordan. Dan Jordan's wife."

I recalled the last time I'd seen Mrs. Jordan. At Pumpkin Fest, where she'd been prancing around the old gymnasium in high heels and tight clothes, looking like a magazine model for a makeup advertisement. This woman couldn't have been the same lady.

"Dan said at coffee that she'd had the flu really bad," Kenny went on. "Said she ended up with…Bell pall? Something like that. Man. I wonder what happened?"

I shook my head. It was hard to bring together the picture I had in my head with the one who had been standing in front of me.

You need to pray for her.

Okay, then. I crossed my cardigan sweater over my front. God was never wrong when it came to telling me who to pray for.

"Here we are." Kenny cornered my wheelchair into my room. My roommate, Verna Stolz, was crocheting one of her never-ending stream of doilies. Kenny turned me at a right angle to her, then put his hands in the small of his back, stretching big. "Well, I'd better get a move on. If there's—"

"Kenny!" Cindy hurried into the room a that moment. "I just talked to Pete. He said Diane called and her water has broken. He was supposed to find you. Go!" She waved as if her hands would move Kenny faster. "Go! Go!"

"All right, already." Kenny took the time to heave a big sigh. "I've done this before, you know." He ambled toward the door with a smile. "My little boy is on the way!" He rubbed his hands together as if he couldn't wait to hold Kenny Jr. "One more all-star for the Pearson team."

"Have you ever delivered a baby in a car?" Cindy was a nurse. She knew what could happen.

"Okay. Yeah. You're right." Suddenly, the new papa was moving, sounding nervous. "Renae and Billy are at school. What about Paige? What are we going to do with her? Oh, man." He scrubbed at his face, pulled his cap off, and then tugged it back on. "I thought I was ready."

Cindy stepped beside him. "I'll ride home with you. If it looks as though Diane will be able to make it to Carlton, I'll bring Paige back here with me. I'll pick up the other two after school. Someone will cover for me. We'll figure something out." She put a hand on Kenny's back. "It's going to be fine, but we need to go now."

Kenny was nodding. His head looked like one of those funny spring-headed Chihuahua dogs that bobbled along on the back dash of a car.

Start praying, Ida.

An odd hand of worry pressed against my heart. This wasn't the kind of reminder I'd expected from God just now. My prayers for new babies, and new papas, were usually filled with happiness. This urging from God was different.

I swatted at the air with my hand. "Get. Go on, now."

Finally, in this strange new home of mine, I had important work to do. Praying for Jan Jordan. Praying for Kenny. Or was it the baby I was to pray for? Maybe all of them.

"Mooff." Both my hands hurried them toward the door.

The sooner they left, the sooner I could start my prayers.

Kenny

"We're almost there!" My frantic announcement was met with a slow, deep moan from the passenger side of the car.

"Mmmmmmmm…Uuuuuuuuu…"

"Breathe, Diane. Breathe!" I spun the steering wheel, practically two-wheeling the corner to the Carlton hospital. I sucked in a deep breath of my own as the emergency entrance came into view. "We're here!" I slammed on the brakes. At least now, if the baby came, there'd be someone who knew what they were doing.

I honked the horn of the car and then jumped out. I wasn't sure if I should run inside the emergency room and yell, "I need a doctor outside!" the way I'd seen plenty of gonna-be dads do on TV or if I should go around to Diane's side of the car and…and what? Deliver a baby?

I raced through the automatic doors leading into the emergency room. Four people in chairs stared at me wide-eyed. I must have looked spooked. Okay, so I was.

"Where's a doctor?" I asked, flipping my head from side to side, ready to grab the first white coat I saw.

Out of nowhere two men who seemed to belong there stood in front of me. "Do you need something?" the green-scrub-suited one asked.

"My wife!" I pointed outside. "A baby!" At least I managed to get out what was important.

The two men ran outside, calling for a gurney. I relaxed. Someone else was now in charge of delivering my little boy. This was turning out to be just like *ER*. I looked over my shoulder for Dr.

Carter, Diane's favorite TV doctor. A gurney whizzed by me, popping my television fantasy. This wasn't TV, this was real!

⌁

We'd made it to a delivery room. I was in as much of a sweat as Diane. Her obstetrician, Dr. Deaver, had come to check on her twice already. I hadn't had to drive like a maniac, after all. For being in such a hurry, this was taking a long time. "Is everything okay?"

Dr. Deaver looked up from his examination of Diane's...well... progress. He pushed the short stool he was crouched on away from the exam bed and stood up. "Everything is coming along nicely." He stripped plastic gloves from his hands as he spoke, turning to throw them into a nearby garbage can. "I would have expected from your previous history," he cast a glance at my poor wife, "that this baby would want to get out of there a little faster. But," he smiled slightly and shook his head, "I've learned Mother Nature has her own timetable."

"So-oo do-es...God." Diane forced the words out between Lamaze-trained breaths of air.

Dr. Deaver nodded. "Yes. I've learned that, too." He put a hand on Diane's sheet-covered knee. "Hang in there. This baby will be here soon enough."

"So-oo, every-thing's ok-ay?" I found myself matching Diane breath for breath and was becoming a little dizzy. I forced myself to inhale deeply against her panting.

"Everything's fine." Dr. Deaver patted my shoulder. "The nurse will keep a watch on things and call me when the baby is ready to deliver. It shouldn't be too much longer."

"Heh-heh," I said rubbing my hands together as the doctor left the room. "Just a little bit longer and Kenny Jr. will be here. Atta boy. Come to Papa, Slugger."

Diane rolled her eyes at me. She was between contractions and could scoff at what I knew for a fact. "You do realize this baby has as much a chance of being a girl as a boy? I didn't have an ultrasound, you know. It could be either."

"Nope," I said. "It's a boy." I sat in a chair and laced my hands behind my head.

"Kenny, wishful thinking won't change what's inside here." She patted her stomach.

"Nothing's going to need changing except a diaper. It's a boy."

My statement was met with a sharp intake of air. Diane began panting again. Time would soon enough prove me right. I stood by her side, a hand on her arm.

"*Don't.*" Quick breath. "*Touch.*" Another. "*Me.*"

All righty. I took away my hand. We'd been through this before. Soon. Very soon we'd be holding our new son.

～

"The head is crowning." Dr. Deaver wasn't nearly as excited as I was. He looked up from his perch at the far end of the bed. "Everyone doing okay?"

"Just great!" I gave him a thumbs-up.

"Speeee-ak forrrr yourrrrrsellllllfff." Diane pushed along with the words.

The nurse leaned over. "A couple good pushes like that and we'll have a baby. You're doing great."

"I've got a head." Dr. Deaver started calling the play-by-play. "Tuuurning. Here are the shoulders. Come on. A good push now, Diane. There… There…" A small, wet, suction sound. A baby! "It's a boy!"

"Ha!" I yelled into the room. "I told you!" I did a little end zone dance on my end of the playing field.

A frail cry that grew louder. Downright ornery.

Diane pushed her chin back and grinned up at me. "You were right."

"Darn tootin' I was!" I was already imagining the bragging I was going to be able to do down at the station. Bubblegum cigars for everyone.

Dr. Deaver handed my baby linebacker off to a nurse. "We need another push here, Diane. Then we'll be finished."

Even though there was still action on the playing field, I was watching what was going on over on the sidelines. The nurse was clearing out the baby's nose, gently wiping his body with a damp cloth. My little guy was as red as a San Francisco 49er's uniform. Kenny Jr. Ah, I liked the sound of that.

"There. Got it." Dr. Deaver handed a silver basin off to another nurse and sat back. "Congratulations," he said to both of us. "You got your boy. Any—"

"Doctor." The nurse interrupted. "Could you step over here?"

Except for the soft squalls coming from my son, the room suddenly grew eerily quiet.

"Is something wrong?" Diane lifted her head off the pillow, craning her neck to see what was going on. When no one spoke she said, nervouslike, "Kenny?"

All I could do was repeat her question. "Is something wrong?"

One of the nurses shot a worried glance over her shoulder. "Everything's fine. The doctor is checking your baby over. We do the Apgar test on all new babies. There's nothing to worry about. This is normal procedure. We check for color, respiratory rate, heart rate, muscle tone…"

She was babbling. A sneak play to divert our attention to what was really going on. I walked over there. If something was happening to my son, I wanted to know about it. Now. "What's—"

Holding a hand to my chest, the nurse ran interference. "Mr. Pearson. We need to let the doctor do his job."

"It's okay," Dr. Deaver said, his voice resigned. "This is his son."

Two steps and I was there, looking down at my little boy. He looked fine. His face a little smushed, his body a little red, but for a baby who had just done a ninety-yard run down a birth canal, he looked fine.

"I can't see anything wrong," I said, looking first at the doctor and then at the two nurses.

"What's *wrong*?" Diane's voice was tinged with fear.

"It's okay, Diane," I replied with what I hoped was a reassuring glance over my shoulder. Whatever it was couldn't be too terrible.

After all, our baby was breathing, kicking, and crying softly. A quick glance accounted for all his fingers and toes. "I don't understand. What—?"

"Mr. Pearson," Dr. Deaver began. A warning flag started waving in my mind. Not a good sign when he'd been calling me Kenny for years. "Uh, Kenny," he corrected. I breathed a little easier. Not for long. "I want you to look at some things." He gestured to my son with his hand, brushing his large finger across my baby's face. "Do you notice the flat facial profile and the depressed nasal bridge?"

Well, sure I did. "All our kids have looked kind of…" I searched for the word, found not a technical one, but a word that would do, "*squished* when they were first born." I let out a nervous, low chuckle. "Hey, look at me." I pointed a finger at my face. "I'm not the greatest-looking guy in the world. So, he takes after me. It could be worse."

Dr. Deaver ignored my diagnosis. "You will also notice the upward slant of the eyes and the epicanthal folds here." He pointed to the inside corners of the baby's eyes where the skin was folded over. Tiny pleats. "Then there's this." He picked up my son's small hand and turned his palm up, uncurling the miniature fingers, pointing to a deep crease across the flat of his hand.

"I've got that too," I said a bit too loudly, holding up my hand to prove my point. "It's called a 'life line,' right?" I was no doctor, but that much I knew. I looked at my palm, where two deep lines grooved my hand. I looked at my son's, where only one deep furrow marked his palm. "What's the big deal? I don't get—"

Dr. Deaver knew better than to argue with a lummox like me. "All these symptoms, along with the muscle hypotonia and some notice-able hyperflexibility lead me to believe your child has Down syn-drome." He paused as though waiting for me to explode. Say something. When I didn't, he added, "Of course I'm going to run some tests to confirm the diagnosis. The first one we'll do is a kary-otype, a study of the chromosomes. That will be the definitive test."

"I don't get—I don't—I—" I combed my fingers against my face. I looked over at Diane, lying exhausted on the bed and silently crying. She'd heard. In three steps I was by her side, my hand holding hers.

I spoke for both of us. "Does this mean he's…" I filled my lungs with what felt like false courage. "Does this mean he's…retarded?"

The nurses tended to the baby as Dr. Deaver moved to Diane and me. "There are many misconceptions about the abilities of children with Down syndrome. Like all of us, each child is unique. It will take some time for us…for you two, to fully know the physical and intellectual functions of your child." He looked down at his hands. "I'm sorry. I know this is not the outcome you had planned. But I think you will—"

"The outcome we had *planned?!*" I snorted at the doctor. "We didn't even *plan* on having this kid. He just *happened!* And now… this?" I waved my arm in the direction of the baby as unsaid words bombarded my mind. *Embarrassment. Shame. What was everyone in Brewster going to think? Say behind my back? "Kenny Pearson couldn't even have a normal kid! Their kid is retarded."*

"Couldn't you have figured this out ahead of time?!" I lashed out with words I could say. "Couldn't you have done something to prevent it?"

"Well…had we suspected problems we could have done an ultrasound. Run some other tests." How could Dr. Deaver sound so calm? I knew. This wasn't *his* kid! He continued defending himself. "The results of the tests, however, would not have changed the outcome of the pregnancy. Down syndrome cannot be prevented," he paused, and then added, "unless the pregnancy is terminated."

"No!" Diane spoke for the first time since we'd been given the news. "I don't care what those tests would have shown. I would have had this baby no matter what!"

No matter *what?* How could she say that? Couldn't she imagine what the people in Brewster were going to say about our kid? I could already hear every word and then some. What would the kids in school say? If he was even smart enough to go to school. *No matter what?* No…I couldn't say that. I pulled my hand out of hers and crossed my arms over my chest, armor against the anger and disappointment that were warring inside my body.

Out of the corner of my eye I could see that the nurses on the side-lines had finished wiping off the baby. They'd tightly wrapped him in a blue blanket and put a blue knit cap on his tiny head. They were cooing over him. Smiling. Making faces. As if he were a normal kid.

Normal kid. Ha! He'd never be normal. Never.

One of the nurses picked up the bundle and turned our way. "Would you like to hold your son?" she asked, holding him out to me.

My arms felt glued to my chest. Quickly, I shook my head. No. I didn't want to hold him. Couldn't.

"Here's your mama," the nurse said, tucking the baby next to Diane. Already his tiny head was rooting around for a meal.

Sure, another mouth to feed. And who knew what kind of medical bills a kid like this would cause. And for what? He'd never be normal. Ever.

The nurse stood by Diane, tucking her index finger into the baby's tiny fist. "You've got a hungry guy there," she said. "It's hard work being born."

Diane smiled down at the kid. Kissed the skin just under the edge of the knit cap, just as she'd done with our other three when they were born. How could she feel the same way about this one?

The nurse stroked the side of the baby's face with the back of her finger. "Have you picked out a name yet?"

Diane looked up at me. At my eyes that were narrowing themselves into thin, angry slits. Slits that said, "*No.*"

"We're still deciding," she answered, hugging the baby close.

Kenny Jr.

That dream had been shattered. I turned my head away from Diane. Some *junior.*

I swallowed at the lump that had pushed its way into my throat. I wasn't sure if it was anger that was closing my throat or something else entirely.

Ian

"Okay, now I want you to make fish lips for me. Like this." Jodi, the therapist at the nursing home, puckered her lips into a wrinkle-producing "O." Then, using muscles I no longer had control of, she used hers to pull her lips back into a broad, weird smile. "Your turn," she said.

I pushed my lips forward. Well, the left side of my lips, anyway. The right side sort of hung there. Numb meat.

"Good," she lied. "Now try again." She mimicked the motion as I tried lamely to follow along. If Jodi's facial expressions were any indication of mine, I was doing a fabulous job. Unfortunately, I could feel that wasn't true on my side of the table. "Again," she cheered, through her puckered lips. "One more time. Great." She sat back, apparently exhausted with the effort of trying to make my paralyzed face move by osmosis.

I sat back, too. If the past two sessions were any indication, I knew we weren't anywhere near done. Might as well rest while Jodi was. In case anyone wandered into the room while we were taking a break, I brushed the side of my hair forward over my disfigured face.

Monday, Wednesday, Friday. Our sessions started with "e-stim," as Jodi called the electrical stimulation she administered at each of our morning sessions. That painful ordeal was followed by a series of muscle exercises designed to return my face to something that appeared normal. Three appointments counting this one and, even though Jodi insisted I was making huge strides, it didn't feel as if I was making an iota of progress. I had a feeling her false bravado was more for the benefit of the insurance company rather than mine.

Jodi looked up from the notes she'd been paging through. "I think we'll work on your eye next."

I knew the drill. First she would have me look straight ahead. Then, without moving my head, I was to turn my brown eyes as far to the left as I could get them. Then to the right. Look up. Look down. I wasn't sure what effect the exercise was supposed to have on my dropped eyelid. But it was one of the few exercises that felt easy. I wasn't about to complain.

"Good." Jodi said. "Now I want you to work on your own while I get ready for my next client." She pulled a stand-up mirror in front of me. I quickly glanced away.

This wasn't getting any easier. I recalled my first appointment earlier this week. The session Libby had dragged me to kicking and screaming. Well, I didn't actually kick and scream, but I made sure she and Dan knew I was going under protest.

"Ih'm not goh-ing," I'd announced when Olivia stood at my door Monday morning. I'd tried to call her, but somehow my fingers just wouldn't push the buttons. Instead, I paced. Across my living room, back and forth. A caged cat.

When the doorbell rang I made sure to stand so that the good side of my face was what she saw. I didn't care how silly it looked that I was talking to her out of the side of my mouth and looking at her out of the corner of my left eye. What she couldn't see, she couldn't be shocked at.

"Oh, yes, you are." She marched into my house, walked to the closet, and grabbed the first coat she could get her hands on. My knockout red wool.

No! I couldn't wear that; it would attract too many unwanted glances. "Nawt thaat one," I said, automatically walking to the closet and grabbing a different coat myself.

"Great," Libby said as she held the coat for me to slip my arms into. Too late I realized I'd been tricked. "Now," she said, placing a hand on each of my shoulders and speaking over my back. "I'm going to turn you around." Her left hand gently pulled at my left shoulder.

"No-h." I resisted.

She spoke firmly. "Jan, you need to go to your therapy appointment. I told Dan I would take you, and I think you know I am a woman who does what she says. If I have to tackle you from behind and drag you out of here by your…" She paused, and I could feel her body bending slightly to the right, "Nine West loafers, I will."

"They'rle Cole Hahn," I corrected slowly.

I could feel the vibration of Libby's laughter through her hands that were still on my shoulders. A small bubble of something popped at the back of my throat. I swallowed. It wasn't one bit funny. Well, okay. Maybe a little.

I hung my head. "Ih dohn't want to gho." My thick tongue tripped over the words. "I dohn't want anywhone to see mee like this."

"Oh, Jan." Libby's voice was full. She wrapped her arms around me from behind and pulled me into a hug. Softly she said into my ear, "You should be known for the beauty that comes from within." It didn't take the note card she'd sent me to remind me of the verse she'd written. "Will you let me take a look at you?" she said next. "I don't give a darn what the outside of you looks like. I promise I'll just look at your heart."

Even though she couldn't see me, I couldn't help but smile a little, the muscles on the left side of my face tugged the rest of my face into a twisted smirk. If anyone outside my family was going to look at me, I'd just as soon it was Libby.

Shaking my head so that my hair fell over the right side of my face, I slowly turned. I purposely looked off, over her shoulder, my head at an odd angle to keep the veil of hair in place. I gazed at the shelf of knickknacks I had hanging on the opposite wall. I didn't want to catch even the tiniest glimmer of horror on her face when she first saw my distorted features. I braced myself.

Silence. Nothing. My eyes quickly flitted to Libby and then away again. Then back.

She reached up with one hand and smoothed my hair back behind my right ear. "There," she said. "That's better."

I couldn't keep my eyes away. What was she seeing? I looked at her, staring only at the irises of her eyes, no further. She reached both hands up and cupped them around my face, her warm palms cradling my face as if I were a small child. What was she thinking? "Charm is deceptive," she said gently, "and beauty is fleeting; but a woman who fears the Lord is to be praised."

From a place I wasn't familiar with I knew she was quoting from the Bible. There was an odd tug somewhere deep inside. She hadn't gasped. She hadn't turned away. I could feel my eyes fill with tears. "Thawnk you," I whispered back, lowering my eyes and letting the tears finally fall.

~

There were advantages and disadvantages to living in a town the size of Brewster. The good thing was that I could quickly get to my dreaded therapy appointment and didn't have to sit in a large waiting room being gawked at by strangers. The bad thing was that anyone I was likely to see, I would know.

Libby held open the large glass door leading into the nursing home and motioned that I should go in first.

"Thawt's okay," I said, stepping backward, "you leead the way. I dohn't even know where the therawpy room is."

"Well, I certainly do." Libby had already described the large therapy room to me. The room she'd spent time in when our friend, Anne, was taking whirlpool treatments for the radiation burns she'd received during her treatment for breast cancer.

Libby confidently led the way down the long hall of the home. I tagged a half step behind, hoping that if anyone noticed us they'd be distracted by my elegant friend and simply not see me. I was silently thankful that Brewster's only physical therapist had her office at the Brewster Nursing Home rather than the local hospital. It made sense. This was where most of her clients lived, after all. People whose droopy faces mirrored mine...but only after they'd added forty years and a stroke or two.

A few residents in wheelchairs stared after us, their blank faces an eerie reminder of what I must look like. One old woman using a walker reached out her hand as we passed by. *No!* I silently screamed as Libby stopped and took the woman's hand. The longer we stood in the hallway, the more likely someone I knew would walk by. I looked at the gray linoleum tiles beneath my feet.

"Frieda! Hello!" Libby sounded genuinely glad to run into this old woman.

I glanced through the strands of my hair. This woman named Frieda was smiling back at Olivia so hard her face had practically curled in on itself.

"I remember when you were this high." The woman took her hand out of Libby's and motioned to a spot near the top of her walker. "Your dad and my Harold were the best of friends, and you would tag along with your dad like a knee-high shadow."

"I know," Libby said warmly. "You've shared that with me before, and I never get tired of hearing you tell me about it." She paused and picked up the old woman's hand again. "I was too young to remember that story, but thanks to you, I'll never forget it now."

My eyes shifted to Libby. Was she serious? Could she even believe the rambling of a woman who was possibly senile? Weren't most of the people who lived here detached from reality in some form or another?

"Who's your friend?" The woman asked, obviously not as detached as I'd assumed.

"Oh! I forgot," Libby said. She turned and said, "This is Jan Jordan. Jan. Frieda Wald. An old friend of my parents. And a friend of mine."

Frieda reached out a wrinkled hand. Automatically, I thrust mine forward. It was more a firm grasping than a handshake. As if she wanted to hang on and not let go. As though I were an instant new friend. I stared at our clasped hands and found myself squeezing her hand back in a communication I didn't quite understand.

"She's a pretty one," Frieda said.

Well, of course, Frieda was taking her feelings for Olivia and putting them into the hand she'd offered me. I felt an odd disappointment. Anyone could clearly see how beautiful Olivia was. I suppose looking at me reminded Frieda of how opposite we looked. "Yes," I mumbled, anxious to move down the hall. "She is pwetty."

I felt Libby's hand on my shoulder. "Frieda is talking about you, Jan."

My eyes shot up. Frieda was looking at Olivia, nodding in agreement. I didn't know what I was supposed to say. Her eyes were old. She probably couldn't see well.

She recognized Olivia right away.

My heart did a queer shuffle. "Thawk you," I said as best I could, still not quite believing the watery-eyed assessment of this old woman.

Libby gave Frieda a hug. "I'll stop by and visit you soon," Libby said as we walked away.

She's a pretty one. She's a pretty one. The four words kept time with my feet as we walked the remainder of the hallway. Words so similar to the ones my mother used to say. I knew they weren't true any longer, but somehow the words gave me courage I didn't feel on my own.

This was it. The appointment I dreaded as much as anticipated. If there was a cure for me, it might be inside these walls. Libby paused to let me go first. Head down, I rounded the doorway leading into the physical therapy room. "Owwuch!" Metal and shoe leather rammed into my shins. I jumped back, my eyes quickly taking in an old woman in a wheelchair and Kenny Pearson pushing it. What was *he* doing here? He belonged at his gas station, not here in the physical therapy room of the nursing home. I had always enjoyed flirting with the overweight teddy bear when I stopped by for gas. He was the kind of guy whose face I could read like a picture book. It had been no secret that he obviously thought I was something. Something mighty fine.

But that was before. I quickly turned my face back into the hallway. I didn't want to see what he might think now.

With perfect timing Libby stepped forward. Thank goodness it was her old neighbor, Ida Bauer, in the wheelchair. Their quick conversation provided a distraction so I could quietly slip around them and into the room.

"Hi! I'm Jodi." A young woman stuck out her hand. "You must be Janine Jordan!" The enthusiasm of my therapist's introduction didn't transfer to me.

"Just Ja-awn," I said, shaking her hand without smiling. I angled my face slightly away from her. She didn't need to see all the damage to my face all at once.

"Glad to meet you, Jan. Let's move over to the table here and we'll get started." She turned to Libby. "You're welcome to wait over there." She pointed to an uncomfortable-looking vinyl chair beside a small table with two beat-up magazines on top. "Or," Jodi perked up; it was obvious the next option was better, "you can walk down to the dining room. They've always got a pot of coffee going. Jan can meet you there when she's done."

"Ah, coffee," Libby said. "You said the magic words." She held up the paperback book she'd brought along. "Take as long as you need."

Jodi walked behind a metal-legged table and took a chair, motioning for me to sit opposite her. "I have your doctor's notes here. I'm going to do an assessment and then we'll get started."

There wasn't much to assess. What there was she could do with her eyes. My right eye was at half-mast, as if my lip were hauling it down with a pulley.

"I haven't had much opportunity to work with younger clients in your condition," Jodi babbled as she pulled a three-ring binder in front of her. "I'm really looking forward to our sessions."

If her comment was supposed to be encouraging, it wasn't. It only served to remind me what an elite group I belonged to. An exclusive group of deformity.

She did call you younger.

As if that mattered anymore. What good was there in being young if I looked like this?

She's a pretty one.

I remembered the way Frieda had looked at me, and there wasn't even a drop of makeup to mask what she saw. And still she'd said, "She's a pretty one." As if she wasn't seeing just the outside of me.

"First of all," Jodi's words directed my attention back to her. "I'd like you to say the vowels for me. I want to listen to hear how much your speech has been impacted by the paralysis."

I cringed. I didn't like that word. Paralysis. *Ick*. I wished she wouldn't say it so...so... At all.

"Okay, repeat after me. A-E-I-O-U."

"Aww-Eee-Iyy-Oo-U." When I concentrated it didn't sound so bad.

"Good!" Jodi made some scratches with her pen. "Now I want you to do this." She wrinkled her nose and sniffed. A huge rabbit.

I did the same. Well, not the same. The right side of my nose felt as though it had been injected with a permanent dose of Novocain. I'd make a lousy rabbit.

"Now, let's see how you do on this." Jodi stuck out her bottom lip, a three-year old with a huge attitude.

I pushed my lip out, too. Make that half my lip. I could feel the tug as the left side of my lip yanked at the right. Urging it to cooperate, but it had an attitude all its own and wasn't going anywhere.

"Um-hmm," Jodi said less enthusiastically. "Now this." She stuck out her top lip.

For some reason the top of my lip went along with the idea just a fraction better than the bottom lip had.

"That's great!" Jodi said smiling.

I wouldn't have called it anywhere near great, but if she could spot an encouraging sign, I wasn't about to talk her out of it.

"Now I'd like you to blow on this." She handed me a whistle.

Yeah, right. I was going to shriek away on a whistle, a siren calling others to run to the scene of this awful carnage. I hesitated before picking it up. Maybe just a tiny puff of air to show her I was trying. I took a breath, put the whistle to my lips, and blew. I needn't have worried. The feeble sound that came from the toy was pathetic. I took a deeper breath and tried again. Air gushed from the side of my mouth, missing most of the whistle. The tiny *tweak* I managed was barely what I'd call a sound. A slight breeze could have done just as well. I looked away from Jodi. No need to know from her expression what a failure I was.

She didn't comment. Instead she passed me a glass of water with a straw and said, "One more test. Take a sip for me."

Without looking at her I leaned my head forward, grasped the straw between my fingers, and slipped it between my lips. I cheated a little, favoring the good side of my mouth. I drew the liquid up the straw. I felt the coolness on my tongue first, then my chin. The tepid water made a puddle in front of me on the table. I couldn't even drink out of a straw!

I pushed the glass away, the liquid sloshing dangerously near the rim of the glass. I didn't care if it spilled! I bit at my bottom lip, my attempt to keep instant tears at bay. I blinked, my left eye moving rapidly, my right barely moving, as if it had no idea what it was supposed to be doing.

I plopped my elbows on the table and dipped my head into my hands. I couldn't do anything! I was no better than a toddler at the tasks I'd been asked to do. A failure at them all. A soft sob threaded through my throat. Just like the rest of my body, the tears I'd tried to master did what they wanted. They ran down my face, one dripping from my chin and joining the puddle of water I'd already caused with my dribbling.

"Jan," Jodi said softly, reaching out to touch my arm, "it's going to be okay. This is only the assessment. We haven't even started the exercises. I have a feeling you're going to do really well. Overcoming something like this is hard work. But you can do it."

"Ih dohn't think Ih cawn."

"Oh," Jodi said, a lightness to her voice that wasn't there before, "I think you're going to be very surprised at what you can do. God does some amazing work around here."

Through my tears I glanced up at her, surprised she would give credit to God and not take it herself…if there was ever going to *be* any credit to take in my impossible case.

"Really," Jodi said. "You're going to be amazed. I promise." She held up three fingers in the old Brownie salute.

I knew she was trying to encourage me, and yet the miserable way I'd failed at the simple tasks she'd had me do kept my eyes filling with tears. I swiped at my cheeks with the backs of my hands. "Ih'm sowrry." I didn't know what else to say.

"Don't worry," Jodi said handing me a tissue with a smile. "We're used to tears around here. I actually like to see a little frustration. It means you're trying."

I turned my brimming eyes to her, checking to see if she was telling the truth.

As if she could hear my doubt, she nodded. "And to cry like that you must be trying *really* hard." She winked.

～

Today was Friday. My third appointment. Libby had insisted on driving me, using the time, she said, "to catch up with my friends in the nursing home." She had left me to walk the long hall by myself, telling me to pick her up in Frieda Wald's room on my way out.

Jodi had guided me through basically the same routine she'd used to assess me, my ability as limited as the first day. I could feel tears stinging the corner of my lazy eye.

As if for me, Jodi breathed a deep sigh. "Let's take a little break," she said. She looked at her watch. "If you don't mind, I'm going to get one of my other therapy patients going on some exercises on the other side of the room. I have an appointment in Carlton this afternoon," she explained. "So I have to leave work early today. I'm trying to make up for lost time."

I shrugged one shoulder. I didn't care. I was pretty sure whoever her patient was would be old enough to mind their own business, or maybe not be able to see all the way across the room to even notice I was sitting here.

Jodi pulled a stand-up mirror my way. "When you feel you've rested a bit, why don't you practice your vowel sounds in the mirror. I'm going to go get Ida."

I'd hardly had time to become discouraged before Jodi was back with a woman in a wheelchair. Jodi made the introductions as she walked into the room and maneuvered the chair into a spot on the opposite side of the large room. "Ida, this is Jan Jordan. She's a new client of mine. Jan, this is Ida Bauer. She's one of our residents here at the home."

Without thinking, I'd turned in the direction of Jodi's voice as she entered the therapy room, exposing the distorted side of my face to the newcomer. Quickly, I turned away, using the mirror to look over my shoulder and catch a glimpse of this woman who used to be Olivia's neighbor.

"Goot morning, Chan." I could see Ida's thin hand rise from the arm of her wheelchair in a friendly wave.

"Mohrn-ning," I mustered, my accent not nearly so pronounced as hers. I focused my eyes back onto my mouth in the mirror. I only hoped Ida had to concentrate as hard on her exercises as I did on mine. I didn't have energy to waste on idle chitchat.

Since when? You have spent most of your life chatting about not much of anything.

Ouch. I winced into the mirror. Well, at least my left eye did. It was surprising how many false things I'd noticed since the diagnosis of my palsy. The eyebrow pencil I'd used religiously could just as well be thrown in Joey's old Crayon box. Along with much of the rest of my makeup. Pomegranate Red lipstick did absolutely nothing for me anymore. Unless you counted drawing attention to lips that needed hiding an asset. I'd taken to wearing a lip-toned gloss these days.

In an effort to pass some of the long hours on my living room couch, I'd picked up the cheap novel I'd been reading before I'd become sick. The words were dead on the page, the plot as thin as the paper it was printed on. Why hadn't I noticed before?

I'd thrown the book aside and turned on the TV, flicking from station to station, trying to find something that would hold my interest. Take my mind off myself and my troubles. Lose myself in someone else's idea of entertainment. Game show, tennis match, cartoons, game show. Soap operas where magic crystals and serial killers were so far removed from my reality that I couldn't bring myself to watch.

After TV and trashy novels, there wasn't much left to fill my time. My new life felt very empty. I found myself actually looking forward to my sessions with Jodi, but I'd turned down Libby's suggestion to stop at Vicky's for coffee. Going out in public was something I wouldn't be doing anytime soon, if ever again.

I stared at my droopy face in the mirror. Snippets of conversation between Jodi and Ida mingled with my thoughts, my facial exercises forgotten. Some concentration. It was all I could do to keep my attention attuned to my vowels as Ida Bauer jabbered to Jodi.

"I don't know vhat's going on," Ida was saying. "Kenny ran off on Montday cuss the bapy wass on its vay. Ant now," she flopped both her hands in her lap.

I strained my ears trying to catch the rest of the sentence. Sure, when I tried *not* to listen I heard every word, when I wanted to hear, I couldn't make out a sound. What had happened? I remembered that Diane Pearson was pregnant and due any day. But that had been before I'd become sick. Had she had the baby? What did she have?

A conversation I'd had with Libby when she'd driven me home from my Wednesday appointment came back to me now.

Libby couldn't help but notice my red-rimmed eyes when I'd met her after my frustrating therapy session. If she did notice, she didn't comment. She'd simply put a hand on my back and guided me outside to the car.

"Feel like going for a drive?" she asked as she backed out of the parking space.

Nothing in Brewster was too far apart. If she drove me straight home it would take all of a minute. The long, endless expanse of my couch, and my day, loomed in front of me. "Shure," I mumbled, more glad for the simple outing than I sounded.

Libby took a left out of the parking lot, threading her way through a few city blocks while I hung my head in case anyone looked to see who was riding with Olivia Marsden. She stopped at a stop sign and then turned onto the highway that led out toward Brush Lake. For the first time in what seemed like ages, I looked out the windows, watching snow-covered hillsides dance by the car. There were brown patches here and there. A flock of ducks, or geese, high in the sky. They were back in North Dakota early this year. Maybe spring wasn't far behind. Mid-March sunlight poured into the car. I leaned my head back against the headrest and closed my eyes. My illness and its aftermath, the struggle to understand what had happened to me, and, more pressing, what would happen to me, left me suddenly exhausted. A heavy sigh filled my chest as I struggled against the tears that pressed at my throat.

I felt the car slow down and turn, gravel crunching under the tires. I opened my eyes. The ice-covered lake was off in the distance, sunlight turning the frozen surface a lovely pale blue. I didn't have to worry about anyone seeing me out here. Nothing was expected of me. All I had to do was enjoy the view. I could finally relax my guard. An unexpected bubble of what felt like joy, mixed with tears, expanded inside me. I turned to Libby. "Thawnk you," I said softly. I couldn't prevent the satisfied smile that tugged at my lips, twisting them into what I hoped looked like happy. I wasn't sure I knew what happy even meant anymore.

"Beautiful, isn't it?" Libby's words seemed to include the frozen lake, the gauzy white clouds that floated above, and, strangely, me, too.

All I could do was stare out the window and nod. I could see why she would think the view in front of us was incredible. But how could she possibly think I was beautiful, too? Me. Looking the way I did. Disfigured. Distorted. Ug—

I made you.

Out of the corner of my eye I quickly glanced at her. She hadn't heard that, I hoped. Had *she* said the words? It didn't seem so. She was driving slowly, her eyes on the road ahead. I looked back out the window, not so much seeing as listening.

When you were in your mother's womb, I fashioned you. I created you. I have a plan for you.

Where were these thoughts coming from? I was no student of the Bible, but these sure sounded like Bible words. I tried to remember just where my Bible was. The last time I used it might have been when I attended a women's study at church. But when had that been? I didn't go every month. Not nearly. The only way someone could call me *religious* was that I religiously made sure I attended the luncheons and the fun events. But the boring Bible study nights? I was unexpectedly ashamed at my record of attendance. Even so, something must have sunk in.

Or I haven't given up on you.

A finger of wonderment tickled my breastbone as chills ran down my arms. What kind of plan could God have for someone like me?

I'd have to think about that later when I was trying to pass the rest of the day on my couch. Right now Libby was pulling into the deserted parking area near the lake. Apparently enough other people drove out here during the snowy winter months that the snow was well packed, even melting a little this morning. Libby put the car into park and let it idle. Warm air coming from the heater was the only sound.

"You know," she said, focusing her eyes off somewhere in the distance, "when I was struggling with my depression last year, I kept expecting there would be some pill or shot or therapy that would instantly make me better."

That was exactly what I'd been hoping for with this Bell's palsy. It had happened overnight, and I wanted it *gone* overnight. I thought no one else could understand how I felt. But here was Libby, saying exactly the thoughts I hadn't put into words.

I'd never questioned Olivia about that time in her life. Was it only last year? It seemed longer ago than that. She'd been hospitalized for depression, and at the time it was easier to avoid her. Just like I'd avoided our friend, Anne, when she'd been sick. I hadn't known what to say to Olivia or what to do. Knowing me, I'd more than likely stick my foot in my mouth and say something that would make her feel worse. At the time I'd rationalized it was best to leave Olivia alone, give her space to get back to normal.

Now, after the weeks I'd spent alone, brooding about what had happened to me, agonizing over how awful my life would be, and comparing those feelings with how I felt today, being out of the house, being here with Libby...I understood I hadn't been much of a friend to her at all.

Maybe being a friend means you don't have to say anything.

The silence between Libby and me was more comforting than any words I could imagine. I looked down at my hands, wondering if there was any way I could begin to make my failing up to her.

Of course, she couldn't know all the thoughts her simple sentence had stirred inside me. After a short pause she said, "Do you know what the first sign was that I was improving?" She didn't wait for an answer, but simply said, "It was when I stopped thinking so much about myself and my own problems, and started noticing what was going on in the lives of the people around me."

Oh... I turned my head to look at her. Did she somehow know I'd just been wondering how I could be a better friend to her? Did she—

"JODI, PHONE CALL ON LINE ONE." The loud words over the intercom startled me back to the therapy room at the nursing home. I looked into the mirror in front of me and tried to concentrate on my exercises as Jodi picked up the phone near me. I heard her say, "I'll get right back to you." She hung up the phone, looked at me, and then looked at Ida Bauer. "Think I can leave you two troublemakers alone for a minute? I need to run to my office and grab a file."

"Acht," Ida said from her far corner, "iff Chan vill behavff, so vill I."

After Jodi left the room, silence separated us like a wall. Even so I could hear Ida's soft groans as she pulled at the weighted handles Jodi had placed in her hands. I recalled the snippet of conversation I'd overheard moments ago that had sent my thoughts wandering. *Kenny left because the baby was coming...*

Should I ask if the Pearsons had had their baby? What they'd had? I didn't know Ida very well. Barely knew Kenny, either, except for the times I stopped for gas. And what if I started talking to Ida? Would she say something about my mangled speech? The way I looked? Suddenly, starting a conversation felt as risky as a bank robbery.

"Do you know what the first sign was that I was improving? When I stopped thinking so much about myself and my own problems and

started noticing what was going on in the lives of the people around me."

Maybe wanting to talk to Ida was a sign I was getting better. I glanced into the mirror. No, my face hadn't been miraculously healed, but still the question pushed at my lips. I peeked at the old woman through the angle of the mirror. What if Ida didn't want to talk? What if she couldn't understand my thick speech? What if—

She's lonely, too.

I stared at myself in the mirror, the odd thought reflecting in my wary eyes.

She's lonely, too.

Unexpectedly, my eyes filled with tears. Wherever this thought had come from, it touched a spot deep inside me. I hadn't dared think the thought until now, but this isolated cocoon of a life I'd been living was lonely beyond words.

That would be a first. You without words.

Amid my tears a wry smile tugged at a corner of my mouth. The quirk of fate in my situation suddenly seemed clear. I'd spent years chattering my life away to anyone who would listen...and now I was bound by a mouth and tongue that would hardly move.

Maybe it's not a quirk of fate.

What— What else could it be?

You should be known for the beauty that comes from within... When I stopped thinking so much about myself...

I closed my eyes and took a deep breath, waiting while the swelling in my throat released its grasp. I spoke slowly, forming the words as best I could. "Dihd Kenny and Di-aane have their baby?" I turned the good side of my face slightly toward Ida so she'd know I was talking to her and not the mirror in front of me.

She didn't hesitate for a second. "Dat's vhat I'd like to know." She shook her head as she continued to move her arms on the pulley contraption hooked to the wall. "No vun aroundt here seems to know anyting. Andt my niece, Cindty, hasn't been into vork since Montday. Acht! If I couldt valk I'd marched right out uff here and findt out vhat's going on." She yanked at the handles in her hands with more strength than I thought she had. "If I vas shtill liffing in my house I'dt—" She interrupted herself to ask, "Didt you hear vhat happened? Vhy I endted up in here?" At my quick shake of my head, she rolled her chin through the air and started anew. "It vass Halloveen andt…"

What had ever made me think Ida might not want to talk? Words spilled out of her thin lips as if my simple question had broken a high-walled dam. I found myself turning my chair so I could face her square on. Hear every word she said as if we were long-lost friends. Let her story soak into the void where my heart had sadly thumped. I felt a tiny smile tug at the right corner of my mouth, a muscle a week of therapy hadn't budged until I'd spoken to this odd companion of mine.

I'd never known listening could feel so good.

Ida

I didn't mean to talk as if my words were a herd of stampeding cows running for the barn in a lightning storm, but once I got started, just like those scared cows, I couldn't seem to quit moving. I told Jan all about the hours I'd lain on my kitchen floor. About how I'd made my peace with God and had been ready to die. And how God appeared not to have my home in heaven ready for me yet.

"So's, here I sit," I said, letting my tired arms rest on the edges of my wheelchair for a moment. "Heaven's not ready for me, so I get to pass the time down here until Godt calls me home." I shook my head. This wasn't the first time discouragement had gotten the better of me. "It's hardt to know vhat Godt vants from an oldt voman like me. I'm not much goot for anyting anymore."

Jan looked at her bright pink fingernails for a second and then back at me. She spoke slowly. "Yo-u are good come-pahny for me. I think tha-at's some-thing."

I was glad she talked slow. Some of these young people foamed at the mouth so fast my old ears couldn't keep up with them. I had no trouble keeping up with Jan's careful words. I felt a blush creeping into my wrinkled cheeks. She'd called my blabbering *good company.* "I thank you for that," I said, grateful for the little gifts God gave me each day.

It was time to close my mouth and open my own ears. "How goes it witt you?"

Jan looked puzzled for a moment, and then the left side of her mouth turned up in a half smile. "It goh-es," she said, a dance in her eyes I hadn't seen there before. She flicked her hand near the mirror on the table behind her. "Ih'm suppoh-sed to be prwac-ticing the wowel sounds, but I think tawlk-ing to you will ahcom-plish the same thing."

"Vell, den, you talk andt I'll vork on my foots excercises." I pressed the toe of my right foot onto the floor, wincing at the dull throb the small effort sent up my leg. "Dis vay Chodi can't be madt at us."

"Doh-es that huu-rt?" Jan asked, her left eye scrunching in empathetic pain.

"A little," I admitted as I lifted the pressure from my foot. "But Godt doesn't promise us a life wittout pain. That's safed for our heavenly home."

"Tha-at heavenly ho-ome you tawlk about souwnds lovely." Again, Jan gave me her lopsided smile.

"Oh, it vill be," I said.

And then, there I was, off to the races again, my mouth moving as fast as my mind, telling Jan all about my Christian upbringing on the farm. How I met Fred. The baby we'd lost. Our move into town. My years alone after he died. The many ways God had stood by me over the years only to find myself here at the nursing home, good for nothing except taking up space until He called me to Himself.

"Oh! But thawt's nowt true," Jan chimed in when I'd come up for air. "Loo-ok at how-w you've hel-llped me with mm-y exercises too-day."

"Talking your ears off vas no help to you. Vhat wouldt Chodi say?"

"What do you mean, 'what would I say?'" Jodi asked as she hurried into the room with a thick file tucked under her arm. "Have you two been getting into mischief?" She dropped the file onto the end of the table and put one hand on her hip, shaking a finger at me. "Ida, if you've been running a marathon while I've been out of the room, you're in trouble."

"The only race I've been running is vitt my moutt, andt it's all Chan's fault. She's a goot listener."

Jodi laughed while Jan looked down at her hands. She raised her eyes to mine, a softening at the corners I couldn't understand.

"Well," Jodi said, walking my way, "I think you've both put in your time today. I'm sorry I was gone so long. It's been one of those days." She unlocked the brakes on the wheels of my chair. "I promise I'll work you hard at your next appointment." Jodi swiveled my chair away from the wall.

"Dat's a promise I von't mindt if you break. Not vhen I haff goot company like Chan to wisit witt."

Jodi glanced at the clock on the wall. "Oh, man, I'm way behind schedule. I'll get you back to your room, Ida, and then I'm on my way to Carlton. Jan, be sure to do your facial exercises at home."

"I-h can puu-sh Ida baack to her roo-mm."

"That would be great!" Jodi swung the handles of my wheelchair in a gentle curve toward Jan and off we went.

Jan walked as carefully as she talked, as if she were afraid moving me too fast might break me. Knowing these young people had better things to do than walk slow as a turtle down the hall of a nursing home, I teased over my shoulder, "At dis rate I'm going to miss lunch. I'm a tough oldt voman. You can go faster if you vant." Jan was probably regretting her offer to take me back to my room.

She started walking a fraction faster, and then she slowed down again. "I-h dohn't have much else plaa-nned for to-day. I-h guess Ih'm in no hurr-y. Unn-less you are?"

"The only ting I'm in a hurry to do iss to meet my Lordt, andt until He calls my name I'ff got all the time in the vorldt. If you don't mindt bapysitting an oldt voman, you can valk as slow as you vant." I reached a hand up, over my shoulder and patted at the air. As if Jan had read my mind she stopped pushing my chair and slipped her hand under mine as her other hand moved to rest on my shoulder.

Supple young skin curled around my papery fingers. A warm hand rested with heavy comfort against the crook of my neck. How long had it been since someone had held my hand? How long had it been since someone had touched me because they wanted to, not because they were helping me in the toilet or were being paid to scrub me in the bath? A watery warmth pricked at the corners of my eyes. If the good Lord called me home right now, I wasn't so sure I wanted to let go.

I'll push Ida to her room.

Where had those words come from? Certainly not from my selfish mind. When had it ever occurred to me to help Jodi out of her hectic schedule? Or to spend more time with someone I barely knew? In former days I wouldn't have dreamed of pushing a wrinkled old woman down the hallway of the local nursing home. There were people who were *paid* to do tasks like that. I had better things to do…things like shopping and gossiping with my friends or getting my nails done. I looked down at my pink polish. Those things had happened another lifetime ago. I wasn't the same person anymore.

The words were out before I knew I said them. *I'll push Ida to her room.* The handles of the wheelchair faced me as quick as a blink. And there I was, pushing an old woman down the hall, proof itself that I was no longer Jan Jordan…at least not the Jan Jordan I'd come to know in the past forty-three years.

Who was I now that I no longer had my looks to define me? Now that I couldn't rely on a fluttering of long lashes to get my way? Now that I couldn't even get my mouth to flash a quick, flirtatious smile? Automatically, as if mirroring my thoughts, one side of my mouth turned up, trying to imitate my old smile. I felt a tug at the right side of my mouth as the paralyzed muscles refused to cooperate. I had no idea who I was going to be after this whole episode was over. If it ever was over.

"Ih'm in no hurr-y," I found myself telling Ida as I pushed her down the long hall. My whole day stretched in front of me, a boring expanse of hours in which I would do nothing but sit and feel sorry for myself. Anything was better than the plans I had. Spending a few more moments with my surprising companion was a welcome relief.

Oh, no! Someone was walking toward us down the long hall. Someone young, from the looks of their shape and their gait. Someone who might know me. I released my grip on the handle of the wheelchair, reaching to brush my hair forward, to cover the slack side of my face so whoever it was couldn't see me full on. Instead I found my hand wrapped around Ida's, her skin as cool and thin as the cucumber slices I used to place on my eyelids to take away puffiness.

Her quick grasp onto my fingers surprised me. As the young stranger veered off into a room, I took my other hand off the handle of the wheelchair and set it against her neck to balance myself. The soft folds of skin in the crook of Ida's neck felt like pleats of fine fabric. I rested my hands against her flesh, marveling at the gossamer feel of her skin. I would have never thought old skin could have the texture of goose down. I'd imagined it hard and calloused...and saggy. Not soft and welcoming the way a velvet drape might feel.

What else don't you know about growing older?

Good question. In the not-so-long-ago past, I thought I knew it all. Had my whole future figured out. I would have cosmetic surgery to keep me looking younger, and if I needed it again a few years down the road, so be it. My nails would be manicured, my makeup impeccable. Anything to keep up the appearance of youth...and push away any thoughts of what came...well, later.

Somewhere along the line, my plans had taken a drastic tangent. A course no makeup or surgery would cover. Now, other than holing myself up at home, I had no choice but to explore the few options I had.

"Do you-u have tii-me for a cup of coff-ee?" I asked Ida, remembering Jodi's instructions to Olivia when she'd delivered me to my first appointment. *They've always got a pot of coffee going.* Anything was better than sitting at home on my dull couch watching mindless television programs.

"Acht!" Ida said, releasing my hand. "You'ff saidt the magchic vord. I vouldt luff a cup uff coffee."

So, there I was, making a U-turn in the middle of the Brewster Nursing Home, pushing Ida towards a coffee urn and myself toward who knew what?

One thing I should have remembered from all my years of living was that everyone is just a little bit lonely, no matter what they look like on the outside of their skin.

Take Jan Jordan, for instance. My feeble eyes had no trouble seeing across my coffee cup that she was a beauty, even if half of her face was a little bit droopy. Even that strange illness she'd had couldn't disguise what God had blessed her with in the beginning. To look at Jan, someone plain all her life like me would think a person like her had the world by the tail. She was a *knock out,* as Fred would have said. And to hear her tell it, she had plenty of other blessings besides.

"My-y husband, Da-an, has been wonn-derul through all this." She gestured her fingers toward her face and then wrapped them around the ceramic coffee mug on the table as if hanging on for dear life. "So paa-tient. My-y soo-n, Jow-ey, is a goo-od kid. He never gets inn-to trowuu-ble and has never saa-id a worr-d about how I look…now." Her eyes stayed glued to the tabletop.

I was adding up her blessings as she talked. A husband who loved her and a son who wasn't a troublemaker. And plenty of friends. You'd think a woman like that would have a basket overflowing with thank-yous. But, at my age, I knew everyone had a story they didn't share with just anyone. I understood my role was to simply sit here and listen. If God wanted Jan's story told to me, my heart was ready to hear it.

Looking around the empty dining hall, I rubbed my fingers through my thinning hair. It would be full within the half hour but now, except for the cooks bustling about in the kitchen, the room was deserted. God had arranged it so Jan would have my undivided attention. Goodness, you'd think an old woman like me would be all listened-up by now. The things I had heard over the years would keep the angels busy full-time. It seemed I never lacked for something to pray about. Jan took a deep breath. It appeared I had some more listening to do. Probably more praying, too.

"I-h know I-h should be glaa-d that I'm still heall-thy." Jan stared into the dark brown liquid in front of her. "But... youu-u see..." She stopped trying to speak and shrugged her shoulders, looking up at me with tears in her eyes.

I reached out my hand and pulled hers off of the coffee mug she was grasping, wrapping my fingers around her warm hand. "Chust say vhatever you're holdting inside, Chan. These ears are oldt enough not to be surprissed by much. In Chames ve're toldt to tell our proplems to each odder so vee can pray for each odder and be healted." I squeezed her hand. "You talk andt I'll pray."

She hung her head, sighed deeply, and then spoke. "All my lii-fe Ih've gotten by on my...my..." She glanced quickly at me, and then she flicked the fingers of the hand I wasn't holding through the air. "Thiss souw-nds so shallow. I've gawt-ten by on my loo-oks." A puff of air from her slack mouth lifted her long bangs. "I-h dohn't have... I'hm not pretty anymohre. I-h dohn't even knohw who I am when I look in-n the mirror. It's like I'hve lost myself." A dry sob shook her shoulders.

Dear Lord, hold her heart as tightly as I'm holding her hand. She needs You.

"Oh, childt, you're not lost. Godt knows exactly vhere you are. Vhy, there's even a story in the Biple about somevun chust like you."

She looked up at me then with a mix of puzzle, wonder, and tears on her pretty face. "Therw-e is?"

I nodded and then wiggled my head from side to side. "Vell, okay," I said, smiling just a little, "it's about a lost sheeps. But if you readt the Biple you know many times Jesus tells stories about us using tings like sheeps to make His point."

I thought I could see a tiny twinkle behind the tears in Jan's eyes. Or maybe it was doubt. "Maa-ybe you-u should tell me the stowry."

"I can do that. But den you shouldt go readt it in the Biple for yourself." That way she'd know I wasn't making the story up.

"If I ca-an find my Bible."

"Vell, if you can't you can borrow mine. I know those oldt stories like the back uff my handt." I traced my thumb across the back of her smooth hand. "You see, there vas this man who had a flock uff a hunderdt sheeps, and one uff them vandered off. Now you'dt tink witt that many sheeps he vouldtn't even know one vas missing…but he didt. Right avay. So he left the ninety-nine other sheeps and vent off to search for the vun that vas lost. Andt do you know what he didt vhen he foundt it?"

Jan shook her head.

"Vhy, he rechoiced as if that vun lost sheeps vas the only vun he hadt!" I squeezed Jan's hand, hoping she felt the gladness, too. "Vhen I vas a little girl I usedt to tink that story vas really about sheeps. I usedt to tink about that vun sheeps climbing up andt down sharp rocks and *baaa'ing* for its mama. But I learnedt better. The story iss really about us. If you're feeling lost, Chesus is looking for you right dis wery minute. Don't vorry, Chan. He'll findt you."

She closed her eyes as if she were praying. I hoped she was, but just for some insurance I spoke up, "Iss it okay if I pray for you?"

She nodded. "I-h caa-n use all the hell-p I can get."

I bowed my head. "Dear Lordt," I said, "You haff a—"

"Oh! You-uu mean-nt right now?"

I looked up at her, quickly understanding she hadn't expected me to pray out loud over the coffee cups. "Godt has time to listen right now." I held out my other hand for her to hold. "Shouldt vee talk to Him togedder?"

She slipped her hand into mine, looked quickly to either side of us, and then smiled shyly with one side of her mouth. "I-hve nevv-er don-ne this before. Sorry."

"You neffer haff to apologize for praying." I bowed my head. "Dear Lordt, You haff a lost sheeps at this table. A sheeps that iss crying for its Master." I paused, imagining Jan wandering through a brown, steep, and hilly place, calling out for help. "You haff a green, grassy place all ready for her to lie down in andt rest. Leadt her to it, Lordt. Leadt her to You." I squeezed both of Jan's hands. "Amen."

She squeezed mine back. "Ah-men." As she slid her hands out of mine she looked quickly around. "Tha-at was nice. Tha-ank you. I-h shou-uld ge-et home. Will I-h—"

"There you are!" My niece-in-law, Cindy, was walking across the large dining area toward us, her director of nursing badge hung straight as a crosswise stickpin on her uniform. "I was about ready to call out the National Guard."

"There you iss, too. You haffn't been at vork all veek. I vas getting vorried. Vhere haff you been? How comes nobody vouldt tell me vhat vas going on? Did Kenny and Diane haff their babby?"

"Slow down, Ida." Cindy stepped to my side and rubbed her hand in small circles between my shoulder blades. Her touch felt good. "I see you have a new friend." She nodded at Jan.

Jan gave a half smile as she turned her head slightly away from Cindy, looking at her out of the corner of one eye, hiding the right side of her face behind a veil of sandy blonde hair.

"Didt Kenny and Diane haff their bapy?" I wasn't going to wait one minute longer. Right away, when Cindy pulled out a chair from the table and sat down, I knew something wasn't right. "Vhat's wrong?"

Cindy picked up my hand and held it tightly in hers. She glanced quickly at Jan.

"I-h can go-h." Jan pushed herself away from the table.

"No!" I said, louder than I meant. "If dare's a burden coming, I vill needt help to share it. Tell me," I said, looking straight at Cindy. "I can't pray about someting if I don't know vhat it iss."

"There's good news…" Cindy paused. "And not so good news." Again she hesitated.

I was getting fed up with the waiting. "Chust tell it all to me." If she thought I was too feeble to handle bad news, she had much to learn. God had been with me through the loss of my child, my parents, and my husband. My siblings, too. And the deaths of too many friends to count. My life had held sickness and sorrow. Whatever Cindy was holding back I could handle…with His help.

Cindy pressed her lips into a grim smile. "The good news is that Kenny got that little boy he wanted."

"Praise Godt," I said, smiling. "But now ve're going to haff to listen to his boasting."

"I don't think Kenny is going to be doing much bragging." Cindy was shaking her head ever so slightly. "The baby has Down syndrome, and Kenny's not taking it well."

"Iss the bapy healthy? Iss Diane all right?"

"Yes, they're both doing fine."

"Vhat den iss the proplem? Vhat iss this Down syndrome?"

"Do you remember Roger Winter? John and Alma's son? They've moved now, but they used to live on your same street."

"Rodcher? That sveet boy? He vas alvays at my doorshtep asking for licorice."

"He had Down syndrome. Same as Kenny's baby."

"All children are the same in Godt's eyes."

"Try telling that to Kenny. He's taking this as a personal failure. He won't even help Diane pick out a name for the little guy."

"You tell Kenny to get ovfer here and wisit me. I'll talk some sense into him."

"I don't know if he'll come. He's hardly been around since he brought Diane and the baby home from the hospital. He isn't even going down to the station. He spends most of the day…somewhere. Ben thinks he's driving out in the country. It's as if he doesn't want anyone to see him."

I could see Jan's head turn Cindy's way, the slack side of her face partially revealed. "Why wouu-ld that be?"

"Beats me. I suppose he thinks having a child with a handicap is shameful somehow. Who knows what Kenny's thinking?"

"Acht!" I said, waving a hand through the air. "Vee are all born vitt handicaps; some you can chust see better than odders. Kenny's handicap iss hiss tick headt. That childt deserves chust as much luff as hiss tree udder kidts. Maybe more. That bapy iss Godt's gift, and he's here to teach uss someting, uff that you can be sure. Godt doesn't make mistakes."

Jan was silent as she looked intently at me. Finally, she moved her eyes to Cindy and spoke. "Whh-o's running the staa-tion?"

Cindy tugged at her earlobe. "Thank goodness Pete's stepped up to the plate. That's one miracle in all this. Who'd a thought that kid would ever work this hard? He's been going into the station at the crack of dawn and staying until closing time. Kenny's lucky he hired him."

"Luck hass nuting to do vitt it." I nodded my head firmly at Jan and Cindy, noticing the room had suddenly filled. As if a dinner bell had sounded, the dining room was bustling with wheelchairs and walkers. A few well-placed arms assisted nursing home residents to their tables.

Cindy stood. "I've got to get back to my office."

"You tell that Kenny to come see me or I'll roll my chair trew the snow to hiss house. I'll talk some sense into hiss tick headt. Tell him to bring that new babpy along, too."

Cindy put a hand on my shoulder. "Well, until he gets over here, you'd best keep praying." She turned to go.

"No vorries there. As long as I breathe I'll keep talking to Godt."

"Is it luunch time alrew-dy?" Jan glanced at the shiny gold watch on her wrist. "I'hd better go, too." She pushed back her chair but didn't stand. Instead she reached a hand forward and wrapped her fingers around mine. "Thaa-nk you for this morr-ning. Ii-t's the firr-st time a morr-ning has flow-wn by in a-ages." She smiled, her lovely face lighting in a way I hadn't seen before. One side of her mouth drooped, but I hardly noticed for the gleam in her eyes.

I held on to her hand long and hard. This was a young woman whose heart was lonely. A woman who needed my prayers as much as Kenny. I released her hand with a squeeze. It was turning out to be a busy day. I had lunch to eat.

And some hard praying to do.

Kenny

"When you go to the station, could you stop by Magner's and pick up some groceries for me?" Diane was pacing the kitchen, burping the baby. Paige sat under the table sucking her thumb. Renae and Billy were getting their coats on for school.

"I'm not going to the station." I opened the sports page of the *Carlton Gazette*, pretending to study the scores as if there would be a test. The words were nothing but a blur in front of my eyes. Nothing much interested me these days. I could feel Diane glaring at me. "What?" I looked up at her, annoyed. *Leave me alone.*

Diane threw me a *look* back and then kissed Renae and Billy on the cheek. "Have a good day," she said as they went out the door. I could hear the forced enthusiasm in her voice. "Paige, do you want to watch cartoons?" Diane followed Paige into the living room.

I closed the paper. No use pretending anymore. I sunk my head into my hands, staring at the table through my fingers. It was brown, the color of everything this past week.

"Kenny, you at least have to go to work and take care of the bills." Diane was back. Quickly I reopened the paper. I should have known her suggestion that Paige watch cartoons was nothing but a plot to get a two-year-old out of the kitchen. The fact that I hadn't figured it out sooner was just proof of how stupid my whole life was. I couldn't do anything right.

Admit it, Kenny. You couldn't even father a normal kid.

I shook my head against the thought. Part of me knew it was wrong, but more of me knew it was all too true. I was a screwup all the way around.

253

"Well then...here." Diane was holding the baby toward me. "If you're not going to go down to the station and earn an income for us, I will. In case you don't remember, we have four kids to feed."

I pushed my chair away from the table. It scraped across the floor, a shrill grating that echoed my feelings and startled my abnormal son. He let out a thin cry. "No!" I said a little too loudly. "I'm not gonna stay with the kid. I'll go—"

Diane's eyes narrowed as she drew the baby to her chest. "He's not *the kid*." Icicles were warmer than her voice. She turned her back to me.

"I'll go to the station." My voice was icy, too. I leaned over the table, folding the paper into a neat rectangle, and then I quietly pushed my chair under the table. Diane was mad enough to make a federal case over my usual messy habits.

She continued to pace the kitchen, carefully keeping one cold shoulder lifted in my direction. "We're going to have to name this baby sometime." I could hear tears trying to push through her words.

I kept silent, watching as the little head of my new son peeked over the edge of Diane's shoulder. Brown, almond-shaped eyes seemed to stare right through me. What kind of name would fit a misfit?

He's not a misfit anymore than you are. Than anyone. All people have purpose.

I blew a puff of air through my nose at the thought. I had no purpose other than to mess things up. And I'd done a good job of it this time.

As I tossed the newspaper into the basket where Diane liked to keep them until garbage day, she walked out of the kitchen with the baby, murmuring soft-somethings into his ear. Part of me wanted nothing more than to pull Diane to me, wrap my arms around her, and mend this broken place between us. I wanted her comforting words to fall on my ears, too. Wanted the support she'd always given me no matter how bad I'd screwed up. But this time was different. No amount of hugging would change the fact that my son wasn't normal. A permanent piece of evidence showing what a mess-up I was.

I shoved my arms into my jacket. I could already hear Marv Bender grilling me about the new baby. All I'd need was for him to get the details that the kid had Down syndrome and it would be all over Brewster by lunchtime. *Kenny Pearson has a misfit for a kid.* I made up my mind. If Marv's school bus was parked outside the station I'd drive around town until he left.

That could take the whole morning. You know how he likes to hang out there.

Suddenly I missed my job. The guys. Missed the joking and teasing that went along with the daily gossip. But there was no joke about this news. What I missed was my old life. The way it had been. Simple. Uncomplicated. It would never be that way again.

Kenny, your life has never been simple. You just never dealt with the problems. You let Diane handle the bills. You pushed any problems aside as if you were tucking them under that greasy old piece of carpet you wipe your feet on at the station.

What problems?

See? That's your problem. You let Diane worry about how to pay the bills. Worry about the kids. Did you ever once take one of the kids to the doctor if they were sick? No. You pleaded, "the station," and let Diane handle the burden. You never looked to expand your business. Bring in a little more income for your family. As long as you could play ball, gab with the guys, and fix an engine now and then, you thought life was good—

It was good!

Was? What makes you think it isn't now?

Well...I've got this new kid.

You've held three other "new" kids in your arms and you thought life was good then.

But, this kid is...is...*different.*

He will have joy in his life. And sorrow. He will love and be loved back. How is that so different from you? From anyone?

He's...he's...

Special?

I wasn't going to say that.

He is. Just as you are.

I'm not special. I'm nothing but a screwup. I'm—

A child of God?

"Kenny, answer the phone! I'm changing the baby's diaper." Diane's reminder jerked me out of the strange conversation I'd been having with myself.

No...not with yourself. With Me.

I shook off the odd chill that ran down my back and grabbed up the phone.

"Are you coming in today?" It was Pete.

"Maybe. Why?" Maybe I wouldn't need to stop at the station. Maybe I'd simply drive around town, take a run out to Brush Lake, be gone long enough so Diane would think I'd spent time at work.

Kenny, grow up.

What?

Grow up.

Suddenly, it was if my Aunt Ida was speaking straight into my head. *Vhen I vas a childt I spoke and tought and reasoned as a childt does. But vhen I became a man I put avay the childish tings.*

How many times had I heard her say that old verse? She repeated it to me almost every time I tickled the kids until Diane told me to stop. Even sometimes when I told Ida the score of a softball game my team had won and bragged about the home runs I'd hit. There she'd be, saying, "*Put away the childish things.*"

What was wrong with a guy having a little fun?

Nothing is wrong with having fun...provided you've taken care of your responsibilities first. Your wife... Your kids...

"I need to make some fuel deliveries. I've already put them off a day." Pete's end of the conversation broke through my thoughts. "Marv said he can sit here while I make a run if you can't make it in." Pete's voice grew muffled, as if he was speaking so someone nearby couldn't overhear. "But if anyone needs to pay for their gas with a credit card while I'm gone, I don't think Marv can handle it."

All I needed was to go into the station and have Marv waiting there for me. A bobcat ready to pounce. Waiting to chew on all the details about my new kid. Hardly able to run to Vicky's fast enough to spit out the juicy news until it spread all over town.

Nope. Not gonna happen. "Let Marv sit there. It'll be fine. Diane needs me. My kid…my kid…Well, Diane needs to rest and needs my help." There. Pete didn't need to know more than my white lie.

Put away childish things.

"I'm going out," I yelled to Diane, zipping up my Kenny's Super-Pumper jacket as if I were going to head straight to the station. Before I could put my hand on the doorknob, the phone rang again. I said a quick prayer that it wasn't Pete telling me Marv couldn't sit there after all. "Hello?"

"Kenny, it's Cindy." Ah, my sister-in-law. She'd want to talk to Diane for sure.

"I'll get—"

"You're just the person I wanted to talk to."

Great. What would Cindy have to talk to me about? I hoped Diane hadn't asked Cindy to *talk* to me. With her nursing background, Diane thought Cindy had the answer to just about any problem that came along. It would be just like the two of them to cook up a plan to somehow psych me into thinking having an abnormal kid was…well, normal. I knew better. No amount of talking would change my mind. I had words ready at the tip of my tongue. I planned to nip any convincing she might try in the bud. *I was just on my way out.* That should handle anything she had to say. In fact, it might be smart of me to cut her off before she could get started.

"I was just on my way out the door," I said smugly. There.

"Perfect," Cindy countered. "Aunt Ida wants to talk to you. I'll tell her you'll swing by." With that she hung up.

So much for my brilliant plan. I pulled on my gloves, remembering all over again that it was my fault Aunt Ida was in the Brewster Nursing Home. More proof of how everything I did just messed things up more. Which reminded me…I hadn't checked on her house in over a week.

Kenny, you're nothing but a loser all the way around.

Who knew what mid-March in North Dakota would do to an empty house in that period of time? I jogged outdoors and hopped in the pickup. It felt good to have a purpose. Something I needed to do. Something where I didn't have to run into anyone. Ida's house was the perfect hideout.

I drove my pickup through the finger drifts that had blown across Ida's driveway during the past week. *You should have come and shoveled.* Another reminder of where I had failed.

I marched through the light covering of snow and let myself into the house. Man, it was seriously cold in here! I hurried over to the thermostat. The thermometer hovered near freezing, not at its usual fifty degrees. I tromped into the basement and over to the furnace. Sure enough, the fuel gauge rested on empty.

I slapped the side of the fuel tank as if my hand might jolt it into action. What I should have been slapping was the side of my dense head.

Nothing. Absolutely nothing you do is right.

I walked through the basement, pulling faded strings to switch on bare light bulbs, carefully checking water pipes that zigzagged across the ceiling, looking for a break in the lines. Maybe one lucky thing would happen today and the water pipes would have held. I couldn't see any sign of a leak downstairs.

I hurried upstairs and checked the water in the toilet. It wasn't frozen. Yet. If I called Pete now, maybe I could catch him before he left the station with the fuel truck. I could get him over here pronto and get the furnace running again. Avert a small disaster, a big plumbing bill, and Ida's chewing out.

I picked up the phone and punched in the station phone number. It took me a good minute to figure out I was holding a dead receiver. Of course, I'd had the phone disconnected when Ida moved out. Once again, as I slammed down the phone, I could almost hear Ida speaking out loud, "*Dummkopf!*"

Dumbhead, was right. I was going to have to stop by the station after all.

Well, there was nothing to do but go on in. Marv's yellow school bus was pulled up to the curb, proof positive that he was lurking inside. I sat outside the station in my pickup a moment longer, putting off the inevitable. The fuel truck was gone, which meant Pete was out making deliveries. I'd taken a quick loop around Brewster, hoping to track him down, but he was more than likely on a run out in the country.

I rolled my eyes up into my head, took a deep breath, and yanked on the door handle. I was as ready as I'd ever be to face Marv's nosy questions.

As I opened the door of the station the smell of oil and gas was sweet perfume after being away for over a week. I didn't realize how much I'd missed it until the scent yanked at a place deep in my big gut.

"Hey," I said to Marv as I walked around him, avoiding his eyes. I didn't want to invite conversation. All I wanted was to sit down and breathe in what I'd missed. I lowered myself into the saggy office chair behind the desk and picked up a stack of mail. Quickly I flipped through the pile, tossing junk mail as I went. I could feel Marv's unasked questions bouncing off my chest, careening in sharp angles off the side of my head. I kept my eyes on the envelopes in my hand. Marv sipped loudly from the Styrofoam cup in his hand.

The driveway bell sounded. Automatically I stood up, ready to run outside.

"Want me to get that?" Marv was standing, too.

I glanced out the window. Vince Bender was idling his Buick by the pumps. He'd be pumping me for the latest if I went out there to fill his tank. "Thanks," I said as I sat back down.

I sorted through the rest of the mail, putting the bills in one too-big pile. I looked around the small office space. I didn't even know where Diane kept the station ledger or the checkbook. Maybe all that stuff was at home. I riffled through the neat stack of charge slips stuck on a spindle near the cash register. It looked as though Pete had been busy this past week. The only trouble was...who was going to write up the invoices to collect all those charges? Diane was still moving slow from having the baby. I also knew the doctors had scheduled a variety of appointments to assess the kid's…well, to check him out. I'd told Diane I wouldn't be going along. The way I'd been acting didn't lend itself to asking for small favors, like doing the station's books this month. Or big ones. Like putting up with an oaf like me.

I ran my fingers through my hair. I couldn't help the way I was feeling about this kid. You could tell he was different by just looking at him. Weird shaped eyes in a flat little face. A nose and mouth that were…I couldn't describe what it was exactly, he was simply—

Special?

I closed my eyes against the sudden lump in my throat. I didn't want any kid of mine going through life being teased and talked about.

Then you'd better treat him the way you treat the other kids.

How could I treat him as if he were normal when he wasn't?

What's normal?

Being like everyone else.

Are you like everyone else?

No.

Would you want to be? Don't you think life would be awfully boring if everyone were the same? You might be surprised at where this child might lead you.

"Need some change." Marv walked into the station with a twenty-dollar bill hanging off the edge of his fingers. He punched at the cash register as if he'd been doing this all his life…or at least for the past week…and pulled out three ones. "Be right back," he said as a wash of cold air took his place.

With any luck I would be out of here before Marv came back in. I grabbed a pen and scrawled a note to Pete. *Fill my Aunt Ida's fuel tank ASAP!!!* There, that should do it. I'd go over and restart her furnace this afternoon. I took a piece of tape and fastened the note to the cash register drawer where Pete couldn't miss it.

Too late. Marv was on his way back inside. I stuck my eyes into the mail as if it were classified information. He picked up his coffee cup and meandered his way around my chair to the coffeepot. I could hear the thin stream of liquid filling the cup, then the pot being put back on the burner, then Marv taking a long, loud sip. Maybe, if I was lucky, for once Marv would keep his big mouth shut. Then again, maybe he'd heard all about the kid and didn't know what to say.

I realized suddenly this was exactly what I was afraid of, a whole *lifetime* ahead of me wondering what people were thinking. I wasn't sure what was worse…what they might say out loud…or what they wouldn't say at all.

Jan

For the first time in three weeks I threw back the covers and jumped out of bed. A finger of anticipation tickled in my chest. Olivia was coming over for coffee this morning and I had things to get ready. I tiptoed toward the bathroom.

"Are you okay?" Dan rolled over and looked at the clock. He was always the first one in the house out of bed. For all he knew this was an early-morning bathroom break for me. The past weeks I'd been lying in bed, or on the couch, until mid-morning. No wonder he assumed I might not be feeling well.

"I'hm fine," I whispered into the still-dark room. "I wahnt to make some bawnaa-na bwread. It's haas to bake for an hour. I-hw thought Jow-ey might lihke some befowre he goes to scho-ool."

"Are you sure you're okay?" Dan lifted himself onto an elbow and turned on the light.

I squinted as I turned my head away from the bright light. I couldn't help but smile a bit. Considering my sluglike existence the past weeks, his concern was justified. "I'hm fine. Libby ii-s coming ohver this mohrning. For coffee."

"She is?" Dan sat all the way up. "How'd that happen?"

I shrugged one shoulder under my silky nightgown. "I-h invi-ited her."

"Great," Dan said lying back onto the bed. He tucked his hands behind his head, smiling in a goofy sort of way. "That's great."

⁓

It felt strange to be working in the kitchen. A good kind of strange. I flipped the banana bread out of the pan onto a cooling rack, enjoying the sweet aroma that filled the kitchen. I'd never been much for cooking or baking. I'd perfected roast beef and potatoes only because my guys liked to eat. And I was an expert at tearing lettuce greens for the salads that were my steady diet. But today I was aware of a sense of satisfaction that accompanied the measuring and mixing I'd done. I found myself anticipating serving Joey and Dan warm banana bread for breakfast and then sharing a slice with Libby later this morning.

When you become more aware of others instead of yourself, that's when you'll know you're getting better.

Libby's words echoed. I bent down and smiled into the small, decorative mirror that hung near the kitchen door. No, I wasn't better. The right side of my mouth still drooped like a limp lettuce leaf.

Healing comes in a variety of ways.

Well, the "way" I wanted was so that I could see it.

My way is best. Trust—

The thought was interrupted as Joey jumped and hit the top of the doorframe with his hand as he bounded into the kitchen. "Wow, Mom, what gives?"

"Bawnaa-na bread." I motioned my hand toward the golden loaf as though I were a small-town Vanna White. "Waa-nt some?"

Joey hesitated, looking at me as if an alien had taken away his real mom. Warm banana bread versus pour-your-own cereal didn't take much thought. "Sure!" He yanked out a chair and sat at the table, scanning the sports section of the paper as I poured a glass of milk and cut a thick slice of the steaming bread.

"I should get the camera," Dan said as he walked into the 1950s-like scene.

On another day his comment might have irritated me, but today I was willing to share my rare sense of well-being. "Bawnaa-na bread?" I was June Cleaver with a speech problem.

Dan grinned. "Sure."

Joey glanced up from the sports section, pointing to the action shot on the front of the page. "Cool, huh, Dad?"

Dan didn't even look at the paper. Instead, he stared straight at me, his eyes crinkled at the corners. "Very cool, son. Very cool."

It was more than enough.

⟿

"I-h can haa-rdly believe Emily is almowst done with her firr-st year of…" I worked my mouth hard to get the word out, "coll-llw-ege." Jodi would have been proud.

"I can't either." Libby broke off a piece of banana bread and popped it into her mouth.

"Howw-w is she handling…coll-ege?" The word was easier this time.

Libby's eyes widened as she motioned that she needed to swallow first. "Good! She was homesick at first. But then, so was I." She lowered her voice as if there was someone who might overhear. "For about three hours." She laughed as she took a sip of coffee. "You know, the Bible says there's a time for everything, and it was time for Emily to leave home. She was ready…and so was I. I just didn't know it until she left."

"Thaa-t's interess-ting." I tried to imagine four years from now when Joey would be graduating. I couldn't imagine. "Whaa-t's the best part?"

"Oh, my, how long do you have?" Libby held up one hand and started ticking off reasons as she lifted each finger. "No hairspray all over the bathroom sink. Her bed stays *made*. I don't lie awake till all hours wondering what she's doing and when she'll be home." She sat back in her chair and folded her arms over her chest. "Time."

"Tii-me?"

Libby nodded her head as she wrapped her hands around her coffee mug. "I didn't realize how much time I spent thinking about the kids, sitting in the bleachers at ball games, doing laundry…until it wasn't there to do anymore." She took a sip of coffee, then continued. "Don't get me wrong, I loved it *all* at the time. Well, maybe not the laundry. But, like I said, there's a time for everything, and now, after all these years of being…" she made quote marks in the air, "'*Mom*,' I get to be '*me*.'"

I put an elbow on the table and my chin in my hand. "Aa-nd who is Lii-bby?"

She looked at me for several long seconds before answering. Long enough to make me wonder what she was thinking. Long enough for me to realize I'd never asked her such a personal question before. Long enough for me to realize I really did want to hear her answer.

When you start thinking about others instead of yourself…

"Who is Lii-bby?" I repeated, reaching for the silver coffee thermos. I really did want to know.

She watched as I refilled her mug, took a sip, and then spoke. "Well, I'm still *mom*, and still *wife*, but there's this whole block of time where I get to simply be *me*. She paused as her eyes focused somewhere outside. "Even I'm still discovering *who*, exactly, that is." She looked back at me. "It's kind of fun." The corners of her mouth turned up in an impish smile. I could feel one side of my lips struggling to match the curve.

Libby took a breath as if she was about to say something, but instead she picked up her cup and slowly sipped from the rim. Normally I would have filled the silence with empty chatter, but since my life had been so isolated these past weeks, I had nothing to say. I sipped my coffee as I waited for her to say more.

She put her cup down and stared into the liquid as if debating about what to say next. Her voice was tentative. "Did I tell you I finished writing my book?"

"You-w did?!" A surge of excitement filled my voice. She'd written a book? An entire book? I'd never known anyone who'd written a book.

You wouldn't have cared before.

"When-nn did you-uu finn-ish? How-w long ii-s it? Whaa-t's it abouu-t?" Even as I struggled to quickly say the words, I remembered Libby had mentioned her book to me before. Why hadn't I thought to ask more about it those times?

Because you were wrapped up in yourself.

"Whaa-t nn-ow?" I had so many questions.

"Hold on." Libby was laughing, shaking her head. "One question at a time, please."

"Okaa-y." I stopped for a breath. "When-nn did you-uu finn-ish it?"

"Well, I typed '*The End*' just before Emily left for college."

"And you-u didn't say aany-thing unn-til now?" How could Libby keep something like that quiet? If I had written a book, I would have blabbered the news to anyone who would listen.

Not if they were someone like you…someone who didn't know how to listen.

I felt a blush of embarrassment climb up my neck. How many other things didn't I know about my friend because I'd been too busy talking about nothing? What had I missed that Dan or Joey might have wanted to share with me? My slow, thick tongue was turning into a bulky blessing.

Ahhh…you're beginning to understand.

Suddenly I wanted to know everything there was to know about Libby's book. "Tell me whaa-t ii-t's abouu-t." I leaned forward, pushing my hair behind my ears as if to catch every word. The appearance of my slack face occurred as an afterthought. Well, it was too late now. Libby had seen it full on and she hadn't so much as flinched.

She stared at her hands. "It's about Anne."

Oh. I felt a sudden tightening of my throat at the memory of our fated friend.

"Our" friend? You weren't much of a friend to Anne.

I cringed as a flash of memories of that awful time played through my mind. The way I'd run off to manicure appointments rather than face my pregnant friend and her breast cancer diagnosis. I remembered the way Olivia had stuck like superglue to Anne during it all. Surely Libby could have used a friend during that time. If I'd been too afraid and immature to deal with Anne's serious issues, I could have certainly been a better friend to Libby. A friend who would have listened to her fears about Anne.

I reached out a hand and took Libby's in mine. "Waa-s it har-wd? Wrii-ting about thaa-t time?"

She turned her hand so our fingers intertwined. "Actually," she said, "it was a bit like having her back again for a while." She sighed as the warmth of our hands blended together. She was quiet for a bit, then she smiled. "Thanks for asking."

Why did I feel like crying?

Maybe it's for all the things you've missed by not asking. Not listening.

Libby squeezed my hand, then let go and picked up her cup. "So," she asked looking at me over the rim, "How are you…really?" Her steady gaze penetrated.

A flood of words rushed to my tongue, but for once in my life it seemed much too much effort to speak them. I tilted my head to one side, lifted a shoulder. "I-hm oh-kay." It wasn't that I had nothing to say, frustrations to share, or fears of my own, it was just that I had something much more important on my mind.

"Caa-n I ree-ad youwr book?"

Libby put down her cup. "Are you sure you're all right?" There was a twinkle in her eye. "If I remember correctly you once told me the only books you ever read are romances." She examined her fingernails. "My book is…is… Well, put it this way, it's not a romance. It's… Parts of it are *hard*. It's about Anne's cancer." Once again her eyes pierced mine. "But mostly it's about friendship. Are you sure you want to read it?"

Now it was my turn to examine my fingernails. Her words, *"mostly it's about friendship,"* laid heavy against my chest, as if pressing me, measuring me, in some odd way.

I thought about the way Libby had shown up on my doorstep three weeks ago, dragging me to speech therapy in spite of my protests. The way she'd walked me down that long hall as if she wasn't one bit embarrassed to be seen with someone who looked the way I did. I remembered the many times over the past years when I'd breezed in and out of our friendship, always expecting Olivia to be there for me, never once thinking that she might need me to be there for her. I recalled a conversation…was it almost a year ago?…when Libby had confided her struggle with depression. I'd blown off her comment and blabbered about the blues I had every month. When she'd ended up in the hospital, I hadn't so much as sent a card. I knew now about the kind of depression she'd been trying to tell me about.

I could feel tears filling my eyes, and I might as well have stuffed cotton balls down my throat for the way my vocal cords suddenly swelled. I blinked, sending those tears down my cheeks. I swallowed hard and then looked up at Libby. "I-h wann-t to read youwr book. I-h think I-h ha-ave a lot to leawrn abouu-t friennn-dship."

It was a start.

Ida

"Vhat a sveetie." I smoothed the backs of my fingers across the feather-soft cheek of Diane and Kenny's baby boy. He turned his head my way as if ready for an early supper. Diane had put a pillow on my lap as I sat in my wheelchair and then laid the baby in my arms. How long had it been since I'd held a baby? Maybe since Paige was born more than two years ago. I wished Fred were here. He always loved babies. I could feel tears filling my eyes as I gazed at the miracle in my lap. That was one good thing about being an old woman. I no longer cared when my emotions spilled from my eyes. I was just glad I was alive to feel them. Balancing the baby, I carefully pulled a tissue from the cuff of my cardigan and dabbed at my eyes. "Haff you picked out a name?"

Diane rolled her eyes from her nearby perch on the bed in my small room at the home. "I'm about ready to throttle Kenny. The hospital called twice. They finally sent out a birth certificate that says '*Baby Boy Pearson*' in place of a name. We need to write to some state office when we finally decide and amend the birth certificate." Diane closed her eyes for a moment. "I don't know what I'm going to do. I've never seen Kenny like this. I mean, the guy can be stubborn…"

"Like an oldt mule."

"Exactly." Diane shook her head. "But this is different. He sits around the house doing absolutely nothing. If I ask him to hold the baby, he makes some excuse why he can't, and then he gets up and leaves for a while. Pretty soon, he's back home just sitting." Diane sighed. "He's hardly spending any time at the station. Pete, the guy who works there, calls the house every day. I don't know how much longer Pete will put up with running our business practically by himself. And I don't know what we're going to do, make that what *I'm* going to do, about the station bills."

The baby yawned and stretched, turning in a way that had me grabbing for his blanket to keep him from rolling off my lap. Quickly, Diane reached out a hand.

"Are you getting tired of holding him?" she asked.

"Neffer." I fluffed at the pillow to nestle the sleeping baby nearer to me. "Vhat is habbening witt the station?"

She tucked both hands under the sides of her blue jeans. "Ever since Kenny bought it I've done the book work. The guy is great with an engine, but lousy when it comes to paying bills."

"Godt giffs us all gifts."

"Yes, but He doesn't put more hours in the day." Diane wrapped a hand around the back of her neck and pushed her head into it. Her voice grew thick. "I don't have the time…" she paused as she took a deep breath, "or the energy to look after the kids, run the station, and," she gestured at my lap, "take on all the special appointments this baby is going to need." Now it was her turn to have her eyes fill with tears. She wiped at them with the back of her hand. "I'm sorry. I didn't mean to do this." A soft sob escaped her lips. "It's just been so ha—rd." She cried for real now. Hiding her head with her hands over her face.

I wanted to reach out and comfort her. Wrap the body that held her tender heart in my wrinkled arms. But with the baby on my lap and sitting in a wheelchair it was impossible to do. "Lordt," I said softly, "comfort dis young mother. Holdt her in Your luffing arms. Giff Kenny eyes to see how to be a goot husband andt a heart…" Diane cried harder as I spoke, "to luff this childt as much as You luff his mama."

There was a time in my life when Diane's tears would have made me uncomfortable. But I had long ago learned that tears could be healing in a way that keeping them inside wasn't. I sat quietly as Diane's held-in emotions spilled from her eyes. I had time. Plenty of time. If the good Lord was giving me the gift of her tears, I would sit here as long as needed.

I bowed my head, watching the sleeping infant in my lap, silently praying for his mama and his daddy. And for this innocent child who would need every bit of the love I already felt for him.

Diane sniffed loudly and pulled several tissues from the box on the nightstand by my bed. She blew her nose and then wiped under her eyes and down her cheeks.

"I'm sorry," she said, leaning over to put the tissues into the small plastic garbage can by my bed.

"Tears are goodt."

"I didn't know I had all that bottled up inside." Diane filled her lungs with a deep breath and then blew it out. "Whew. That felt surprisingly good."

"I toldt you."

She stood. "I'd better get going. I need to swing by the station and at least pick up the bills. Maybe I can find some time tonight, after the kids are in bed, to get at them." The circles under her eyes underlined how little energy she would have later this evening. She bent and scooped the baby into her arms, leaving my lap feeling as if something good was missing.

"Vill you tell Kenny I vouldt like to see him?"

Diane nodded, weariness behind her smile. "I'll try. He doesn't seem to hear much of anything I say these days."

I reached out and put a hand on her shirtsleeve. "Then I vill pray that the Lordt wouldt open Kenny's plugcked ears."

Diane laughed. "You do that. If anyone can get through to Kenny, it will have to be God." She shifted the baby into one arm and leaned over to hug me. "Thanks for listening to me blubber," she said.

"Acht," I said waving her away. "Vhat else does an oldt voman haff to do, anyvay?"

It seemed all I was doing these days was praying.

Now I had the new baby to add to my growing list. That precious child, with almond eyes and flattened little face, as if a baker had formed him from soft dough and then tapped him on the nose and said, "There you go." He was born with God's blessing, but also with afflictions we humans didn't understand. He would need more prayer than the other children.

I opened my Bible and pulled out the piece of paper I kept there to mark my page. *Precious Baby* I wrote near the bottom. Oh, my. This list was getting long. Too long to trust to my ancient memory to recall each day.

I held the list toward the window, catching the late afternoon light. So many who needed my prayers. At the top were several names I'd drawn a faint line through. Friends and relatives who had passed away, but who I still liked to remember in prayer now and then, thanking God for the ways they had blessed my life.

Further down the list was Jan Jordan. I'd started praying for her before I even knew who she was. I remembered well the day she skirted around my wheelchair to enter the therapy room for the first time. Her troubled countenance cried out for more help than I knew Jodi could give her. God had told me to pray and I had. Little did I know those prayers would turn out to be for my newest friend.

I'd been praying for Kenny since he'd been born. He and his twin brother, Ben, had peppered my prayers for...what was it already? Thirty-six...seven? Could it be thirty-eight years? Those two had given me a run for my prayer life when they were teenagers. But they'd grown into two fine men, even if I did have to get perturbed with Kenny's stubborn streak now and then. Of the twins, he was the one I could count on to look in on me after my Fred died. Ben was too busy to think of his old aunt, but Kenny always found a minute. Not always the exact minute I wanted but, eventually, things got done.

Now, I found myself bowing in prayer for him more than I ever had. It was one thing to pray a child through adolescence, something else entirely to pray a grown man through discouragement.

Somehow this seemed harder.

Kenny

"I'm going to run an air bomb over to Mrs. Bechtle's. She's got a flat." Pete stood in front of me as if waiting for permission. "Think you can handle things while I'm gone? It'll only take me a few minutes."

I nodded slowly. Since when had Pete taken to asking *me* if I could handle things?

Since you checked out. Left him in charge for the past three weeks.

Pete hopped into the old beater pickup I kept for emergency runs like this and drove off. I wandered out of the station office into the garage. The air was warm and thick. Somehow Pete had figured out how to work the used-oil burning stove I'd rigged up. There was a red vehicle on the hoist I didn't recognize. I felt a strange churning in my gut as I realized I had no idea what needed to be done on the Ford. Water pump? Oil change? Rotate the tires? The thought of any of it seemed exhausting.

I looked around at new mufflers stacked in boxes along one side of the garage, at the air reel hanging over my head. There was a stack of dirty rags in one corner and a bikini-clad girl on a calendar hanging on the back wall. None of it seemed familiar. None of it sparked my interest. Not even the skimpy bikini. Diane would be happy. She nagged me about that stupid calendar every year.

I roamed the oily garage, looking for something to do, half-hoping some car part would grab my attention and take my mind off its dull brooding. All I could think about lately was my kid. My kid with a condition called Down syndrome. I knew everyone in Brewster would simply call him "retarded."

Retarded.

I picked an old rag off the counter and threw it hard on the floor. *I hate that word.*

Bad memories?

Yeah. I stuffed my hands into the pockets of my jeans and kicked at the rag on the floor. I remembered all too well the taunts I'd heard out on the elementary playground. *Retard. Retard!* Just 'cause math was hard for me. I'd stood at the blackboard for what seemed like *hours* trying to divide or multiply or whatever impossible problem the teacher had assigned me to do. Couldn't she tell how humiliating it was to stand there while my classmates snickered behind my back? My only defense was to become the class clown. If they were going to make fun of me, I'd give them some other reason to laugh.

Retard! I could still hear the whispers. Man. Kids could be so mean. Teachers, too. No kid should have to put up with that.

So…what are you afraid of? That your kid will have to live with those same words? Those same feelings?

All his life! I kicked hard at a tire propped against the wall. The contact with thick rubber felt good. I kicked it again. And again. Until the muscles in my leg were spent.

At least I had enough brain power to go to mechanic school. When I married Diane I had the math problem taken care of, too. I handled the work; she handled the money.

I pulled my foot back, ready to kick the tire again. My kid would *never* have a break. No one to run interference for him.

That's why I gave him to you.

My throat closed as I braced my throbbing foot against the top of the tire instead of kicking it. I rested my forearms on my lifted knee and bent my head. *I don't want that kind of responsibility. It'll hurt too much to watch my kid—*

It's not always what you *want that's best.*

The driveway bell rang sharply inside the garage. I jerked my head up, almost knocking it against the muffler boxes sticking out from the wall. I didn't want to wait on a nosy customer, but I didn't exactly like the thoughts I'd been having, either. Anything was better than thinking about my new kid. I hurried outside.

"Hey, Kenny." Donny Klein stepped out of his pickup, nodding his head in a way I knew meant "fill it up." "It's good to see you back…" His words trailed off as if suddenly he'd remembered the reason why I hadn't been at work.

The kid.

A weird quietness hung between us. I stuck the gas nozzle into the side of the truck, then grabbed the window spray and a rag and got busy.

"Gas prices hanging steady, I see."

"Yup." For all the checking I'd done they could have skyrocketed or bottomed out. I might be making a killing. Or losing my shirt.

That'd be nothing new.

I stepped on the running board and stretched my arm across the window. For the first time in months I noticed my bum shoulder wasn't clenching up on me. Maybe these past weeks of rest had done some good.

I use all things for good. I stretched my arm as far as I could reach. Pushing my luck. Testing. It was as if Aunt Ida were standing by my shoulder today, repeating the Bible verses and advice she'd quoted all my life.

Not Aunt Ida. Me.

Who? Had I said that out loud? Quickly, I glanced at Donny. He was staring up at the overcast sky. I cleared my throat. If I wasn't careful, I would start talking back to the unusual voice that had befriended me today. "Think it'll snow?"

"I'd rather have rain. Spring's late this year." Donny cleared his throat. "Sure could use the moisture." The automatic shutoff on the gas hose snapped. Donny reached for his wallet and started walking toward the office.

I topped off his tank. Maybe he was as relieved as I was that this uncomfortable encounter would soon be over. I didn't need a four-year degree to sense his unsaid words. I had no doubt he was as curious as everyone in town about my kid. Why didn't he just ask?

Why don't you just tell him? You could use the support of friends right now.

Friends? I had no friends. Even my twin brother, Ben, had shuffled his feet as if he were running a football drill when he'd stopped by to see the baby. The *one* time he stopped by. I twisted Donny's gas cap tight and headed into the station. As soon as Pete got back I would head home. At least there I didn't have to squirm through awkward silences, wondering at unasked questions.

What about Diane?

Diane didn't have an unasked question in her life. If she thought something, she said it. At least I knew where I stood with her.

Not so firm a foundation the last I checked.

I was squirming again. Aunt Ida's Bible verses were coming out of my ears today.

Not Aunt Ida. Me...

Maybe I should go talk to Pastor Ammon. Nah. I shook my head as I opened the station door. I wasn't a pastor-talking kind of guy.

Then talk to Me.

Hoo-boy. I needed to get a grip. Collect Donny's money and head home. A long nap on the couch was what I needed more than anything. Time to dream about absolutely nothing.

⁓

Where was Pete? I looked, again, at the clock on the wall, double-checking it with my wristwatch. He'd been gone thirty-five minutes. More than enough time to put air in Mrs. Bechtle's tire so she could drive it to the station and get it patched.

I watched a ragtag line of cars pass by on the highway. For the first time in my life I hoped none of them needed gas. I straightened a couple candy bars and then checked the pop cooler. Full. Pete was running this place as if it were his own.

It will be if you don't snap out of this funk. Start taking responsibility...

I plopped myself into the lumpy office chair behind the counter, checking my watch again. The couch called me.

Two neat stacks of mail were pushed next to the cash register. I picked one up, tossing the grocery fliers and junk mail into the garbage can. I quickly sorted through the second pile and was left with a handful of first-class mail. Like a turtle, I tucked my neck into my shoulders when I saw the return address of my bulk fuel supplier. *Second Notice.* No doubt Diane hadn't had time to pay for the last shipment he'd delivered. I cringed as I imagined what was inside the other letters. Insurance premiums? Vendor bills?

No use just imagining. I stuck a thumb under the flap of an envelope from the bank and ripped it open. *Overdraft Notice.*

Wasn't life just peachy? I put my head into my hands. My life seemed to be crumbling around me. I was nothing but a loser. A failure. A no-good...*retard.*

As if I were back in junior high, a flash of hot anger burned in my chest. I was *not* a retard! I felt like slugging someone until I realized that someone would be me. I'd called myself that horrible word. I kneaded the tight muscle at the crook of my neck. My life was nothing but a mess. A complete and total mess. What was I going—

Go to the bank.

Oh, yeah, right. Go to the bank and let some teller lecture me about being overdrawn. Ha! That was the last place I wanted to go.

You can't get away from your troubles by running...only by facing them. Go to the bank.

I shoved the overdraft slip into the pocket of my jacket. The only place I planned to go was to the three cushions on my couch.

~

"Kenny, Paul will see you now." Nancy hung up the phone and motioned me back toward Paul Bennett's corner office.

After Pete had returned, I'd taken a drive around town to kill time, detouring a block out of my usual swing to avoid the entrance to Vicky's and the possibility of someone waving me down for coffee. How I'd gotten from the station into the lobby of the bank waiting to see the bank president I had no clue.

Paul stood as I walked into the office and quickly came around the side of his desk. "Kenny," he said, pumping my hand, "it's good to see you. Have a seat." He closed the office door, settled himself into his chair, and then pushed a button on the phone. "Hold my calls, please." He leaned forward in his chair. "How are you doing?"

Oh, man. I wondered if he had any idea what a loaded question that was. Had he heard about my kid? Was he asking about the overdraft notice I had stuffed in my pocket? If Paul was like everyone else in town, he knew about my kid but wasn't talking…at least not to me. He must mean my bank balance. My *negative* balance.

I looked down at my folded hands, at my thumbs that were twitching as if they were two agitated worms. "Not so good." I reached into my pocket and pulled out the bank slip. "I'm sure you know about this," I said, laying the crumpled paper on his desk. "Diane has always done the books and what with…" I stopped and cleared my throat. I wasn't about to get into those details with my banker. I took another stab at it. "I've never been good with numbers and Diane has been…" I swiped a hand through my hair. Man, there was no getting around it. The subject of my new kid was an elephant sitting in the middle of the office.

"Kenny," Paul said, leaning forward on his arms, "it's okay. I know you're going through a challenging time right now. I'm glad you came in to talk to me."

"I didn't—" I started to say. Tried to explain how I hadn't planned to come to the bank at all. "I—" I lifted my palms and let them fall into my lap. Suddenly I had no words. I felt my throat growing tight. I swallowed. I was either going to cry on my banker's shoulder…or choke to death trying not to. I coughed into my hand.

"Life is full of things we didn't plan, isn't it?" Paul folded his hands on the desk top. "I can't wait to ask God a few questions of my own." He paused and then went on. "I bet you have one big question for Him right now."

If my throat wasn't fully clogged before, it was now. How did Paul know about that? About how mad I felt at God? So mad I hadn't even dared *think* about what I wanted to tell the Big Guy. I rubbed at the tingling in my nose.

His voice was gentle. "God can handle your questions, Kenny."

A dry sob escaped from between my lips. I disguised it as a cough, pointing to my throat as if I'd had a cold all week.

He went on. "I don't know why some people are blessed with perfectly healthy children and some are given a child with extra challenges."

Well, there. If I'd thought Paul wasn't going to talk about my kid, I'd been wrong. The elephant was out of its cage. I hung my head.

"Life isn't going to be easy for your child." His voice was so gentle it was almost as if he was patting me on my back with his words. "But I have a feeling that God has given you this little boy because you are the perfect dad for him."

I swung my head up. Me? The *perfect* dad? In my life I'd been a lot of things…a mess-up, a loser, a sports nut, a fool. As hard as I tried, I'd never been a perfect anything.

Paul was nodding as if there was no denying it. "God doesn't make mistakes, Kenny. Take my word for it. He's got a plan and you're part of it."

Once again I dropped my head. This time it wasn't from some sort of shame I felt. This time it was in humility. I'd come here expecting a lecture on bad business management, instead I'd gotten…I wasn't sure what I'd gotten, but whatever Paul had said, it felt good.

Kind words are like honey.

There was Aunt Ida, again. Or maybe in all those Sundays Diane had dragged me to church something had actually sunk in through my daydreams.

I looked up at Paul. I could feel my mouth working, trying to find words to tell him what his words meant to me. For the first time in three weeks it felt as though at least one person in town understood.

Diane knows. Aunt Ida might have an idea. And don't forget Me. I know exactly how you feel. Talk to Me, Kenny…

"Thank you," I said to Paul. My voice was hoarse. I didn't care. "Thank you."

He seemed to understand. At least he didn't ask me to explain what I was thanking him for.

"Now…" He reached for the crumpled overdraft slip lying in front of me. "About this." He held it up, waving it slightly.

Reality again. "Diane…" I shifted in my chair. Tried again. "Things are such a mess…this new kid…" What was there to say other than I hadn't been tending to business?

Grow up, Kenny. Take responsibility.

I took a deep breath. Blew it out. I could feel a line of dampness forming along my upper lip. "I've let things slide. Having this baby and then finding out that he was—" The words clogged my throat. I pushed them out. "That he has Down syndrome…I haven't been handling it well." A wave of heat flushed up from my chest into my face. Man, I was hot. I shrugged out of my jacket. "I was used to Diane doing the books at the station, paying the bills."

Say it all.

I cleared my throat. "I'm lousy at numbers." Quickly I looked at Paul, looked away. "Always have been." I dipped my head as if I expected him to throw the overdraft slip at my dense head.

"Everyone has gifts," is what he said. "You work with your hands. Diane and you have made a good team, but I imagine she has her hands full these days."

"Yeah, and my attitude hasn't helped." I couldn't believe how strangely good it felt to confess this stuff. Say it out loud where it wasn't hidden deep inside like a secret bomb.

"Who's been making the deposits since you've been away from the station?"

Good question. Slowly I shook my head. "I'm not sure." Man, where had I been these past weeks? What had I been thinking?

Obviously, you haven't been!

"I suppose Pete? Diane? Oh, man." Once again I hung my head. Lifted it. "I don't know."

Two inches. I felt two inches tall…if that. How could I have been so stupid to think Diane could take care of three big kids, a baby who needed extra care, a lummox like me, *and* keep up with the station books? And all I had to do was lie around the house and mope? Or drive around in the country and pretend nothing was wrong? As if that would make anything better. It didn't even help *me* feel good.

Take responsibility. Grow up, Kenny.

I sucked in a breath as if I'd been underwater, and then I looked to Paul for a lifeline. "Where do I start?"

Paul sat back. "Okay, your first step is to go back to the station and talk to Pete. See if he's made regular deposits. Let me check something." Paul swiveled his chair and punched at the keyboard by his elbow. He lightly tapped his index finger against a key until the screen changed. "The deposit history this past month looks spotty. From the look of it, I'd guess Pete has a stash of cash and checks for you to tend to."

I only hoped he did.

Or business could have dried up without you there to tend it.

Once again a mix of anger and shame flooded through me. This time I knew the only person I had to blame was myself. "Anything else?" I needed all the help I could get.

"You're going to have to get your books in order so we can see where you stand. Get everything deposited. Make a list of your collectibles and your outstanding bills."

Already my head was spinning with numbers I couldn't quite see. I ran a finger around the crew neck of my sweatshirt. "Okay," I said, my voice as unsure as my math.

"Kenny?" Paul waited until I looked him in the eye. "You aren't in this alone."

I quickly nodded my head, oddly grateful for my banker. I stood up, pushed my arms into my coat, and shook his hand. As I walked through the lobby of the bank and out the double doors toward my truck, Paul's words kept repeating in my mind. *"You aren't in this alone."*

I got into the truck and turned the key, sitting for a moment before shifting into gear. *"You aren't in this alone."*

I looked over my shoulder and pulled away from the curb. My head felt clearer now. I would go to the station and gather up the bills. Hopefully cash and checks, too. Somehow I'd make sense of it all.

How is a retard like you going to make sense out of numbers he doesn't understand? How will you ever make sense out of having a retarded kid?

Don't call him a retard!

Unexpectedly, anger and tears mixed together. I blinked hard, grateful Brewster's main street was practically empty. What was I going to do? About the gas station? About my kid? I drove past the station. No way was I going to let Pete see me like this.

I drove out of town onto the highway, going nowhere. Just like my life. I hit the heel of my hand against the steering wheel. What was I going to do? I was stupid. My kid was... No! I wasn't going to go there.

And then, a garden of words that had been buried deep down... *"I have a feeling that God has given you this little boy because you are the perfect dad for him."*

Perfect? I was so far from perfect it wasn't funny. Hot, thick tears streamed through my three-week stubble as I drove down the highway.

Then another sentence from before. *"You aren't in this alone."*

I wasn't in this *alone?* Ha! I snorted through my tears. I sure was. Diane was falling in love with our new baby. And probably falling out of love with me. Who else was there?

I scrubbed at the tears mixing into my whiskers. Who would want to love a fat scruff like me anyway?

"Huh?" I said out loud. Too loud. "Who??!!"

For the first time today there was no Aunt Ida advice. No quiet thought to answer my question. It was just me. Good old Kenny.

Good old good-for-nothing Kenny.

I wasn't going to look at myself any sooner than I had to. I concentrated on an anatomy poster on the far side of the therapy room, keeping my eyes away from the mirror as Jodi finished scrawling some notes. She was distracted, her day apparently going not much better than mine. All I'd had to do was open my eyes this morning and I knew it was going to be a bad day.

"Don't forget," Dan said, standing at the foot of the bed and tightening his tie, "I'll be staying at the Comfort Suites." He bent and picked up his overnight bag. "My meeting ends around four tomorrow. If I get out of there right away I should be home for supper."

I nodded and then swung my feet over the side of the bed. I'd been dreading this overnight meeting of his for a week. It would be the first time I'd be on my own with Joey since all this had happened. A part of me knew how ridiculous it was for me to be worried...after all, it wasn't my legs or arms that were paralyzed. I could get around just fine. But, other than my therapy appointment, I wasn't going anywhere these days. Dan had been my shield, of sorts. Without him a few blocks away today and tomorrow, I felt as if I would be floating in space, tethered to nothing.

"Bye." Dan leaned in for a kiss.

I closed my eyes, concentrating on making the fish lips Jodi had taught me. The right side of my mouth hung limp. Some kiss.

"You'll be fine." He squeezed me to his chest with one arm and kissed me quickly on the cheek. "I've gotta run."

That had been two hours ago. Two long hours ago.

"Mom!" Joey hollered through the bathroom door. "I'm late! I need a ride to school."

My first thought was that it would be hard to drive him to school with a paper bag over my head. My second was that I couldn't drive him wrapped in a towel, fresh from the shower.

At least you're getting your sense of humor back.

It wasn't a joke.

I ran a comb through my wet hair, jumped into a pair of jeans, quickly buttoned a blouse, and prayed I wouldn't get pneumonia in the cold car.

Joey was already waiting, slapping his hands against the dashboard, a crazed drummer. I stuck the key in the ignition and turned it. Nothing. I turned it again and pressed on the gas. Silence.

No! Now it was my turn to slap the dash. "Starwt!" I said, tears already pushing into my throat. I turned the key again. Nothing but a dull click. I leaned my head against the steering wheel. How could this be happening today? Any other day of the year Dan would be here with his car as backup. But today...

I turned to Joey. "You'll hawve to run."

Give the kid credit. All he said was, "Good thing I'm out for track, huh?"

I sat in the cold car, my wet hair slowly freezing. I wasn't about to run to my therapy appointment at ten.

You'll have to cancel it.

My stomach dropped at the thought. The long hours of the day stretched ahead of me. My therapy appointment was the only bright spot in it. I wouldn't even be able to look forward to Dan coming home tonight.

You could call Libby for a ride. Or walk.

The nursing home wasn't that far away. Nothing in Brewster was. I'd called on Libby enough. If I dried my hair, bundled up, and put on a pair of oversized sunglasses, no one would see enough of me to notice anything wrong.

You need to get the car fixed.

It could wait until Dan got home. I walked back into the house.

Dan won't be back until tomorrow night. By the time he can check it out and make arrangements to get it fixed, it could be another couple of days before you can drive it. More appointments to walk to.

Well, then, I'd walk.

"Ready to get started?" Jodi was standing across from me, her eyes darting to the clock on the wall and then back to me. It seemed she wasn't even going to sit down and coach me this morning. Possibly she was seeing the pointlessness of all this, too.

Briefly, I closed my eyes, readying myself for the facial exercises I already knew weren't doing any good. The cold morning walk had cleared my head. Made me all too aware that the window-of-opportunity for likely healing of my Bell's palsy was past.

What was it the doctor had said? *We see the majority of improvement in the first two weeks.* I was heading into four weeks of treatment. It didn't take a genius to do the math.

"Let's start with brow lifts." Jodi raised her eyebrows and then lowered them, reminding me of what she wanted me to do. She left me to practice by myself.

The first glimpse was always the worst. In my mind I was still unmarked. Still the "Jan" I remembered. I pulled my eyes toward the image in front of me. The familiar stranger in the mirror.

I stared into the silver glass, at the side of my face that dripped like cold syrup. Other than trips to the home for therapy, I hadn't left the house once. Dan and Joey had taken over the grocery shopping. I'd had Dan call Elizabeth's that first week and tell my manager I had some "health issues" and wouldn't be in for some time, and I'd simply stayed home from Joey's band concert. Dan and Joey had gone without me, even though in the past it had been me prodding Dan, telling him we really did have to go listen to the junior high band mangle familiar tunes. I'd canceled a hair appointment with Jacob last week, too. Only after losing an argument with Dan when he refused to cancel it for me.

"It's Jaan Jordan," I said carefully when Jacob came on the line. "I whon't be able to keep my appoynt-ment."

"Jan. Jan," he'd said as breezy as always, "you know your cut needs regular shaping to keep it looking fresh. Do you want to reschedule?" I could hear him flipping through the pages of his appointment book. "You're due for highlights, too," he added.

"No." I thought fast. I needed to do this in as few words as possible. "Ah'm going to let mhy hailr gwow out."

Jacob was silent. Probably wondering if I was getting my hair cut in Carlton these days. Or if I was drunk. Better he thought I was blasted rather than disfigured. And, so what if my standing spot was taken by someone else? I might never need a haircut again if all I was going to do the rest of my life was to sit in my living room and watch television.

Still, Jacob had been fabulous to me—and my hair—over the years. I didn't want him to think it was something he'd done. I spoke slowly, trying to incorporate all the tricks Jodi had been trying to teach me. "Mhy hailr needs a whest." I tried to sound light. Funny. The way Jacob and I always bantered with each other. "I'll call you when I caahn't stand it anymorhe." My attempt at flippancy fell flat.

Tears filled my eyes. Thank goodness, he couldn't see me. A mangled face and swollen red eyes. He'd run screaming, for sure. It was better this way.

I looked at myself in the mirror Jodi had placed smack-dab in front of me. I had my doubts that trying to make deformed fish lips was going to have any lasting effect. If I had to look like this for the rest of my life, I would simply— I gave my head a quick shake. I'd cried enough tears and discovered they didn't help. For now I had to jump through the hoops, pretending I believed in the benefits of physical therapy.

"Goot morning, Chan." I didn't need to turn my head to know Ida was here. We'd developed a tentative friendship, but I didn't feel like talking to anyone right now. "How are you today?"

"Fi-nnne," I answered very slowly, watching my lips in the mirror. I didn't say anything more. Maybe she'd get the hint.

"You don't soundt fine."

So much for hints. I lifted my left hand enough so I knew she could see it and waved it side to side in the air.

"Badt day?" she asked.

Without looking at her I nodded.

"Yah, some days are like dat." I could see in the mirror that she was using her arms and thick-soled shoes to roll her wheelchair to her usual corner of the therapy room. "Vell den, I von't bother you witt my oldt voman chattering. Sometimess ve needt quiet to sort out our toughts. I vill talk to Godt about you insteadt. You shouldt try it, too."

If only I had half the faith in prayer that she did. I could almost hear what she would say to that. *Haff faitht like a mustardt seedt.* I was starting to think the way Ida talked. I felt a small smile tug at the corner of my mouth. The first bright spot in my lousy day.

I couldn't pray as easily as Ida, but I did manage a sentence. *Lord, if You can hear me…please listen to Ida.*

I looked back to the mirror and tried to lift my eyebrows. The left rose with ease, the right side was a poor imitation of a good try. I was conscious of Ida working in her corner, probably pleading with God to smite my lousy mood.

"Concentwate." I found myself murmuring with my thick tongue as I lifted my eyebrows once again. This time the right side rose enough that there was an actual wrinkle in my forehead. A smile tugged at the left side of my lips. I could imagine Joey giving me a high five. *"Way to go, Mom!"* I gazed into the mirror and did it again. Two wrinkles! I tried again. Woo-hoo!

I leaned back in my chair, suddenly exhausted by the effort such a small movement had taken. The irony of my accomplishment didn't escape me. I'd spent most of my adult life trying to keep wrinkles away. Now I was trying my darndest to make them appear. I closed my eyes, recalling the miniature triumph. I'd actually made wrinkles in my forehead! I couldn't wait to show Jodi.

Wrinkles? You're rejoicing over a wrinkle? That is the first *time in your life you've ever been happy to see a wrinkle. What's the matter with you? Wrinkles mean* old.

Wrinkles mean your exercises are doing what they're supposed to. Your muscles are starting to work again.

Don't buy that. Wrinkles mean old. Old means death. Period.

I rested my forehead in my hands, the emotion of my small victory was warring with the mindset I'd lived with for years. What was I supposed to do? The exercises that would cure me created the very thing I'd run from my whole life.

I pressed my head further into my hands, as though pressure could chase away what was wrong and leave me with what was right.

"*Don't be concerned about the outward beauty that depends on fancy hairstyles, expensive jewelry, or beautiful clothes. You should be known for the beauty that comes from within, the unfading beauty of a gentle and quiet spirit, which is so precious to God.*"

I felt a lump push its way into my throat. I'd read the words Libby had written to me in her note card so often I knew them by heart. The quiet combination of phrases somehow brought comfort to my lonely days on the couch. They brought comfort again now. A comfort so great it made me weep. I didn't want to cry here.

I felt a hand on my shoulder. "Jan? Are you okay?" It was Jodi, the very person I didn't want to see me like this.

I nodded into my hands and then shook my head. I didn't know if I was okay or not. I raised my red-rimmed eyes to her, imagining what I must look like to her young, perfect eyes.

She rubbed a hand across my back. "It's okay," she soothed. "The exercises are hard. You need to be patient."

"Iht's not thaat," I said, my tears making my tongue heavier. "I dahd it."

"What?" she asked, not understanding.

I took a breath and concentrated. "I diiid it," I repeated carefully. "Waatchs." I sat up straight, looked at a button on Jodi's shirt, took another breath, and held it. *You can do this,* I told myself. Slowly I willed my eyebrows upward. I could feel the way the right brow raised just a fraction of an inch. The important thing was, it was raising. I held it there and turned my eyes to meet Jodi's. Her eyebrows were practically lifted to her hairline, a big grin across her face.

I expelled my held breath as if I'd just swum the English Channel underwater. Jodi clapped her hands together as though she'd won a million bucks. But I knew who the real winner was.

I grinned back at her, the left side of my mouth wide and free, the right not nearly as lifted, but equally happy.

"You did it!" Jodi leaned over and gave me a quick hug. "You just made my day. Now, you keep practicing. I need to run down to the nurses' station for a minute."

I turned back to the mirror. Anxious to practice my new skill. One wrinkle. Two. I did it again. Deep inside my heart was jumping for joy. *Don't be concerned about outward beauty…be known for the kind of beauty that comes from within.*

My awful day suddenly turned inside out. I wanted to share what I was feeling. "Iii-da," I said getting out of my chair and walking over to hers. I hoped the lopsided grin on my face didn't look too goofy. "Waatchs." I bent my knees so my face was at her level. "Here." I pointed to my eyebrows. *Up. Up.* Silently I cheered myself on. It was as if a tiny key had finally unlocked a muscle, releasing it to rise ever so slightly.

I'd been concentrating so hard I didn't notice Ida's expression. I did now. Her eyebrows practically stood at attention, as if they'd been helping mine. "Dii-d you see?" I asked.

"Praise the goot Lordt!" Her grin matched mine. "Answeredt prayer iss so delicious." She smacked her lips together as though she could taste my victory. "I am wery hapby for you, Chan."

Her words were meant to bring me joy, instead they popped the bubble I'd been floating in. Ida was sharing my joy from her wheelchair. She'd been in this therapy room almost every minute I'd been here…probably days and weeks longer. Maybe more. While I was busy crowing about my sudden progress, Ida hadn't made any of her own. Never once, in the weeks I'd been coming here, had I thought to ask about her healing. What the goals of *her* therapy were.

I laid my hand on her sweater-covered arm. "Leht's get to worrrk ohn you."

"Acht!" She waved my suggestion away with her other hand. "I can pray chust as vell sitting down as shtanding up." She paused and then added softly, "But it vouldt be nice to valk again. Not be such a burden to the peoples here."

"Then whaalk you whill'll," I said, as if my healing could somehow be shared with her.

Kenny

No use putting it off any longer. I shifted the pickup into reverse, tossed my arm over the seat, and backed out of the snowy approach where I'd finally stopped when I couldn't see to drive any further. Lucky for me, the country roads surrounding Brewster were even less busy than the streets in town.

I shifted into drive. I felt drained. Crying was as hard as pulling an engine. Harder. When I worked on a vehicle I didn't have to think. Well, at least I didn't have to think about the kind of stuff crying made me think about.

My kid. Diane. The overdraft at the station. With one hand I tugged my cap off, scratched at the thin hair at the top of my head, and then pulled it back on. What was I going to do?

Loose gravel crunched under my pickup tires as I pulled off the country road onto the highway that led back to Brewster. I had to start somewhere. Between Diane and my kid, I didn't know where to begin. The station would be the easiest. Well, not *easy.* I yanked my cap off again and hit it against the seat before tugging it back on. Paul had said to make sure all the deposits had been made. Make a list of my receivables. That would be a problem. Only Diane knew who owed us money.

I heaved a breath into the cab of the pickup. I felt like a swimmer who was too far from shore. Short of breath. Arms heavy. No horizon in sight. I wasn't even sure where solid ground was anymore. If there was such a thing as solid ground. The tears I'd thought were gone shoved their way into my throat, closing it so I could hardly breathe. I was drowning. Drowning.

Someone help me!

I am your foundation.

A choked sob pushed past my tongue. How could I grab onto what I couldn't see? How could I stand when there was nothing under me?

I am your foundation. You are not in this alone.

There it was again. The same phrase Paul had said at the bank.

Suddenly, a hot coal of anger seared its way across my chest. As hopeless as I'd felt, now I was angry. Only this time I wasn't thrashing in uncharted water, I knew exactly who I was mad at.

"God!" I shouted into the pickup. "*You!* Why did You do this? Why am I in this mess? Why did I have a kid who is—" A loud, racking sob filled the truck. "No!"

I'd thought I was done with crying. I wasn't. The pickup slowed to a near crawl as hot tears once again streamed down my face. *Why? Why!* My lips moved but no sound came from my clogged throat.

It's okay, Kenny. I can take it. Give it all to Me.

I had no choice. There was nothing left to hold back. He already had my tears and my anger. My immature bumbling through life. He knew it all.

I gripped the steering wheel until my knuckles were white. "It's *Yours*," I said, flinging the words into the air. If God wanted the mess that was my life, He could have it. "Take it! See what You can do with it!"

⌐

I drove into Brewster's city limits surrounded by an odd quiet. I hadn't expected God to swoop down and instantly change my life, but I had expected something. Not just riding back to my old life in my old pickup. My grip on the steering wheel loosened slightly. "Now what?" I spoke the words aloud, as if I really did expect Him to answer.

I pulled into the driveway leading to the gas pumps, drove around the side of the garage and parked the pickup. I glanced into the rearview mirror, checking to see if I looked as drained as I felt. I did. I pressed my fingers against my eyelids, hoping that somehow the redness would vanish. I could always say I was coming down with a cold. As stuffed as my nose felt, it might not be a lie. I tugged the brim of my cap down low. That would have to do.

I pulled open the door handle and stepped out of the truck. The whole town seemed quiet today. With any luck I could go inside, grab up the bank deposit, and be on my way without seeing anyone but Pete. If my timing was right, he would have his head buried under a car hood out in the garage. I wouldn't have to talk to a soul.

I slammed the door of the pickup, the sound echoing in the crisp springlike air. I looked around at a pile of spare tires stacked along the side of the garage. Scrap metal parts that laid in a jumbled mess...a lot like my life. So much for throwing my problems at God. I had no choice but to carry on by myself.

I took a step toward the station. Two. And that's when I heard it again. The words that had been dogging me all morning. *You are not in this alone.*

I stopped walking toward the office and looked up at the sky. If God wanted it all... If I wasn't in this alone...

"Prove it," I said, my eyes narrowing. "Prove it."

Ida

I'd almost given up on the idea of walking. These past months at the home had brought so many changes in my life, one more hardly seemed worth complaining about to my heavenly Father.

Over the years I'd had to give up many things. Small things, such as wearing dresses that zipped up the back. Or Sunday shoes with narrow heels. And I couldn't remember the last time my back had been soothed with soft-scented lotion. I knew the Lord didn't give a hoot for any of those things...but it was surprising how much I did. Turned out those were the least of my worries.

It was the bigger things that caused me to call on the Lord for His mercy...and love. The big things that caused my faith to be tested and grow. I'd long ago turned over my ache for a child. The Lord had provided nieces and nephews, especially my Kenny, to fill that empty spot inside of me. Losing Fred was akin to having a part of my heart torn away. But, again, the Lord was there, comforting in the night when the hours were the longest. Sending friends and my work at Vicky's café to fill up my daylight hours. In the past ten years my eyesight had faded. Enough so I felt most comfortable driving only during the day and later, not at all. Reading was a dance with the lightbulb, trying to find the right angle that would help the words jump off the page and into my clouded eyes. No wonder God had helped me commit so many Bible verses to memory. He knew I would need them. I'd also lost most of my longtime friends in the past years. But here God was, sending me new ones...tenderhearted workers here at the home. Even loud Wendy had worked her way into my heart with her goodness. And my newest unlikely friend, Jan Jordan. When it came to giving up walking, I understood. I didn't like it, but I understood. God always had a plan. Maybe He wanted me to sit and meditate in a way I never did when I had my two good feet under me.

So it surprised the dickens right out of my old body when Jan stood in front of me and said, *"Then walk you will."* She was a cheerleader who didn't seem to think the game was lost. I didn't have the heart to tell the poor child my legs might be done with their earthly walking. If it made her feel useful to cheer me on...well, I had nothing better to do.

I held out both of my hands to her, grateful that she could see past my wrinkled shell to a place I couldn't. She wrapped her pretty painted fingernails around my furrowed hands as if she were going to pull me right up out of my chair.

"Ih-h down't think Joh-di will mind if we work togewther. Do you?" She squeezed my hands. "Ih'll practice my tawlking while you practice your walking."

Her unplanned rhyme tickled at my ears. A bubble of unexpected delight pushed its way into my throat. "I tink vee can talk Chodi into it."

"Talk me into what?" Jodi's timing was on the money. "What are you two cooking up?"

Jan turned to Jodi. "Ih-m gowing to hellp Ida learn to walk."

"What are you trying to do?" Jodi asked, laughing. "Work me out of a job?" She walked close to where I sat and Jan stood. "I think it would be great for you two to work together. We don't always have time around here to work with our patients beyond their time in the therapy room." Jodi turned to Jan. "Any extra time you can give to strengthen Ida's muscles would be great."

"Thenn it's done." Jan smiled at me.

My eyes hadn't improved an iota in the past minute, but I could swear I saw the right side of her mouth turn up just a hair. God was at work. I could feel it in my old bones.

Kenny

I stopped with my hand on the knob of the station door and took a deep breath. *What was wrong with me?* The tears I'd cried all morning still hung at the back of my throat, threatening. I was hoping I wouldn't have to say more than a few sentences to Pete as I gathered up the bank deposit and tried to find the other information I needed. Then I could head back home. Not that home was much of a retreat anymore, but at least Diane would be busy with Paige and the baby. I could set myself up at the kitchen table and try to figure this mess out. With any luck, Diane would look over my shoulder and make sense of it all for me.

I turned the knob. No response. I tried to turn it again. It was locked. Even though I knew better, I looked at my watch. The only time this door was ever locked was after nine at night and on Christmas Day. I jiggled the knob again, and then I took a step back from the door, casing the doorway as if I were a detective on *CSI*. My eyes landed on a small note taped to the inside of the window.

Back in twenty minutes.

I put a hand in the crook of my neck and pressed my head back against it. Hard. Great. Just great. Pete decided to take a twenty-minute break in the middle of the morning. Apparently, since I hadn't been around to keep an eye on him, he was doing whatever he pleased. On *my* dime. He'd sworn he was clean, but if he was off smoking a joint somewhere...I looked over my shoulder at the highway that ran by my front door. *Wonder how many customers I just lost?*

Who said I wasn't in this alone? Good thing town was quiet this morning. I shoved my hand into the pocket of my jeans and pulled out my key ring. Well, at least I didn't have to worry about talking to Pete first thing. The speech I was concocting to tell him he was fired chased any tears right out of my throat. I unlocked the door. The smell of coffee mingled with oil. At least he knew enough to keep the coffee going.

I poured myself a cup and then walked through the small office space. The cooler was nearly empty, humming away in a monotonous solo. One Salted Nut Roll laid crookedly in an otherwise empty box. The Sen-Sen box was completely empty. A few Butterfinger bars and M&M's mingled with half-empty boxes on the rest of the shelves. It looked as though I was going out of the candy business.

For all you know, maybe you are. Completely out of business.

Then I remembered. Over the past three weeks I hadn't been around when the candy and pop guys stopped by for refills and reorders. Without me to tell them what to bring, or a payment for my order, they would drive right past on their way through Brewster.

Once again, anger stabbed through my chest. I hadn't asked for any of this. Not a shabby gas station in the middle of nowhere. Not a grease monkey kind of job. Not a brain so stupid it could hardly make sense of a bank statement. And not another kid, much less one with Down syndrome.

I grabbed the Salted Nut Roll in one hand, tore off the top of the wrapper with my teeth, spit the red paper onto the floor, and crunched down. There. That was better. My teeth ground away at the chewy candy. I swallowed. Took another bite.

You can't solve your problems by eating. Taste My food. Trust Me.

I looked down at the half-eaten candy bar in my hand, at my stomach hanging over the waistband of my jeans. Out of shape. Sort of like my whole life. Suddenly, the candy tasted like crusty cotton balls. I set the bar on the counter, trying to wash down the unexpected lump in my throat with cool coffee.

God, I told You it was all Yours. This whole mess of my life. What am I supposed to do? What do You want from me?

You are not in this alone.

Yeah, right. Aunt Ida might say God talked to her, but if this was God, He might as well be speaking Greek. I walked around the back of the counter and shuffled through the mail stacked near the cash register. The more I thought about it, I couldn't fire Pete. Not unless I wanted to spend every waking minute dodging comments from gas customers. Maybe I'd sell the place.

And do what?

We could move to Carlton. I'd get a job working for someone else. Somewhere no one knew me.

Someone will always know you.

I closed my eyes. Yeah, that was the trouble. No matter where I went, I'd always have to live with myself.

And with Me.

I looked at the clock on the wall. I had no idea what time Pete had left, but it had been at least fifteen minutes since I'd driven up to the station. I pulled off my cap and ran my fingers through my hair. What would I do if he quit? Maybe he was getting fed up with me, too. Even I could hardly stand myself. My lousy attitude about everything. Work. The kid. Me.

I wandered out into the garage. For the first time I could remember, there wasn't a vehicle in either stall. No wonder I was overdrawn at the bank. The little business I had was drying up. I could mess things up without even being here.

What am I supposed to do? Huh? What?!

I shoved my hands into the back pockets of my jeans and hung my head. For the first time all morning, even the voice that had tried to comfort, tried to give direction, was silent.

There was a sound behind me. I turned around. Pete stood in the doorway between the office and the greasy garage.

"You're here," he said, his jaw set in a defiant way.

"I could say the same about you."

"Well, at least I show up every morning and not just when I feel like it." He was staring me down.

I turned my eyes to a grease spot on the floor. I didn't want to tell him that the times I did show up at the station, even then I didn't *feel* like it. "Where were you?" I didn't like the suspicious challenge in my tone, but it was too late now.

Pete took a step toward me. For a moment I thought he might give me a push. Something. I took a step backward as he walked past me and started straightening junk that had piled along the side wall over the years. "Where were you?" I asked again, my voice as harsh as before.

He turned and gave me a narrow look over his shoulder, and then he turned back to the junk. "What's it to you?"

Now I was the one who felt like shoving someone. I put my clenched fists on my hips. "This is my business, in case you've forgotten."

There was a long silence, then Pete straightened and turned to face me. He looked me slowly up and down. "Then start acting like it."

I could feel the muscles clenching alongside my jaw. "It's my business," I repeated, dumbly.

Pete took a step toward me. "Take a look around." He waved one arm around the empty garage, paused as if debating what to say next, and then he spit it out. "Do you think I'm an idiot? You're not at home with your new kid like you've been telling me. I see you driving around town all day when you're not here. You're alone in your old truck. Who do you think you're fooling? You aren't going to *have* a business if you keep this up. Or a family."

I could feel a hot flush spread into my neck. "Keep what up?" As if I didn't know.

Pete snorted through his nose. "What you're doing." He paused. "Or should I say, *not* doing."

"What's that supposed to mean?"

Pete rolled his chin through the air. "Oh, man. If you only knew what you're doing."

"What are you talking about?" Finally, a question I really did want answered.

"Look at me." Pete took both his hands and hit them against his chest. "Do you want your kids...Billy?...to turn out like me?"

I didn't have a clue what he was raising his voice about. Who was this punk anyway to tell me anything? I didn't have to listen to this. I turned to walk back into the station. Get back in my pickup. I heard a couple steps behind me and then felt a hard hand on my shoulder. Suddenly I was turned around, facing Pete nose-to-nose.

"My dad died eight months ago." His voice was tight, as if I had my hands around his throat trying to hold the words inside. "Do you know what that does to someone like me?" He stared into my eyes as if I should know the answer to his question. "Do you know what that means?" His voice was a challenge. A taunt.

I broke his gaze. "Uh, no. I guess I don't."

"It means…" He swallowed hard. "It means I don't get a chance to tell him I'm sorry for being such a lousy kid." Pete dropped his head quickly.

Oh, man. "I'm sorry."

He looked back at me. "Not sorrier than I am." His voice was softer now. "My dad bailed on my mom and me when I was about Billy's age. I didn't understand why he left. I thought maybe it was something I did. Like 'cause I didn't pick up my toys or go to bed when he told me to that he got sick of me and left. Turns out he was fooling around on my mom, but I didn't know that then. All I knew was that he was gone. He tried now and then to be a dad to me, but he got remarried and had this whole other family, and there I was, the left-out kid. I started acting up, getting into trouble at school. I guess maybe I started out trying to get my dad's attention." Pete scuffed his boot across the cement of the garage floor. "I don't know exactly why I thought my dad would come back if I acted like a jerk. Pretty soon, that's just who I was. Pete West, troublemaker." His eyes flashed when he met my gaze. "You know my reputation."

I nodded.

"You took a chance by hiring me. How come?"

I lifted a shoulder. "Mike left. Diane was pregnant. I needed help." It had been as simple as that.

Or not so simple. There was that voice again.

Pete cleared his throat. "When my dad died last summer, it was a huge wake-up call. No matter how bad I acted, my dad wasn't *ever* going to notice me anymore." He blew a puff of air through his nose. "What was I supposed to do now?" He held his hands out toward me. Dropped them. "I could waste the rest of my life trying to get back at my dad. For what?" Pete shook his head. Changed gears. "I did a lot of thinking." His tone lightened. "Which isn't easy to do when you're smoking dope." He flashed me a lopsided smile. "Don't worry, I'm not doing that junk anymore." He grew serious. "I decided the only way I could get back at my dad now was to make something out of myself. Make the people who knew him, knew me, proud of me. Or something." He looked down at the greasy floor. "It sounds kind of stupid to say it now. But it made sense then. But how was I going to do that when I had no college? No skills? And a reputation for trouble?"

Pretty much like me, except for the trouble part.

"I knew I needed to start by getting a job. Any job. And keep it for a while. But how was I going to do that? Everyone in Brewster knew what a mess-up I was. And then you…" He scuffed at the floor. "Out of the blue you offered me work." He cleared his throat. "A chance."

The way I remembered it, Pete had been in the right place at the right time. He had been the one to help *me* out.

It didn't seem the time to argue over who was right. Maybe, in some strange way, we both were. Now it was my turn to clear my throat and keep my mouth shut.

He went on. "You've got great kids, Kenny. When they stop down here and joke around with me, it's not really *me* they're here to see. It's *you.* Can't you see when they're laughing with me, they're looking out of the corner of their eyes at you? Trying to see if you're proud of them? All they want is your attention."

I'd missed that completely, but I knew what he meant. It was easy to remember the times Ben and I had played ball out in the driveway, somehow timing our makeshift game so that we were blocking the driveway right when our dad was coming home from work. It was two kids screaming, "*Watch us, Dad. Watch us.*"

What had Renae or Billy or even little Paige been trying to tell me these past weeks and I hadn't been around to hear? Or see? I'd been so absorbed in my own sob story that I was giving them one of their own.

Pete took a deep breath and let it out slowly, as if what he had left to say needed his complete concentration. "I know you guys just had a baby and that he's not...not...well, *normal.* But he's still your kid. He's not going to turn out to be anything if you don't pay him some attention. Look what you did to me."

"What I did to you?"

"Yeah, look at me. I wasn't exactly what you'd call first choice when it came to hiring, but you took a chance on me. And look..." He waved his hand around the station. "I kept this place going while you weren't here. I filled gas and fixed some motors. I changed a muffler on Marv's school bus. I even hauled gas out to Paul Bennett's place this morning."

So that's where he'd been.

"I wouldn't have been able to prove any of this stuff to myself, or anyone else in Brewster, if you hadn't given me a chance."

Pete bit at his lip and then said, "The way I see it is, there's way worse things than being retar—not normal."

So...he'd heard. The whole town had heard. I wondered what they thought.

Pete didn't wait for my wondering. "When you're not normal, nobody expects that much from you, so everything you do is kind of a big deal. But what's *worse* is when you've been given the same chances as everyone else and you screw them up all by yourself." He tapped himself on the chest with an index finger. "That would be me."

And me.

The outside driveway bell sounded. Pete glanced outside. Automatically, I turned my head to look, too. Marv was driving the school bus past the pumps and parking it alongside the building. He didn't need gas, but he did need coffee.

Pete pushed his next words out quickly. "Can't you see? You're not in this alone. You've got a wife and your kids. And, remember, when your Aunt Ida used to stop down here almost every day? She was a blast. You've got her, too. And…" he nodded his head toward Marv, who was shuffling toward the office, "you've got all kinds of friends here at the station. They're worried about you, Kenny. But if you keep doing what you're doing…not showing up at work, not giving any attention to your wife or your kids or your friends, they're going to start making a life without you. Believe me, I don't think you want that. I had a life without my dad and it's…" His voice cracked. "It's not good."

It was my turn to look at the grease spot on the floor. Breathe deeply while a wave of emotion beat against my body. I looked up at him. "For a punk, how'd you get to be so smart?"

One corner of his mouth turned up. "When I figure that one out, I'll tell you." Pete reached out, tapped my upper arm once, and then stepped around me. "I'll go see what Marv wants."

I stood alone in the empty garage, my brain swimming. I wasn't sure what part of what Pete had said I should think about first. But I did know the five words he'd said that hit me hardest. Like a softball to my chest.

You're not in this alone.

Suddenly, I knew what I needed to do. I headed for the side door, where I could slip out of the garage without passing Marv or Pete. Pete's words had given me a chance.

⌒

"Diane?" I hurried into the house, anxious to simply see her. I had a lot of explaining to do. A lot of thinking still ahead of me. But I couldn't do any of it without my wife. "Diane," I called, again. The house seemed very quiet.

Oh, Lord, I found myself praying as I peeked into the living room and then walked into the kitchen, *please let her be here. I need her. I* walked down the hall, looking into rooms I could already sense were empty. I'd been such a jerk. For all I knew she had packed up and left me. But then, Diane could be as stubborn as me. I doubted she would give up on our marriage without a fight. She was so much smarter than me.

Maybe she was getting groceries. Maybe the baby had a doctor appointment over in Carlton. Of course she would have taken Paige with her. Wherever she was, I wished I was with her.

I looked at my watch. There would be time to say what I had to say when she got back. Right now, there was another place I needed to go. Another person I needed to see almost as much as Diane.

~

I could hear laughter coming from the room before I got there. I stopped just outside Ida's doorway, listening to Diane's laughter. Ida's, too. When was the last time I'd heard either of them laugh? I closed my eyes for a second, wondering what else I'd missed these past weeks.

Another ring of laughter. Another voice in the room I couldn't place.

Suddenly, I felt afraid. Afraid that my presence would put a cloud over the fun. I'd been in a world of my own making these past days. A miserable world. A gray planet without sun. Without friends. Without family. Especially without Diane.

Me, too?

Yes, without God, too. It had been pure misery to live with only myself and my depressing thoughts. I didn't want to do that anymore.

You are not in this alone. Take a step.

I took a deep breath. Stepped forward, toward the laughter.

I stood in the doorway simply taking in the scene in front of me. Paige was sitting on the floor at Aunt Ida's feet, twisting Ida's shoelaces as if she already knew how to tie a pair of shoes. She was only two, but I could see that time wouldn't stand still waiting for me to catch up. Diane was sitting in Ida's wheelchair. Ida was in her recliner holding our little boy in her lap. He looked as content as if he'd just finished off a bowl of Cheetoes. Behind Diane stood Jan Jordan, a hair brush in one hand, working hard on Diane's thick hair.

I coughed. Stepped into the room.

"Daaaaad!" Paige scrambled off the floor and barreled into my knees. I caught her under her arms and swung her high, into the air. Her giggle was a long-awaited gift. She snuggled into the crook of my neck.

"Kenny." Diane had turned. Stood up.

I blurted the first thing that came to mind. "What have you done to my wife?"

As if I'd pointed, everyone in the room turned and looked at Diane. Her hair stood out from the sides of her head as if she'd stuck her finger into an electrical outlet. We all burst out laughing.

I stood Paige on her feet, marveling at how good it felt to laugh again. As if worries and burdens were rolling off my back. I walked toward Diane. Jan stepped near Ida, patting at her hair, making her look as if she'd just stepped out of a beauty shop.

"Hey, babe," I said, throwing an awkward arm around Diane, hoping against hope she wouldn't shrug away from my sideways hug. Instead, she leaned into my chest, wrapping her arms around my thick middle.

"Hi, yourself," she said looking up at me.

Ida caught my glance. "Chust vatch who you're calling bape." Her eyes twinkled. Laughter, again.

Why had I stayed away from these people? The people who loved me most in the world? Just went to show what a *dumkopf* I'd been. How much hard work I had ahead of me.

Paige tugged at the leg of my jeans. What was it Pete had said? *They just want your attention.* I bent over and picked her up again. Hugged her close. She struggled in my arms. Leaned back. "Dis," she said, taking my cheeks in her chubby hands. She turned my head, tipped it, then touched her nose to mine. "Ko kiss," she said.

I looked to Diane for an explanation.

"Eskimo kiss," she said as if reading my mind. "Her new thing."

"Ahhh," I said, understanding how much I had missed. How much I had to look forward to. I leaned in and brushed my nose against my daughter's.

"Baby." Paige pointed to my almond-eyed boy lying in Ida's lap. "My baby."

I followed her gaze to my new son and then looked at Diane. "Mine, too," I said. I handed Paige to her mom. "Can I hold him now?" As if I needed to ask permission.

I could see Diane's eyes start to fill. She nodded. Her hair was a bush around her face, but I hardly noticed. She always cried when she was happy. She looked beautiful no matter what.

I leaned over and scooped my boy into my hands. His little arms flapped as I picked him up. As if he was afraid I would drop him. But I didn't plan to. Not ever again.

Pete's words swirled through my mind. *What's worse is when you've been given the same chances as everyone else and you screw them up all by yourself.* God knew, and I did, too, just how badly I'd messed up so much of my life. I'd been so wrapped up in myself, in the sports I played and watched on TV. I'd been so tied to the station I hardly had time for my family. Inside I shuddered. I knew all too well that half my time at work was spent drinking coffee and gabbing with Marv and the boys. I spent less time fixing engines and hauling fuel. If I tended to business a little more, added some convenience items like the station down the street…who knew? Maybe I could afford to hire another person in addition to Pete. Spend more time with Diane, Renae, Billy, and Paige. And this little guy. I pulled back the blanket and nudged my little boy under his chubby chin.

Paul's words came to me now. *I have a feeling that God has given you this little boy because you are the perfect dad for him.* I sighed. I probably would never be a perfect anything, but what I *had* been doing hadn't been working all that great. I glanced over at my aunt. I knew exactly what she would say. *Have faitht like a mustardt seedt.* I smiled down at my son. If all it took was that little bit…well, that much I had.

I nestled him into the crook of my arm and touched his soft cheek with the back of my finger. I watched as his mouth began to work, as his tiny fingers spread out and then wrapped themselves around my index finger. Funny, this didn't feel *not normal* at all. It felt exactly like when I'd held Renae. Billy. Paige.

I looked at my son. Looked at Diane.

It felt exactly like love.

Ida

How could so much happen in one single morning? When I saw Kenny standing in the doorway of my room, it was as if God had taken a bushel basket of my prayers and tipped it bottom-side up over the top of my white head.

I had sat on the edge of my bed that morning, my bones creaking as usual, just as I had thousands of other mornings. I lifted the curtain to look outside. Fred used to tease me about my silly habit. "Do you think the sun won't come up until you look for it?" There it was, as dependable as God's grace. I thanked the Lord for another day, another chance to see Him at work. Another day to wonder why He was keeping me on earth.

After I washed my face, I sat in my small recliner, read my Bible, and then talked to God. My heart had been heavy this morning. It seemed there wasn't much purpose for an old woman like me. A body to take up a bed is all I felt like most days.

I bowed my head. "Oh, Lordt," I whispered, "I'm sorry for feeling discouragedt. But some days I don't understandt vhy You don't take me home vitt You. Is it a sin to vant to sit at Your feet?"

I knew very well my discouragement was over my nephew Kenny. He hadn't been to see me in nearly three weeks. The longest time in my long life that I could ever remember not seeing him. I had a hunch what was keeping him away, and that was making me pray all the harder.

Dear Lord, brace up Kenny's heart. He so badly wanted a little boy. A boy to name after himself. Disappointment is a sorrowful thing. Open his heart, Lord. Show him Your plan. Show him Your love. Let him return to You. I paused and then added, *and to me.*

Soon the routine of the day took over. My roommate turned in her bed and said, "Guten morgen." Not long after that we were being called to breakfast in the dining hall. Before I knew it, Rebecca, one of the aides, had come to take me to physical therapy. My three-times-a-week chance to visit with my new friend, Jan.

I was looking forward to seeing her today. She knew, as well as I, about discouragement. I prayed daily for her, too. To be so young, so beautiful, and then to have an affliction that reminded you every time you looked in the mirror. I could live to be a hundred and I wouldn't understand God's plan.

I could tell the minute I came into the therapy room that Jan was as downhearted as I. Some days were like that. I angled myself into my corner and set about praying for her as I started my toe pressing exercise. I hoped at least one of us would have something to smile about this day. I prayed that it might be her.

I had nothing to credit but answered prayer when Jan stood by my wheelchair fifteen minutes later and said, "Ida, watch." There went her eyebrows, both of them, up and up. Her smile spread to me. God was good to let me know He'd been listening.

When she offered to push me back to my room I had to bite my tongue to keep from saying "Praise Godt" right out loud. I didn't want her to know that I'd noticed how much she kept to herself. I'd learned that concentrating on others was the best way to heal whatever ailed a person. And I considered her offer just another signal from God that He was at work in her life. As she took the handles of my chair into her hands, I closed my eyes. *Praises, Lord. Big praises.*

"Here vee are." I pointed to the left so Jan would know where my room was. "Ovfer der." I motioned to the far side of the room, to my bed by the window.

My roommate was gone for the morning. More than likely getting bathed while I was at therapy, then Verna would be attending the weekly Bible study in the chapel at the home. I usually went too, but I had a notion that today God would say it was okay to do His work right in my room.

Jan parked my wheelchair and then took a seat on the edge of my bed. "So, thii-s is whewre you live."

I could see her eyes taking in the two quilt-covered single beds. Verna's rocking chair. My recliner. Our small fridge, there so we could have our own treats now and then. My bulky yellow tape player from the State Library sat on a table near my bed. Books on tape helped me pass many an hour when my mind was too busy worrying to count my blessings. And the Bible tapes were as if I was being read to by God Himself.

"Do you-w like it here?"

"Dis iss my home now. It's cozy." I didn't miss the sideways look Jan was giving me, a look that wondered if I was telling the whole truth. I nodded my head at the question in her eyes. "Vell, yes, I miss my little house on Ninth Street. Dat vass home for too many years for me to forget it like a shnap." I didn't even try to snap my fingers. There was a time when I was the best finger-snapper in school, but arthritis had put the kibosh on that talent years ago. "I madet up my mindt dat I vouldt be hapby vhereffer Godt vanted me. So…" I held out my two hands. "Here it iss."

"I-h wish," Jan said, looking down at her folded hands, "that I-h couwld be as trr-usting as you." She looked up at me. "With God." Two words that suddenly came out of her mouth as clear as daylight. "With God," she repeated, her eyes looking off to the side as if she were trying to see the clear words for herself. She turned her wide eyes to me.

"I heardt," I said.

Tears fill her eyes. "Two surpwises this morwning."

"Blessings."

"Yes." Her lopsided smile agreed with me. "Bll-essings." She reached toward my bedside table. "Wouuu-ld you minn-d?" She picked up a hair brush. "Ih'd love to fix youwr hair for you."

I pushed at my thin, white hair with my fingers. It didn't seem there would be much anyone could do with the fluff on my head, but she was welcome to try.

Jan maneuvered my wheelchair in front of a wall mirror hanging above the dresser that sat low beside the double closet on one wall. She picked up the brush and began brushing through my hair with long, slow strokes. Oh, my. I could feel tension I didn't know I carried falling away from my body like loose hair. I closed my eyes. When was the last time anyone had taken the time to tend me like this? Brushed my hair? Only when Fred was alive. I would sometimes sit on the floor, leaning my back against the front of his favorite chair. We would watch Lawrence Welk on the television and Fred would brush my hair while Bobby and Sissy did their fancy dances. Oh, my. I'd forgotten about that. I could feel a relaxed smile spread across my face. Memories were so precious. *Thank You, Lord, that I can still remember.*

I let my mind wander around in my past as Jan lifted sections of my hair and began gently tugging at them with my brush. For once I wasn't counting the minutes until lunchtime, waiting for something, or someone, to come along and brighten my day. I was happy to simply sit here and let Jan minister to me.

This is for all the times you were like Martha. Now you can sit and be like Mary. Let Me tend to you. God spoke quietly into my heart, using Bible stories I'd memorized to sooth me like a balm.

"Take a looo-k." Jan's voice had a curious sparkle to it.

I opened my eyes. "Acht!" There I sat, my white fluff teased into a rats nest all around my head. An old woman with her finger in the electric box. "Acht der liebe!" I couldn't help but laugh out loud.

Jan waved the brush and laughed, too. "Trwust me." She began to work at small sections of my hair, smoothing over the top with the brush, then her hand. I closed my eyes again, listening as she began to talk.

"Did you-u ever worry about grwowing old?"

For some reason I knew she wasn't asking for an answer, she was trying to make sense of something for herself. I sat quietly. Waiting while she sorted things out.

"I-h used to examine my face every mowrning and every night. Looking for wrwinkles, for some sign that I was getting old. I-hm not sure what I thought *old* would do to me. Just that it was something bad."

I wasn't sure if her speech was improving as she stood behind me, or if the Lord was letting me hear her talk the way He heard her.

"But now, since…this." She waved the brush in a circle around her face. "I-h don't know. It's as though God is trying to tell me that therwe are much worse things in this world than wrinkles." She paused and met my eyes in the mirror. "Do you know what I mean?"

I didn't need to speak, only nod my head.

"If He was twrying to get my attention, He did a good job." She started working on my hair again. "I-h used to be so busy running from errand to errand. Off to my job or to get my hair and nails done that I never took the time to think about what kind of life I was living." She stopped smoothing my hair while she smiled to herself. "I'hve had a *lot* of time to think these past weeks. A *lot*."

I waited for her to say more. Finally, I asked, "Andt vhat haff you tought about?"

"About how use-ll-less all that time I-h spent looking for wrinkles was." She paused with the brush in the air, then continued slowly combing through my thin hair. "About all the silly things I-h used to blabber about. Now, since it's been harder for me to talk, I-h have to think about what I say. Decide if it's worth the effort." Catching my glance in the mirror, she raised both her eyebrows at me…the right one only slightly lower than the left, but definitely raised. "I-h found out I didn't have all that much to say that was worth talking about."

"Godt hass such interesting vays to show us His vill for us."

Jan gazed at me in the mirror. "I-hm finding that out." She patted the sides of my hair with her hands and then looked around the room. "Do you hawve any hairwlspray?"

"Vhat do you tink dis iss? A beauty shop?"

"Ih-m going to brwing some next time I come." She picked up my left hand. "Ih-m going to brwing some nail polish, too. The men around here wohn't recognize you by this time next week."

"Vell," I teased back, "den you'dt better teach me to run insteadt uff chust valk."

Jan turned my chair around and bent in front of me. She tucked one side of my hair behind my ear. "There." She straightened my light blue cardigan and then buttoned the top two buttons, tugging on the hem so it laid flat on both sides.

There was a soft knock on the door. Both Jan and I turned our heads toward the sound as little Paige came running into the room ahead of Diane and the baby.

"Eyyyy-daaaa." Paige stopped just short of running into my thick-soled shoes.

"How'ss my fafforite liddle girl?" I reached my hand out to touch her soft, flyaway hair. She tossed a stocking cap into my lap before running and pointing to the candy jar I kept on my dresser. "Tootsie," she said plain as day.

Diane laughed. "You try and teach kids manners, and look at her. Not now, Paige. It's too close to lunchtime."

I waved my hand at Jan. "You giff her vun. Who else do I get a chance to shpoil?"

When Diane had entered the room I could see Jan quickly tilt her head away from her, but now she turned to face her. She stuck out her hand. "I-hm Jaa-n." She laughed as she realized she was holding out the hairbrush. Quickly, she moved it to her left hand.

"Oh, I know who you are." Diane waved at Jan's outstretched hand as if they'd been friends for years.

"I wasn't sure if you…" Jan pushed a stray hair away for her eyes, smiling shyly at Diane.

"Tootsie!" Paige was on her tippy-toes, trying to reach the candy jar.

"Do you-u mind?" Jan pointed to the candy jar with the hairbrush.

Diane rolled her eyes. Laughed. "It won't be the worst thing she's ever eaten before lunch. Go for it." As Jan pulled a Tootsie Roll out of the jar, Diane looked at me. "Ida, you look beautiful today."

Self-consciously I reached up to touch my fancy hair. "Chan did it."

"Well, she did a good job."

They both stood there looking down at me. Jan broke the silence. "I-h guess Ih-ll go now."

"No," I said maybe too loud. "You shtay and wisit." I looked at Diane. "Chan iss my new friendt." I didn't tell Diane that she was the first person I had seen Jan speak to outside of the therapy room.

"Is thaa-t youwr new baby?" Jan peeked at the little boy inside a blue blanket.

"This is Pearson." Diane loosened the wrapping. "At least that's his last name. We haven't quite decided what to call him. I have a husband who—"

"He's so-ow cuu-te." Jan was running a finger along the side of his face. "Caa-n I hold him?"

"Sure." Diane didn't bother to finish her sentence about her stubborn husband. God hadn't answered that prayer yet. It appeared He hadn't changed Kenny's bullheadedness one bit since Diane's last visit. She handed Jan the baby.

"A person forw-gets how prwecious they are." She touched him softly. "You'rwe verwy lucky."

"I know," Diane said, looking down at her hands. "I wish Kenny could see that."

Jan took her time before saying slowly, "Sometimes gifts come in paa-ckages we down't expect."

I had a feeling in my bones that Jan wasn't talking only about this baby.

"Ida," Jan said, "woull-d you like to hold him?"

I held out my arms.

"It might be easier if you-w sat in yourw recliner." Jan held out a free hand to help me make the short switch and then gently laid the baby in my lap.

Diane plopped herself into my wheelchair, putting her loafers onto the footrests of the chair. "This is the first chance I've had to put my feet up all day. Feels good. Now, Ida, if I could only look as beautiful as you, I'd have it made."

My arms were full so I motioned with my chin. "Let Chan vork on your hairs. Ve'll look like tvins!"

Jan held up the hairbrush. "Are you braa-wve enough?"

Diane waved a hand near her hair. "Have at it. There's not much you can do with this mop."

As Jan began brushing through her hair, Diane closed her eyes. I could almost see the worries of the day fall away from her face.

I looked down at the little boy in my lap. Jan was right when she said he was an unexpected gift. At my age I never thought I would be holding a baby again, and here I was with one in my lap. God was so good.

I jiggled my knees a little, thinking this way of rocking a baby would make Jodi proud of me. The motion felt much the same as the exercises she put me through. This was much more fun.

Bless this little one, Father. I looked down at Paige, over at Diane. *Mend the broken place in Kenny's heart. Restore this family.*

"Mommy funny!" Paige pointed at her mom.

Diane opened her eyes. "Oh!" Her hair stood at attention as if a five star general had walked in the room. We burst out laughing.

"Don'wt worry," Jan said, tangling Diane's hair even more. "I-hill fix it."

"This is nothing," Diane said, closing her eyes again. "One time when Renae was little, I let her play with my hair. Before she was done I had to go to the beauty shop to get the hairbrush *cut* out of my hair." She sighed deeply. "As long as you keep the brush *in* your hand, I'm fine."

There was a soft cough from the doorway. Kenny. I breathed a prayer. *Oh, Lord, heal the broken place inside of him.*

"Wow." Kenny just stood there, his jaw open wide.

I saw Jan quickly turn her head away, then slowly angle it back toward Kenny. Kenny bent to pick up Paige. He took a slow step into the room. "I hardly recognized you."

I hoped with all my heart that Kenny was talking about Diane's fluffed-up hair and not about the slight droop on Jan's face. Kenny walked into the room, the first time I'd seen him since his little boy had been born. He looked tired. Scruffy. As if he'd been run through the mill. But at peace in some way I couldn't explain. Something about him had changed.

Except for Paige's soft chatter, silence hung as though a thick quilt had covered the room. As if we were all waiting for something, but no one knew what it was. *Oh, Lordt, give someone some words.*

"What did you do to my wife?"

We laughed at the wild bush of Diane's hair. At Kenny's surprise. God had planned ahead to break the ice between us.

Kenny walked over and hugged Diane. An embrace that seemed to tie them together in a way only God could see. He looked at me holding his son and then back at Diane. "Is it okay if I hold him now?"

She didn't speak, only nodded her bushy head as Kenny bent down and lifted the warm bundle from my lap.

He held his small child in the crook of his elbow, touching and stroking his face in a way that seemed to say, *"Welcome little one. I'm your daddy."* He moved to the edge of the bed, sitting on top of the thick quilt I kept folded there.

He looked up, staring into Diane's eyes for a long moment and then he looked over at me. "I've thought of a name for this little guy." He turned his eyes to the bundle in his arms. "I'd like to name him...Fred. After my uncle."

After my husband.

"If that's all right with you?" He glanced quickly between Diane and me. "I know we talked about naming him..." Kenny swallowed hard, "Kenny Jr. But there's already been a Kenny Jr., and I plan to see our other little boy up," he nodded his chin beyond the ceiling, "there someday." Again he looked between us.

My throat closed with warm tears.

Diane spoke for me. "I think Fred is perfect."

Finally, I pushed out my grateful words. "I tink so, too."

My God was so good.

When had my life suddenly become so full?

I looked around Ida Bauer's small room in the nursing home. There in her recliner, sat Ida. Diane Pearson was in Ida's wheelchair waiting for me to finish styling her hair, her daughter, Paige, was patiently at work trying to undo the zipper on the side of my brown boot. And there sat Kenny on the edge of the bed, holding his new son.

I should have felt out of place. After all, I wasn't related to any of these people. In truth, I hardly knew them. But I didn't feel that way. I felt as if I was exactly where I was supposed to be at this moment in time. Exactly where God had planned.

A fullness filled my chest. Happiness of a sort I'd never felt before. Contentment. I turned the hairbrush in my hand and then began smoothing Diane's thick hair. Underneath her sweatshirt and jeans she was beautiful. High cheek bones. Striking eyes. But that wasn't all. I could tell just from the short time we'd visited that there was even better stuff inside her. A way of making people…me…feel like an instant friend. Kenny had gotten himself quite a catch when he'd married her.

I caught Diane's eye in the mirror. Ventured a crooked smile.

"This looks *great*," she said, smiling back. "Kenny might have to take me on a date tonight. No use wasting a new hairdo." She winked into the mirror.

Without thinking, I winked back. *I winked back!* My right eye had winked with no effort at all!

"I-h could watch the kids," I offered, suddenly feeling so very generous.

Diane laughed. "Be careful. I just might take you up on that."

"I-h could," I said, already imagining Joey playing with Paige.

"I've got a roast in the Crock-Pot," Diane explained. "But if you'd like to stop by for coffee one of these days, I could use some adult conversation."

Conversation. My odd speech didn't bother her. But then, I didn't need to be the one always talking to have a conversation. I'd learned these past weeks that sometimes listening was as good as talking. Better. "I-h would like that. Ver-wy much."

"Great!" Diane tucked one side of her styled hair behind her ear.

I reached down and tucked the other side. "You-w have such a beautiful face. You-w shoulwd show it off."

Diane rolled her eyes, blushing at my comment. "Not much to show off when the only people who see my face most of the day are under the age of three."

"Hey!" Kenny chimed in from his perch on the bed. "Don't I count?"

"No," Diane said, "you don't." She waved her fingers over her shoulder at him. "You have me memorized. You don't even see the outside of me anymore."

You don't even see the outside.

The words struck me, an embrace of my heart. Wasn't that exactly what the verse Libby had shared with me meant? Somehow it took on new meaning coming from Diane.

You're right, I don't see the outside. Neither do the people who love you.

I could feel a lump push its way into my throat. I gave Diane a light squeeze on her shoulder to let her know I was done, then I walked to the far end of the bed from where Kenny was sitting with his new son in his arms and sat down myself. I needed some time to sort this out.

My eyes settled briefly on each person in the room, searching their faces to see what I really saw. Was I looking at just the outside? The face the world saw? Or was I able to see something more? The kind of seeing-but-not-seeing Diane had talked about? When my eyes landed on Ida, I examined her face. There! For an instant I could see the fine wrinkles that lined her cheeks, the loose skin that hung around her neck, but when I blinked those things were gone, replaced with a face I had come to love over the past weeks. A face that glowed when she talked in her funny German way. Eyes that sparkled, making her seem more sixteen than eighty-two. *Eighty-two.* Numbers that meant absolutely nothing when it came to knowing who this wonderful woman really was. It was a mystery I knew I would think on for some time.

I listened to the easy conversation flowing around me. The way Diane and Kenny seemed to be teasing each other, catching up with each other in a way I didn't quite understand. Their bantering turned to more everyday conversation, Kenny asking Ida question after question. It seemed they had some catching up to do, too.

For once I didn't feel the need to chime in with any tidbits of my own. Listening was enough. Simply sitting here. Quietly sitting. It was enough.

My mind wandered back over the month just past, further back... to the years that had brought me here. How wasteful so much of my time seemed now. All those silly appointments, hair and manicures, facials and pedicures, all trying to erect a shell the people who loved me didn't see anyway. I could see so clearly now that it wasn't the treatments in themselves that were bad. It had been my attitude toward them. I hadn't scheduled a manicure as a way to keep my peeling nails in shape or even as a simple treat to myself, a way to relax from the pressures of daily life. Or even to look nice for Dan. I'd kept all those appointments because I wanted people to look at me and think, "My, look at Jan Jordan. Isn't she hot? Look at her pretty nails. Look at the way the light bounces off her hair. Look at her. Look at her..."

I shuddered now at how empty my motives had been. I could see also how those appointments had been a hollow attempt to add meaning to my shallow world. They had made me feel important and busy in a way that seemed ridiculous now.

This past month had changed all that. I found myself smiling down at the quilt that covered Ida's bed. I wasn't quite sure how what I'd thought had been the absolute worst time of my life had somehow turned inside out to become possibly the best. In the past few weeks I'd come from lying in a fetal position on my couch to this place right here where I felt surrounded by friends. Friends of a sort I'd never had until…this. It was another mystery I would have to examine.

Libby and I had grown closer these past weeks, too. Connecting in a way we hadn't in all the years that marked our friendship. She had dropped her novel off at my door a few days ago, saying, "You're only the second person I've dared share this with. I hope you like it. You read. I'll pray."

The heck with my lopsided grin. I'd laughed out loud. It was so like Libby to trust God so openly. I had no doubt her prayers would mingle with the words I would read. I reached out and hugged her. Not a quick, artificial hug. This time I held her close in a way I never had before. "Youw-r words are safe with me," I said into her ear.

They were more than safe. I'd found myself reading intently, Libby's words going from the page to my eyes and directly to my heart. Even if her story about her friendship with Anne would never be published, I had a feeling maybe God had her write it down especially for me. A journey of friendship I was just beginning.

Bits of the conversation flowing around me began to poke through my thoughts.

"Fred—Freddie—" A laugh. "It's weird finally having a name to call him."

"Here, Paige, play with this. That's right, comb your hair. So pretty."

"Pete's pretty much been in charge." That from Kenny.

"Freddie has a bunch of tests scheduled next week." Diane.

"The station books are a mess." Kenny again.

"I-h cawn do books." Who'd said that?

Suddenly, everyone in the room turned my way. "What?" I said, realizing quickly that I'd spoken without thinking. Old habits were hard to break. I held out my hands, palms up. "I-h used to be a bookkeeper at a jewelr-wy store. In the mall." They were still staring at me. "Before Dan and I-h were married." As if that made any sense.

"*You were* a *bookkeeper?*" Unbelieving Kenny.

"I-h've always been good with math." I shrugged one shoulder. "Besides, it was a good way to get a discount on some grweat jewelrwy."

Diane laughed. "As a woman, I understand completely."

Kenny scratched at his head as if trying to push the unlikely picture into an image that would fit. He spoke slowly. "Would you like a job?"

A *job?* At a gas station?

A million thoughts ran through my brain. What would Dan say? What would my hours be? It had been a while since I'd kept books for anyone. Could I still do it? What about the way I looked?

They don't see that.

At a gas station?

"Can I-h get a discount on gas?" I winked my right eye.

"Oh, so that's how it'll be." He smiled. "If you can do my books, I'll even throw in an oil change. For free." As if that sealed the deal. "Stop down at the station later today and let's talk."

Just then I remembered. "My car. Cawn you fix my car? It wouldn't starwt this morning. I-h walked."

A crooked smile lifted Kenny's cheek. "Already asking for favors. I can see it now. Next it'll be candy bars. Then Mountain Dew—"

"Diewt Coke," I added.

Kenny laughed as Freddie yawned loudly, stretching his short arms as if trying to include us all in his tired embrace. He settled for Kenny's index finger.

"Ida? Are you ready for lunch?" Rebecca, an aide at the home, stepped around the doorframe. "Oh, my. Is it your birthday? You have quite a crowd here today."

Ida waved her comment away. "I don't needt a special day to haff wisitors. My family iss velcome any oldt time."

Her family.

Me.

She'd included me.

Ida caught my eye. I could swear one of her twinkling eyes winked as she raised her wrinkled hand and let it rest near her heart. She rubbed the spot ever so gently, as if she were sealing me in there along with the others.

Who would have guessed all my misery would lead to...this?

I use all things for good.

Oh, yes. He certainly did.

I lifted my right hand, pressing it over my heart, a mirror image of her's. Sealing her inside of my heart, too. A woman who felt like a grandmother, a mother, a sister...a friend.

I could hardly imagine what the days ahead...the *years* ahead, might hold. But suddenly, I couldn't wait to find out.

Though it cost all you have, get understanding...

Epilogue

"Happy birthday to yoo-uuu. Happy birthday to yoo-uuu. Happy birthday, dear Aunt Ida-aaa. Happy birthday to yoo-*uuu!*"

"Acht!" I waved away their silliness, but my heart danced along. They were the people most precious to me, standing and sitting around me with goofy party hats on their heads. The kids were tooting on those old-fashioned roll-out noisemakers till their ears were red. Renae and Joey Jordan, who were old enough to think that sort of thing was babylike, were the worst of the lot. They were using the feathers on the end of the paper rolls to tickle the noses of Billy, Paige, and little Freddie in his walker. Their giggle-screams filled the room. *Pop!* There went one pink balloon. I had a notion none of the colorful balls would be left by the end of the afternoon.

That was okay. God said to make a joyful noise, and we were doing just that.

Renae came near me, waving the paper whistle between her teeth like a loose tooth. I ducked my head, playing along. When I looked up again, there it was, a feather on the end of my nose.

"You silly goose." I reached out to tickle her side. Her young body curved away just ahead of my fingers and then leaned back in, almost as if she wanted me to catch her. There wasn't much to playing get-away with an old lady in a wheelchair. I tickled her side, her clear laughter twining with the others in the room.

"How old are you, Aunt Ida?" Billy was a second grader now. Smart with numbers like his mama.

"I'm eighty-four," I said, hardly believing it myself. "Can you count dat big?"

Billy grew serious. "I think so." Off he loudly went. "One…two…three…"

Diane gently turned him so that he was counting more for himself than the whole bundle of us. She rubbed a hand across my back. "How are you feeling today?" She knew this past year had not been my best. My constant friend, Art…arthritis. A bad cold in November, followed by the flu. And legs that simply would not walk. There was a time during my sickness with the flu that had just about taken me. I was ready, but it appeared the good Lord wasn't.

"Today iss goot," I said, reaching up to hold her warm hand. "Iss goot."

"Is Ida okay?" There was Jan at my side. She, too, was well aware of what this past year had held.

"She's goooot," Diane said, teasing with her copycat talk. "Think everyone is ready for cake?"

Jan looked around the light-filled room. This was one of my favorite rooms in the nursing home. Windows from the east and south made most any day feel as if summer were just around the corner. Billy was climbing on top of a chair. Before his mom could grab him, he jumped off. "I think this cr-wew is ready for anything," Jan said. "Give me a minute, though. I want to make sure the party girl is r-ready for pictures."

"I'll get the cake," Diane said.

Jan knelt by my chair. She tucked a strand of my white hair behind one ear, then smoothed over the rest of my hair with her hands. Next she adjusted the shoulders of my new, pink dress and tugged at the hem of my white cardigan. She turned my strand of pearls so that it was just so. "There," she said, leaning back to take a look. "You look beautiful."

"Tanks to you."

"Thanks to me…" she hesitated, and then added, "and God." Jan's faith had blossomed like a daisy this past year. Along with her speech. And our friendship. She picked up both of my hands and held them in hers. "He made you so beautiful, Ida. Long before I ever got my pink fingernails on you."

I looked down at our four hands. Bright pink fingernail polish on all twenty fingers. No one but us knew that our toes matched, too.

I squeezed her hands. "I luff you, childt."

"And I love you." Her eyes filled. Now our eyes matched as well. "Are you ready to blow out some candles?"

"I don't know iff I haff dat much air in me."

Just then Paige squealed like a stuck pig. Jan turned to see the commotion, then looked back at me. "I think you'll have plenty of help."

⌒

The afternoon sun was calling it a day. And so was I. Birthdays were wearing on an old body like mine. Even the kids had tired out. Renae was reading a book in the corner of a couch. Billy and Joey Jordan were sitting on the floor, playing some kind of game on small contraptions they held in their hands, moving and wiggling as they punched at the buttons. They'd showed me the small screens, the object of the game, but my eighty-four-year-old brain didn't quite understand it all. I nodded as if I did. Paige had curled up in her mom's lap with her yellow blanket. She was asleep now. Something that sounded awfully good to me.

Only little Freddie was still ready for a party. He'd napped through much of the earlier hoopla. Now he was fidgeting, wanting to crawl out of Kenny's arms.

"Ida," Kenny said now. "I've been saving one last present for you."

I shook my head. "An oldt voman like me doesn't needt anyting more." They had already given me new slippers when my old ones were perfectly good. I'd carefully folded the purple wrapping paper and given it back to Diane. She could use it again. And, in an envelope they'd given me a certificate for a permanent and a haircut with the beauty shop lady who came to the home. What more could I use? "It shouldn't be anyting bic," I said. "I hardly haff shpace in my little room."

"Oh," Kenny said. "You'll have room for this. Watch." He stood a squirming Freddie onto the soles of his tiny white tennis shoes. Freddie's little eyes grew wide and he waved his hands. Kenny turned him my direction. "Hold out your arms, Ida."

I rested my elbows on the armrests of my chair and opened my fingers.

"Say, 'come here,'" Kenny coached.

I looked at Kenny and then at Diane. They were both smiling. They'd been saving this for me all along.

"Vhat? Vhen?" I had prayed so hard for this child. For the health problems that came along with his Down syndrome. For the teasing I knew would be part of his future. I'd prayed for his parents, his two sisters, and Billy. That their hearts would be big enough to love him no matter what. I knew for a child like this, many things came slowly. He was well over a year and still he hadn't walked. So, lately, I'd been praying especially for that, too.

"Say, 'come here.'" Again, Kenny coaxed.

"Fred," I called. "Freddie. Come to Ida."

He put one foot out, wobbled, and then swayed forward on the other foot, catching himself just in time. I leaned forward, as if I could catch him if he fell. There was no need. He rocked a bit. Stepped. Once more. Again. Oops! Down he went, but before he could squawk, Kenny had him back on his feet. Back on his way to me.

Freddie's almond eyes locked onto mine, much the same as my own Fred had looked to me when he needed help. "Come. Come," I urged.

He swayed and staggered, a miniature sailor with sea legs. He held out his hands and danced the last four steps. Touched my hands, and then grabbed on for dear life with a grin an old woman would never forget. Everyone except sleepyhead Paige clapped their hands. Kenny was there to sweep Freddie into my lap.

"You didt it!" He clapped his chubby fingers together as though he knew exactly what he'd done. I turned my eyes first to Kenny and then to Diane. "Dat vas the best present."

Answered prayer always is.

I held Freddie's warm body in my arms, his head snugged against my bosom for a long second. Then he was ready to get down again. Ready to practice his walking some more. He toddled away. I was willing to trade my old legs for his. He had so many places left to go in his life. I was content to sit and watch.

And pray.

My tired eyes gazed around the room. At Jan and Diane packing up what was left of the snacks. Those two. I hadn't known enough to pray for their friendship, but God had brought them together even when I prayed for them each alone. I watched as the kids slipped their arms into jackets. Daily I lifted each of them to the Lord. Especially Freddie. He needed extra care. And then there was Kenny. My Kenny. The closest thing to the son I'd never had. Oh, how I prayed for him. Harder than for any of them. God had heard. Kenny was turning into a fine, fine man. A husband. A father. A friend.

Maybe this was why God had left me on this earth. These people still needed my feeble prayers.

Not feeble, Ida. Mighty.

~

"The kids are out in the car. We're ready to go. Are you sure you don't want any supper?" Kenny had helped me out of my wheelchair and onto my bed. I sat on top of my quilt, anxious to lay my head on the white cotton pillowcase and close my eyes. It had been quite a day.

"No supper," I said. "If I get hungry later I vill ask for a bowl of chiggen soup." I looked over at my roommate, Verna, sleeping on top of her bed. She'd grown so hard of hearing this past year it hardly paid to keep our voices down this late in the day.

Kenny took a seat in my wheelchair and faced me squarely. "I have one more thing I wanted to talk to you about."

I held up one tired hand. "No more presents."

"No." Kenny looked down at his knees. "This is something else." He looked up at me. "I think there is someone interested in buying your house."

My old house? The place I'd lived most of my years? I could feel my eyes grow wide, my eyebrows a puzzle. "Now?" It had sat empty for so long. "Who vouldt vant it?"

"Vicky Johnson has been looking at it."

"Wicky?" It didn't make sense. "She already has a house. My place vouldt be too small for her husband and kidts." I knew her family well. Her husband, Dave. The kids, Angie and Sam. I should know them. I'd worked off and on for Vicky since she'd bought the local café. I taught her how to make pie crust for the Pumpkin Fest pies and filled in behind the cash register when she was short of help. She was one of the hardest workers I knew, yet she'd still found a few times to stop by and visit me here. She'd never breathed a word about looking at my house. Why would she be interested in my old place?

My thoughts raced around my mind like wild horses, until one idea stopped them all in their tracks. Oh, no…it couldn't be. She and Dave weren't…? *Oh, Lord, don't let it be so.* I had to know. "Are Wicky andt Dafve…?" I couldn't think how to finish the impossible question.

Kenny knew what I meant. He shook his head. "No. They're fine as far as I know. Vicky said she has a business idea for your old house that she's been thinking about for a while now. She didn't say more. But she did make an offer." He breathed deep and cleared his throat. "Are you ready to sell it?"

Was I?

He hurried on. "If you're not, I don't mind looking after it one bit. If you aren't ready to let it go, I'll tell her no and be done with it."

My home. The place where Fred and I had lived and loved and argued and made up. The place where we'd laughed. The place where he'd died. I'd expected to die there, too. But God had another plan for me.

I took Kenny's hand in mine, a tightness at my throat I swallowed against. "Dat iss not my home anymore than dis room iss. Godt is preparing a place for me to liff. You go aheadt andt tell Wicky she can haff it witt my blessing."

Kenny squeezed my hand. "I had a feeling you'd say that." Once again he cleared his throat. "I kind of hate to see the old place go. We made a lot of good memories there."

I had a notion he was remembering churning homemade ice cream over the basement floor drain. Hot cocoa with big marshmallows on cold winter evenings. Chinese checkers. Jigsaw puzzles. Tickles and hugs. Oh, there were so many good memories made in that house.

But it was time to let go. Not of the memories. If the good Lord was willing, I would have those tucked inside my heart until I saw Him face-to-face. As long as I had the memories, I could let go of the house. Let go of things from my past that were binding me to this world.

I was ready.

More than ready.

The mansion God had planned for me would soon be done.

I squeezed Kenny's fingers, then let go. It was time for him to go home with his family. "Tank you for the loffly pardy." I reached up and put my wrinkled hand on his cheek. "Godt bless you, Kenny."

He stood, leaned down, and kissed my cheek. Whispered in my ear, "God bless you, too, Aunt Ida."

Oh, but God didn't have to…because He already had.

Mightily.

Oh, so mightily.

I laid my head against the pillow. *Ahh, Lord, thank You for rest.* My tired bones ached and, after the commotion of the afternoon, my ears were ringing as if they had bells in them. I thought back over the day, about the young people who had so much energy, about little Freddie who had so many tests ahead of him.

Why, Lord? Why him? I would have gladly given up some of my long years to make his life smoother. Why?

Queen Esther.

What?

Queen Esther.

Oh, I remembered well the story of the biblical queen who saved a nation by daring to speak up to the king. But what would a beauty like her have to do with someone so plain as me?

Think, Ida.

I retold the story in my mind. Remembering how Esther, too, questioned what she was being asked to do. Just as I was questioning God about my purpose here.

What? What was the rest of the story? *Think, Ida. Think.*

The words crept quietly into my mind and then into my heart. A whisper. I knew now what it was God meant me to know.

Who can say but that God has brought you here for just such a time as this? You are to pray, Ida. Just keep praying.

So, that was it. He wanted my prayers.

I still had work to do.

As tired as my mind had been a minute ago, I was suddenly as wide awake as a rooster in the morning. If God wanted me to pray, I would. As long as I had breath in me I would raise up the peoples around me.

I closed my eyes and folded my hands over my sweater. I would pray until I fell asleep in the good Lord's arms.

Oh, Lord, You are my Shepherd… Just as You are Jan's, and Kenny's, and Diane's, and Freddie's, and…

Kenny

"No...over a little bit. To the left."

"Here?" I looked over my shoulder, which wasn't easy to do on a ladder while holding something so heavy. Pete was on another ladder holding the other end.

"A little more. About three inches."

Three inches? Three inches. As if anyone would notice three inches. I turned my head to face the station and rolled my eyes. I knew better than to argue with the woman.

"Guess you need to push it my way, Pete."

"Gotcha. Ready?"

"Okay!! Stop! There!" Jan Jordan stood out near the curb, waving her hands as if she were a movie director, trying to get the same view drivers would see as they drove past the station. I hoped they would think enough of our new sign to swing on in.

"Perfect."

"Hold tight to your end, Pete. I'm gonna try and grab a couple nails." Lucky for us the old part of the station had a wooden framework at the top of the building. It would have been much harder to hang this sign on the new metal end.

With one hand I put two nails between my lips and then grabbed the hammer hanging from the back of my belt. "Steady now." I pounded the top of the sign first. Then the bottom. That should hold 'er till Pete could take care of his end. Once we had it stabilized I'd get some steel screws and fasten 'er in tight.

"Hang on, Pete. I'll just climb on down here..."

"Careful." Jan was behind me, steadying the ladder from the ground. When I'd hired her, I thought I was getting a new bookkeeper, not another woman to keep me in line. But, between Diane and Jan, I didn't make a move they weren't in cahoots about. It was a bit like having two mother hens pecking at my back. Cautiously I climbed down, one rung, two, three...I bit at the insides of my cheeks. Truth was, it felt kind of good to have people care so much about me. I looked up at Pete, down at Jan...but I'd never tell. They'd tease me until I'd cry "uncle."

I moved my ladder over, closer to Pete. "Here, I'll climb up and hold the sign steady while you pound your side in."

"You guys gotta take a look at this." Jan was back on the curb. "Move the ladders away first and then come see."

"I'll move 'em," I told Pete. "You go have a look."

As soon as we were both on the ground again, I tipped the ladders onto their aluminum sides and leaned them against the building, then I walked to join Pete and Jan. They were standing on the curb, looking up and smiling as if they were in a toothpaste commercial.

"Doesn't it look great?" Jan motioned for me to take a look myself.

I turned, knowing exactly what I'd see.

K & P's SuperPumper
Gas—Snacks—Videos—Bait—Repairs
Friendly, reliable service...with a smile.

Jan had made us add that last line. "It'll make people smile," she'd said. Out of the corner of my eye, I glanced at them. It looked as though she was already right. Again.

I turned and read the sign once more. K & P's SuperPumper. Ken and Pete's. If Billy ever wanted to join me in the station, I'd worry about a new sign then. For now, I wasn't sure if the pressure I felt in my chest was from the tacos Diane had made for lunch or from something else altogether. It had to be something else. Heartburn never felt this good.

I held out my right hand to Pete. "Hey, partner."

He pumped my hand right back, blinking as fast as changing gas pump numbers when the hose was on high. "Just wait. My mom is gonna be here with her camera any second."

"Well, until she gets here…" Jan leaned down and dug a camera out of the duffle bag-sized purse at her feet. "You two get over there. I want a picture myself. Go on." She shooed us with her hand. "I'm going to have this enlarged. We'll frame it and hang it behind the cash register."

"Hey," I said, positioning myself under the "K" of the new sign. "Whose business is this, anyway?"

"Be quiet and smile." Jan flashed us both a stupid grin.

It wasn't hard to smile at all. What was harder was to understand how it had all happened so fast.

Just then the first customer of the *new* K & P's SuperPumper pulled in for gas.

"I'll get him," Pete said.

"I'll take a picture." Jan was hurrying to the front of the vehicle with her camera, scouting for the best angle.

"I'll put the ladders away," I said to no one.

It was weird, and good, not to have to do everything myself. I dragged the two ladders around back, into the small storage shed near the alley. I clicked the padlock shut and then started walking back to the front of the station. I paused as I rounded the corner, taking time to take it all in. Pete had spent much of yesterday sweeping the concrete driveway clean. He'd pushed that broom as though he were brushing away more than just sand and pebbles.

I took off my cap and scratched my head before pulling my cap back on. I guess having an investment in a place made a person look at it differently. How it all came about was something of a puzzle. One I was still working to solve.

Jan had started doing the station books the same week we'd named little Freddie in Ida's room at the home. I couldn't afford to hire a bookkeeper but, as Diane told me, "We can't afford not to."

As much as Diane wanted to help out, with Paige still at home all day, and all of Freddie's special needs, she was already burning her candle at both ends. I'd watched the kids most of a week while Diane and Jan put their heads together to get the books back in order.

"You need more income," Jan said point-blank one late evening at the station. Renae was watching the kids at home. Diane, Pete, Jan, and I were babysitting our own set of troubles. "You need to stay on top of your account receivables. And you need to find a way to increase sales."

Well, duh. Even I knew that. But how?

She was full of ideas. "For one thing, you could add video and DVD rentals. The upfront cost shouldn't be that much if you hook up with a rental outfit. All you'd need is some shelving and a place to keep them. It would increase foot traffic in here, too. And there," she pointed to my brown Mr. Coffee machine, "you could add a cappuccino machine next to the coffee. And you could definitely use a better selection of snacks."

"And bait," Pete had added as if we'd been talking about fishing all along. "There are a lot of people who stop in here for gas who say they're going fishing. We could get some coolers and—"

"Wait. Stop." I held up both palms. My head was swimming. Full of minnows swishing through their ideas. "Just where would I put all this stuff?"

"Well, if it were up to me..." Jan stood up and walked to the far wall. "I'd bump this wall out. You've got the property all the way to the corner. You could add another twenty feet or more. Get the bathrooms inside, along with a couple more coolers and shelves. You could put a self-service beverage island right where I'm standing."

I could see it, and yet I couldn't. Either she was brilliant or she'd lost her mind. "And just where will I get the money to pay for all this if I'm already half broke?"

I could see Diane biting the corner of her lip, something she always did when she was thinking hard. "We could take out a second mortgage on the house."

"Do you have any equity in the station?" For a blonde, Jan was ruining any dumb-blonde jokes I ever planned to tell.

I rubbed at the back of my neck. "I don't know if it would be enough. And Renae will be needing money for college in just a couple years. And Freddie—"

"I have some money." Quietly, Pete spoke. We talked right over him until he said it again. "I have some money."

"Pete," I said, trying not to make it sound as though I were talking to Billy. "We're talking big bucks here." I mean, the kid was in his early twenties and still living with his mom. We weren't talking allowance money, and what I paid him sure wouldn't fund much of anything.

"Well," his voice was soft, "when my—" He stopped, cleared his throat, and tried again. "When my dad died last year he…he left me some money. Kind of a lot. Mom made me put it all in the bank. She said I should save it for something special, like a house. Or college." Pete scratched a finger at a spot on the counter. "What she really meant was that I shouldn't waste it on…drugs." His eyes darted a look at each of us. "I don't think I'm going to be going to college anytime soon. But I wouldn't mind—" He lifted one shoulder. "You know." He circled his hand as if drawing a circle around the station…a new, bigger station. Around all four of us.

Diane and I traded glances. Jan had her eyebrows raised as if to say, "This just might work." I turned to Pete and dipped my chin. He nodded right back as if it sealed the deal.

And here we were. K & P's SuperPumper was open for business.

I picked up a crushed pop can from the outside corner of the station and carried it back into the office. Pete was at the till, ringing up the gas fill, Jan was busy at the new coffee island, checking to see that the pots were full. Diane would be here in a few minutes with plates full of cookies…and the kids. I looked at the clock. I needed to run to the home and pick up Ida. Our open house was about to begin.

The door opened. In walked Marv. I shoulda known. He'd never pass up free coffee. Or cookies. He walked to the pot and poured himself a cup, leaned back against the wall, and took a sip. "It's hot." Coming from Marv, that was as good as it came.

It was the same-old, same-old, and yet it was all brand-new. Go figure.

～

"Kenny! We need you over here. Your event is about to start."

Quickly, I jogged to the starting line, taking a post on the inside edge of the track. I knew we probably weren't going to win this race, but that wasn't the point. I stuck out my hand and slapped five. "You can do it, Alex."

He grinned wide. "Ah know. Ah know."

"Runners at their marks!"

"Steady pace," I reminded, as I jogged off. I would meet him at the finish line. He nodded, his eyes focused on the race ahead.

"Set...Go!"

Alex took off along with the other runners. I ran ahead, keeping an eye over my shoulder. "Go, Alex. Go!"

He stumbled. Caught himself. Kept running. I could hear others along the track, in the bleachers, cheering on their favorite runners. I caught a glimpse of Diane on the sidelines, holding Freddie in her arms, yelling for Alex, too. I was at the finish line now. Waiting. Yelling. "Run, Alex, run!"

Billy was at my elbow. "Go! Go! Go!" He was red in the face from screaming so loud.

The front runner crossed the line, the second, the third. Billy kept shouting. So did I. "Come on, Alex. You can do it!" He stumbled again.

The fourth runner. The fifth. Finally, Alex crossed the line. Dead last.

It didn't matter. That wasn't the point. The point was that he'd run the race before him.

"You did it! You did it!" yelled Billy.

I opened my arms wide so Alex would know how proud I was of him. How proud we all were. He staggered into my chest, throwing his arms around me. I held on tight.

As an "Official Hugger" at this Special Olympics event, I wondered just who, really, had won the race? The first-place finisher? Alex, simply for persevering? Or me...for coming the farthest? Maybe we all had.

I clapped Alex on the back. "Good job!"

"Ah did it!"

"You sure did!" A high five before he trotted off to his parents.

I walked over to the sidelines where my family was waiting. I nodded at some of the people from the support group for parents of kids with Down syndrome that Diane and I had joined in Carlton. Once a month we made the drive. More often we got together for potlucks and games with our kids. All of the kids. All with their unique abilities. I'd learned Freddie's future was more hopeful than I'd dared dream. With proper health care and schooling, he might be able to live on his own someday. Hold down a steady job. Have friends. Love God. Be happy. Not so different than the dreams I had for any of my kids.

I lifted Freddie from Diane's arms into mine. No, my dreams for my kids weren't much different than the ones I had even for myself. For anyone I loved.

I looked into Freddie's almond-eyes, seeing there a trust so deep that I knew, without a doubt, God had planned this for me all along. Paul Bennett's words of more than a year ago confirmed what I knew to be true. *I have a feeling that God has given you this little boy because you are the perfect dad for him.*

I pulled my son close to my chest. "I love you, kiddo."

He pulled back, patted at my cheeks with his chubby hands. "Daa-aad."

He'd been saying his first word for two weeks. My heart was suddenly full to bursting.

That's how much I love all my children. You, too, Kenny.

I looked up into the cloudless sky, watching as a single bird cut through the air high above. *I know, Lord,* I silently whispered. *Now I know.*

Jan

"This color would be fabulous with your brown eyes." I dabbed a bit of the khaki-green shadow on the back on my hand, stealing a glance at my watch at the same time. Twenty minutes and I could be on my way back to Brewster. Home.

"I don't know…" My twenty-something customer twisted her lips. "I mean, *green?* Are you sure that's what's in?"

"It doesn't matter what's *in*," I coached. "What matters is what makes the most of what God gave you. And your eyes are definitely a feature you want to highlight. They're great." Maybe it wasn't politically correct to talk about God at Elizabeth's makeup counter, but I really didn't care. Spending so much time with Ida this past year had rubbed off on me. I'd learned one of the advantages of growing older was being able to say pretty much what you wanted…and get away with it. Another was that when God came first, a person could hardly help but mention Him now and then.

"Okay," said my young customer. "I guess I'll try it."

"Did you need anything else?" It was store policy. I had to ask.

"Well…" She pushed her tongue over her teeth. "I was thinking about getting some foundation. But it might get to be too expensive." She glanced down at her slightly worn purse. "What do you use? Your makeup is…flawless." It was a word right out of *Cosmo* magazine.

"Oh, goodness." I touched my fingertips to my face. Apparently, she didn't notice the slight droop of my mouth, or the way my right eyelid sometimes turned lazily downward. "I use…" Oh, heck with Elizabeth's policy. I leaned forward, speaking low. Elizabeth's might not approve of what I was about to say. "Your complexion is so beautiful. I wouldn't cover it up with anything. Wait until you're older."

"Are you sure?" A small smile played on her glossed lips.

"Yes. I'm sure. I'm a good twenty years older than you. I need a *little* help." Now *there* was something I would have never pointed out before. "But you?" I shook my head. "Less is more." I winked. It was my new philosophy.

"Thanks." She pulled a twenty dollar bill from her purse. Smiled.

I turned to ring up the sale. Ten more minutes and I'd be on my way home. Life was full these days. Hectic…but full. Joey had a baseball game tonight. I'd spend the evening outside on a bleacher with Dan. Tomorrow I was meeting Libby for lunch at Vicky's. She was going to bring along her friend from Carlton, Katie Jeffries. I hoped we'd have a chance to talk about Libby's book. I was on a mission to make sure she hung in there until those words got published. But, knowing Olivia, we'd talk about most everything *but* her and her book. I was learning from her that the mark of a great friend was listening. Not talking. Sometimes she did it too well. And I didn't. But I was learning.

I handed the young woman her change and then wrapped her eye shadow in tissue paper and dropped it in an aqua-blue bag. I didn't do much shopping anymore. I didn't have time. But, when I did, I knew how nice it felt to take home something pretty. "Here you go. Enjoy."

I put away the samples I'd pulled out and then cleaned fingerprints off the counter with a soft cloth and a spritz of window cleaner. There. All set for the next shift.

"Been busy?" Here was Amy, right on time.

"Not too." Summer days in North Dakota were too precious for spending inside. I pulled my purse from under the counter. "Have a good night."

After spending most of the day in the air-conditioning in the store, it felt good to climb into my sun-warmed car. I adjusted my sunglasses and then lowered the window, putting my elbow on the ledge. There weren't many days in this state a gal could do that. I flipped my hair over my shoulder and backed out of the parking space.

Suddenly I heard something. A wolf whistle. At me? Was someone I knew nearby? I shifted into park, looking around for a familiar face in the parking lot.

The only people nearby were a group of college-aged guys. One of them gave me a thumbs-up.

Me? I flashed a thumb back and then threw back my head and laughed out loud. If they only knew.

I headed out of the parking lot, merging onto the highway that would lead me back to Brewster. A year ago I would have basked in the attention of those too-young guys all the way home. While a whistle certainly felt good, I had so much more to think about these days.

I rolled the window back up and turned the radio on softly. My one-day-a-week job at Elizabeth's was over for this week. Monday I had spent the morning at Kenny and Pete's getting the weekend receipts in order, making the deposit, paying bills. I'd go in again on Thursday and get things ready for the weekend. Do the deposit again. Get change. Straighten out the candy bars. Something the guys never thought to do. The videos, too. Then I'd pour myself a cup of coffee and stay and visit for a while. Marv would be there for sure. We'd talk about *Casablanca* or *Breakfast at Tiffany's*.

I smiled to myself. I'd never have guessed Marv had a love for old movies. And an encyclopedia-like knowledge of *The Three Stooges*. But then, when had I ever taken time to talk to someone like Marv? His plaid shirts would have been enough to make me chalk him up as someone uninteresting.

I glanced in my rearview mirror. Switched lanes. Talk about passing judgment. I shuddered to think of all the preconceived ideas I'd had about people. Lipstick that didn't match clothes. A tie that was tied two inches too short. Scuffed shoes. A bad haircut or teased bangs were enough to send me on a tangent.

I'd learned many of those ideas from my mother…but I'd also invented plenty of my own. This past year had somehow paled those silly notions. It had even changed my mother. Or maybe it had changed the way I saw her. Through a different sort of lens. A more forgiving one.

It was surprising, and a huge weight off my shoulders, to realize how much this past year had changed me. My birthday was approaching in a few short weeks, and I was actually looking forward to it for the first time since I'd turned twenty-one.

I'd gained so much spending time with Ida this past year. Listening as she talked about the many losses in her life. Standing by, grieving along with her as several of the people living in the home who we counted as friends passed away. Well…I had a new appreciation for every year…every *day* that God had chosen to give me.

I looked out the window at the golden fields racing by my windows. Hay bales stood ready for winter feed. *Thank You, Lord, for today.*

A warm feeling filled me. Ida had taught me to pray this way. Sentence prayers, she called them.

I thought ahead. Or was it behind? I had four important jobs now. Four? Make that five things that made up my days. The first, of course, were Dan and Joey. They had been my anchor during the time I was sure I was drowning. Then there were my friendships with Libby, Diane, and several others. I hardly had time to stay caught up with all of them. But that was half the fun. Squeezing in walks, coffee, Bible studies, and even phone calls while we cleaned our kitchens. We made sure each other was doing okay. Third was my job at Kenny and Pete's. I rolled my eyes. Who'd a thunk it? Me? A bleached-blonde fashion diva working at a gas station! God had a sense of humor, for sure. Fourth, my job at Elizabeth's, which I only continued to do because it helped with number five. My volunteer work at the home.

I pushed up my blinker, slowing down to exit the interstate, to merge onto the highway that would take me home. Wednesday was turning into my favorite day of the week. The day I took the products Elizabeth's agreed to donate and went to the nursing home to pamper the residents.

I'd had Dan and Joey haul an old recliner from our house into the small, closetlike room they'd found for me at the home. A coat of lavender paint, two large mirrors, and some silk flowers had turned the room into a mini spa. I'd bought a pink fleece blanket to cover the chair and that is where I did my work. If you could call it that. It felt more like...more like a...ministry.

Warm tears pushed at my eyes. I blinked them away, marveling at how easily my right eye worked. I no longer saw Jodi for therapy, only to say "hi." *Thank You, again, Lord.* How much I'd taken for granted until this past year. It was no longer a time I viewed as a trial. Now, I called it a gift. Pure gift.

On Wednesdays I would stop to see Ida first. I'd push her to the lavender room she called the "shhpa." Then I'd help her transfer from her wheelchair into the recliner. I'd lay the chair back, put some soft piano music on the CD player and tell her, "Think of something happy."

"Dat's not hardt vhen I'm being treated like a qveen."

Not many of these hardworking farm women in the Brewster Nursing Home had ever had a facial. Much less someone to file and polish their fingernails.

"How are you?" I'd ask her as I gently rubbed moisturizer into her soft skin.

"Godt iss goodt," she'd say.

"Yes," I'd agree. "He is."

Then we'd chatter away, catching up on Kenny and the kids, on what meals reminded her of younger days...chicken and dumplings... and meals she would rather have skipped. "Chust becuss I'm Cherman doesn't mean I haff to luff sauerkraut!" I laughed when she got feisty. She did, too.

It was an honor I never would have dreamed of. To be privileged to touch these fascinating women in such a personal way. To run my hands over their wrinkles, the lines I now understood were badges of honor. They'd *earned* every one of them, and they were beautiful. All of them.

You are, too.

Yes…that, too. Working with these older women had even helped me understand my longing hadn't been for a baby, so much as for another person to love. Someone besides me. I knew God had given me this rocky path for a reason. What kind of victory would it be to climb a mountain that was flat? It was the steep and hard trails that brought triumph. Each week I thanked God, again and again, for bringing me to this glorious peak.

I pulled my car into the driveway, pausing while the garage door cleared the way. It was my last chance to remember before I began the next "shift" of my day. Make that night. I rolled down the window. Breathed in the warm, evening air.

There they were, the five important things that made up my life. *Five? What about Me?*

Ah, God was teasing me again. *Be patient. I'm getting to You.*

I ran into the house and tossed my purse on the counter. Read the note. *Meet you at the game. Love, Dan.*

I dashed upstairs, shedding my sweater as I ran. I stopped and took a breath. I had time. The game didn't start for another twenty minutes. Dan always went early to watch Joey warm up.

I buttoned my white cotton blouse and slipped into a pair of jeans, almost ready to run off to the baseball diamond. Sit with my husband. Watch my son. Life was good.

I leaned forward and looked into the mirror, swiping Pure Plum across my lips, brushing Rhubarb blush across my face. The face I had grown to love, not pick apart.

You said there were five things? What about Me?

He wasn't going to let me forget. But, He didn't need to worry. I hadn't.

I fluffed my hair. Spritzed on Dan's favorite perfume. Now, I was ready. I would walk to the ballpark and ride home with my husband.

I stuck my lipstick in my pocket, folded a tissue, and tucked that in, too. In the past year I'd done so much changing. If God was wondering where He fit in…well, I couldn't begin to count God as number six…or number one. I'd always been good with math, but this was a problem I couldn't solve.

There was no numbering when it came to God. It wasn't a problem. It was a pleasure.

I stepped out the door and began walking into the early evening sun. He was so much a part of it *all*, there was no separation. No numbering.

If I had to describe it…I'd have to talk about makeup.

Makeup?

I hurried my steps. The game would start soon. *Yes, God. Makeup.*

It felt as if during this past year I had pealed off the layers. All the masks. All the makeup I'd worn for so long. I hadn't realized it at the time, but I was uncovering… discovering…who I really was beneath it all. All those years I'd thought I knew who I was. *You're the pretty one.* But I hadn't. Not even close.

I did now. This was better. So much better.

All those years, deep inside, my heart had beat steady and strong. As if it knew. As if it had been marking time. Simply waiting for the moment. The moment when I finally knew who I really was. When I became Jan. The Jan I'd somehow always been, but hadn't truly known until this awful, glorious year.

Jan.

No makeup to hide behind. No fancy name. Simply the person God had created me to be.

I heard the crack of a bat. The cheer of the crowd. I ran the last steps, not wanting to miss a second of whatever God had waiting for me.

Me.

Jan. Always Jan.

"Woo-hoo!" I yelled as Joey rounded third. "Woo-hoo!"

My cheer wasn't just for Joey…it was for my whole life!

I was running toward so much more than a ball game. It was as if I was running toward life itself.

I held out my arms as if I could embrace the air. As if I was hugging life.

Joey was running toward home and in some oh-so-wonderful way…so was I.

A Note from
Roxanne Sayler Henke

Dear Reader,

I hope you enjoyed *Always Jan.* I turned fifty during the writing of this book. (That number used to seem *so* old...it doesn't anymore.) It seemed like the perfect time to tackle the topic of aging.

My dad was diagnosed with cancer when I was ten years old, so the idea of "mortality" was on my mind at a very young age. While I was growing up, we had a rash of too-young deaths in our community, and I learned early on that life is very precious.

Now that I am fifty, I realize how very "young" my dad was when he died at age fifty-four...when I was seventeen. Every day is precious. Too precious to waste complaining about aches and pains, about a flabby stomach, or about sagging skin. Our time is better spent embracing each day. Loving those around us. Growing closer to God.

My hope is that this story has helped you understand the value of every precious day. And that when you come to the end of your days, you will realize they were only the *beginning* of something even more wonderful!

Warm regards,

Roxy

Always Jan
Conversation Questions

1. Talk about vanity. What is the difference between wanting to look nice and being caught up in the way you look? What is the hardest for you to accept about aging?

2. At the beginning of the book, Jan received her validation from looking good. Do you know people like this? Are you like this? In what ways?

3. At the beginning of the story, what are Kenny's priorities? Talk about what constitutes a healthy interest in fun activities outside of work and when they become a problem. Do you know people like Kenny? In what ways are their lives out of balance? How can they bring it into balance?

4. What could Kenny's wife, Diane, have done to make Kenny understand her needs?

5. Discuss the different ways people of different ages view time. Is either view more, or less, important?

6. Did Ida depend too much on Kenny to help her? What are some ways an older person can ask for help, yet be mindful of the demands on a younger person's time?

7. Ida lived a life of faith. Talk about how her faith helps her as her life progresses. How did Ida's simple faith affect those around her? Have you known someone like Ida? How could you be more like her?

8. Part of aging is a realization that you are "grown-up." Are you grown-up? Explain when you knew...or what it will take. Discuss how difficulties can mature us.

9. Discuss the ways the difficulties that happened to Jan and Kenny helped them grow. Were they better for the struggle? In what ways? What difficulties in your life ended up making you a better person?

10. Is it easier for older people to accept difficulties in life? Harder? Why? How do younger people typically cope with troubled times?

11. Discuss the changes in Jan through the course of the story. How did this affect the people around her? Dan and Joey? Libby? Kenny? Diane? Ida?

12. Did your mental image of Jan change during the course of the story? Did you find her more, or less, attractive as she dealt with her struggle? Why?

13. Talk about Pete. What brought about a change in him? Discuss the way Kenny's struggles ultimately helped Pete.

14. Do you dread getting older? Or do you look forward to it? Why? Why not? Discuss the advantages and disadvantages of growing older. Most people seem to concentrate on the disadvantages of aging. Are there things you look forward to as you age?

15. Think of the many intricate ways God worked to bring these three (four, counting Pete) unlikely friends together. Are there relationships in your life where you can spot God's hand at work?

One More Thing

I would love to hear from you!
You can e-mail me through my website at:
www.roxannehenke.com
or directly at: roxannehenke@yahoo.com
Thanks for joining me once again in Brewster, North Dakota.
Wishing you good books and time to read them!

Roxy

Harvest House Publishers
For the Best in Inspirational Fiction

Roxanne Henke

COMING HOME TO
BREWSTER SERIES
After Anne
Finding Ruth
Becoming Olivia
Always Jan

Mindy Starns Clark

THE MILLION DOLLAR
MYSTERIES SERIES
A Penny for Your Thoughts
Don't Take Any Wooden Nickels
Dime a Dozen
A Quarter for a Kiss
The Buck Stops Here

Sally John

THE OTHER WAY HOME SERIES
A Journey by Chance
After All These Years
Just to See You Smile
The Winding Road Home

IN A HEARTBEAT SERIES
In a Heartbeat
Flash Point
Moment of Truth

Susan Meissner

Why the Sky is Blue
A Window to the World

Linda Chaikin

Desert Rose
Desert Star

Craig Parshall

CHAMBERS OF JUSTICE SERIES
The Resurrection File
Custody of the State
The Accused
Missing Witness
The Last Judgement

Debra White Smith

THE AUSTEN SERIES
First Impressions
Reason and Romance
Central Park

Lori Wick

THE TUDOR MILLS TRILOGY
Moonlight on the Millpond

THE ENGLISH GARDEN SERIES
The Proposal
The Rescue
The Visitor
The Pursuit

THE YELLOW ROSE TRILOGY
Every Little Thing About You
A Texas Sky
City Girl

CONTEMPORARY FICTION
Bamboo & Lace
Beyond the Picket Fence
Every Storm
Pretense
The Princess
Sophie's Heart

Roxanne Sayler Henke lives in rural North Dakota with her husband, Lorren, and their dog, Gunner. They have two very cool young adult daughters, Rachael and Tegan. As a family they enjoy spending time at their lake cabin in northern Minnesota. Roxanne has a degree in Behavioral and Social Science from the University of Mary and for many years was a newspaper humor columnist. She has also written and recorded radio commercials, written for, and performed in, a comedy duo; and cowritten school lyceums.